Barely a Bride

As a founding member... iffin,
Viscount Abernath... ying
as long as possible... ff to
war, he knows he ... nd a
wife—fast . . .

Just days later, he marries the lovely Lady Alyssa. For a
man who will always be wed to his freedom, she seems a
perfect—and perfectly undemanding—bride. Intelligent
and self-sufficient, she craves her independence just as
much as Griffin loves his. A loveless marriage of convenience is exactly what they both desire. But when he returns from war two years later, he is not the man he once
was—and she is no longer the girl he married. Scarred to
his soul, all Griffin wants is to lose himself in the warmth
of Alyssa's embrace. But to win his wife's heart, he must
now woo the bride he left behind . . .

"Historical romance fans are fortunate to have a treasure
like Rebecca Hagan Lee." —*Affaire de Coeur*

Don't miss her other delightful novels . . .

The Marquess of Templeston's Heirs Trilogy

Once a Mistress
Ever a Princess
Always a Lady

A Hint of Heather
Whisper Always
Gossamer

Turn the page for more acclaim for Rebecca Hagan Lee . . .

Barely
a Bride

Rebecca Hagan Lee

B

BERKLEY SENSATION, NEW YORK

This is a work of fiction. Names, characters, places, and incidents either are the product of the author's imagination or are used fictitiously, and any resemblance to actual persons, living or dead, business establishments, events, or locales is entirely coincidental.

BARELY A BRIDE

A Berkley Sensation Book / published by arrangement with the author

PRINTING HISTORY
Berkley Sensation edition / August 2003

ISBN: 0-425-19124-9

A BERKLEY SENSATION™ BOOK
Berkley Sensation Books are published by The Berkley Publishing Group, a division of Penguin Group (USA) Inc., 375 Hudson Street, New York, New York 10014. BERKLEY SENSATION and the "B" design are trademarks belonging to Penguin Group (USA) Inc.

PRINTED IN THE UNITED STATES OF AMERICA

10 9 8 7 6 5 4 3 2 1

This book is dedicated to the memory of
Murphy's Sweet Jaime Lee
23 July 1989–06 October 2002

❧

*My devoted little miniature schnauzer
who kept the same office hours I kept and who listened
to the plots of twelve books and helped me write
eleven and three-quarters of them.*

*She was the essence of unconditional love and boundless
courage wrapped in a tiny salt-and-pepper package,
crowned with bright black button
eyes shining with mischief.*

I miss you, Monkey.

Official Charter of the Free Fellows League

On this, the seventh day of January in the year of Our Lord 1793, we, the sons and heirs to the oldest and most esteemed titles and finest families of England and Scotland, do found and charter our own Free Fellows League.

The Free Fellows League is dedicated to the proposition that sons and heirs to great titles and fortunes, who are duty bound to marry in order to beget future sons and heirs, should be allowed to avoid the inevitable leg-shackling to a female for as long as possible in order to fight the French and become England's greatest heroes.

As charter members of the Free Fellows League, we agree that:

1.) We shall only agree to marry when we've no other choice or when we're old. (No sooner than our thirtieth year.)

2.) We shall agree to pay each of our fellow Free Fellows the sum of five hundred pounds sterling should any of us marry before we reach our thirtieth year.

3.) We shall never darken the doors of any establishments that cater to "Marriage Mart" mamas or their desperate daughters unless forced to do so. Nor shall we frequent the homes of any relatives, friends, or acquaintances that seek to match us up with prospective brides.

4.) When compelled to marry, we agree that we shall only marry suitable ladies from suitable families with fortunes equal to or greater than our own.

5.) We shall never be encumbered by sentiment known as love or succumb to female wiles or tears.

6.) We shall sacrifice ourselves on the altar of duty in order to beget our heirs, but we shall take no pleasure in the task. We shall look upon the act in the same manner as medicine that must be swallowed.

7.) We shall install our wives in country houses and keep separate establishments nearby or in London.

8.) We shall drink and ride and hunt, and consort with our boon companions whenever we are pleased to do so.

9.) We shall not allow the females who share our names to dictate to us in any manner. We shall put our feet upon tables and sofas and the seats of chairs if we so choose and allow our hounds to sit upon the furnishings and roam our houses at will.

10.) We shall give our first loyalty and our undying friendship to England and our brothers and fellow members of the Free Fellows League.

Signed (in blood) and sealed by:

The Right Honorable Griffin Abernathy, 17th Viscount Abernathy, aged nine years and two months, eldest son of and heir apparent to the 16th Earl of Weymouth.

The Right Honorable Colin McElreath, 27th Viscount Grantham, aged nine years and five months, eldest son of and heir apparent to the 9th Earl of McElreath.

The Right Honorable Jarrod Shepherdston, 22nd Earl of Westmore, aged ten years and three months, eldest son of and heir apparent to the 4th Marquess of Shepherdston.

Prologue

"The French have abolished their monarchy and there is talk of war. Six whole days! England will have need of us soon. We are prepared. Our pact is formed. The Free Fellows are born."

—GRIFFIN ABERNATHY, JOURNAL ENTRY, 07 JANUARY 1793 A.D.

DERBYSHIRE, ENGLAND
The Knightsguild School for Gentlemen

They slipped away in the dead of night.

The three young men moved quickly, quietly, weaving their way through the rows of identical iron cots in the dormitory of the Knightsguild School for Gentlemen. Three young gentlemen enrolled in the school—scions of the oldest and most prestigious families of England and Scotland—carried with them paper, pens and ink, sealing wax, leftover stubs of candles, a paring knife, a yellowed bit of newspaper printed with the seditious writings of the colonial rebel, Thomas Jefferson for inspiration.

The business they were about was serious, and their dreams of becoming England's greatest heroes were not to be taken lightly. Heroism required dedication—dedication to honor and to one's country—and dedication required sacrifice. The heroes they read about and dreamed of becoming were dashing figures willing to forgo the comforts of family and home, of wives and of children, in order to fulfill their destinies. True heroes remained free of encumbrances in order to make the ultimate sacrifice. Griffin, Colin, and Jarrod prepared to do likewise.

There would be no more long, tearful nights filled with empty longing for the familiar comforts of home and hearth. No more waiting in vain for letters from loved ones. No more tender hearts thoughtlessly trampled by ignorant females who looked down their noses at lesser titles and dwindling fortunes, who blamed the son for his father's shortcoming, who thought more of the title than of the boy.

Wrapping themselves in blankets to ward off the bitter January chill, the boys headed toward the storeroom behind the kitchen. They moved with great stealth and cunning, tiptoeing out of the dormitory, down the stairs, past the schoolrooms and the refectory, toward the vast kitchens and the little-used storeroom behind it.

The candle stubs they carried barely illuminated the way, but perhaps that was just as well for the work they were about had to remain a secret. Even from the other boys.

"Damn!" Griffin Abernathy, the seventeenth Viscount Abernathy, swore as his candle stub guttered and hot wax dripped onto the back of his hand.

"What happened?" Colin McElreath, the twenty-seventh Viscount Grantham asked in a loud whisper that bespoke his Scottish heritage.

"My light's gone," Griff answered. "You'll have to lead the way."

"Quiet! Both of you!" Jarrod Shepherdston, the twenty-second Earl of Westmore, warned. "You're making enough noise to wake the dead. And if we get caught, there will be canings all around."

"We've suffered canings for lesser crimes," Colin answered, cupping his palm around the candle flame, shielding it from the draft as he changed places with Griff. "Without complaint."

Griff nodded at Jarrod. "You've never minded canings before."

"And I don't mind them now," Jarrod retorted. "What I mind is missing the puddings." He stared at his friends.

"It's bad enough that they practically starve us to death in the name of discipline, but you know that in addition to caning us, the headmaster will take away our puddings—for at least a fortnight, if not more."

Jarrod's companions nodded. They didn't object to suffering through the painful canings Mr. Norworthy, the headmaster, administered nearly as much as the other punishment he inflicted.

The founder of Knightsguild had been a military man, and the school was run accordingly. Meals were served on a strict regimen of two full meals per day, at breakfast and at the nooning. Breakfast consisted of porridge, tea, and toast, and the nooning meal consisted of boiled meat and vegetables. The students did not receive an evening meal. Soldiers in the British army were only allotted two meals a day, and what was good enough for His Majesty's soldiers was good enough for the boys who would grow up and replace them. Evening meals meant paying a staff to work extra hours to prepare it, and even if Knightsguild had provided another meal, it could not have compared with the meals the boys enjoyed at home.

Only Saturday tea came close, and that was only because Mr. Norworthy had a voracious sweet tooth. Saturday tea was the one event the boys all looked forward to. The pastries, cakes, biscuits, and puddings served in place of the noon meal were the highlight of their existence at Knightsguild, and forfeiture of the puddings was the most effective punishment the headmaster had yet devised.

Norworthy had learned long ago that growing young men never willingly gave up dessert.

Griffin grinned at Colin, then at Jarrod. "Then we'd better not get caught." He nudged Colin in the shoulder and urged him forward in his best imitation of a Scottish burr. "Lead on, Macduff."

"McElreath," Colin growled. "My name's McElreath, not Macduff."

"I was paraphrasing Shakespeare's *Macbeth*," Griff told him.

"A play Englishmen seem to find so fascinating."
Colin smirked. "I suppose you think that because he
wrote about them, Shakespeare knew all there was to
know about the Scots?"

"Not about everyone." Griff grinned once again. "Just
their mad kings."

"Quiet!" Jarrod pushed past both of them and pinned
Griffin with a look. "This *was* your idea," he reminded
him. "Do you want to get us caught?"

Griff shook his head.

"Then keep quiet," Jarrod ordered. "Or your blather-
ing will sink us all."

"It may have been my idea," Griffin defended, "but
we all embraced the idea, and we all agreed to it."

"That's true," Jarrod said. "But you thought of it because of *him.*" He nodded toward Colin. "Because he
went and got his hopes dashed and his heart trampled
by a *girl.*"

"Colin can't help that the fact that Esme Kelverton's
father broke Colin and Esme's marriage contract because
Lord McElreath can't gamble worth spit."

"I canna blame Sir Preston," Colin interrupted, his
Scots burr thick with emotion, "for wanting the best for
his daughter. And there's no doubt that with my father's
ill fortune at the card tables, my prospects have dimmed.
The only thing I'll inherit is a title and a mountain of
debts." He took a deep breath and fought to keep from
crying. "But I canna help but feel bad about Esme.
We've been betrothed from the cradle. I thought she
cared more about me than about my prospects."

Jarrod let out a contemptuous snort. "You'd do better
to learn it now. Nobody cares about *us.* We're eldest
sons. We're supposed to stay alive because as long as
we're breathing, the family line is safe. We're supposed
to breathe, but we're not supposed to live. The only
thing anyone cares about when it comes to eldest sons
is their titles and prospects," Jarrod pronounced, staring
at Colin and Griffin as he imparted the wisdom his extra
year of life and his higher rank had afforded him. "And

there's no use sniveling about it because, you see, *girls* are the very worst sort of snobs. They have no choice. They have to marry a man with good prospects. To do anything less is to disappoint the family." He drew himself up to his full height. "Better to do as we've decided and swear off girls altogether."

"That's right," Griffin chimed in. "Who needs them?"

"Not us." Jarrod reached around Griff and gave Colin a *keep your chin up* punch in the arm. "We're going to be the three greatest heroes England has ever known! And no girl is going to stop us!" He smiled at the others. "Now, let's attend to what we're about. Follow me. I'll lead the way."

"Go ahead." Colin grinned. "You always do anyway."

Jarrod led the way through the kitchens to the storeroom. He set his candle on the brick window ledge, took out the paring knife, and carefully sliced through the leather cord holding the wooden latch. Once he gained entry, Jarrod pushed the door open and stepped inside.

Griffin and Colin followed.

The heat from the kitchen ovens on the other side of the brick wall kept the storeroom warm enough for the boys to shed their blankets. They folded the blankets into neat, woolen squares to use as floor cushions before pulling a battered wooden crate they had hidden in the storeroom into place to use as a table. When the crate was situated to everyone's satisfaction, the three companions placed their collective offerings of pen and ink, paper, candles, knife, and sealing wax on it and set down to work.

By the time they emerged from the storeroom, an hour or so before the breakfast bells rang, the three boys had formed a pact that bound them together and made them brothers. They had formed a secret society guaranteed to protect them from further pain wrought in the name of love and family and had fashioned a charter to govern it. And their composition was worthy of Thomas Jefferson's best efforts.

They called it the "Official Charter of the Free Fellows League," and as they pricked their thumbs with the paring knife and eagerly signed their names to each of the three copies of the charter in blood, Griffin, Colin, and Jarrod swore to honor the agreement as long as they lived.

Chapter 1

"Massena has been appointed to command the French in Portugal. The purchase of my commission in the Eleventh Blues is complete. My regiment leaves for the Peninsula in eighteen days. Tomorrow I've an appointment at White's to inform the earl. My future has begun."

—GRIFFIN, LORD ABERNATHY, JOURNAL ENTRY, 18 APRIL 1810 A.D.

WEYMOUTH HALL
London, April 1810

"*You sent for me, sir.*"

Griffin, seventeenth Viscount Abernathy, stood facing his father, the sixteenth Earl of Weymouth, in the study of his father's London town house. He was separated from his father by a wide expanse of dark, polished mahogany and a much darker, wider gulf of doubt brought about by age, familial differences, and the inherent conflict between a man and his heir.

"I sent for my heir," the earl snapped.

Griff inhaled, counted to twenty, then slowly expelled the breath. "I am your heir, Father."

"Not for much longer."

So that's how it was to be. As an only son and an only child, Griff was quite accustomed to his father's repeated attempts to use guilt as a means of manipulating him. His father's methods were tried and true, but Griff had long ago grown weary of the tactics. It would be nice to think that his father had sent for him because he wanted Griff's company. Just once.

"And why is that? Are congratulations in order?"

Griff asked. "Have I an older brother I've never met?"

"Don't be ridiculous! If I had another son, you'd be the first to know about it."

"I would rather think that Mother would be the first to know about it." Griff gave his father a slight smile. "Or your mistress."

Lord Weymouth failed to find the humor in his son's remark. "However much we might like it, your mother is not increasing."

"I am disappointed to hear it."

"It isn't for lack of trying," the earl continued. "I can assure you of that. And of the fact that I have no need of a mistress. Your mother keeps me quite busy and quite satisfied in that regard. But no matter how often we try or how creative we become, we fail to accomplish our goal. Ours has never been a prolific family, and it seems that Lady Weymouth and I were quite fortunate to produce you."

"I am delighted you feel that way." Griff struggled to maintain a neutral countenance. His father had many admirable traits, but a sense of humor wasn't counted among them.

The Earl of Weymouth was a brilliant man, but careful and methodical. He was quiet and observant, paid enormous attention to detail, and rarely deviated from his planned course of action.

Griff had never heard his father mention the possibility of having intimate relations with his mother or with any other woman. Oh, he knew that his parents had had intimate relations at least once. The consummation of their union had, after all, resulted in his birth, but like most offspring, Griff didn't want to hear the details, nor could he begin to imagine his father as a lover, creative or otherwise. He blocked the mental image that threatened to ruin his perception of his parents and turned his attention back to what his father was saying.

"We are *delighted*"—Lord Weymouth used the same word Griff had used, proving to his son that he did have a fully developed sense of irony, if not a fully developed sense of humor—"enough with your presence on earth and in our lives that we've no wish to see it extinguished prematurely."

"You heard?"

"Of course, I heard. Did you expect that I wouldn't?" Lord Weymouth picked up a heavy ledger and slammed it upon the desktop.

The loud crack of leather against wood echoed through the quiet room. Lord Weymouth frowned, then pushed away from his desk and stood up.

His size was intimidating. Standing head and shoulders above almost every man he knew, Weymouth used his size to his advantage, but that tactic no longer worked with Griffin. The boy hadn't so much as flinched at the sound of the ledger hitting the desk or displayed any hint of childish emotion when his father stood up from behind his desk. Weymouth recognized the fact that his son was a grown man. Griff had sprouted up and filled out while away at university and was now able to look him in the eye. In truth, his son looked down in order to look him in the eye, a fact of which Lord Weymouth was inordinately proud. It was quite clear to Lord Weymouth that even in his stocking feet, Griffin easily bested his height by a good inch or so.

Except for age and the difference in height, the two of them were very much alike physically. Griff had his mother's brilliant blue eyes and hair a lighter shade of brown, but there was no denying that he was his father's son. His shoulders and chest were equally broad, and the earl found, much to his chagrin, that Griff was more fit. His waist was trimmer, and his hips and thighs were well muscled from hours spent in the saddle instead of behind a desk.

The earl fought to keep from grinning from ear to ear. His son was a man he could be proud of. Was proud of. But that didn't keep him from wanting to throttle him. Imagine his only son and heir choosing—choosing—to take up a commission as a major in the cavalry.

"I knew you'd hear about it," Griff admitted. "I just didn't expect you to hear about it quite so soon."

"So soon?" Weymouth came perilously close to

shouting. "You accepted that commission a sennight ago. I only learned of it this morning."

"I did ask that my decision be kept quiet until I had a chance to discuss it with you," Griffin offered.

"And when did you intend our discussion to take place?" The earl's tone had taken on a biting edge, a biting edge that had been known to quell far greater men than his son.

"If you'll check your appointment calendar, sir, I believe you'll find your secretary assigned me the hours between four and six tomorrow at White's."

Weymouth reached over, flipped open his appointment book, and discovered that his son's name had, indeed, been duly noted for the hours of four to six at White's on the following afternoon. "You could have discussed this with me *before* you accepted the commission. Or did you keep it secret because you feared I would withhold my approval?"

"I have reached my majority," Griff reminded his father. "I don't fear your displeasure or require your approval."

"You are my heir," the earl replied. "My only heir. Have you no sense of duty?"

"England is at war, Father," Griffin said.

"I know England is at war!" Weymouth barked. "I see the results of it every day at the War Office, and I've no wish to see my heir's name added to the casualty lists."

Griff straightened his shoulders and stood at attention. "I had hoped that you would be pleased that I had decided to serve my country in her time of need."

"Pleased?" Weymouth snorted. "I'd be *pleased* if you would forget this nonsense. I'd be *pleased* if you'd sell your commission to someone else and let them serve in your place."

"So the Earl of Weymouth's heir can be spared? So someone else's heir's name can appear on the casualty lists?" Griff glared at his father.

Weymouth glared back. "Yes, dammit! Better theirs than mine."

"Have you so little confidence in my ability to survive?" Griffin asked.

"I have every confidence in your ability to survive," Weymouth said, "as long as you stay home where you belong. We're not talking about fox hunting or stalking stag or hunting expeditions spent traipsing across the wilds of Scotland with your friends. We're talking about war."

"I know what war is, Father."

"Do you?" Weymouth mused. "I wonder. I wonder if anyone who hasn't experienced it knows what war is."

"Then let's just say that I know where my duty lies."

"Your duty lies with your family, with tending and preserving what your mother and I have tended and preserved for you."

"And what of Bonaparte and the threat he poses to England and to our way of life?"

"What of it?" Weymouth demanded. "Bonaparte is more of a threat to our family and our way of life if you go to serve against him than he would be if you stayed home and watched him conquer the whole of England."

Griff recoiled, shocked to the core by his father's words. "I cannot believe you would forfeit your country so willingly."

"I am a great deal more willing to forfeit my country than I am to forfeit my son."

"You mean your heir," Griff corrected.

"I mean my *son*, dammit!" Weymouth stared at that son, daring him to contradict. "And I cannot believe that you would willingly forfeit your future and your family's future in order to become cannon fodder for the French." He ran a hand through his hair. "Cavalry. Bloody hell. I could understand the navy. I could even understand a commission as one of Wellesley's aides. But the cavalry . . ." He shook his head. "It's foolhardy. It's vainglorious. It's the most dangerous—"

"It's my strength," Griff said softly. "I sit a horse better than any man you know."

Weymouth nodded. "You sit a horse better than any man I've ever *seen* or ever hope to see."

"The army needs cavalry officers."

"Yes," the earl agreed. "And the reason the army needs cavalry officers is because we have more than our share of idiot generals who insist on getting them shot to hell. You're tall enough to be a grenadier. And you'd have a better chance of staying alive."

"I intend to serve my country," Griff said. "I mean to help defeat Bonaparte, and I have to go with my strength in order to succeed." He looked at his father, silently begging the earl to understand. "I've spent my entire life playing at soldiers, memorizing military tactics and stratagems. I may be tall enough, but I don't fancy a position in the grenadiers, lobbing grenades at the enemy lines until some sharpshooter picks me off. I prefer to take my chances with the cavalry. It's what I know best. If you were twenty years younger, what would you do?"

Weymouth nodded. "I would do exactly what you're going to do." He met his son's gaze. "I would provide for the future of my family name and line by finding myself a suitable bride and getting myself an heir on that bride *before* I go off to war. And if I were you, I'd begin right away."

"You must be joking!" Griff exclaimed.

"On the contrary," the earl replied. "As you are quite aware, I have a considerable reputation for not having been born with a sense of humor. This isn't a joke."

"But, Father, be reasonable—"

"I am being reasonable," Weymouth snapped. "Far more reasonable than you are being. I, at least, would tend to the details of the family. I, at least, would provide my parents with a grandchild to take my place as heir to the family land and titles in order that they not become extinct should something happen to their only child."

"But to marry some poor girl and get her with child in order to leave her a widow—" Griff broke off as the magnitude of his decision and the possibility of his not returning home from war suddenly became a reality.

"I'm not suggesting you marry a poor girl or that you

leave her a widow," Weymouth told him. "An heiress will do just as well. And as long as you're going to be a husband and a father, you might as well return from the war alive and healthy and whole." He smiled at his son for the first time since Griffin arrived. "It's the least you can do for your family."

"You aren't serious."

"I thought that we had established that I am quite serious. I suggest you start the quest for your bride at Lady Cleveland's soiree this evening." Weymouth flipped through his appointment book as he spoke. "You only have two weeks."

"I'm not going to spend my remaining fortnight attempting to locate a bride."

"You will if you expect to be married before you leave," his father countered. "You only have a fortnight plus four days before you're scheduled to report to your regiment. It will take at least a day to negotiate the wedding settlement and another two days to plan and execute the wedding and a wedding breakfast for a hundred or so of our closest friends."

Griffin stood his ground. "I am not getting married."

"Fine," the earl agreed. "Sell your commission and turn your attention to Abernathy Manor. It is desperately in need of upkeep. The house and the lands are on their way to ruination."

"Abernathy Manor will have to endure a bit longer without my attention," Griffin said. "I'm joining His Majesty's Eleventh Blues."

"Then you'll want to choose a bride." His father's tone of voice and the look of steely determination in his eyes brooked no argument. "Otherwise, I shall be forced to select one for you."

"You can select a wife for me, but you can't make me repeat the vows."

"I won't have to," Weymouth said grimly. "You will repeat your wedding vows willingly, or you will find yourself summarily cashiered out of the Eleventh Blues. You'll be dishonored, disgraced, and disowned."

"You can't disown me," Griffin reminded him. "You have no other heirs."

"Then I'll cut you off without a penny."

"Fine," Griffin replied. "I'll make my own way."

"You do that," Weymouth told him. "You're young and strong and smart; you can earn a living for yourself. But that task might not be so easy for the three hundred souls at Abernathy Manor who find themselves dependent upon your income—"

"You would close the manor and turn everyone out?"

"I would tear down the manor and put sheep on the place without batting an eye," Weymouth promised. "It's less costly and a much more efficient use of the acreage." He glanced at his son, gauging Griff's reaction. "What do I need with another manor house? I have Weymouth Park, the London town house, and a hunting lodge in Scotland to keep up."

"That's blackmail."

"Of course it is," the earl agreed. "And the reason it's used so often is because it's effective. Don't look so glum," he advised his son. "While it's true that you'll be giving up your bachelor ways, you'll be able to rest easy in the knowledge that in addition to acquiring a bride and an heir, your noble sacrifice has secured the livelihoods of three hundred or so deserving souls."

"I'll have your word that Abernathy Manor and all its inhabitants will be well taken care of," Griffin demanded. "Whether or not I return from the war."

"You have my word . . . so long as you take a bride and get an heir on her before you leave."

"What if I take a bride but fail to leave her with an heir? I can't promise I'll be able to fulfill that duty in a few days' time."

Weymouth looked his son in the eye. "The sooner you find a bride, the more time you'll have to work at it."

"I could still fail," Griff reminded him. "You've failed to produce another child. And, as you said, not for want of trying."

"You'll have to do better than your mother and I have been able to do."

"What if I succeed, and the child is a girl?"

"Ownership of Abernathy Manor reverts to me. Our letters patent make no allowances for firstborn females."

"You could have the letters amended by parliament."

"I could," the earl said. "But I prefer that my son return to England and fulfill his duty to his family."

"Even if that means returning from the dead?"

"Whatever it takes to accomplish the deed," Weymouth pronounced. "I will accept nothing less from my son and heir."

Chapter 2

"Since I've no wish to marry, I've decided to ignore the fuss of the London season and devote my energies to improving the gardens here instead. I've designed four new flower beds already, and I wish to experiment with the application of varying strengths of fertilizer from the stables."

—LADY ALYSSA CARROLLTON, LONDON, 1810

GROSVENOR SQUARE MEWS
Three blocks away

"*You aren't supposed to be in here, miss.*"

Lady Alyssa Carrollton started at the sound. She dropped the heavy metal fork she'd been using to muck the stall of her favorite hunter and whirled around to find Abrams, the head groom, standing in the door of the stall.

Abrams doffed his cap.

"Abrams!" Alyssa gasped, pressing a hand to her breast in an attempt to still the rapid beat of her heart. "You nearly frightened me half out of my wits!"

"I didn't mean to startle you, miss," Abrams apologized. "But you aren't supposed to be here, and certainly not decked out like that." He nodded at the hem of her girlish riding habit.

Recognizing the censure in Abrams's tone, Alyssa glanced down at the skirt of her stained and dusty habit. The garment was at least four years old, threadbare in places and straining at seams in others. She hadn't wasted a moment worrying about propriety or her appearance until she realized the seams of her bodice were pulled taut and that the hem of her dress barely reached the calves of her oldest pair of riding boots.

"Your abigail should have retired that habit to the rag bin ages ago," Abrams replied, his disapproval more than apparent.

"She did." Alyssa bent to retrieve her fork. "*I* recovered it from the rag bin because I needed it."

Abrams's look of disbelief spoke volumes.

"I *had* to have something to wear to muck the stalls." She stared at the groom. "I tried to borrow a pair of trousers from one of the grooms, but he refused."

"Of course he refused!" Abrams exclaimed. "Any lad working here would refuse such a shocking request from the young lady of the house. And every lad here should turn his face to keep from seeing you in that."

"I know it's a bit shorter than is completely proper," Alyssa admitted, "and snug in places, but I can't very well wear a good dress, now can I? And the fact that this one is old is what makes it perfectly suited for the task at hand." She reached for the rope handle of the muck bucket and tugged, pulling it closer to the stall door.

"There is no task at hand for you, miss." Abrams bent to help her. "Lady Tressingham ordered us to keep you out of the stalls and as far away from the stable as possible."

"That's ridiculous!" Alyssa sputtered. "How does she expect me to tack up Joshua if I cannot enter the stalls?"

Abrams bit the inside of his cheek to keep from smiling at her bluff. "Beg pardon, miss, but your mother expects *us* to tack up Joshua and bring him to you. Young ladies fortunate enough to employ grooms do not tack up their own horses."

"But I always tack up my mount at home," Alyssa argued.

"That's the country, miss. This is London, and the rules are different." Abrams paused. "As you well know. Besides, Joshua isn't in his stall, and you weren't tack-ing him up with a fork and a muck bucket." He allowed himself a knowing grin.

"I intended to ride," Alyssa bluffed. "But Joshua was gone. And as his stall needed cleaning, I thought I'd lend the stable boys a hand with their chores."

"I beg to differ, miss, because I know you weren't going to ride alone," Abrams countered. "Or leave the house dressed like that."

"Who would notice what I wear at this time of morning?" she challenged.

"The gentlemen riding along the Row would certainly notice," Abrams replied. "Your father among them."

"My father wouldn't notice if I paraded down the Row dressed as Lady Godiva." Alyssa winced. The truth hurt. But Abrams had been in service to the Carrollton family for more years than she had been alive, and there was no point in dissembling or pretending. The truth was that Alyssa doubted her father would recognize her, much less notice her clothing. He had little regard or time for human females. His attention was tuned to the breeding mares in his stables and the bitches in his kennels. Although he appeared to be quite fond of his wife, the Earl of Tressingham barely acknowledged Alyssa, her three older sisters, or their growing families. Not one of his four daughters commanded the attention he devoted to his horses and hounds. With the exception of his wife, females needed hooves or paws to claim Johnny Tressingham's attention, and Alyssa had neither.

Abrams cleared his throat. "But others would. So I'd say that it's a lucky thing that I removed temptation from your path by instructing young Ellis to take Joshua and accompany Lord Tressingham on his jaunt through the park, thereby saving you and Lady Tressingham a heap of embarrassment." He lifted the muck bucket out of Alyssa's grasp and hefted the contents onto a wooden cart. "Now, if I could only do that with the stalls."

Alyssa shot him a look of wide-eyed innocence.

He shook his head. "I'm on to you, miss."

"On to me?"

Abrams nodded. "You didn't come here to ride. You

came here to gather Joshua's leavings to use in the gardens."

"Well, how else am I going to get it?" she demanded.

"I can't answer that, miss."

"Mother forbade the gardeners' helpers from collecting it from the stables for me, and she forbade the grooms from delivering it to the greenhouse." Alyssa heaved a sigh of frustration. "She knows I need fertilizer for the garden."

Abrams clucked his tongue. "That may be true, miss, but *you* can't be in here collecting it."

"*I'm* the only one left who can," Alyssa answered. "She's forbidden everyone else."

"She's forbidden you as well," Abrams reminded her. "Your mother ordered us to keep you out of the stables so long as we're in London."

"What am I supposed to do if I'm invited to go riding?" Alyssa asked.

"You send word to the stables to have your mount saddled and a groom ready to accompany you at whatever time you wish to depart." Abrams winked at her. "And none of this crack of dawn stuff . . ."

Alyssa frowned.

The head groom continued. "The early morning hours along Rotten Row are reserved for the gentlemen. Ladies ride the Mile at a more sedate pace and at a later hour."

"Why should I have to wait until ten o'clock in the morning to ride when I'm accustomed to riding at daybreak?" Alyssa demanded.

"Because you're a young lady, miss, and only the gentlemen ride at that time of morning."

"Joshua will be kicking down his stall long before ten o'clock in the morning."

"I'll see that young Ellis attends to Joshua's exercise before you ride him," Abrams told her.

Other than digging in the garden and puttering around in the kitchen, exercising Joshua at the break of dawn when most of the world was still asleep was the thing Alyssa loved best. "I don't want young Ellis attending to Joshua's exercise. I don't want anyone attending to

Joshua's exercise or to his keeping except me," Alyssa complained.

"I understand, miss," Abrams said, "but rules are rules. And a young lady from a fine family must protect her reputation. Riding with the gentlemen during the early morning hours is a surefire way of endangering it."

"So, I'm to be denied the pleasure of riding."

"Not necessarily." Abrams eyed her disreputable habit. "But if you ride, you're to be properly outfitted, properly seated, and accompanied by a groom."

Alyssa groaned.

"Those are Lady Tressingham's orders, miss. And she ain't going to brook any opposition. You must be on your best behavior, or you will be forbidden to ride at all." Abrams softened his gaze. "And attending to your best behavior means that you're to forget about cleaning stalls and appropriating the horse leavings."

"What am I going to do about the gardens?" she asked. "I've already designed the new beds and started transplanting the pink rhododendrons—"

"You're going to be a most obedient daughter and leave the designing of the new flower beds and the transplanting of the pink rhododendrons to the gardeners employed to perform those tasks."

"Mother . . ." Alyssa breathed, recognizing the scent of her mother's perfume seconds before she heard her voice. Alyssa looked up to find her mother standing in the center aisle of the stable perfectly coiffed and immaculately dressed in a pale blue muslin gown topped with a dark blue pelisse. "You're awake—I mean—" Alyssa stumbled over her words. "What brings you here?"

"At this ungodly hour?" Lady Tressingham smiled. "I might ask the same of you." She sniffed, wrinkling her nose at the pungent odor emanating from the wooden cart. "But the smell speaks for itself."

"I can explain—"

"I don't require an explanation. As I haven't yet reached my dotage, my eyesight, my hearing, and my sense of smell are quite acute." Lady Tressingham lifted

an eyebrow at her wayward daughter. "However, I *do*
require that my daughter and my servants obey my instructions. Rhododendrons or no rhododendrons."

"But, Mother . . ."

"Drop the fork, *Alyssa*." Lady Tressingham's softly
spoken words were tempered with pure iron will.

Alyssa swallowed her words of protest and dropped
the fork.

Lady Tressingham unfastened the dark blue pelisse
she was wearing and handed it to her daughter. "Put that
on."

Alyssa obeyed without protest, slipping her arms into
the pelisse before fastening it over her riding habit.

"Now, bid Abrams a pleasant good morning, then turn
and march out of the stable and back into the house."

"Good-bye, Abrams." Alyssa turned and started out
of the stable, then glanced back over her shoulder. "Will
you see that the—"

"Not a another word," Lady Tressingham cautioned,
punctuating her words by waggling her index finger at
Alyssa.

"But, Mother, there's no sense in letting perfectly
good *fertilizer* go to waste. . . ." Alyssa was fair to bursting with indignation.

"Fertilizer!" Lady Tressingham's voice rose an octave
and she fought to bring it back down to its normal register before continuing. "I don't care about fertilizer! I
care about you! I care about your future, your reputation,
and your prospects. Servants talk, Alyssa. They tattle to
other servants. Servants who work for other families.
Good families. With sons. Go. Now." She pointed toward the expansive lawn separating the house from the
stables where a small army of gardeners and their assistants clipped the boxwood borders and worked the soil
in the spring beds. "Abrams has his instructions. And
you have yours. So don't so much as glance at the gardens or open your mouth again until we reach the safety
of your bedchamber."

Lady Tressingham rang for Alyssa's abigail as soon as they reached Alyssa's bedchamber.

"You sent for me, miss?" Durham bobbed a curtsy as she entered Alyssa's bedchamber.

"*I* sent for you," Lady Tressingham announced, stepping around Alyssa's curtained tester bed and into view.

"Beg pardon, milady." Durham bobbed another curtsy. "I did not realize you were within."

"Or that my daughter has been *without*, apparently," Lady Tressingham commented dryly.

"Ma'am?" Durham blinked at Lady Tressingham's tone of voice, then smothered a yawn with her hand.

"Go below and bring up a breakfast tray of toast and hot chocolate, then draw a bath for Lady Alyssa," Lady Tressingham instructed. "Oh, and stoke the coals before you go. My daughter has a habit to be rid of."

"Beg pardon, milady, but housemaids are charged with stoking the coals. I am a ladies' maid."

Lady Tressingham narrowed her gaze at the maid. Durham had come highly recommended, but it was quite obvious that the maid was oblivious to the tension in the room and to the reason her presence had been requested. The woman appeared to be as thick as treacle pudding. And with a ladies' maid like that, it was no wonder Alyssa managed to sneak out of her bedchamber dressed in rags like a street urchin. "Oh, for heaven's sake!"

Durham threw up her arm, shielding her face as if from a blow, as Lady Tressingham strode across the room and picked up the fire poker.

"I'm not going to hit you!" Lady Tressingham announced, bending before the fireplace, stirring the smoldering coals to life. "I'm going to stoke the coals while you"—she glanced at the maid—"go down to the kitchen and order the hot water for my daughter's bath and fetch my breakfast tray."

"Yes, milady." Durham bobbed a final curtsy, then jerked open the door and scurried out of the room. "Right away, milady."

Lady Tressingham turned to her daughter. "And you—"

Alyssa bit her bottom lip and glanced down at her feet in a vain attempt to appear contrite.

Lady Tressingham wasn't fooled. "Look at me." She frowned at Alyssa.

Alyssa obeyed.

Lady Tressingham held out her hand. "My pelisse, if you please."

Alyssa shrugged out of the garment and handed it to her mother.

"Now," Lady Tressingham pronounced. "Take off that habit."

Alyssa moved toward the dressing screen standing in the corner of the bedchamber.

Lady Tressingham shook her head. "Here. In front of the fire where I can see you."

"But, Mama . . ." Alyssa felt her cheeks flame with embarrassment.

"*Now,* Alyssa."

Alyssa unbuttoned the bodice of her riding habit and slipped it off her shoulders, then stood clutching the well-worn fabric in her hand. She let out a sigh. Her old riding habit had served her well. And replacing it would take a bit of doing. Alyssa glanced at the massive cherry wardrobe dominating the wall opposite her bed. Her winter clothes were packed away in the attic of their country home, but there had to be something she could use, something dark, something she might have worn for mourning. She bit her lip once again. But what? There hadn't been a death in the family since they'd come to London. And if there had been, they wouldn't be in London. The family, out of respect for the dead, would have forgone the season and returned to the country. Still . . . the maids wore black. Perhaps she could trade one of the many pastel muslins her mother had ordered for the season to one of the maids for a dress in nice serviceable black—

"No."

Alyssa glanced at her mother. "Pardon?"

"No to whatever it is you're thinking," Lady Tressingham said. "Now, hand over the bodice and take off your skirts and that threadbare chemise."

"Mama!"

Lady Tressingham studied the color staining Alyssa's face and neck. "You undress in front of Durham."

"I do not!" Alyssa protested. "I use the screen."

"I'm your mother, Alyssa. I've seen you in the altogether."

"Not since I've grown up."

Lady Tressingham smiled. "Have you? Judging from your grubby appearance and your behavior, I'd say it's a matter of debate as to whether or not you *have* grown up."

"You know perfectly well what I mean."

"Do I?" Lady Tressingham tossed the bodice of Alyssa's riding habit into the fireplace. She snapped her finger. "Your skirt, Alyssa."

Alyssa unfastened her skirt and stepped out of it, glaring at her mother as she did so.

Lady Tressingham ignored her. Scooping the skirt from the floor, she folded it neatly and then tossed it onto the fire.

Alyssa watched in horrible fascination as the coals burst into flames that consumed the fabric. "I am not a child."

"Yet you persist in behaving like one," Lady Tressingham countered.

"There is nothing childish about pursuing one's dreams, Mama."

Lady Tressingham smiled. "You dream of mucking stalls and digging in the soil?"

"I dream of designing gardens like Capability Brown and Mr. Repton. I dream of inventing new ways of doing things and improving the way we live."

Lady Tressingham laughed. "We're members of the ton, Alyssa. One cannot improve upon the way we live."

Alyssa kicked the porcelain chamber pot beneath her bed. "Maids must haul water from the kitchen up three flights of stairs in order to fill the bathing tub and empty the chamber pots we keep hidden beneath our beds."

Lady Tressingham nodded. "Yes, my darling girl. Maids do those things. And they're grateful for the work and the money it provides. You should be grateful for the fact that because you're a lady and a member of the ton, you're above that. You've a reputation to protect and an old and honorable name to uphold. You're a Carrollton. The daughter of the Earl of Tressingham. You've no need to haul water or empty chamber pots or muck stables or dig in the dirt. And no one expects that you should perform menial tasks."

"There is nothing disreputable about performing menial tasks," Alyssa argued. "They're necessary to our current way of life."

"Indeed, they are," her mother agreed. "But why do those things if one can afford to hire someone else to do them?" She reached out and pinched Alyssa's cheek. "You're a lady, Alyssa. The only task you need worry about performing is finding a suitable husband." She held out her hand. "Chemise, stockings, and boots, please."

Alyssa sat on the edge of the bed and tugged off her boots.

"No need to frown, my darling girl," Lady Tressingham said. "I'm not going to burn your boots. Just your chemise and stockings. I intend to keep your boots locked away so that you won't be tempted to use them. And from now on, you'll behave like the lady you are. You'll dress in the pretty dresses I bought you and attend all the lovely gatherings to which you've been invited. The only gardening you're going to be doing is arranging flowers in vases, and there will be no more trips to the stable."

"What about Joshua?" Alyssa asked. "Are you going to forbid me to ride?"

"Of course not," her mother answered. "If a gentleman asks you to accompany him on a morning ride, you'll be allowed to do so, as long as your father or I am present."

Alyssa groaned.

"And don't think that misbehaving or disobeying my

orders will result in being sent home to the country."
Lady Tressingham eyed her daughter. "Oh no, my darling, we'll simply redouble our efforts to transform you
into the Incomparable Beauty of the Season as I and
your sisters were, and when we've succeeded, your father shall choose the man he thinks will best suit you—
unless, of course, the duke of Sussex has acquiesced to
his mother's wishes and offered for you as he should
have done for one of your sisters." She paused. "Undergarments, please."

Alyssa stripped off the rest of her clothes and watched
as her mother added them to the flames. "I don't want
anyone to offer for me."

"Of course, you do," her mother protested. "Because
the only alternative is to live out the remainder of your
life taking orders from your father and me and from your
married sisters and their families once we've gone to
our reward." Lady Tressingham smiled. "Marry, Alyssa.
Marry well. Give your husband his heir and a spare.
Then you will have earned the right to do as you please.
Even if what you're pleased to do means mucking stalls
and designing gardens."

A knock sounded at the door.

"Ah," Lady Tressingham sighed. "My breakfast and
your bath." She walked over to Alyssa's wardrobe, removed a dressing gown, and carried it back to Alyssa.
"It's a gentleman's world, my darling. And marrying
well is your best way of succeeding in it. Being a spin-
ster is no life for you—not if you wish to pursue those
dreams of yours."

Alyssa frowned.

"No need to make such a face at me. I've only your
best interests at heart. You may believe there's no reason
for you to marry, but eventually, you'll see the wisdom
of it." Lady Tressingham arched a brow at her daughter.
"And you'll have plenty of time to ponder the notion,
since you are forbidden to putter in the gardens or
grounds or frequent the stable for the duration of the
season."

"For the duration of the season?" Alyssa was aghast

at the idea of not being able to garden or to ride unchaperoned for the next ten weeks. "I'll go mad."

Lady Tressingham smiled. "I don't think so, my darling. We've had an eccentric or two in the family, but no strains of madness."

"I'm likely to be the first," Alyssa muttered, sounding more like a rebellious ten-year-old than a young lady in her second season.

"Well," her mother drawled, "I believe the condition can be cured with a proposal from a gentleman of wealth and impeccable breeding." Lady Tressingham narrowed her gaze at her daughter. "Get yourself betrothed, Alyssa. Find yourself a suitable husband, and I'll gladly allow you to dig up and rearrange every flower bed on the place."

Alyssa pinned her mother with a look. "Have I your word on that?"

Lady Tressingham heaved a dramatic sigh. "Yes," she confirmed. "You can dig right up until time to dress for your wedding."

Chapter 3

"Earlier this month, our great enemy, Napoleon, married Marie-Louise of Austria in order to secure an heir for the throne of France and to form an alliance with Austria. It seems I must marry and do the same—on a less exalted scale—if I wish to take up my commission in the cavalry. My search for a suitable bride has begun."

—Griffin, Lord Abernathy, journal entry, 23 April 1810

Griff was rapidly running out of time.
    It had been nearly a week since his father's ultimatum, and he was no closer to finding a suitable bride than he had been when his father had insisted he do so.

Because a cavalry officer was expected to provide his own horses and provisions, Griff spent nearly every waking moment preparing for war. He journeyed to Newmarket and visited Tattersall's, inspecting the horseflesh before he purchased the three horses he was obliged to take with him. The rest of his time was spent at his tailor's and his boot maker's, where he endured fittings for uniforms and boots. He purchased camp furniture and a comfortable campaign tent as well as supplies and clothes for his groom and for his personal manservant.

His days had been so full that Griff had barely made appearances at the rounds of balls and parties to which he had been invited. And none of the young ladies at any of the parties he'd attended had made him consider staying long enough to dance with them.

Acknowledging the fact that he needed help, Griff

called an emergency meeting of the Free Fellows League on the afternoon of the sixth day. He sent personal notes to the members asking that they meet in one of the private dining rooms at White's.

They did not disappoint him.

Griff rose from his seat and greeted his friends and cofounders of the League as Colin, Lord Grantham, and Jarrod, Lord Shepherdston, entered the gentleman's club at the appointed time. He poured three snifters of brandy from a bottle smuggled in from France by way of the Cornish coast, then handed one to Jarrod and one to Colin before raising his own.

"To the Free Fellows." Griff proposed the toast, then tossed back half the liquor in his glass.

"To the Free Fellows," his friends echoed.

But Jarrod raised an eyebrow at Griff's uncharacteristic behavior. Griff never tossed back brandy—especially fine French brandy they had gone to a great deal of trouble to smuggle into the country. French brandy of a vintage meant to be savored. "Problems?" he asked.

"You might say that," Griff answered. "I am, after all, about to become the first Free Fellow to relinquish his status." He downed the rest of his brandy in one swallow.

"Say again?" Colin sputtered.

"We heard you'd been busy making the rounds about Town," Jarrod commented, dryly. "But we didn't know you'd been *that* busy. . . ."

Griff nodded. "I've been ordered to secure a bride before I join my regiment."

"Ordered?" Colin repeated. "By whom? Your commanding officer?"

"First by my father," Griff answered. "And then, by my commanding officer." He pulled a letter from his pocket and handed it to Colin.

Colin unfolded the sheet of paper and read aloud. "To Major Lord Abernathy from Colonel Sir Raleigh Jeffcoat. Major Abernathy, the note contained herein is a direct order from commanding officer to subordinate ordering you, as the only son and heir of the Earl of Weymouth, to attend to your marital obligations and fulfill your duty to your family before you join the regiment."

Colin stopped reading and handed the letter to Jarrod, who continued reading. "His Majesty's Army does not make a practice of commissioning members of the peerage who are their family's only sons and heirs because His Majesty's Army has no wish to play a part in the extinction of a great family name. You are further informed that should you decide to disavow this direct order, your commission will be declined and the price of your commission shall be forfeited."

"Well, that's a first," Colin announced as he stood at Jarrod's shoulder and studied the colonel's signature and seal. "The army usually prefers its officers to be bachelors. I've never known it to actively order a man to marry before."

Jarrod snorted. "His Majesty's Army didn't order Griff's marriage; his father did. And this must have cost him a pretty penny." He gave a low, admiring whistle.

"I knew he had powerful friends in the War Department," Griff muttered. "I just didn't know how powerful his friends were or how determined he would be."

"Judging from this unprecedented order, I'd say the earl is very determined to have his way and that his powerful friends are probably the highest in the land." Jarrod tapped the letter against the edge of the table. "Lord Jeffcoat can be bought, but not cheaply."

"It doesn't matter." Griff groaned. "My choice is the same in any case. Give up my bachelorhood or give up my commission."

Although both of his friends currently held army commissions, they worked with Lieutenant Colonel Colquhoun Grant, who had served as General Wellesley's intelligence officer and was quite adept at breaking French codes. Jarrod and Colin had proved similarly adept at ferreting out information and at code breaking and had been assigned to gather intelligence for the army. Currently, both remained headquartered in London.

Griff knew that Colin and Jarrod supported his decision because they understood how much it meant to him. Serving in the Horse Guards was all Griff had ever dreamed of doing. Joining the cavalry and fighting the French had been his greatest ambition, and although he'd managed to keep it a secret from his father until now, Griff had been on the waiting list for a commission since he'd left university.

When a vacancy finally opened up, Griff had been quick to purchase it. Unfortunately for Jarrod and Colin, that vacancy had been in a regiment bound for the Peninsula. Griff was ready to leave, but his friends were not. They were still trying to come to terms with the fact that Griff had accepted a commission in the Eleventh Blues, a regiment sure to become a part of General Wellesley's major push to topple Bonaparte from the French throne.

Griff set his empty glass on the top of the sideboard, then reached into the inside pocket of his jacket and removed two thick parchment packets. He handed the envelopes to his friends. "I believe the recorded wager was two hundred pounds." He frowned. "I trust paper currency is sufficient."

When they'd reached their majority, each of the Free Fellows had wagered an additional two hundred pounds on who would be the first to marry. Two hundred pounds in addition to the five hundred they had agreed to forfeit in the Charter. Griff had bet on Jarrod, because Jarrod had been the first to inherit his father's title.

Jarrod had wagered that Colin would be the first to marry, because Colin was always short of funds and desperately needed to marry an heiress to help restore the family coffers.

Colin had wagered on Griff. Not because Griff needed money or because he was likely to inherit his title any time soon, but because Griff had always been the most tenderhearted of the three and the most romantic.

Although he desperately needed the cash, Colin was reluctant to accept it. He glanced down at the envelope, then back at his friend. "Griff, you don't have to do this." He attempted to press the money back into Griff's hand.

Griff shook his head, refusing to accept it. "A wager is a wager, Colin. Take the money. You won it fair and square."

They had made their first wagers when they formed the Free Fellows League. Griff and Colin had been nine years of age, and Jarrod had been a year older. They had had to wait until they were old enough to join the venerable gentleman's club in order to record the wager on the betting books at White's. Recording the original wager and adding to it had been the first order of business the day they became members. Now, nearly seventeen years later, Griff was paying his debt.

"Who's the future Lady Abernathy?" Jarrod asked.

"I have no idea," Griff answered honestly. "Only that there is going to be one. And if I don't choose a bride for myself, my father will choose one for me."

"You've no young lady in mind?" Colin was stunned.

"None." Griff sighed. "I'm going to war. Besides, I had no intention of going against our League rules. I didn't intend to marry at all and certainly not before I reached the age of thirty. Unfortunately, my father is determined to secure the succession."

"Of course he is," Jarrod said. "You're an only child, and it's natural that your father make demands of you in order to insure his family name and holdings not become extinct."

Griffin glared at him.

Jarrod held up his hands in a sign of surrender. "I'm not saying I agree with his method. I'm simply saying that I understand why he's employing it."

"I understand it, too," Griff admitted. "That's what makes my decision so difficult." He looked at his friends. "I want to do right by my father and my family, but I am determined to be my own man. My own *cavalry* man."

"So," Colin cut right to the heart of the matter. "I guess that means you're getting married before you leave. How long do you have?"

"A week."

Jarrod swore. "How in the bloody hell do you expect to find a suitable bride in one week's time? Especially when you've spent your evenings cavorting with the ladies at Madame Theodora's."

"*I* haven't been to Madame Theodora's in over a week," Griff retorted. "And you know it, or you would have seen me there."

None of the Free Fellows kept mistresses, choosing to frequent several very discreet, very select, houses of pleasure instead.

"Unlike the two of you," Griff continued, pinning his friends with a knowing look, "I've made at least a cursory appearance at every ball, rout, musicale, and soiree to which I've been invited for the past six days."

Colin tried to keep from shuddering and failed. "I heard you were among the crush at Lady Cleveland's the other night, but I thought it must have been a mistake."

Griff shook his head. "It *was* a mistake, but not a case of mistaken identity. If someone told you they saw me there, they were telling the truth. I did make a brief appearance."

"And no one caught your eye?" Colin asked.

Lady Cleveland's party was one of the highlights of the season. It was crammed with carefully chaperoned young debutantes all vying to catch the attention of the wealthy gentlemen. Unfortunately, there had been such a crush of people there that Griff had opted to leave as soon as possible in order to make way for some other poor bride-questing bachelor.

"Plenty of women caught my eye, but none of the sort I should be seeking as a wife." Griff paused for a moment, reconsidering. "There was one young lady." He'd only caught a glimpse of her from across the room. He had seen her again, two nights later, at Lady Dorrance's musicale, but he hadn't spoken to her. Nor had he gotten her name. He'd only seen her twice. But she had caught his attention. "Unfortunately, I've no idea who she was."

"I know just the girl you're talking about," Jarrod

drawled. "Pale blond curls? Big blue eyes? Flawless complexion? Pink lips? Weak mind? Eager mama?"

"You're loads of help." Griff scowled. "Especially since you know more than half of the debutantes this season fit that description."

"More than half the debutantes fit that description every season," Jarrod said. "And except for the eager mama, the knowledge I've gleaned from observing you at Madame Theodora's would lead me to believe that that's the sort of girl you would choose. It does appear to be your usual preference."

"My usual preference has nothing to do with it," Griff snapped. "I'm searching for a *wife,* not an evening bed-mate."

Jarrod raised his eyebrow in question, then shrugged his shoulders. "You're the one searching for a bride."

Griffin felt the color rise in his face. "You know what I mean," he said. "There is a difference in amusing one-share self with a woman with whom you share a bed and breakfast and little else and selecting a woman to share the remainder of one's life. My lady must possess a brain and a few more talents. She must meet a higher standard than my usual bedmates."

"Spoken like a true Englishman," Colin scoffed. "I'd rather my bedmate possess the brain and the talents. All I require of my wife is a pleasing face, a relatively slim form, and a very fat dowry."

"Spoken like a true Scot," Jarrod retorted. "And it's lucky for you that unattractive girls are often equipped with fat dowries. But we're looking for Abernathy's bride-to-be."

"The one for whom he failed to get a name," Colin reminded them. "Unless he manages a better description than the one you supplied, I've no notion how we intend to find her." He turned to Griffin. "Can you describe her?"

Griff could. Right down to the last detail on the dress she was wearing, but he didn't care to share that bit of information with Colin or with Jarrod. "I would know her if I saw her again."

"Are you sure?" Colin asked. "You only caught sight of her twice."

"I'm certain of it," Griff replied as Colin and Jarrod exchanged knowing looks.

"Then we'd better get busy before someone else snaps her up," Colin said.

Griff was suddenly wary. It was one thing to ask for help; it was quite another to have his friends assume command of the mission. "What do you have in mind?"

"We considered going door to door," Jarrod teased. "To ask if the young ladies of the house would step forward and make themselves available for your careful inspection . . ."

"But that would take too long," Colin added. "So we decided the most efficient way was to go home, change into our court dress, and make use of the Almack's vouchers we've received." He laughed at the grimace that crossed Griff's face.

"Surprised you didn't think of it yourself," Jarrod teased.

"I did," Griff said wryly. "But I hate knee breeches and buckled shoes, and after avoiding the place all these years, I knew better than to go alone. That's why I invited the two of you."

Chapter 4

"I have enlisted the aid of my brothers in arms, and together, we have formulated a plan of battle."

—GRIFFIN, LORD ABERNATHY, JOURNAL ENTRY, 24 APRIL 1810

"*Leaving so soon?*" Jarrod asked as he cornered Griff in front of a row of densely fronded potted palms separating the refreshment tables from the designated dance floor.

"So *soon?*" Griff arched an eyebrow. "It seems as if I've already spent an eternity here in Free Fellows Purgatory."

Jarrod chuckled. "It may seem like an eternity, my friend, but in reality, we entered Almack's hallowed doors less than an hour ago."

"You're joking!" Griff exclaimed. "I've already fended off a half dozen marriage-minded mamas and their offspring."

"You're not supposed to fend them off," Colin said, coming up to join them with two glasses of watery orgeat in hand. "The whole point of being here is to find a bride."

"I thought the point of being here was to do what has to be done so that I might join my regiment," Griff answered.

"Call it what you will," Colin told him. "But you're here to find a wife." He glanced at Jarrod and down at the glasses. "Sorry, old man, but I could only carry two, and I had to fight my way through the crowd to get these." He handed a glass to Griff and kept one for himself. "It's abominably hot in here."

It was. And Jarrod was as hot and thirsty as the other two Free Fellows, but he shuddered at the sight of the watery liquid. "None for me, thanks." While Almack's was the place to see and be seen while bride hunting, the patronesses' idea of refreshments suitable for unmarried ladies left quite a bit to be desired. He turned to Griff. "Grantham's right. You came because you have to secure a bride as soon as possible if you want to join your regiment. Any sign of her?"

"None." Griff took the glass Colin offered and downed the orgeat. "Damnation! I can't believe I thought this was a good idea or that the two of you agreed to come here tonight. It's worse than I thought it would be. I don't want a bride. I don't want to get married. All I want is to join my regiment. All I want is to fight for England." He glared at the other two. "I'm a founding member of the Free Fellows League. I want to remain a Free Fellow. I *am* going to remain a Free Fellow. I cannot believe I thought I could actually go through with this. . . . What the devil was I thinking?"

"No bride. No regiment," Jarrod declared. "That's what you were thinking."

Griff shook his head. "I was thinking that I could choose the young lady who caught my fancy, offer her nothing but my name, my title, and my property, sail away without a backward glance, and still call myself a gentleman."

"You can," Colin assured him. "You can call yourself a gentleman and a Free Fellow as long as you don't forget your oath."

"My oath not to marry?" Griff asked.

"Your oath not to marry unless you have no alternative except to marry," Jarrod answered. "And the fact is that unless you're willing to give up your military career and our mission to defeat Bonaparte you have no alternative."

"I've no wish to be any young woman's husband, or

jeopardize our mission. And forcing this decision upon me isn't fair to either of us," Griff said.

Jarrod shrugged. "What is ever fair in life? That's the way these things are done. You know it, and the young lady you choose will know it. That's all that matters."

"Is it?" Griff demanded. "Do you think they really understand? Do their mamas explain that this is all business?" He swept his hand out in a gesture that encompassed the whole of the assembly room's female population. "Or do these young ladies believe, no matter what their mamas tell them, that *their* marriages will be different. That *their* future husbands will love, honor, and cherish them? And if they believe in romance, what are the odds that I will find a young woman who won't be brokenhearted when she learns I'm never going to love her. Or one that won't mind being left all alone while I go off to war?"

Colin chuckled. "You might be surprised."

Griff lifted an eyebrow.

"Virginal young ladies of good family are generally thought to find the marriage bed messy, uncomfortable, and shockingly distasteful—especially on their wedding night," Colin elaborated.

"How many virginal young ladies have you bedded?" Griff demanded.

"None," Colin admitted cheerfully. "I try to steer clear of marriageable young ladies *and* virgins. But I'm told—"

Griff snorted.

"Ask any of your newly married friends," Colin insisted. "They'll tell you."

"Not if they're gentlemen," Griff protested.

"Besides," Jarrod added, joining the discussion, "we don't have any newly married gentleman friends. We're Free Fellows. Remember? And Abernathy's right. No gentleman is going to discuss his bride's reaction to the pleasures of the marriage bed."

"That's the point I'm trying to make," Colin reiterated. "Gentlemen don't discuss it. But Abernathy's bride might be very happy to see him ride away, because most young ladies view the marriage bed as a chore that must be endured. According to everything I've heard, young *ladies* seldom find *pleasure* in the marriage bed."

"Then their husbands are ignorant fools," Griff pronounced. "I'm neither."

"Right you are," Jarrod clapped him on the shoulder. "You're an unlucky devil, at the moment, because you're forced to marry, but you've never been accused of being a fool or of being ignorant in the ways of pleasuring a woman." Jarrod took Griff and Colin's punch cups out of their hands, then turned and set them beneath the drooping fronds of a potted palm. "Now," he said, rubbing his hands together in anticipation of the hunt, "let's go find your viscountess-to-be."

None of them noticed the slightly red-faced young lady emerge from behind the potted palms and hurry to the refreshment table in search of orgeat and Lady Cowper.

"There you are!" Lady Tressingham exclaimed as her youngest daughter reappeared with two cups of orgeat. "I thought you might have gotten lost on your way to the refreshment tables or . . ." she added in a sarcastic drawl, "decided to redo all the floral arrangements."

Alyssa bit her bottom lip, then turned a speculative eye on the jumble of vases packed with poorly arranged flowers and greenery. "Of course not."

"Well, you could have done so," her mother accused. "It took you so long."

"There was a crush around the punch bowl and I—"

"Never mind." Lady Tressingham took the cup of orgeat. "You're here now. I was afraid that you would miss all the excitement."

What excitement? Alyssa studied the mass of men and women crowded into the assembly rooms. The only exciting thing that had happened so far was that she'd accidentally overheard a fascinating conversation between three gentlemen who called themselves the Free Fellows.

A secret League fighting against Bonaparte. She hadn't meant to eavesdrop, but she had had no choice in the matter, except to embarrass them by making her presence known. Not that Alyssa would ever breathe a word of what she'd overheard to her mother . . . especially since the conversation she'd heard was private and clearly unfit for her innocent ears. Her *virginal* ears . . . virginal ears that couldn't help wondering, all of a sudden, what pleasures the marriage bed held and how many young brides were cursed with fools for husbands—

"Ouch!" Alyssa frowned as her mother elbowed her in the ribs once again.

"You haven't heard a word I've said. Now, pay attention," Lady Tressingham ordered. "And smile. He's looking straight at us."

Alyssa frowned. It seemed nearly everyone in attendance at Almack's Assembly Rooms had been looking at them all evening. At least, that's the way her mother made it feel, for she had elbowed Alyssa in the ribs and whispered the same order over a dozen times. Alyssa was certain she'd have a black and blue mark there tomorrow. "Who is it this time?"

"Him." Lady Tressingham pointed discreetly with her fan.

Alyssa followed her mother's direction and saw a lone figure standing in front of the potted palms. She wondered if he was the one the other men had addressed as Abernathy. "Who is he?"

"The Duke of Sussex," her mother answered.

She was disappointed, but Alyssa paid closer attention to the rest of what her mother was saying. "The Sussex House gardens duke?" She hadn't seen him since they were children, but Alyssa had had the privilege of touring his gardens on several occasions. They were, in a word, magnificent, despite the fact that she found the formal design and the statuary a tad too old-fashioned and perfect, a tad too predictable for her taste. Still, the gardens and grounds redesigned and planted by Capability Brown were a model for every budding gardener to strive toward.

Lady Tressingham frowned. "Of course the Sussex House gardens duke. He owns Sussex House. It's been in his family for generations and you could be part of that family." Sometimes she genuinely despaired of her daughter. How she could have given birth to a creature who was always digging in the dirt and puttering about was beyond her. One would almost think Alyssa was born of yeoman stock instead of some of the bluest blood in all of England. "Honestly, Alyssa! Trust you to think of his gardens instead of his property and title. *Everyone* is buzzing about their appearance here tonight, and all you think about is the duke's gardens." She elbowed Alyssa in the ribs once again. "First the duke and now them. It's so exciting! Keep smiling!"

"Who?"

"The two viscounts and the marquess," her mother explained with an excited, almost giddy edge to her words.

"What is so exciting about two viscounts, a marquess, and a duke at Almack's?" Alyssa asked. "Everyone in society comes here. The rooms are packed with viscounts, marquesses, and dukes."

"Not with *these* viscounts, marquesses, and dukes," Lady Tressingham told her. "They've never been known to darken the assembly room doors. There have been rumors, but I didn't believe it possible. . . . Still, if Sussex, Shepherdston, Grantham, and Abernathy are here, they've come looking for brides. I wonder which one it is or if they've all decided to marry."

"Did you say Abernathy?"

"Of course, my little Incomparable." The countess shivered with excitement. "Lady Cowper and the other patronesses are beside themselves with anticipation and joy. This is a first, my darling girl. History is being made and we are here to play a part in it."

Alyssa groaned at her mother's histrionics. But Lady Tressingham took no notice. "These are four of the wealthiest and most eligible gentlemen in London." She paused. "Well, *three* of the wealthiest. I've heard that Viscount Grantham is a bit pressed for cash, but no matter. He'll find a suitable heiress."

"How can you be so sure?" Alyssa was intrigued in spite of herself.

"There aren't that many eligible viscounts left. What untitled heiress or heiress from a recently titled family wouldn't want to marry a viscount whose family name and titles date back to the time of Macbeth?"

"I'm sure there must be one or two besides me," Alyssa answered. "I cannot be the only forward-thinking girl in London."

"You read too much," Lady Tressingham said flatly. "And you think too much. It puts silly notions in your head." She took hold of her daughter's chin and turned Alyssa to face her. After quickly pinching color into Alyssa's cheeks, Lady Tressingham placed her hands on Alyssa's shoulders and turned her toward Lady Cowper. "Take a good look at them, my darling, and tell me that you wouldn't be flattered to have any one of them single you out for a waltz."

Alyssa looked, and what she saw made her jaw drop open in a most unladylike fashion.

"Close your mouth, dear," her mother advised, "or use your fan to cover it. You'll draw flies."

Lady Tressingham was gratified to see that for once her daughter did as she was told. "Forget the marquess and the viscounts and concentrate your attentions on the duke. Her Grace, the duchess, has often reminded me that she intends to have the best for her son. And my girls are the best."

Alyssa nodded in absentminded agreement, but she barely spared a glance for the tall, elegantly handsome man. Her attention was focused not on the duke but on the man in the center of the group of three.

He was staring at her, and Alyssa could feel the heat of his gaze from across the room. It wasn't the first time she'd caught him looking at her. She'd seen him at Lady Cleveland's earlier in the week and then again, two days later, at Lady Dorrance's musicale. She remembered him, remembered the expression on his face when he looked at her and the heat reflected in his brilliant blue eyes. His was a face a woman dreamed about. And although she hated to admit it, Alyssa had found herself dreaming about it ever since she'd first seen him at Lady Cleveland's ball for the simple reason that *he* was unforgettable.

Chapter 5

"Although normally deadly dull and unremarkable this early in the season, my accidental discovery of the existence of the Free Fellows League has made Almack's quite the opposite tonight."

—LADY ALYSSA CARROLLTON, DIARY NOTATION, 25 APRIL 1810

"*That's the one,*" Griffin said, nodding at the girl standing with her mother across the room.

Jarrod groaned.

"What is it?"

"You don't want that one," Jarrod answered.

"Of course I do," Griff responded, narrowing his gaze at Jarrod. "Why? What's wrong with her?"

Although he tended to avoid the ton as much as possible, Jarrod knew everyone in it and all the latest *on-dits* about them. "Beyond being a bit more rational than most any female I've ever met, there's nothing wrong with *her.*"

"Then what's the matter?" Griff demanded. "Who is she?"

"Lady Alyssa Carrollton."

Griffin wrinkled his brow. He knew that name from somewhere. "Carrollton? Isn't that the family name of the Earl of—"

"Yes." Colin nodded. "Tressingham. The one who talks of nothing but horseflesh and hounds. Every time you see him. Bores you silly. Even carries miniatures of his favorite hounds. Tressingham is the one who's always after your father to breed Weymouth's dog to Tressingham's bitch."

"That seems to be what Griff has in mind," Jarrod remarked dryly. "Only in human form."

Griff closed his eyes and slowly shook his head from side to side, as if unable to comprehend the news that the young lady of his dreams was the daughter of the biggest bore in England. "He has a daughter who looks like *that* and he carries miniatures of his *hounds?*" He opened his eyes and stared at Lady Alyssa. "There must be a strain of madness in the family." He glanced over at Jarrod and winked. "Blister it, but I knew there had to be a fly in the ointment somewhere!"

Colin snorted. "Tressingham isn't the only fly in the ointment." He turned to look at the Duke of Sussex. "Rumor has it that the duchess of Sussex wants her for her son's bride."

Griffin looked over at the duke and glared at the immaculate fit of his coat, the snowy white perfection of his four-in-hand, and the sleek fit of his evening trousers. Daniel, the ninth Duke of Sussex, had everything Griffin had to offer and more. Sussex's family name was as ancient and as well respected as Griff's. His title was more prestigious. His estates were grander and his personal fortune greater. Griffin couldn't best him in looks, either, for Sussex was every bit as tall and equally attractive. Some would say more attractive, for Sussex was perfection, elegance, and grace personified, and Griff was too big to be considered elegant. He was merely ruggedly handsome. "Sussex can have anyone he wants."

"So can you," Jarrod pointed out.

"I want *her,*" Griffin answered in a stubborn tone of voice.

"Apparently, so does he," Jarrod said, giving Griff a pointed look.

"Has he offered for her yet?" Griff demanded.

"Not that I've heard," Jarrod admitted. "But he will. His mother . . ."

"He'll have to choose someone else," Griff insisted. "He has plenty of time. The clock isn't ticking for him. He isn't going off to war."

"He may see things differently," Jarrod reasoned. "And the Tressinghams are sure to choose a wealthy duke over a wealthy viscount. Look around. The room is filled with lovely young ladies. Do yourself a favor and choose someone else. Someone who doesn't interest you."

Griff was incredulous. "Why would I do that?"

"Because you're a Free Fellow," Jarrod reminded him. "You took an oath. As Free Fellows, *we shall never be encumbered by sentiment known as love or succumb to female wiles or tears.*"

"I'm not in love," Griff said. "And I've yet to meet the girl, so I can't be succumbing to female wiles or tears."

"Maybe not," Colin added. "But you're in danger of breaking another oath." He stared at Griff and recited from memory, *"We shall sacrifice ourselves on the altar of duty in order to beget our heirs, but we shall take no pleasure in the task. We shall look upon the act in the same manner as medicine that must be swallowed."*

Griffin groaned. "We took those oaths before we knew what we would be sacrificing. . . ." He looked at his friends. "We were too young to have any practical carnal knowledge. . . ."

"An oath is an oath," Jarrod said. "And a gentleman always keeps his oath."

"Especially when that oath was signed and sealed with blood," Colin reminded him.

Griff sighed. "I *am* keeping my oath—as much of it as possible under the circumstances. I've no wish to relinquish my Free Fellows status. I don't want to marry a stranger. But since circumstances compel me to do so in order to get an heir, I'd like to choose from the best *breeding*"—Griff winced as he said the word—"stock." He found the idea of choosing women as if they were cattle personally distasteful, but that was the way in which these things were done, and he couldn't change tradition at this late date. The fact was that he *was* marrying in order to get his family an heir and as far as his father, the Earl of Weymouth, was concerned, only the best breeding stock would do.

Colin looked at Jarrod. "He has a point."

"Yes," Jarrod agreed. "He does." He turned to Griff. "Her father may be a tremendous bore, but Lady Alyssa is a beauty, and her family name is as old and honorable as yours. She'll bring a handsome dowry into the marriage, and she certainly looks capable of producing an heir."

"And we didn't say that we couldn't find our wives attractive, only that we couldn't love them or succumb to female wiles," Colin elaborated. "As to taking pleasure in the physical act . . ." he shrugged his shoulders. "I suppose that's for each of us to decide for ourselves." He grinned at Griff and then at Jarrod. "After all, we *were* only nine and ten at the time."

Jarrod relented. "Then we're agreed. The charter can be amended. If we have to marry, we ought to get some pleasure out of it." He reached over and clapped Griffin on the back. "Let's find Lady Cowper and arrange an introduction before Sussex does. He's more likely to win her than you are. But at least you'll know what you're losing."

"Isn't he divine?" Lady Tressingham lifted her fan, shielded her face, and glanced across the room at the man staring back at them. He smiled, and she answered back with a practiced flick of her wrist, expertly employing her fan in the art of flirtation. "Isn't Sussex the most attractive man you've ever seen?"

There was no doubt that the Duke of Sussex was attractive, but there was something more appealing about the man on his right. "The duke is quite attractive, Mama," Alyssa answered dutifully. "But tell me, who are the viscounts, and which one is the marquess?" She tried to sound as if her question were born of polite curiosity instead of a sudden, aching need to know.

Lady Tressingham gave a pained sigh. "You should have been studying your Debrett's instead of refolding all the linens and making a pest of yourself with the housekeeper and the staff. Did you bother to memorize the pages I marked? Or any of it? Haven't you been listening to anything I've said during the past few weeks? I cannot believe I reared such an ignorant daughter."

Alyssa looked her mother in the eye. "I'm not ignorant, Mama. Just indifferent. Since I didn't intend to marry, it made no sense to waste time memorizing information I didn't need. And when you insisted I reconsider my decision, I decided to wait to memorize the pages of Debrett's that will apply to me once you and Papa decide who I'm to marry."

"That's very sensible," Lady Tressingham admitted, "except that you need the information before you choose a husband. Otherwise, how will you know what you're getting? What if the duke doesn't come up to snuff and offer for you?" Lady Tressingham frowned. It didn't bear thinking on, but it was possible. After all, young Sussex had failed to offer for her three other daughters despite his exalted mother's wishes.

"Quite right, Mama, but I knew there was no need for me to worry about that because I knew you were very familiar with Debrett's and I didn't know about the duke or his mother's plans. Besides, I was busy gaining other knowledge—housekeeping knowledge every *bride*"— Alyssa said the magic word—"needs. Now, will you please tell me which viscount is which?"

"The only real housekeeping knowledge a bride needs is how to supervise a staff," Lady Tressingham insisted stubbornly. "Your Debrett's would be of more use in this situation. Now that you're well on your way to becoming the Incomparable Beauty of the Season, you suddenly care about the knowledge you should have already gained from Debrett's."

"Yes, Mama, *now* I care. But even if I *had* memorized Debrett's, it wouldn't help, because Debrett's doesn't include likenesses, and no one wants to look or feel ignorant in front of a prospective suitor's companions," Alyssa replied quickly, praying her mother would supply the necessary information without further comment because she didn't like dissembling. Especially to her mother. "And it's obvious that those three men are friends, so tell me, who is who?"

Her mother sighed once again. "The one on the left is Viscount Grantham. The one in the center is Viscount Abernathy . . ."

Good heavens! So that was Lord Abernathy . . . Abernathy who wasn't ignorant or a fool, but who was a sworn Free Fellow. Whatever that was.

"I had no idea Sussex was a part of their group. He's a year or so younger." Alyssa turned her attention back to what her mother was saying. "Shepherdston, Abernathy, and Grantham are boon companions, and now it seems that Sussex is as well. . . . Of course, that will probably change after your marriage. It is always understood that once a gentleman marries, he relinquishes his previous friendships with his *unmarried* friends and begins a new life with his wife and *their* friends."

"How horrible!" Alyssa was shocked.

"You say that now," Lady Tressingham said, "but you'll feel differently when you're a duchess. Look up and smile. He's headed this way."

"A duchess?" Alyssa blinked. "I don't want to be a duchess."

Chapter 6

"I've met the future Viscountess Abernathy. We appear to share similar sensibilities. I've no delusions of grandeur. Fortunately, neither has she."

—GRIFFIN, LORD ABERNATHY, JOURNAL NOTATION, 26 APRIL 1810

"*And I, for one, am relieved to hear it.*"

Lady Tressingham gasped. "Where did you come from?"

"According to family legend, my mother and father gave birth to me. Here in London. Some years ago."

Alyssa recognized his voice the moment he spoke. She looked up to find her gaze snared and held fast by the bluest pair of eyes she'd ever seen. Eyes she recognized from two other occasions.

He bowed first to her mother and then to her as Lady Cowper, the most amiable of Almack's seven patronesses, made the necessary introductions. "Lady Tressingham, may I present to you Lord Abernathy?"

The countess nodded reluctantly.

Lady Cowper beamed at the viscount and then at Alyssa. "Lord Abernathy, Lady Tressingham and her daughter, Lady Alyssa Carrollton."

"Lady Tressingham." The viscount lifted her hand and brushed his lips over her knuckles.

"We were expecting someone else," she offered by way of apology.

"I gathered," he said, before lifting Alyssa's hand and brushing his lips against it. "Lady Alyssa."

"My lord," Alyssa murmured.

Lord Abernathy turned to Lady Cowper. "Thank you most kindly for the introduction."

"Not at all, dear boy," she replied. "Glad to be of service. To you both." She gave Alyssa a mysterious smile. "Enjoy yourselves in the waltz."

"The waltz?" Lady Tressingham glanced at Lady Cowper.

Lady Cowper's smile broadened. "Many of our ladies and gentlemen have danced the waltz in their travels abroad. And although it is not generally accepted here in England, we—the other patronesses and I—have decided to be the first to allow one waltz an evening." She turned to Lord Abernathy. "I believe it's next."

Griffin recognized an opening when he saw it. "Do you waltz, Lady Alyssa?"

Alyssa nodded. The dance instructor her mother had hired had taught them all—Lady Tressingham and her four daughters—how to waltz, even though the dance had not yet found acceptance in England.

"May I?" Griffin bowed to Alyssa, then took her by the hand and led her onto the dance floor.

Her thoughts were in turmoil as he whirled her around the room in time to the music. Raising her chin a bit higher in order to meet his gaze, Alyssa found herself staring into the intricately tied folds of his cravat. He was taller up close than he'd looked at a distance and far more handsome. He wasn't as classically handsome as his friend the duke. Lord Abernathy's face was a bit too masculine, his features too strong. But his eyes, as blue as a newborn baby's, were truly gorgeous and succeeded in softening what might have otherwise been too rugged a face.

Alyssa studied the line of his jaw and the tiny indentation in the center of his chin. Although she was certain that he had shaved earlier, the shadow of his beard had begun to darken his jaw. She wondered how his whiskers would feel beneath her fingertips, how they would feel against the tip of her tongue.

"A penny for your thoughts."

Alyssa missed a step and would have stumbled if not for his smooth recovery. "Pardon?"

"You were a thousand miles away." He smiled down at her. "And I couldn't help but wonder what you were thinking."

"You're not a duke." Alyssa said the first thing that came to mind. "My mother is terribly disappointed about that."

"I noticed," he answered. "What about you?"

"What about me?" she asked.

"Have you changed your mind?"

"About what?"

"About being a duchess?"

"Heavens, no!" Alyssa laughed. "The restraints placed upon me by my sex and my position as an earl's daughter are quite enough, thank you. I can barely breathe as it is. I've certainly no desire to add to them by marrying a duke."

"It could be that by marrying a duke and becoming a duchess, the restraints placed upon you would be greatly lessened," Griff offered.

"Not if the duke in question has a powerful mother who, upon his marriage, would be relegated to the rank of dowager duchess." Alyssa may not have seen the duke since he was in short pants, but she'd heard enough about his mother to know she relished control and the power her rank afforded her.

"And is that the state of affairs with the duke in question?"

"Most definitely," Alyssa told him.

"She might take a fancy to you."

Alyssa shook her head. "It's possible, but not very likely. It's been my experience that powerful women do not appreciate having their position usurped, and sharing the same house could prove to be a most unpleasant state of affairs for the usurper."

"I see." Griff pretended to ponder the problem. "In that case, might you consider marrying a viscount?"

Alyssa answered his teasing in kind. "Only if he

comes equipped without a powerful mother and with a garden." She smiled up at him.

"A garden?" He frowned. The mother he understood, but he was puzzled by her second requirement. "Like the Sussex House gardens?"

She shook her head. "Not like Sussex House gardens. They're perfectly magnificent, that's true, but I don't want a garden someone else has perfected. I want to create my own."

"You like to design gardens?"

"I like to garden," she corrected, smiling. "Without an army of gardeners and a hundred years of tradition dictating what I can and cannot do. Unfortunately, I've been forbidden to dig in our gardens for the duration of the season."

"And why is that?"

"A lady of impeccable breeding should not give the appearance of coming from yeoman stock."

"That sounds as if it could only come from a mother."

"My mother," she agreed. "Which is why I'd prefer to marry a man who will provide me with a garden of my own and who won't complain about my desire to dig in it."

Griffin grinned. "In that case, I'm your viscount. My title isn't as lofty, but it's old and well-respected and it comes with an estate, a manor house, acres of parkland, and a rather overgrown and badly neglected garden and," he added for incentive, "a generous income."

"You forgot about the mother," she teased.

"I have one," he admitted. "Lovely lady. Very nice. Looking forward to welcoming a viscountess into the family."

"Oh, well." Alyssa managed a perfect imitation of her mother's dramatic sigh. "The garden sounded too good to be true."

"Did I mention the fact that my father is still very much alive and that he and my mother have a very large, very well-tended estate of their own in a county far away from the one in which my viscountess would reside?"

She had thought, at first, that he was teasing, but the

look in his eyes told her he wasn't. "You're serious. . . ."

"I have need of a bride," he said. "And I want her to be you."

Alyssa didn't find his proposal entirely flattering, nor was she surprised by the suddenness of it. But she pretended to be by quietly, calmly murmuring all the protests she imagined any young lady would murmur at such a time. "Lord Abernathy, we've only just met. I know nothing about you. You know nothing about me."

"I know enough," he told her. "I chose you from the moment I first saw you at Lady Cleveland's."

"This is much too sudden—"

"Not for me," he said. "I don't have the luxury of time for a long courtship. I'm joining my regiment soon."

"You're leaving?" Alyssa bit her bottom lip.

"I'm afraid so. Unless you choose to stay with my parents, you'll be alone at Abernathy Manor." He gave her a rueful smile. "As alone as one can be with fifty servants wandering about the place."

She knew why he was offering to marry her, knew she should be offended at the idea of being his means to an end, but she wasn't the least bit offended. She was intrigued and seriously considering his offer. "How long would you be gone?"

"I'm a soldier," he said. "And we're at war. Who can say? Perhaps months, perhaps years, perhaps forever."

"Forever?" She tried very hard to keep from sounding eager, and she must have succeeded, for he seemed not to notice or find fault with her manner.

"There is always that possibility," he reminded her. "I'm in the cavalry."

The strains of the music faded, and Griff gracefully guided Alyssa to a stop and led her off the dance floor on the opposite side of the room from where they had left her mother.

The assembly rooms at Almack's were deuced inadequate when it came to seeking respite from the crowd. Unlike most private residences, Almack's had no terrace or gardens from which to escape the closeness of the

ballroom. Griff had never been inside the assembly
rooms, but he knew that Almack's was perfectly suited
to its purpose, which was to provide a place for eligible
young men to view and dance with the marriageable
young ladies without danger of compromising them.

The only possible chance of escaping the eagle eyes
and ears of the patronesses and of the Marriage Mart
Mamas lay in finding the ladies' retiring room unoccupied or in slipping behind one of the curtained window
alcoves or behind the profusion of strategically placed
potted palms. Griff decided the ladies' retiring room
would offer the most privacy—provided it was unoccupied and provided Lady Alyssa proved to be a passable actress. "It's uncomfortably hot in here," he
prompted after their dance. "You must feel faint—"

"Not at all," Alyssa protested. *Except when he stands
so close.*

Recalling that she was an innocent, Griff tried again.
"If you feel faint, Lady Alyssa, I'll be happy to escort
you to the ladies' retiring room or to one of the curtained
alcoves behind the potted palms where you might catch
your breath in *private*." He emphasized the word.

Understanding dawned, and Alyssa blushed to realize
that he wanted permission to escort her somewhere private so they might continue their discussion away from
prying eyes and ears. "Oh!" She leaned heavily against
him, feigning dizziness. "As a matter of fact, I do feel
faint, my lord."

"Easy," he cautioned, keeping a hand on her arm as
he pretended to steady her. "Don't overact. I'll have to
burn a few feathers as it is. . . ."

Alyssa wrinkled her nose as he expertly guided her
through the crowd, past the first card room, to the ladies'
retiring room.

The drapes hanging in the doorway were opened, a
sign that the room was unoccupied. But Griff wasn't
taking any chances. He motioned Alyssa inside, then
leaned close to whisper, "Are we alone?"

Alyssa nodded. "Yes."

Griff quickly stepped inside the room and pulled the

velvet drapes partially closed. To pull the drapes completely closed was to risk the chance that someone would notice and come to inquire about the occupant. To leave them completely open ran the risk of having some other lady or some other couple seek respite from the crowd. Partly closing the drapes seemed the best way to insure some privacy without putting Alyssa's reputation at risk.

Griff glanced around, getting his bearings. The ladies' retiring room was large, with medallioned ceilings and numerous gilt mirrors. Upholstered chairs lined the walls, and several velvet-covered low fainting couches were placed about the room. A large circular table in the center of the room held a stack of ladies' handkerchiefs, a collection of decorative smelling bottles, a large metal box of Promethean matches, and several bottles of asbestos and sulfuric acid in which to dip them in order to ignite them. A large china urn held an arrangement of peafowl and peacock feathers for burning.

He pulled out a peacock feather and lifted several matches along with a bottle of igniting fluid, and a bottle of smelling salts and carried them to a table beside a fainting couch away from the door, close to the far wall out of the line of sight of the gilt mirrors, making certain they were at the ready should he be required to use them. When he was certain they were alone and out of earshot of anyone who happened along, Griff took hold of Alyssa's hand. "Will you do me the honor of becoming my wife?"

Alyssa's heart began to pound. She would be foolish to take him seriously. She couldn't take him up on his offer, and yet she thought she might regret it if she allowed this chance pass her by. It wasn't as if she was going to be miraculously delivered from the prospect of being sold into marriage to a stranger. At least, with Viscount Abernathy, she could do the choosing instead of her father. And Alyssa really disliked the thought of being the duchess. The rank of viscountess would suit her much better. She could do as she liked. No one would pay much attention to a viscountess. Not when there were countesses and marchionesses and duchesses around.

"What would you expect of me?" she asked.

"Well, I will require an heir," he said.

Alyssa frowned. She'd forgotten about that possibility.

He gave her a commiserating smile. "*That* is the purpose of marriage for people like us."

"Yes, of course you'll require an heir," she murmured. "And a spare after that one."

"Two sons is the standard for which every man hopes," he said. "But I won't demand it. One will be sufficient. And once the inconvenience of your confinement is over, you will naturally be free to pursue your own interests without the worry or responsibility of rearing a child. I can afford excellent care, and our child shall have the best nurses and nannies."

"I wouldn't mind the responsibility," she murmured. "Or having a hand in the rearing of my child."

"Then, of course, you would have a hand in it," Griff assured her. "The decision would be yours."

Alyssa smiled. "We're speaking of having a child together, and I don't yet know your Christian name."

"It's Griffin," he answered. "My friends call me Griff. But you may call me anything you like."

He grinned at her, and Alyssa felt her heart flutter at the warmth in his brilliant blue eyes.

"Some would call you mad," Alyssa retorted. "I may be one of them. Tell me, Lord Abernathy, why me?"

"Because I have need of a wife, and you are the only young lady I've ever seen who made me believe I was meant to be her husband."

Chapter 7

"I have met the man I am going to marry. He comes with an old title and a neglected estate. He also comes with a commission in His Majesty's Army. With luck, I shall become a viscountess and take up residence at his country estate in time to continue my experiments in propagating and transplanting Capability Brown's variety of pink rhododendrons."

—LADY ALYSSA CARROLLTON, DIARY ENTRY, 25 APRIL 1810.

As an answer, it was perfect.

Alyssa stared at Lord Abernathy's enticing lips. *What a charming actor he turned out to be!* His words, delivered in such an earnest manner, were meant to melt a young girl's most tentative heart. Or an older, more experienced woman's most deliberate heart. They were practiced, calculating words, cleverly disguised as sentiment, and they were—quite simply—the most eloquent argument for accepting a proposal she'd ever heard.

His words were so eloquent that Alyssa's heart seemed to stop at the beauty of them. They were so eloquent that she came within a hair's breadth of believing them.

The fact is that she would have believed him if she hadn't heard the truth spoken from his own lips three-quarters of an hour earlier when she'd stood hidden by a row of potted palms and accidentally overhead the conversation between Viscounts Grantham and Abernathy and the Marquess of Shepherdston—the mysteri-

ous trio who referred to themselves as the Free Fellows
League.

But she had overheard their conversation, and she
knew that—his pretty words to the contrary—he had no
interest in becoming any woman's husband.

She knew because she'd heard him swear it.

And now, three-quarters of an hour later, Alyssa knew
that she would be wise to ignore his eloquent words
because she couldn't possibly believe him. But there was
a part of her—a secret, highly impractical, girlish, and
romantic part of her—that thought how nice it would be
to have a man like Griffin Abernathy whisper those
words and to know in her heart of hearts that he meant
them.

No wonder tenderhearted Lady Cowper had smiled
broadly at her request for a discreet introduction and had
obligingly brought Viscount Abernathy over to make her
acquaintance. Lady Cowper no doubt knew that while
Griffin Abernathy might not bear the lofty title of a duke
or a marquess, he had charm and looks that were certain
to make any young lady's heart flutter.

Including the heart of an Incomparable Beauty.

Alyssa pursed her lips and wrinkled her brow in concentration. She didn't want her heart to flutter. Possess-
ing a heart that fluttered at every handsome gentleman's
pretty whispers was hazardous to one's virtue and peace
of mind. It was also most insensible. And Alyssa had
earned her reputation for being the most sensible of girls.
She didn't want to succumb to the impractical notion of
falling in love. She knew better. She didn't want to think
that she could be susceptible to his charm. She was under no illusions. She was different from the other virginal—the word stuck in her mind like a burr beneath
her flesh—young ladies clamoring for attention. She
hadn't come to Almack's in hopes of snaring a suitable
husband. Alyssa had come kicking and screaming, pro-
testing the injustice of being put on display and sold to
the highest bidder like cattle at auction. Of all the young
ladies present, she had thought herself the least likely to
be noticed. She had thought herself the least likely to

receive undue attention from any of the gentlemen she had spent her first season discouraging. And she had prayed that would continue to be the case. But Alyssa had discovered, to her mother's eternal delight and to her eternal dismay, that she'd been named an Incomparable Beauty.

Unfortunately, Incomparable Beauties were expected to make extraordinary matches, and Alyssa wanted no part of it. She didn't want a husband. Extraordinary or otherwise.

What she wanted—what she craved, above all else—was freedom. An escape from the unrelenting rounds of social calls and parties and routs and balls. And therein lay her dilemma, because the endless rounds of parties would continue unabated unless she found a way off the merry-go-round. There would be no respite from it until the season ended and no escaping into the garden or the stables.

The only hope for a way out was by accepting a proposal from a suitable gentleman.

The question was: suitable for whom? Her mama and papa? Or herself?

"Is that a yes? A no? Or an invitation?"

Alyssa blinked, thrown off balance by the look in his blue eyes and his softly spoken statement as he maneuvered her further into the room, into the shadows, away from the other people wandering in and out of the assembly rooms. "Invitation?"

"I accept." Griff brought his face closer to hers. "Because, in any event, I find the expression on your face and the pucker of your lips fascinating and quite suddenly, irresistible." Leaning forward, he touched his lips to hers.

Griff meant to satisfy his curiosity, to see if her plump, rosy lips were as soft as they appeared to be, but Alyssa gave a startled gasp at the unexpected intimacy, and he took advantage of the opportunity. He teased at the seam of her lips, running the tip of his tongue across it, gently entreating her to grant him full access to the sweet recesses of her mouth.

Alyssa didn't disappoint him. She made a soft sound of willing surrender and allowed him further liberties.

Griff captured her breath, swallowing the soft sigh that escaped her lips as he deepened the kiss. She tasted of orgeat, of barley water and almond flavoring, and the tart sweetness of untutored innocence.

A door to one of the card rooms slid closed, and the sound of the orchestra striking up another tune drifted from the ballroom along with bits of hushed conversation and soft laughter. Griffin broke the kiss.

Alyssa opened her eyes and murmured a protest. "What?"

"Sssh." Griff pressed his finger against her lips, feeling the dampness he'd left there. "We've company." He motioned Alyssa to the couch, then stepped back, turning so that his broad shoulders shielded her from view as another couple started toward the room.

Griff grabbed a match and dipped it into the bottle of igniting liquid. The match caught. A flame shot up from the end of it, and the odor of sulfur filled the air. Griff singed the end of a feather, waved it around for good measure, then extinguished it and the match.

The footsteps outside the door halted. The couple exchanged a few whispers and moved on.

The unmistakable smell of sulfur had signaled that the room was occupied.

Griff exhaled a sigh of relief. It wouldn't have been enough to stop a worried mama, a light-headed deb, or one of the patronesses, but it had been enough to deter another couple hoping for privacy. He glanced around. The fact that he'd been kissing Alyssa Carrollton in full view of anyone who happened to venture into the ladies' retiring room or—Griff crossed the room and peeked around the draperies—across the corridor from anyone in the card room who happened to look up from play, was a sobering thought.

"Are we safe?" Alyssa whispered from behind.

"I am," Griff answered. "But I fear you may be in grave danger."

"From what?" She stood on tiptoe, looking for the menace, trying to see over his shoulder.

"Not what," he murmured. "But whom."

Alyssa leaned back, staring up at his face. "I very much doubt that anyone would dare to accost me with you here to protect me."

"That's true," he replied in a low, husky tone ripe with layers of meaning. "But who will protect you from me?"

Alyssa's breath quickened, and her heart began a rapid tattoo.

Griff stared at her neck, mesmerized by the tiny pulse point rising and falling in the soft, vulnerable hollow of her throat.

"I wasn't aware that I needed protection from you, Lord Abernathy." Her voice quavered, and she pressed her knees together to keep from shaking or collapsing at his feet.

"Then allow me to make you aware." He closed his eyes and pressed a kiss against the pulse beating in the hollow of her throat, then slowly, tenderly kissed his way up the curve of her neck. He nipped at her earlobe, and Alyssa sucked in a breath as a rush of warmth flooded her body from head to toe. Her legs began to tremble, and her knees nearly buckled at the surge of raw emotion flowing through her.

Griff tightened his arm about her waist to keep her from sinking to the floor, then smiled a wicked little smile and breathed against her ear.

The warm, moist air against her earlobe became a current of electrical charges, carrying dozens of tiny shocks that imprinted themselves upon her soul. The atmosphere around them crackled with tension and the stirrings of desire. Her whole body seemed to tingle, and Alyssa marveled at her reaction. She'd never felt anything like it, and she wondered, suddenly, how many other surprises Lord Abernathy had in store.

She didn't have long to wonder, for he flicked his tongue against the pearl drop fastened to her earlobe, before plunging the hot wet tip of his tongue into the shell-like contour inside her ear. She nearly yelped in astonishment as the sudden, startling impropriety of that touch sent her senses reeling. He laved her ear, and Alyssa settled comfortably in his arms, yielding to his naughty breach of etiquette, opening herself up to more of his tantalizing surprises, welcoming the erotic sensation as he sent more shivers up and down her spine.

Griff felt her tremble in his arms and paused briefly to savor the effect, then continued his journey, kissing his way along her jaw until he reached her mouth.

Griff brushed her lips with his—once, twice, thrice—then covered them with his own, paying particular attention to her plump bottom lip as he savored the texture, tracing his tongue over it, memorizing the pattern of the fine lines that marked it. He sucked on her bottom lip, teasing her, tempting her to open her mouth and allow him right of entry and permission to explore.

Alyssa surrendered to temptation, parting her lips, inviting him inside, silently entreating him to deepen the kiss. He complied, moving his lips on hers, kissing her harder, then softer, then harder once more, testing her response, slipping his tongue past her teeth, investigating the sweet, hot interior of her mouth with practiced finesse.

He traced the elegant line of her neck with the tips of his fingers, then tangled his fingers in her hair as he leisurely stroked the inside of her mouth in a provocative imitation of lovemaking. And while Lady Alyssa was ignorant of the language of love, her body was not. It recognized the ancient mating ritual and responded in kind. Her breasts plumped, the tips of them hardening into insistent little points, clamoring to be noticed, and the surge of current that went through her body at the boldness of his kiss settled in the region between her thighs, causing an unrelenting ache for something she couldn't name—something she suspected *he* would have no trouble recognizing or supplying.

Alyssa moaned softly, pressing herself against him in an effort to assuage the aching as she returned his kiss, following his lead, learning the taste of him, the thrust and parry of his tongue and the rasp of his teeth.

He heard her soft moan and somewhere in the midst of kissing her, Griff forgot she was an innocent. He held her close against him with one hand splayed against the small of her back, while he used his other hand to blaze a path with the palm of his hand from the soft curls at the nape of her neck, over her shoulder, down her arm, and between their bodies, gently cupping the soft underside of her breast. Satisfying the ache in his body, Griff pressed her hips to his, allowing her to feel the hard line of his body through the thin silk of her skirts.

He was wedging his thigh between hers when a soft giggle somewhere to the right caught his attention. Blister it! But he'd managed once again to come within a hair's breadth of compromising Lady Alyssa Carrollton— and not just compromising her, but taking her right there. Right then. On the couch in the ladies' retiring room at Almack's.

What the devil had happened to his self-control? His discipline? Griffin broke the kiss and stepped away, struggling to gain control of his raging desire. He looked down at her upturned face, the moisture on her lips, and her blissful yet slightly dazed expression, and decided he would marry Alyssa Carrollton or no one.

Suddenly bereft of his touch and his kisses, Alyssa opened her eyes. Griffin had turned to look over his right shoulder. Alyssa studied the strong line of his lean jaw and felt a compelling urge to sweep her tongue along it. Standing on tiptoe, she attempted to do just that, but his jaw remained enticingly out of reach. She settled for the sun-baked bit of flesh barely visible above his starched neckcloth.

Griffin whirled around, nearly knocking her aside. "What—"

"It's called a kiss, and I was aiming for your jaw, but still, I'm gratified to know you're not entirely unaffected by it," she said softly.

"Sssh," he warned in a husky whisper, reaching out to steady her. "We aren't alone any longer."

"Not again!" Alyssa blew out an exasperated breath.

"I vow this room is as crowded as the ballroom. Isn't there someplace we can go for privacy?"

A vision of his coach popped into Griff's mind. It was dark inside the coach, comfortable, private, and convenient. The seats were upholstered in thick, soft velvet, and the windows were hung with matching curtains. It was parked a block or so down the street, and after he and Alyssa . . . Griffin sighed. After he relieved Lady Alyssa of her virtue, he could see her home. Safe and sound. With no one the wiser and only his offer of marriage between them.

He waited until the latest threat of discovery passed, then took Alyssa by the hand and drew her out of the shadows. "I could take you to my carriage." Griff surprised himself by answering honestly and by half-hoping she'd say yes. "But come morning, your reputation would be in shreds."

"Bother my reputation!" Alyssa exclaimed. "Protecting it has proven to be an endless source of frustration."

Griff laughed. "Reputations are like that. The trouble is that we never realize their value unless we lose them. Only then do we find that they were irreplaceable and that no amount of gold or prestige can restore them completely." He gave her wistful smile. "We'd better get you back to the assembly before your mother decides you've been gone much too long."

"Wait!" She ordered. "How do I look?"

She looked beautiful. Her eyes were luminous, her skin flushed, and her mouth, bee-stung. She looked as if she'd been well and thoroughly kissed. Griff reached out and tucked a stray curl into place. "You look as if you've been kissing a man in the ladies' retiring room."

Alyssa blinked. "Are you certain?"

Griff nodded.

"Can people really tell from looking at me that I've been kissed?"

"Not everyone, but a great many of the people in there"—he gestured toward the assembly room—"could discern it. And not simply that you've been kissed, but that you've been kissing in return."

Alyssa beamed. "How remarkable!"

Griff frowned at her. "Quite remarkable. Very remarkable. Extremely remarkable. Reputation-ruining remarkable."

"Oh, yes, well . . ." Her voice was low, disheartened. "There is that."

"Yes," he murmured. "Unfortunately, there is that."

She brightened suddenly. "How can they tell?"

"Your eyes are bright, your skin is flushed, and your lips are swollen."

"As if I'd been crying?"

Griff nodded. "Your nose isn't red, but other than that, you do look as if you might have been crying."

"That's it," she replied. "If anyone is rude enough to inquire, I'll simply say I've been crying."

He grimaced. "Thereby ruining *my* reputation."

Alyssa was stunned. "How could I ruin your reputation?"

"No one will inquire directly, Lady Innocence. Except, perhaps, your mother. Everyone else will gossip and speculate and offer your reputation up as fodder for the latest *on-dit*. And when they tire of gossiping and speculating about you, they'll want to know what I did to cause your tears. Because I was, after all, the man you were with when you shed those phantom tears. Either way, both our reputations would suffer, and that's something I would prefer to avoid."

Alyssa was quiet for a moment. "Unless I let it be known that I was crying tears of happiness because you proposed."

"That might work." Griff pursed his lips, considering her suggestion. "But, my position as an officer and a gentleman precludes my speaking to you on such a delicate subject until I've spoken to your father."

Alyssa sighed. "I suppose it's just as well," she told him. "Because I rarely cry, and no one who knows me well would ever believe that a marriage proposal would cause me to shed tears of happiness." She glanced up at him from beneath her lashes, and Griff was captivated by her expression. "Do I still look as if I've been kissed?"

" 'Fraid so," Griff murmured, very much aware that she was in danger of being kissed again. And soon.

"Then it will have to be an accident," she replied.

"Pardon?"

"No matter," Alyssa tucked her hand into the crook of his arm and gave him an impish grin. "Shall we?"

Griff checked to make certain the way was clear before preceding her out of the room. He hovered near the door of the first card room, waiting until she appeared, then escorted her back into the ballroom. "If anyone says anything, I'll tell them you felt faint and that I escorted you to the retiring room and burnt a feather to help revive you because the crush was so thick we couldn't get to your mother."

"Don't worry," Alyssa whispered. "No one will say anything."

Griff smiled. "That's what you think. We reek of sulfur and burnt feathers."

"In this crowd, everyone reeks of something." She gave him a glorious smile. "I promise, your reputation is safe with me. I'll take care of everything. Just don't say I didn't warn you."

The teasing note in her voice should have alerted him; still, Griffin was unprepared for what came next. "Lady Alyssa?"

"Oops!" Alyssa slipped the silk cord of her fan off her wrist and let it fall to the floor. It bounced off the toe of Griffin's buckle shoe, clattered against the polished marble, then skidded to a stop inches away.

Griffin automatically bent down to retrieve it. Alyssa did the same, timing it so that they bumped heads with enough force to bring tears to her eyes.

She saw stars and bit her bottom lip so hard it drew blood.

Griff gritted his teeth against the pain. "Your fan, milady." He handed her her silk and ivory fan, then pulled a handkerchief from his waistcoat pocket and dabbed at the spot of blood on her bottom lip. "Nicely done, milady. You managed to bring tears to both our eyes and to disguise your swollen lips—all at the same time."

Alyssa attempted a smile. "It was the best I could do in the midst of an audience and on such short notice. Besides, now I have reason to feel faint."

"Wellesley couldn't have done any better," Griff replied, rubbing his forehead. There would be a knot there tomorrow. He could feel it swelling already. Griff sat back on his heels and was just about to offer Alyssa his hand, when a pair of purple satin slippers stepped into view.

"Lady Alyssa, Lord Abernathy . . . Are you all right?"

Alyssa looked up to find Lady Jersey, the most acid-tongued of Almack's patronesses, standing over them.

Griff pushed himself to his feet and helped Alyssa to hers.

"I'm fine, Lady Jersey," Alyssa answered. "I dropped my fan, and Lord Abernathy was kind enough to retrieve it for me." She looked the Almack's patroness in the eye, daring her to contradict.

Lady Jersey smiled thinly. "Of course he did, my dear. That's to be expected. Lord Abernathy is, after all, a gentleman." She batted her eyes at Griffin.

Griff cleared his throat.

Lady Jersey smiled at him once again. "Lord Abernathy, if you'll forgive me for taking her away from you, I'll see that Lady Alyssa is returned to her mother. I believe Lady Tressingham is looking for her."

Griff gave Lady Jersey his most charming smile. "Thank you, Lady Jersey, but I believe it's my duty and my pleasure to see that Lady Alyssa is returned safely to her mother. If you'll excuse us." He offered Alyssa his arm.

"Thank you," Alyssa whispered as he guided her through the crowded ballroom toward her mother.

"Before I give you back into your mother's keeping, I must ask if we've a bargain?" Griff reminded her.

"Yes," Alyssa said.

Griff nodded. "Then I'll speak to your father as soon as it can be arranged."

Alyssa groaned. "Can we not simply elope to Gretna Green? You have a coach. It would be much less bother than the alternative." *And much more romantic.*

Griff shook his head. "I'm afraid running away to Scotland is out of the question."

"You wouldn't say that if you knew my father—" Alyssa began.

"I *do* know your father," Griff replied. "At least, in passing."

"Then you understand how much simpler it would be not to seek his permission."

"You're forgetting that I, too, have parents to consider," Griff reminded her. "And my parents would consider my elopement a great insult to you and to them. No," he murmured almost to himself. "I won't disappoint them or make them or us fodder for gossipmongers. If we're going to do this thing, we're going to do it properly with a wedding at Saint Paul's and a breakfast to follow."

The wheels began turning in Alyssa's head. "For how many guests?"

"However many you think proper," Griff answered. "You've more experience in this sort of thing than I."

Alyssa narrowed her gaze at him. "I hate to disappoint you, Lord Abernathy, but I'm not quite as experienced as you seem to believe. This is, after all, *my* first wedding, too."

There was no escaping the biting sarcasm in her voice. "I meant that you had more experience attending—perhaps even, participating—in weddings and wedding breakfasts than I," he amended. "I haven't any siblings, and as a bachelor, I rarely attend weddings." The truth was that he had never attended any weddings. "Surely, you know more about how it's done than I. How many guests would you suggest in order to quell gossip and speculation among the ton?"

She tapped her bottom lip with her index finger as she considered his question. "Fifty or so of our closest friends would be a minimum."

"Then invite two hundred," Griff advised.

"That sort of wedding takes months of planning."

"We don't have months," Griff said. "So you'll just have to do the best you can." He smiled at her. "If Wellesley can move an entire army to Spain and Portugal in mere weeks, you should be able to plan and execute the sort of wedding we require within days."

"Spoken like a man who has no experience with this sort of thing," Alyssa retorted, refusing to be cajoled by his blue eyes or his incredible smile.

"I have complete faith in your ability," he added.

Alyssa snorted in an unladylike fashion.

"Would it help if I told you that money was no object?"

She smiled at him. "It might, but you're forgetting about my father. He and my mother have their hearts set on a duke or at the very least, a marquess, for me. He might not consider a viscount."

Griff had forgotten about that. "I've good prospects. I'll take my chances."

"Then you should speak with my mother."

"I can't agree more," Griff said. "Unfortunately, it isn't done. Duty and honor require that I speak with your father."

Alyssa nodded. "More's the pity."

Griff fought to keep from laughing aloud. "It isn't too late to change your mind."

"Are you suggesting I should?"

"No," Griff said. "I'm not." He paused and looked down at her. "I'm quite satisfied with my choice."

"You're certain of that?" Alyssa asked.

"Yes," he said. "Are you?"

"Of course, I'm certain," Alyssa told him. "This is my second season. I had suitors and offers last season, but fortunately my two older sisters received better offers. Since two weddings a season were all my father would agree to finance and attend, I was spared. But if I don't find a husband this season, my parents will find one for me."

Griff met her gaze. "Why me?"

"Why not?" she replied. "You're in need of a wife,

and you happen to be the only gentleman I've ever seen who made me feel as if I were meant to be his wife." She threw his words back at him.

"Touché." He smiled. "Did those words sound as well-rehearsed when I said them to you?"

"Oh, no." She looked up at him. "Quite the opposite. They sounded entirely sincere."

"That's nice," he said. "Because they were." He winked at her. "Make no mistake about it, Lady Alyssa Carrollton, I want you for my viscountess."

Recognizing the gleam in his eye for the challenge that it was, Alyssa met his gaze. "Then don't disappoint me."

Griff almost kissed her on the spot. "I wouldn't dream of it."

He escorted Alyssa to her mother. Lifting her hand as he bowed at the waist, he brushed his lips across the back of it and murmured, "A pleasure making your acquaintance, Lady Alyssa. Thank you most kindly for the dance."

"My pleasure, Lord Abernathy."

He let go of Alyssa's hand and turned to her mother. "With your permission, ma'am, I would like to call upon Lord Tressingham tomorrow in order to pay my respects."

Lady Tressingham eyed him speculatively. "I'll see that he's made aware of your impending arrival," she said. "And now, we shall bid you good night, Lord Abernathy, and good luck."

Griff accepted the dismissal. He bowed once more, then turned on his heel and made his way through the crowd toward the card room.

Alyssa lifted her fan to her face in an effort to disguise the fact that she was following his every move.

"Don't bother, Alyssa," Lady Tressingham remarked from behind her own fan. "He's a dream to look upon, but Abernathy's only a viscount and quite unsuitable as long as there are marquesses and a duke in the running."

Chapter 8

"According to the War Office's latest dispatches, Massena has chosen his field marshals and is preparing for battle. I have chosen my bride and am preparing to marry."

—GRIFFIN, VISCOUNT ABERNATHY, JOURNAL ENTRY, 26 APRIL 1810

Griffin gave his white linen neckcloth a final pat, and then fastened the intricately tied folds of his cravat with a gold stickpin bearing his family crest.

He turned to Eastman, his valet. "Will I pass muster?"

"Most excellently, sir," Eastman pronounced. "You look quite the Corinthian."

Griff exhaled. "About time." After discarding half a dozen waistcoats, jackets, neckcloths, and a variety of pins, watch chains, and fobs, he and Eastman had finally decided upon the perfect combination for the task at hand. A coat of dark blue superfine with brass buttons, a brocade waistcoat, linen shirt and neckcloth, trousers of buff doeskin, and glossy black knee boots. "A uniform would have been much less bother. Hell, turning out in full state kit would have been less bother."

The valet shook his head. "It isn't done, my lord."

Griff grinned at Eastman. "I didn't say it was proper. I said it would have been easier."

Eastman met Griffin's grin with a tiny smile. The only time His Majesty's Eleventh Blues turned out in full state kit was for coronations, the opening of parliament, royal weddings, funerals, and parades, and the preparation for those events generally took anywhere from eight to twenty hours. The fact that his lordship considered turning out in full state kit easier than dressing to meet the father of the young lady he intended to marry was a measure of his apprehension. And the fact that his lordship was scheduled to meet with his own father to relay the outcome of his interview immediately afterward, served to heighten Lord Abernathy's nerves. Eastman imagined that His Lordship would rather face a French cavalry charge.

He glanced at the gold anniversary clock on the mantel. "It's time, sir."

"Pardon?" Griff looked up.

"You asked that I remind you of the time, sir, so you wouldn't be late," Eastman reminded him. "It's time."

Griff nodded. "Is Apollo ready?"

"Ready and waiting, sir." Eastman firmed his lips in disapproval but refrained from voicing it.

Griffin recognized his manservant's expression. "Go ahead," he urged. "Speak your mind."

Eastman looked askance.

"You volunteered to accompany me to war, Eastman," Griffin said. "That more than entitles you to voice your opinion in my presence, whatever the occasion."

Eastman took a deep breath. "I question the wisdom of using Apollo as your mode of transportation. He is, after all, a breeding stallion and not the sort of mount a gentleman usually rides when paying a call upon his intended."

"I'm not paying a call upon my intended," Griff said. "I'm paying a call upon her father in order to ask for his daughter's hand in marriage so that she may become my intended." He flashed a self-deprecating grin. "I'm hoping Apollo will provide added incentive in convincing her father."

"I don't understand the necessity, my lord," Eastman admitted.

"The lady I intend to marry is one of the Incomparable Beauties of the season."

"Congratulations, my lord." Eastman grinned. Lord Abernathy had been quite closemouthed about the young lady. Until this moment, he had yet to offer any hint as to her identity. Of course, that was the proper thing to do. A gentleman did not presume or bandy a young lady's name about until the negotiations were concluded and the wedding notice appeared in the morning paper.

Griffin continued, "Her father is an earl, and the young lady has a plethora of suitors from which to choose—including the Duke of Sussex. Her family may not see the advantages of having their daughter marry me. I am only a viscount."

"A young, handsome viscount. A viscount with an ancient title. A viscount who is wealthy in his own right and heir to the Earl of Weymouth," Eastman listed Griff's attributes.

Griff laughed. "Still a lowly viscount. But one whose father happens to possess one of the finest stables and breeding kennels in England."

Eastman looked puzzled.

"The father of the young lady in question is quite a keen admirer of both."

"I see." And although Eastman was no judge of horseflesh, he knew Apollo was clearly superior to the horses other gentlemen rode. "I don't see how the young lady's father could fail to be impressed by Apollo—or by his rider."

"My thoughts exactly," Griffin agreed.

"Still," Eastman mused, "it seems a shame to have to forgo a carriage ride around the park with your betrothed."

"She isn't my betrothed."

"She will be," Eastman predicted. "Once her pater is dazzled by the splendor of Viscount Abernathy on horseback."

A half hour later, Griffin crossed Hyde Park and rode through the gates of Number Three Grosvenor Square. He dismounted, handed Apollo's reins to a groom, then bounded up the front steps and knocked on the front door.

"Lord Abernathy to see Lord Tressingham," Griffin

announced as the butler answered his knock.

"His lordship is in his study." The butler stepped back to allow Griffin entrance. He closed the front door behind him, then reached for Griff's hat and gloves. "If you'll follow me, sir."

Griff obeyed, following the butler across a polished marble floor, past the curved banisters of the central staircase, down the hall to a pair of intricately carved oak doors.

The butler knocked on the door and announced him. "Lord Abernathy to see you, sir."

Griff waited quietly, glancing around the study, taking note of the floor-to-ceiling bookshelves on two walls and the numerous oil paintings adorning the burled wood pancling on the remaining walls. Griff noticed that the paintings, all skillfully executed, were of horses and hounds. Even the massive oil painting hanging above the fireplace was of a tricolored foxhound.

Griff smiled and offered his hand in greeting as the butler withdrew from the room.

The Earl of Tressingham folded his morning paper and stood up. A jovial and good-looking man who stood a foot or so shorter than Griff, Johnny Tressingham more than made up for his lack of height with a prominent display of brawn. The earl came around his desk, right hand outstretched.

The two men shook hands, and Tressingham offered Griff a seat. "Come in, Lord Abernathy. Sit down and tell me, to what do I owe the pleasure?"

Griffin remained standing, frowning in concentration at the earl's question. "Your daughter, sir."

It was Tressingham's turn to frown. "Which one? I've nothing but gels. Four of them, you know."

Griff hadn't known. Or hadn't remembered. He had been a confirmed bachelor until a few days ago, and there had been no need for him to concern himself with keeping track of which families had marriageable daughters.

"Adelaide, Alyssa, Amelia, Anne. All my gels favor and all of them have names that start with an *A*. Damned if I can keep them straight." He looked at Griffin. "But you understand the problem, of course, seeing as how you're acquainted with them."

"I've only had the pleasure of making Lady Alyssa's acquaintance," Griff answered. "That's why I've come."

Tressingham took a deep breath. "What's the gel done now?"

Griff blinked in surprise. "Something quite extraordinary, really. She managed to catch my eye."

Tressingham snorted. "Nothing out of the ordinary about that. All my gels are lookers."

"I wouldn't know about the others, sir," Griff told him. "Only Lady Alyssa."

"Alyssa. Alyssa. Oh, yes, that one. Filly. Light brown mane, streaked with blond. Nice big eyes. Blue, if I'm not mistaken. Good ground manners. Hasn't been broken to ride. But that's only natural as she lacks an adequate handler."

Griff had to fight to keep his jaw from dropping in astonishment. The earl described his daughter as if she belonged in someone's stable. He cleared his throat. "Excuse me, Lord Tressingham, you appear to be discussing horseflesh. I'm talking about your daughter."

Tressingham laughed, a big, booming guffaw that spoke of a male camaraderie Griffin didn't feel. Tressingham stopped laughing and stared at Griffin. "No sense of humor, eh?"

Griffin tried not to appear affronted. The man before him was, after all, the man he hoped would become his father-in-law. "On the contrary, sir," he answered. "My friends tell me I have quite a good sense of humor."

"No evidence of it," Tressingham murmured. "And who can trust what their friends say? Friends are supposed to minimize your shortcomings and maximize your attributes. If they're loyal. That's their job. Abernathy . . ." He reached up and scratched his brow as if trying to place the family name. "Abernathy. What rank did you say you were?"

"Major, sir, about to take commission in His Majesty's Eleventh Blues."

"Going off to war to fight the Frenchies, eh?"

Griff nodded.

"I suppose someone has to do it," Tressingham said. "And I guess it's all right for younger sons and those unfortunates who've no money to go along with their titles. Or the blighters who actually like the army life." Tressingham turned to the sideboard to the right of his desk and poured himself two fingers of Scots whisky. He looked at Griff and gestured with the whisky decanter. "Join me?"

Griff shook his head. "No, thank you, sir, it's a bit early in the day for me."

Tressingham snorted in derision as if to say there was no such thing, then took a deep draught from his glass. "Go on," he urged. "Explain yourself. Are you going into the army to make your name or your fortune?"

"Neither," Griff answered. "I'm going into the army to fight Napoleon. I'm not a younger son, I'm the heir. And I possess an ancient and honorable title."

"Good for you." Tressingham's offhanded congratulations sounded entirely genuine. "And what rank might that title be?"

"Viscount," Griffin answered. "I'm the seventeenth Viscount Abernathy."

"A viscount, eh?" Tressingham clucked his tongue in sympathy and eyed Griff more carefully. "That's too bad." In his experience viscounts tended to be perpetually short of blunt and always looking to marry heiresses. This one, however, wore a well-tailored coat of dark blue superfine, a snowy white shirt of fine linen, an impeccably tied four-in-hand, a brocade waistcoat, and buff doeskin trousers that molded his long, muscular limbs. He looked exceedingly prosperous. But looks could be deceiving. Beau Brummel always looked exceedingly prosperous, and Brummel was always borrowing money from the Prince of Wales or some of his other more prosperous cronies in order to buy off his creditors. "And you've come about my filly, Alyssa."

"I've come about your *daughter, Lady* Alyssa," Griff emphasized the words *daughter* and *lady*. "And I don't expect to find her in residence in the stables."

"Then you must have Amy or Adelaide or Anne in mind," Tressingham said. "Unfortunately for you and fortunately for me and Lady Tressingham, they're safely married."

Griff shook his head. "I'm not interested in your other daughters. I've come about the unmarried one. Lady Alyssa." Griff paused for a moment. "The one who likes to garden."

"Then surely you know the best place to find her is in the stables." Tressingham blew out an exasperated breath. "She's probably mucking them even as we speak."

"Mucking stalls?"

"For the fertilizer, don't you know? But the gardens at our country house have never looked better. Course, her mother has forbidden her to help out in the stable or work in the gardens while we're here in London."

"Why?" Griff wondered.

"Because the gel cares about little else but gardening and riding, reading and puttering about. Half the time she looks and smells like a stableboy. Which would be fine if she smelt that way because she was riding all the time, but she's experimenting with different types of muck for the gardens. And that's no way to catch a suitable husband. Not in London. Course, she has had a pile of suitors in spite of it." He paused. "But none to suit her mother. Lady Tressingham has her heart set on the Duke of Sussex. You seem like a nice sort of chap, but if you're only a viscount, you've come too late. My other gels married lads who are earls or better. We'll not be settling for a mere viscount for the last one. Especially since my wife and Her Grace have had an understanding since our gels came into the world."

Griff frowned.

"Both of them are determined to make it so. And Alyssa's their last chance." Tressingham still appeared to be a genial host, but his voice had taken on a distinct mercenary tone. "Sussex is a duke. And if Sussex doesn't come up to snuff, there's always Linton. He paid

me a call earlier and he's a marquess." Tressingham
fairly crowed with success. "You're a viscount and a
soldier. Why should I give you any consideration?"

"Linton is a marquess but an impoverished one. He's
looking to marry an heiress for her fortune. I'm not,"
Griff told him. "As I told you earlier, my title is as old
as Sussex's, and I'm as well set financially. Perhaps Abernathy Manor can't compete with Sussex House or its
famous gardens, but I've something better to recommend
me. Something you've been angling to acquire."

Tressingham frowned. He didn't like having a mysterious carrot dangled in front of him by a young man
seeking to court one of his daughters. "And what might
that be?"

"Access to some of the finest breeding stables and
kennels in England."

Tressingham swallowed hard and looked as if he'd
just been handed the keys to paradise.

"I don't keep up with Debrett's," Tressingham admitted, "or frequent clubs other than Boodles, but I
know we've met before." Too vain to don his spectacles
and bring the younger man's face into proper focus, he
squinted at Griffin.

Griff nodded. "We've met on several occasions, but
only in passing."

Tressingham's reaction was typical. He rarely attended social events, and when he did, his topic of conversation was generally horses and hounds and little else.
Although they had met and conversed several times over
the years, Griff had done his utmost to avoid Tressingham partly because Tressingham was a frightful bore
who rarely, if ever, allowed anyone a chance to speak
about anything except his favorite topic.

Tressingham grunted. "Whose get did you say you
were?"

"I didn't."

"Then, I'm asking. Whose heir are you?"

Griff gave Tressingham an inscrutable smile. "I
should think a horse and houndsman and a member of
Boodles, like yourself, would know to whom I refer."

"Weymouth." Tressingham breathed the name in a reverent tone. He looked as if he expected church bells to toll and a choir of angels to descend from heaven singing hymns of praise. "Weymouth has the finest stables and kennels in England. Now I recognize you." Tressingham snapped his fingers. "Abernathy is Weymouth's family name. You're the Earl of Weymouth's get."

"I'm the Earl of Weymouth's *son* and heir," Griff corrected. "And a *mere* viscount because the traditional courtesy title of the Earls of Weymouth's heirs is Viscount Abernathy and Baron Maitland."

Tressingham drained his whisky, set the glass on the sideboard, then walked over to Griff and clapped him on the shoulder. "I agree, my lord." He grinned broadly. "You've much to recommend you."

"I thought you might feel that way," Griff replied dryly, "once you understood that I have more to offer than mere money and a title."

Tressingham pointed to the massive oil portrait of the tricolored foxhound. "Sir Thomas Lawrence painted it," he said. "That's Carrollton's Fancy Mistress. I bought her great-great-grandmother when I was barely out of short pants, and I built my kennel by breeding my females to the best stud dogs I could find. Fancy is the culmination of all those years of careful breeding." He stared at Griff. "Do you realize how many times I've attempted to persuade Weymouth to allow me to breed Fancy to his King George's Prince of a Fellow?"

"Quite a few, I suspect."

"At least a half dozen times this season." Tressingham lifted an eyebrow in a sign of skepticism. "You're absolutely certain that giving you permission to court my youngest gel will guarantee Fancy a breeding to Prince of a Fellow?"

Griff shook his head. "Not permission to court. Permission to marry."

"Marry?" Tressingham was stunned. "You want to marry my daughter?"

"Yes." Griff studied the older man for a moment

longer, then decided to sweeten the pot. "And, as a member of the family, you will, of course, be allowed to align your kennels and stables with the earl of Weymouth's."

"Would your father be willing to put that in writing?" Tressingham asked eagerly.

Griff nodded. "You'll be granted unrestricted entry to Weymouth's kennels and stables, allowed to ride and hunt with the local hunt using Weymouth mounts and hounds if you like, and you shall be granted, in writing, exclusive breeding rights to the earl's prized equine and canine studs and dams." Griff watched Tressingham's eyes light up. "So long as the agreement is written as part of the marriage settlement between your daughter, Lady Alyssa, and myself."

Tressingham stared at Griff for a full moment before responding. "The stables as well as the kennels?"

"The stables as well as the kennels," Griff confirmed.

"Even while you're away at war?"

"Even so. As a matter of fact, I had hoped that since I am preparing to join my regiment, you might consider overseeing the care and management of my breeding stallion, Apollo." Griff paused. "I'm leaving him behind, and my father is too busy with his government work and politics to attend to *his* breeding stable and my own. . . ." Griff let his words fade away.

"I would consider it an honor." Tressingham was fair to bursting with excitement and pride.

"The loan of Apollo would be temporary," Griff clarified. "For the duration of my service abroad. I would, of course, expect to find him munching hay in my stables upon my return." He smiled to ease the sting.

"What happens if you don't return?" Tressingham asked. "Would the agreement become null and void should you be killed in the war and my daughter made a widow?"

Griff frowned. One would think that Tressingham might finally come to consider his daughter's needs above his own. But as that didn't appear to be the case, Griff intended to finalize the deal. Once the marriage contract was drawn up, Griff would ensure that *his* father agreed to abide by and enforce the terms and to protect his viscountess and their child. If Griff failed to return from the Peninsula, the future Lady Abernathy would lack for nothing whether she chose to remarry or not. Weymouth could be counted on to honor all of Griff's wishes and to leave nothing to chance.

Tressingham shrugged his shoulders. "Men are killed in battle and daughters made widows every day. Have I your word as a gentleman that your father would honor our agreement?"

"You have my word as a gentleman that my father would honor any and all agreements between us—so long as you honor yours. You should also understand that if I should be fortunate to have one, my heir would inherit my title and all my possessions—except Apollo. You could keep him with my blessings and thanks," Griff affirmed.

"Done," Tressingham said, beaming at Griffin. "I'll send for my solicitor this afternoon."

Griff nodded. "I'll send word to the newspapers. Notice of my betrothal to your daughter and our impending wedding will appear in the morning editions."

"Agreed." Lord Tressingham offered Griff his hand. "Welcome to the family."

"Thank you, sir. I'm pleased that we could come to an understanding." Griff shook his future father-in-law's hand, then took out his pocket watch and looked at the time. "I've a meeting with my father at his club in half an hour, but I'll return with my solicitor and the preliminary contracts later this afternoon."

"Haven't you any interest in the size of my gel's dowry?"

"I'm sure it's quite handsome." Griff actually hadn't given her dowry a moment's thought.

"It is indeed," Tressingham replied proudly.

"I would not have thought otherwise," Griff pronounced, "from a gentleman of your stature and breeding. Now, if I might trouble you for one of Lady Alyssa's gloves."

"One of her gloves? Whatever for? A keepsake?"

"A measure. I'll be paying a brief call on my jeweler, and I want to be certain the ring is properly sized."

"Of course." Tressingham rang for the butler, relaying his instructions as soon as the man entered the study. "Needham, please ask Lady Alyssa's personal maid for a pair of Lady Alyssa's gloves."

"Gloves, sir?" Needham frowned. Lady Alyssa was notorious for ruining her gloves.

"Yes, gloves," Tressingham confirmed. "A new pair, and have them brought to my study as soon as possible."

"Very good, sir."

"And bring a bottle of my best French brandy." He turned to Griff. "You will join me this time in a toast to your future and to your good fortune?"

Griff smiled. "Of course."

"Good," Tressingham said, waving his hand and shooing Needham out of the study. "Go on, man. Lord Abernathy doesn't have all day."

"Right away, sir."

Tressingham closed the door behind the butler before turning to face his future son-in-law. "If you've no objection, I'd like to take a close look at your stallion in the next day or so. If you're joining your regiment soon, you'll want to see that he's properly settled into my establishment before you leave."

"I've no objection." Griff smiled. "I rode him across the park. He's in your stable even as we speak."

"Excellent." Tressingham rubbed his palms together in anticipation. "I'll walk you out when he's brought around and take a good gander at him then. Unless you've time for a ramble along the Row as another way of sealing our agreement . . ."

"I believe that can be arranged," Griff said. "I'll send a note around to my father's club informing him of my delay."

Tressingham walked over to his desk, pulled out a sheet of stationery and a pen, and handed them to Griff.

Griff wrote a brief note to his father, sanded and sealed it, and handed it to Tressingham. "I intend to call upon Lady Alyssa once the contracts are in order and we've concluded our business. Has she any social engagements this evening?"

Tressingham took the note to give to Needham upon his return. "I believe Lady Tressingham mentioned that she and Alyssa are scheduled to attend Lady Harralson's ball and midnight supper this evening."

"I'll plan my arrival here accordingly," Griff answered. "Unless you intend to act as their escort . . ."

Tressingham shuddered. "Not on your life."

Griff laughed. "Then, you've no objection to my escorting them?"

"None at all, my boy. You're welcome to it." He pinned Griff with a look of glee. "I can't believe my good fortune. Here, I thought the best I could do would be to marry the gel to a duke or a marquess. I never dreamed I would be marrying her to Weymouth's heir. I can't help but think I've gotten the best part of this deal. Strange, your coming along like you did. I had heard you were in league with a circle of confirmed bachelors."

The Free Fellows League. Perhaps they hadn't been quite as mysterious and discreet as they thought. "I was," Griff allowed. "Until I laid eyes on your daughter."

"Well," Tressingham shrugged his shoulders. "To each his own. That's what I always say. And whatever the reason, I'll be as pleased to call you my son-in-law as I would have been to call the Duke of Sussex the same. Probably more so," he admitted. "For Sussex's horseflesh is passable at best, and he doesn't hunt or keep a kennel. He has nothing to offer except a royal title, wealth, and that monstrosity of a house and garden."

And a domineering mother. "And I'll be honored to make Lady Alyssa my wife." Griff looked Tressingham in the eye. "There is one other thing I failed to mention. . . ."

"Oh?"

"Once the contract is signed, my betrothed answers to

no one but me. I'll take full responsibility for her behavior."

Tressingham opened the door to Needham's knock, then stood back to admit the butler. "Suit yourself," he said, removing Alyssa's gloves from the butler's tray before passing them along to Griff. "But not until the notice appears in the morning paper."

"Fair enough," Griff said.

Tressingham turned to his butler and handed him the note Griff had written for his father. "See that this note is immediately sent round to Lord Weymouth at White's."

"Very good, sir." Needham tucked the note away for safekeeping, and then set the tray on the side table. He uncorked the brandy, poured two glasses, and passed them to the gentlemen.

"Pour one for yourself, Needham."

"I beg your pardon, sir?"

"We're celebrating Lady Alyssa's betrothal to Lord Abernathy."

Needham raised an eyebrow. "My understanding is that Lord Abernathy is a viscount."

"Indeed, he is," Tressingham said. "The Earl of Weymouth's viscount." He poured Needham a glass of brandy and handed it to him before raising his own. "To Lord and Lady Abernathy."

"Hear, hear," Needham agreed.

"Thank you," Griff acknowledged the toast and the good wishes behind them.

"And here's to Fancy." The Earl of Tressingham gestured toward the oil painting hanging above the mantel. "And to Prince of a Fellow and the litter of champion foxhound pups we'll be raising come fall."

Chapter 9

"The foundation is set, and my objective is in sight. I shall be taking up my commission and joining my regiment ere long."

—GRIFFIN, VISCOUNT ABERNATHY, JOURNAL ENTRY, 26 APRIL 1810

*G*riff handed his hat and gloves to the doorman at White's, then crossed the entrance hall to the main room where his father sat lounging in his favorite oversized leather chair in his customary place near the fire, a cup of coffee on the small marble-topped table at his elbow. Griff drew up a matching chair and sat down beside the Earl of Weymouth.

"It's done," he announced quietly. "The announcement will appear in tomorrow morning's edition of the *Times.*"

Weymouth gave his son a curt, approving nod. He gestured for the waiter to bring a cup and saucer and a fresh pot of coffee for Griffin. "Who's the lucky young lady?"

"Lady Alyssa Carrollton."

Weymouth frowned. "Carrollton. That's the family name of the Earl of—"

"Tressingham," Griff finished his father's sentence. "Yes, I know."

"You proposed marriage to Tressingham's daughter?" Weymouth fought to keep the incredulous note out of his voice. "Egads, but he has to be the biggest bore in England! I don't believe I've ever heard him speak a coherent sentence that didn't contain references to horses or hounds."

"That may be so," Griff agreed. "But there's nothing boring about his daughter. She's one of the season's Incomparables. Lady Tressingham is thrilled at that accomplishment but her daughter's aspirations run higher."

"I'm not surprised," Weymouth answered. "An Incomparable can have her pick of titles." He pursed his lips. "So she aspires to something higher than a viscountess? Perhaps she wants to be a duchess. I heard a rumor about town that young Sussex was interested in her."

"He was," Griff replied. "As was Linton."

"Bah!" Weymouth dismissed Linton with a wave of his hand. "The Marquess of Linton's a fortune hunter."

"As are half the suitors in London," Griff pointed out.

"Sussex isn't."

"Unfortunately for Sussex, Lady Alyssa doesn't aspire to the title of duchess."

"Oh?" Weymouth was intrigued in spite of himself. The only rank higher was that of royal princess. "What then?"

"A gardener."

Weymouth blinked. "Did you say a gardener?"

Griff nodded. "She enjoys gardening and aspires to design them."

"Then it's hardly logical that she would turn down the opportunity to become the Duchess of Sussex. The gardens at Sussex House are perfectly magnificent."

"Too perfectly magnificent," Griff explained, "for Lady Alyssa's taste. A Whig at heart, my bride-to-be prefers a more natural style of gardening than Sussex could offer." Griff leaned back in his chair, sitting patiently as the waiter carefully filled a cup with steaming hot coffee and handed it to him.

"You mean to tell me that the young lady you intend to marry chose you over the Duke of Sussex because she doesn't care for his garden?"

Griffin grinned at his father. "That's about the gist of it."

Weymouth lifted his cup and saucer from the table at his elbow and took a long, bracing swallow of coffee.

"Don't misunderstand me, my boy, because your mother and I are quite enamored of you and quite certain there's no finer choice of a husband in all of England. But I cannot help wondering if there is a strain of madness or eccentricity in the young lady's family? I mean young Sussex is every bit as handsome as you and a wealthy duke to boot. He has a great deal to recommend him as a suitor. And he hasn't purchased a commission in His Majesty's Horse Guards." Weymouth shook his head. "He would make an ideal husband. I don't understand what her father was thinking. Had I been in his shoes, I would have chosen Sussex."

"I don't know about the madness," Griff said consideringly. "Although I'm quite certain the topic will come up when I meet with Lord Tressingham and his solicitor later this afternoon, but I fear there's definitely an element of eccentricity." Griff paused.

"How so?" Weymouth wasn't overly alarmed. Hundreds of years of selective breeding for aristocratic bloodlines often produced eccentricities in family members. Eccentricities could be managed as long as the other family members recognized them for what they were.

"The walls of his study were lined with oil portraits of horses and hounds. There's a massive portrait by Sir Thomas Lawrence of his prized foxhound hanging over the mantel."

"Then it's guaranteed to be attractive," Weymouth commented. Sir Thomas Lawrence was currently in vogue as the favorite portrait painter of the ton. He commanded exorbitant commissions and earned his reputation as a favorite because his portraits were often so flattering they barely resembled the subject.

"It is," Griff replied. "Prettiest tricolored hound you've ever seen."

"I'm sure he paid handsomely for it."

"Then you would think he'd pay just as handsomely for portraits of his family."

Weymouth winced. "There weren't any Lawrences?"

"There weren't *any*. There wasn't so much as a *min-*

iature of Lady Tressingham or any of his four lovely daughters in sight." Griff stared at his father over the rim of his coffee cup. "Nothing human. Every painting, every sculpture, every tapestry I saw from entry hall to study was canine or equine or both." Griff paused for a moment to let his father absorb that facet of Tressingham's personality. "You said it yourself, Father. The Earl of Tressingham is likely the biggest bore in all of England. He's obsessed with his foxhounds and his horseflesh. The reason he consented to have me as his son-in-law rather than Sussex is because you happen to possess kennels and stables that outstrip everyone else's—including his. And Tressingham desperately wants to breed his prized female to your stud hound."

"What?" Weymouth choked on his mouthful of coffee and came very close to spewing it all over Griff and the red Turkey carpets covering the floor.

"He chose me over Sussex because I guaranteed him that breeding. I assured him that you would happily align your kennels and your stables with his. And that as a member of the family, he would have complete entrée to both." Griff set his cup back on its saucer and reached up and tugged at the folds of his neckcloth. "In short, I bribed him. And when he hesitated, I sweetened the offer by giving him the loan of Apollo for the duration of my service overseas."

"You're parting with Apollo?" The earl couldn't believe it. Griffin had helped bring that stallion into the world, raising and training him himself.

"I'd have to part with him anyway," Griff said. "I'm not taking him to Spain. I'll not risk having him killed in battle. He'll stay here where he's safe, and Tressingham will take very good care of him." He closed his eyes and firmed his jaw against the sudden pang of loss. "Tressingham's an eccentric bore, but he knows the value of prime horseflesh, and he knows how to breed champions. Tressingham was thrilled to get him, even on loan. He'll take excellent care of Apollo. He's convinced he's gotten the better bargain."

"Does the girl know?" Weymouth asked as soon as

he'd recovered his composure and his ability to speak.

"That her father traded her for a black stallion and the promise of a litter of foxhounds?" Griff shook his head. "God, I hope not." He opened his eyes and stared at his father. "Being forced to marry a virtual stranger in order to fulfill one's obligation to one's family is bad enough. She shouldn't have to face the fact that her father didn't give a rip about her wants or needs but thought only to satisfy his own selfish desire."

"The girl means that much to you?" Weymouth was clearly surprised by Griff's vehement reaction.

Griff snorted. "She means nothing to me, sir. I only met her last evening."

Weymouth frowned once again. "But—"

"Let's just say that, contrary to what you and Mother believe, I'm not especially prime husband material for a lady like Alyssa Carrollton. I'm a cavalry officer. She deserves much better than what I'm offering."

"Her family put her on the marriage mart, son. You had nothing to do with that."

"But I'm about to take advantage of it."

"That's true," Weymouth replied. "But you don't have to be eaten up with remorse about it. You made an offer. Her father accepted it. If you think she deserves better than what she's getting, you're to blame because you're the only one who can change it. Give the girl the best you have to give. You're marrying her to satisfy your family obligations so that you can go to war and defend your country, knowing you've done your duty to provide for the future of the family. That's as it should be." He looked Griffin in the eye. "Almost all of us marry for reasons of family and duty. That is how great families survive and prosper. But marrying for dynastic reasons doesn't mean that it has to be all business. Romance the girl."

"Lady Alyssa doesn't appear to be enthralled with the idea of romance," Griff replied. "And quite frankly, neither am I."

Weymouth shook his head in disbelief. "Youth is wasted on the young. Don't be a fool, Griffin. All young girls are interested in romance," Weymouth pronounced. "Whether they know it or not. You've chosen her to be the mother of your child," he reminded his son. "Make certain she gets something out of it."

"She's getting a possible child, a title, an absentee husband, a neglected manor house, and the opportunity to create the garden of her dreams," Griff replied sarcastically. "Not to mention a betrothal ring the size of a bird's egg and a wedding at Saint Paul's. What more could an Incomparable want?"

"Memories."

Griff looked over at his father.

Weymouth met his unflinching gaze. "You're going off to war, son. Make certain that it's worth the pain and the bother. Don't just make a child, my boy. Make memories. Give your bride a reason to look forward to your return and give yourself another reason to return." Weymouth cleared his throat once, and then once more, before shifting the conversation to a safer topic. "Have you presented her with a ring?"

"Not yet."

"I assume your mention of a betrothal ring the size of a bird's egg means you wish to present her with your great-grandmother Abernathy's betrothal ring."

"Not necessarily. I simply used it for reference. I don't make a habit of studying them, but the ones I've seen are the size of bird's eggs. I assumed that any betrothal ring I give her should be large enough to please and impress the future in-laws and the society gossips."

"Well, you're entitled to give her your great-grandmother's ring if you wish. It's in the safe at Weymouth House along with all the other Abernathy and Maitland family jewels."

Griff frowned, uncomfortable with the prospect of weighing Alyssa down with a child and a collection of his great-grandmother's gaudily ostentatious canary diamonds. "The Abernathy jewels belong to Mother," he said.

Weymouth allowed a tiny amused smile to turn up the corners of his mouth. "Only until you marry; then they belong to the Viscountess Abernathy. Your mother understands that."

"I've never really cared for Great-grandmother Abernathy's ring," Griff said. "And I thought Alyssa might like a ring of her own. I thought she might appreciate having a ring that hasn't been used for someone else's betrothal." He took another sip of his coffee. "I've an appointment with Rundell and Bridges Jewelers on Ludgate Hill at four of the clock this afternoon."

The earl widened his smile. "The center stone of your great grandmother's ring is a forty-carat canary diamond. Matching rows of lesser-carat diamonds surround it, and your mother never cared for it, either." He shook his head. "I vow I'll never understand it. Yes, I agree, it's gaudy. But it's worth a bloody fortune. Queens have financed entire armies for less, and our own Prince of Wales salivates every time he sees it."

"Nevertheless." Griff shook his head. "I can well afford the price of a betrothal ring for my bride-to-be, and I would like to buy her something special."

Ever practical, Weymouth replied, "You can always have the stone placed in a new setting."

Griff declined the offer. "I think another type of stone would better compliment Lady Alyssa's hand."

"What do you have in mind?"

Griff shrugged his shoulders. "I haven't the slightest. But I'll know it when I see it."

"I know Rundell is the Prince of Wales's favorite and the jeweler of choice of the smart set, but if he can't accommodate you, try Dalrymple's on Bond Street. I often shop there for gifts to present to your mother, and she always appreciates his unique designs."

Griff glanced up and met the earl's steady gaze, in complete accord with his father for the first time in days. "Thank you, Father. I'll remember that."

"Will you be joining us for dinner tonight?" Weymouth asked, suddenly acutely aware that time was running out. Soon, there would be no more opportunities for long conversations before the fire at the club and morning rides through the park with his only child. Griffin was leaving soon. And he might never return.

"I can't," Griff said. "After my trip to the jeweler's, I've scheduled a meeting with my solicitor and Tressingham and his solicitor in order to draw up the marriage contract and settlement." He looked at his father. "Which I assured Tressingham *you* would honor in my absence and in the event I fail to return from the Peninsula."

Weymouth nodded. "It goes without saying that I would honor your wishes."

Griff chuckled. "It doesn't go without saying to Tressingham. *He* insisted on having it in writing."

"But of course," Weymouth replied, forgetting his reputation for having no sense of humor. "One can't rely simply on a man's word when the prospect of producing a litter of champion foxhound pups is at stake. One must get that promise down in writing."

"Not just in writing," Griff added, "but written into the marriage settlement."

"And whose idea was that?" Weymouth asked.

"Mine, of course," Griff told him.

"And he fell for it?"

"Completely. But then, how could he refuse a chance to ally himself with his idol?"

"Remind me never to bargain with you when it's something you truly want."

"You already have," Griff retorted. "Eight days ago. Everything I know, I learned from you." He grinned at his father. "Like father, like son."

Weymouth's smile grew into a chuckle and then into full-fledged laughter. And the sight and sound of the Earl of Weymouth doubled over in laughter was rare enough to induce other members of the club to stop what they were doing in order to watch.

Weymouth laughed until he cried, then carefully removed a handkerchief from his pocket and mopped his eyes before casually signaling the waiter for a refill of coffee. "What have you scheduled after your meeting with the earl?"

"I've asked for a few moments alone with Lady

Alyssa in order to present her with the ring. And then I'm escorting her and Lady Tressingham to Lady Harralson's soiree."

"Why don't I have Eastman bring your evening things from your town house to Weymouth House? Surely, you can spare a few moments for your mother and me while you're dressing for the evening."

Griff nodded.

"Good. I'm sure your mother will appreciate hearing the news from you tonight rather than reading about it in tomorrow's newspapers."

Griff stood up. "Why don't you and mother make an appearance at Lady Harralson's?" Griff suggested. "Give the ton something to talk about. And give me the chance to introduce you to Alyssa." Griff put up a hand when his father would have spoken. "Nothing formal. Just an introduction. We'll arrange a more formal meeting at Weymouth House later. I'm sure Mother and Lady Tressingham and Alyssa will need to begin preparations for the wedding."

"Agreed," Weymouth said, pushing himself out of his chair, standing to embrace his son. "Your mother and I will meet you at Lady Harralson's later this evening." He gave Griffin a wry grin. "Now, I'd better go inform your mother that we'll be attending." He winked at Griff. "She'll want plenty of time to deck herself out in all her 'official' Countess of Weymouth finery."

Chapter 10

"To make rosewater from the cast-off petals in the garden, gather fresh rose petals from the garden. Place rose petals in deep pot and cover with three cups of water. Simmer for ten minutes. Add one cup of alcohol and pour rose petal mixture through cheesecloth, collecting the liquid into clean, glass bottles. Garnish with sprigs of fresh lavender and a few tiny rosebuds. Cork and store in the wine cellar or buttery until use."

—LADY ALYSSA CARROLLTON, RECIPE DIARY, 26 APRIL 1810

"*Alyssa, this has got to stop at once!*" Alyssa looked up from her task and found her mother standing in the doorway. "I cannot stop, Mama," she said. "I'm in the process of bottling a batch of rosewater."

Alyssa stood in a room off the kitchen before a massive worktable crafted of scarred oak beams where jellies, jams, and preserves as well as all the household cures and remedies were made. She held a heavy stockpot in her hand and was carefully straining a mass of pulpy rose petals through the cheesecloth covering a long-handled pot.

When the bottom container was nearly full of rose-scented liquid, Alyssa set the stockpot aside and lifted the corners of the cheesecloth, allowing the remaining puddle of liquid to flow through the cloth into the container. Alyssa tied the corners of the cheesecloth and dropped it back into the stockpot. She placed a funnel into the neck of the first of a row of empty wine bottles, then lifted the long-handled pot and began pouring the rosewater through the funnel and into the wine bottle. As the level rose in the neck of the bottle, Alyssa removed the funnel. She dropped a sprig of fresh lavender and two or three tiny rosebuds into the bottle as garnish, then corked it and set it at the far end of the table to cool.

Lady Tressingham stared in openmouthed amazement. "Where did you learn to do such a thing?"

"From a recipe book of medieval healing cures, tisanes, and poultices I found in the library at Tressingham Court." Alyssa shrugged her shoulders. "I tried it and liked it and we've been using my rose, lavender, lemon, and chamomile waters here and at Tressingham Court ever since."

Lady Tressingham pursed her lips in thought. The household had been laundering her delicate undergarments and linens in rosewater for years. She didn't recall when it started and never remembered suggesting the idea to Mrs. Batsford, the housekeeper at Tressingham Court, but one day her laundry arrived smelling of roses, and it had continued to this day. She stared at her daughter. "How long have you been doing this?"

"Since shortly before my fourteenth birthday."

"You've been making supplies of rosewater for both households since that date?"

"Well, I waited to see if you liked it. And when Mrs. B told me you adored the rose scent of your laundry, I decided to continue. I make the sachets you like, too." She filled another bottle and corked it.

"Alone?" Lady Tressingham glanced around. "Where are all the kitchen and scullery maids? Why aren't they doing it?"

"I sent them away," Alyssa answered. "I work better alone."

"You shouldn't be working at all," Lady Tressingham cried. "This is a job for the cook or the housekeeper or somebody. . . ."

Alyssa shook her head. "Not at all. According to tradition, it's *your* job."

"Mine?" Lady Tressingham spat out the question as

if she'd never heard a more ridiculous notion. "Impossible."

"In the days of Henry the Eighth and Queen Elizabeth, the ladies of the house kept the herb garden and prepared all the lotions, potions, and remedies the household needed, in addition to their hours spent doing needlework." Alyssa glanced up at her mother. "Since you don't like to garden and appeared to have no interest in preparing the rosewater used on your linens and undergarments, I decided to make it."

"I thought we purchased it," Lady Tressingham admitted. "From a perfumer or a purveyor of toiletries."

"I don't make all the scented soaps or oils anymore," Alyssa said. "Because they take a bit longer and require more work and I haven't had as much time to devote to it since Amy, Addie, Anne, and I started preparing for our London seasons. But I still make all of the scented waters and sachets we use."

Lady Tressingham sniffed the air. "It does smell divine."

"It's your favorite blend," Alyssa told her. "The flowers in the garden aren't just to admire or to cut and arrange in vases; they're used in many other ways."

"That may be so, but the fact remains that you are not the lady of the house or the person charged with this responsibility."

"Why not?" Alyssa demanded. "I'm the person who started it, and I'm the person best suited for the task."

"Because while you may live here, this is not your house or your responsibility. It's mine. And Mrs. Warrick came to me with a bevy of complaints about your presence in the kitchen and your constant meddling with the household staff and chores."

"I'm not meddling, Mama. I'm simply making note of the way things are done to see if there might be a more efficient way of doing it." Alyssa filled another bottle with rosewater, dropped several tiny rosebuds into the liquid, then corked the bottle and set it aside to cool with the others. "Did you know that Mrs. Warrick has the maids fold and store the bed linens in the same manner every time? While Mrs. Batsford at Tressingham Court instructs the maids in different methods of folding and insists that the linens stored in the cupboard be rotated and refolded once every month to prevent wear at the fold lines.

"Mrs. Reynolds, the Earl and Countess of Albemarle's housekeeper, rotates the linen cupboards every three months, and Mrs. Bingham, the Duchess of Kerry's housekeeper, doesn't rotate the linens at all. She replaces them every year."

Lady Tressingham nearly screamed in exasperation. "I don't care how the neighbors' housekeepers' care for their linens. I only care about mine. And that means keeping my housekeeper contented. You cannot continue to harass her with your endless questions about her methods of operation and suggestions for improvement."

Alyssa slid another bottle of rosewater down the table and carefully lined it up alongside the others. "I haven't been harassing Mrs. Warrick."

"You've been questioning her ability and her methods," Lady Tressingham said. "She is the housekeeper, and you are only an unmarried daughter of the house. Mrs. Warrick feels your criticism is unwarranted. Nor does she appreciate your going behind her back and interviewing the neighboring housekeepers about their methods of doing things. She feels that doing so casts a poor light on her abilities. And so, for that matter, do I."

"I haven't criticized Mrs. Warrick's methods or her abilities. Nor have I gone behind her back. I told Mrs. Warrick that I had asked Durham to help me gather information from the neighboring households, so that we might compare notes. And I offered helpful suggestions based on those notes."

"She doesn't need your suggestions, Alyssa. Helpful or otherwise. Mrs. Warrick has been in service all her life. She knows how to run a household."

"She's been in service to our family all of her life," Alyssa pointed out. "She knows how to run a *Carrollton* household. But that doesn't mean it's being run as efficiently as it could be. There are always better ways of doing things, and it's our responsibility to learn them and to incorporate them in our daily lives."

Lady Tressingham heaved another dramatic sigh. Sometimes she wondered if she had actually given birth to Alyssa or if the midwife had somehow switched her child for the wet nurse's. The midwife had recommended the wet nurse, after all. It was true that Alyssa excelled in the ladylike arts of language and sketching and watercolors, of needlework, and playing the pianoforte, but she had an unfortunate curiosity about and a penchant for performing domestic work. "I cannot believe that in the space of a day or so, you have managed to graduate from pestering the outdoor staff to harassing the indoor staff with your endless questions and suggestions."

"How else can I compare methods and decide upon the most efficient ones?"

"Why should you want to do so?" Lady Tressingham countered sharply. "At least until you're married with a home of your own. Then you may interrogate every housekeeper in England if you like, so long as you cease interrogating mine."

Alyssa sighed. Finding a suitable husband and waiting until she was married with a home of her own was her mother's answer for everything.

"I know you don't agree, Mama, but in my own way, I *have* been preparing to manage a home of my own."

Lady Tressingham's face softened, and she smiled at her youngest and most stubborn of daughters. "I know that, my darling, but you've concentrated all of your attention on preparing to manage a home once you're married. You've done very little preparation and given very little attention to the business of finding the man who will marry you and provide you with a home and a staff of your own."

"I did manage to become an Incomparable," Alyssa reminded her mother.

Lady Tressingham narrowed her gaze at Alyssa. "You did what was expected of you. Fortunately, your sisters and I laid the groundwork for you to build upon. Your accomplishment in becoming an Incomparable was as much mine and your sisters' doing as yours," she said. "Had I not been so diligent and had your sisters not made such brilliant matches, you might not have received your voucher to Almack's or been accepted by the ton."

"But I did receive my voucher," Alyssa retorted, "and I've managed to acquire a few suitors along the way."

"That you have." Lady Tressingham smiled. "And the most important one will soon pay a call on your father. If things go as expected during their interview, you should be married before the season is over."

Alyssa let out the breath she hadn't realized she'd been holding. Griffin Abernathy had said he would call, and she believed him because he was a man of his word. Still, the waiting had kept Alyssa on pins and needles all morning. There had been no word of his arrival, and the hours she'd spent at her bedroom window had all been for naught.

Her bedroom faced the rear of the house overlooking the gardens. She'd chosen it for precisely that reason, but at the time she'd chosen it, Alyssa hadn't realized that she would, one day, need a view of the front entrance or the stables. As a result of her unfortunate choice of rooms, she hadn't witnessed the viscount's arrival or his departure, and no one had seen fit to inform her.

After waiting for what seemed like hours for someone to tell her that Viscount Abernathy had called for her, she'd managed to occupy her time by interviewing Mrs. Warrick and conducting an inventory of the linen cupboards.

The inventory had yielded the discovery that the Tressinghams' London residence was dangerously low on the rosewater used to rinse Lady Tressingham's linens. Alyssa had leaped at the opportunity to do something about it and had quickly taken charge of the task of replenishing the supply.

After sending word to the gardeners instructing them

to gather a supply of rose petals along with a few rose-buds and fresh lavender from the garden, Alyssa selected the items she needed, ordered the stockpot she customarily used filled with water and set to boil, and prepared a work space at the massive table in the room off the kitchen. Once the basket of rose petals arrived, Alyssa began the process of making bottles of rosewater.

She poured the last of the liquid from the pot into a bottle, then set the pot aside and corked and labeled the final bottle. Satisfied, she surveyed the fruits of her labor. Twenty-six bottles. That wouldn't be enough to last to the end of the season, but it would do until there were enough rose petals from the garden to make another batch.

But now that her task was done, Alyssa desperately needed something else to do. Something else to occupy her mind as well as her hands. Why was it that daughters were the last to know what their future held in store? There must be something else she could do. Something the housekeeper wouldn't object to.

Perhaps she could inventory the supply of beeswax candles on hand or make out the menu of refreshments to be served during the remainder of the season's morning calls. Surely, Mrs. Warrick wouldn't object to that.

Alyssa sighed. She knew her mother and the London housekeeper wished she were more like her older sisters. Amy, Adelaide, and Anne were all quiet, unassuming beauties that didn't question their places in the world.

But Alyssa was different. She had always yearned to make the world a better place for the people she loved. She couldn't sit and embroider and make polite conversation with her sisters and the other ladies who came to call, not when she knew there were so many other more important things that needed to be done. She had learned early on that she was a doer. She was a person who needed to be needed but who also needed to be up and about and doing the things she felt she should do.

And today, she felt she needed to keep busy so she wouldn't have to worry about the outcome of Griffin Abernathy's interview with her father.

"Your sisters have all married well, but as a duchess, you shall best them all."

Her mother's words interrupted her thoughts. Alyssa frowned. "Duchess?"

"Of Sussex, no less. I told you, Her Grace and I have had an understanding for years." Lady Tressingham's voice quivered with excitement. "She assured me that His Grace would pay your father a call. I can hardly believe our good fortune. It's too good to be true."

Alyssa fervently hoped her mother was right. She hoped becoming the Duchess of Sussex was too good to be true. Was it possible? Had Lord Abernathy broken his word? Had he changed his mind about offering for her?

"His Grace paid a call on Papa?"

Lady Tressingham frowned. "Not yet. But he will. Imagine, my daughter the *duchess.*"

Alyssa couldn't imagine it. Not after kissing Griffin Abernathy at Almack's. And she hoped she never had to.

"Has Papa had any other visitors today?" Alyssa tried to sound nonchalant, but her mother wasn't fooled.

Lady Tressingham drew her brows together in a wrinkle-inducing frown she ordinarily avoided at all costs. "Yes, he has" she answered. "Lord Linton and the young viscount. But, Alyssa, you must know that His Grace is the only suitor your father and I will consider. I doubt your father wasted any time sending Lord Linton and Lord Abernathy packing."

"Are you certain?"

"I know he sent Lord Linton home disappointed," her mother answered. "And he was about to dispense with Lord Abernathy."

"Oh."

"Don't sound so disappointed. You've a wonderful future as duchess ahead of you."

"I had hoped—"

"For more suitors?" Lady Tressingham interrupted. "Of course, you did. All Incomparables do. But in this case, it isn't the quantity of suitors that matters, it's the quality. You've garnered proposals from two members of the ton in one morning. That is quite an accomplishment."

"Mama, you don't understand—" Alyssa began.

Again her mother cut her off. "Of course I understand. I was young once. But you mustn't read more into it than there is. The men who have offered for you are all honorable gentlemen from old and noble families, but everyone knows Lord Linton has shallow pockets and is looking to marry an heiress with deep ones. And as for Lord Abernathy . . . Well." She sighed. "Lord Abernathy would be the undisputed catch of the season if we didn't have an understanding with His Grace."

"Is it set?" Alyssa asked. "Has Papa accepted an offer from His Grace?"

Lady Tressingham bit her bottom lip. "I don't know if the details have all been ironed out. But I know your father sent for his solicitor some time ago." She exhaled. "I haven't spoken to him about His Grace's offer thus far because your father was still closeted with Lord Abernathy when I came looking for you."

Alyssa let out a breath. "Then there's still hope."

"Hope?" Lady Tressingham was surprised. "For what?"

"That Lord Abernathy will prevail."

"Lord Abernathy?" Lady Tressingham's voice rose. "I don't want Lord Abernathy to prevail!"

"I do."

The girl was utterly baffling. "You would choose to be a mere viscountess rather than a duchess?"

"I would choose Lord Abernathy over His Grace," Alyssa said.

Lady Tressingham blinked, momentarily speechless. "A viscountess." She shook her head. "You have obviously taken leave of your senses. Why? What have you against His Grace?"

"I've nothing against His Grace," Alyssa told her. "I've yet to be introduced to him."

Lady Tressingham grimaced. "You saw him from across the room. He was making his way toward us when Lady Cowper appeared with Abernathy."

"I saw him," Alyssa said. "I didn't speak to him."

"No," Lady Tressingham confirmed. "Because you were too busy dancing with Lord Abernathy. Egads! But there is no comparison, my darling. Sussex is divine. Abernathy is merely handsome."

"In your opinion, Mama." Alyssa met her mother's disapproving gaze without flinching. "I think otherwise. I think Lord Abernathy is divine and His Grace merely handsome. Besides, I've no wish to be the Duchess of Sussex."

"I don't believe it!" Lady Tressingham threw up her arms in a gesture of dismay, often used with great success in operas and ballets. "I know you've very little experience mixing in the highest circles, but that's nothing to be afraid of. You'll become accustomed to having people bow and address you as Your Grace in no time."

"No, I won't," Alyssa protested.

"No matter." Lady Tressingham dismissed Alyssa's refusal. "The duke will help you settle in. As your husband, he'll smooth the way for you and see that you learn all you need to know."

"His Grace will have to find someone else to help settle in as Her Grace. I won't need it. Because I don't intend to become his duchess."

"Whether you intend to become the Duchess of Sussex or not is of little consequence at this juncture," her mother told her. "Because your father and I intend it for you. Believe me, Alyssa, once you get used to the idea, you'll thank us for attending to your best interests."

"I'm not going to be the Duchess of Sussex," Alyssa said firmly. "I'm going to be Viscountess Abernathy."

Lady Tressingham's laugh was sharp and mirthless. "While it's apparent that Lord Abernathy did his best to sweep you off your feet during your illicit waltz last evening, it's best that you forget about him. I'm quite certain that your father has sent him packing by now."

"Don't underestimate Lord Abernathy, Mama," Alyssa warned. "He asked me to marry him last night, and I don't believe he'll be as easy for Papa to dismiss as you seem to think."

Lady Tressingham gasped. "He should know better than to propose to you without first asking your father."

"Of course, he knows better. But that didn't stop him from asking me."

"You refused, of course."

Alyssa shook her head. "I accepted."

"No matter," her mother declared. "You're a female. You cannot marry without your father's permission. And your father will not grant Lord Abernathy permission to marry you. I've chosen Sussex for you. Your father understands the benefits of allying our family with His Grace's. He won't disappoint me."

Alyssa looked her mother in the eye. "I would like to think that for once Papa wouldn't disappoint *me*."

"I wouldn't count on it, my dear."

"Then I'll count on Lord Abernathy. He'll find a way to keep his promise."

Chapter 11

"I have made a formidable enemy in my future mother-in-law. She wanted Sussex for her daughter. As a viscount, I will never measure up."

—GRIFFIN, VISCOUNT ABERNATHY, JOURNAL ENTRY, 26 APRIL 1810

Griff sat silently as the two solicitors—his and Lord Tressingham's—hammered out the terms of the marriage contract and the marriage settlement. He listened as the two men argued each point of the contract, negotiating compromises, until both parties reached a satisfactory conclusion. Changes in the terms of the contract were noted, and after two hours of haggling, the solicitors pronounced the documents ready to be signed.

Griff heaved a sigh of relief as he watched Tressingham scribble his name at the bottom of the document. Griff added his signature to the parchment, signing it with a flourish.

"Well done, my boy!" Tressingham slapped him on the back. "Well done."

Griff opened his mouth to speak, to ask for a few moments alone with Alyssa, but Tressingham was quicker. He walked over to the side table and poured two glasses of brandy. He handed one to Griff and lifted the other in a toast. "Here's to our long and mutually satisfying alliance!"

Griff frowned. Good grief! Tressingham made it sound as if Griff had just become engaged to marry him, rather than Alyssa.

"Drink up, my boy!" Tressingham urged, his jovial generosity returning now that legalities were over. "Did you bring the betrothal ring?"

Griff swallowed a mouthful of brandy and nodded.

"Good." Tressingham walked over to the bell and pulled it.

The butler appeared almost immediately, and Griff decided that he must have been waiting outside the library door. "Tell Lady Tressingham and the gel that I wish to speak to them."

"At once, sir."

"And tell them to make it on the quick," Tressingham added.

Griff waited until the butler exited the room to speak. "I requested a few moments alone with Lady Alyssa," he reminded his future father-in-law. "I should like to present her with her betrothal ring in private."

"Plenty of time for privacy after all the preliminaries have been taken care of." Tressingham turned to Griffin, rubbed his palms together in anticipation, and said. "Where is it?"

"Where is what?" Griff asked.

"The ring, boy. The ring." He grinned. "I hear the Abernathy family has a magnificent betrothal ring with a big yellow diamond."

Griff nearly groaned. He should have realized Tressingham would have heard of and expected to see Great-grandmother Abernathy's ugly canary diamond betrothal ring. He looked at Tressingham steadily. "I've selected another, more suitable ring for Lady Alyssa."

Tressingham winked. "Big diamond still at the jewelers, eh? Well, it happens to the best of us. But it's damned decent and smart of you to remember to bring another more *suitable* ring for the gel. Still, it isn't every day that two great families, such as ours, become allies. Not every day that a gel like Alyssa—" He broke off as Needham opened the door.

"Lady Tressingham and Lady Alyssa, my lords," Needham announced, stepping back to allow the ladies to precede him.

"Do something with your hair," Lady Tressingham whispered to Alyssa. "And for goodness' sakes, smile. You're about to become a duchess."

As far as Alyssa was concerned, becoming a duchess was nothing to smile about. But she reached up and touched her hair and discovered that a mass of baby-fine curls had escaped from their pins while she labored over the boiling pot of rosewater. She smoothed the tendrils into place as best she could and rubbed her damp palms down the front of her dress. She stared down at her toes and took a deep breath, preparing herself for whatever lay ahead.

"What is *he* doing here?"

Alyssa breathed a prayer of thanks to God and all of her guardian angels for the note of irritation in her mother's voice, for it could only mean that the man waiting inside the library with her father was not His Grace.

Praying that it was Lord Abernathy, Alyssa straightened to her full height, held her head high, and beamed, hoping that, this time, her papa had managed to live up to her expectations.

"Here you are, my dear." Tressingham ignored his wife's rude outburst. He opened his arms wide in a gesture of welcome and goodwill.

Lady Tressingham surprised Griff by stepping into the circle of her husband's arms.

Tressingham gave his wife an affectionate hug. "That's my girl," he pronounced, opening his arms wide once again and gesturing for his daughter to join them in a family embrace. "Come here, Alyssa, and say hello to Lord Abernathy." Tressingham gave his daughter a nudge in Griffin's direction.

Alyssa did as her father instructed. "Hello, Lord Abernathy."

"What is *he* doing here?" Lady Tressingham asked again, this time in a stage whisper.

Tressingham shushed her. "All in good time, Puss."

Griff stared at Alyssa, nearly dumbfounded by the sight and the scent of her as the memories of the kisses they'd shared in the ladies' retiring room the night before came roaring back. He sucked in a breath. Her light brown hair curled in tiny ringlets about her face, and her cheeks were pink, providing her flawless complexion with a most becoming blush. He would never have believed it possible for any woman to look as if she'd just spent all morning or all evening making love with a man—unless she had. But Alyssa Carrollton had that flushed, slightly disheveled look about her that set his heart racing and sent blood pooling in his groin. And her scent . . . she smelled of roses. Acres and acres of roses. Fields of roses. The scent emanated from her hair and her dress and her skin as if she were made of rose petals instead of flesh and blood. He'd never smelled anything as softly delicate or as powerfully erotic, and Griff knew with a certainty that he would never again be able to smell the scent of roses without thinking of Alyssa. His mouth went dry, and Griff fought to form the simple words he needed. "Hello, Lady Alyssa."

Alyssa couldn't stop smiling. He was every bit as gorgeous in his buff doeskin trousers in the light of her father's study as he had looked in knee breeches, stockings, and buckle shoes beneath the bright gaslight in the ballroom at Almack's. But it was her memory of the way he'd looked beneath the softened gaslight in the ladies' retiring room that was the most powerful. It seemed impossible, but she was quite certain he was more handsome now—for he was standing before her after having spent the majority of the afternoon in the company of her father negotiating for her hand in marriage.

"It's a pleasure to see you again, Lord Abernathy." She kept her voice low, but she couldn't keep her bottom lip from trembling.

"You knew I would come." He focused his attention on her mouth and the way she bit her lip to stop its tremor.

"I knew you would come," she answered, "but I didn't know if you would prevail."

He smiled at her. "Then, you've much to learn about me, my lady."

"Have I?"

"Yes," he answered. "And a lifetime in which to learn it."

"Enough!" Lady Tressingham's single word broke through the rosy haze and soft conversation surrounding Griff and Alyssa.

"Enough suspense," she continued, glaring at Lord Tressingham. "I want to know why Lord Abernathy is here and His Grace, the Duke of Sussex, is not."

Lord Tressingham took a deep breath. "I decided to accept Lord Abernathy's offer and grant him our daughter's hand in marriage."

"What!" Lady Tressingham practically vibrated with outrage.

"Lord Abernathy is about to become our new son-in-law," Lord Tressingham repeated in a firmer, no-nonsense tone.

"We agreed, Johnny." Lady Tressingham ignored the no-nonsense tone in her husband's voice and continued to take him to task as only a wife could do. "We agreed that His Grace was the best husband for Alyssa." She shot a disapproving look at Griffin. "Lord Abernathy is from a fine family, and I am certain that he possesses many admirable qualities—not the least of which is a desire to marry our daughter—but the fact remains that he is only a viscount, while His Grace—"

"I know we discussed it, Puss. I know we decided upon His Grace. I know young Abernathy is only a viscount. But he's the Earl of Weymouth's viscount."

"What has that to do with anything?" she snapped, before the answer began to dawn. Lady Tressingham closed her eyes for a moment and gritted her teeth, then glanced up at the portrait of Fancy hanging over the mantel. She eyed Griffin with renewed irritation mixed with the tiniest hint of admiration. Outranked and outmatched by His Grace in every way that counted, Lord Abernathy had found a way to stack the deck in his favor. "Weymouth owns—"

Tressingham beamed at his clever wife. "King George's Prince of a Fellow."

"I see."

Everyone who was anyone in the ton knew Johnny Tressingham's obsession. Few, except for his circle of loyal cronies, could tolerate it. Most wondered how his wife managed to do so. But few members of the ton understood the depth of love the former Miss Penina Sykes felt for her husband. When they'd met, she was in her first season. He was Lord Carrollton then, and heir to his father, the Earl of Tressingham. She was a poor relation by marriage of the Viscount deLancere. Her status, or lack of it, hadn't mattered to Johnny. He'd been instantly smitten. And if it had taken her a fraction longer to fall in love with him, it had only been because she couldn't believe her good fortune. Johnny was the kindest and gentlest man she had ever met. A man who understood his shortcomings as a husband and who went out of his way to please her in other ways, especially at night in the marriage bed. He was the first man she had ever met who treated her with kindness, who treated her as if she were more than the sum total of her looks. Johnny Tressingham treated her as an equal. He admired her not just for her beauty but also for her brains, and he had always been proud of her. Proud that she was clever and accomplished, and so well liked and accepted. And, although he didn't know how to show it, Johnny was equally proud of the four daughters they'd produced, never once expressing disappointment or displeasure over the lack of a son and heir. If he loved his horses and hounds as much as he loved her, Lady Tressingham thought that was a small price to pay for all he had given her. She was angry at his decision, but she wouldn't stay that way for long. He hadn't deliberately set out to thwart her ambitions; he'd simply succumbed to his great obsession. She could forgive him for that because he loved his horses and hounds with as much abandon as he loved her. He couldn't help it. Johnny never did anything in half measures. He wasn't made that way, and she had long ago learned to accept and appreciate it.

"And wait until you see the new stallion munching hay in our stables. . . ."

Lady Tressingham fought to keep from smiling at Johnny's boyish excitement. But she felt no such compunction about Lord Griffin Abernathy. She narrowed her gaze at her husband. "In order to win our daughter's hand in marriage, Lord Abernathy gifted you with a stallion?"

"Not just any stallion," Tressingham told her. "But his prized *breeding* stallion. One of his father's famous Thoroughbreds of pure Arab descent." He glanced at Griffin. "And Lord Abernathy didn't *give* him to me. He *entrusted* Apollo to me to care for and to manage while he's away at war."

"How fortunate for Lord Abernathy that you were willing to accept such a great responsibility." She turned her glare on Griffin.

"Indeed, it was, ma'am," Griffin responded to her challenge. "But entrusting Apollo into your husband's capable hands is nothing compared to the trust Lord Tressingham has shown in entrusting the care of Lady Alyssa to me."

"I *trust*"—Lady Tressingham emphasized the word—"that my daughter will have as much to gain as my husband."

"I trust that *she* will find it so," Griff replied.

"Well." Lady Tressingham injected a note of cheer she didn't feel into her voice. "It isn't every day that a young woman is granted the right to wear a man's family heirlooms—especially when they're beyond price." She narrowed her gaze at Griffin once more. "I trust that my daughter will be taking possession of the Abernathy diamonds?"

"Of course," Griff answered. "The necklace, brooch, bracelet, and diadem will all belong to her—as soon as she becomes Lady Abernathy."

"And the betrothal ring?" Lady Tressingham asked.

Griff looked Lady Tressingham in the eye. "I prefer to present Lady Alyssa with her betrothal ring in private."

"That is out of the question, Lord Abernathy," Lady Tressingham replied. "You should appreciate the fact that while my daughter is unmarried, she will remain uncompromised."

"I do appreciate it, Lady Tressingham, but our society *does* grant engaged couples a few unchaperoned moments." He stood firm. "This is one of them."

Lord Tressingham intervened. "Come, Puss." He took his wife by the arm. "Lord Abernathy has just purchased the right to spend time alone with our daughter."

"But . . ." She gave a token protest.

Lord Tressingham smiled at his wife. "It will be all right, Puss," he said, glancing at Griffin. "Lord Abernathy is a gentleman. He'll not be compromising our gel with her parents in the next room." He led Lady Tressingham to the door of the library that connected with the lesser salon where he paused. "You've a few minutes out of sight of the parents," he said, winking at Griffin. "I suggest you put them to good use."

"Johnny!" Lady Tressingham protested as he escorted her through the door.

"Now, Puss," he soothed. "They're young and engaged. So what if he steals a kiss or two? I did the same with you."

Griff waited until Lord and Lady Tressingham left the room before turning to Alyssa.

"So," she drawled. "You traded a prized breeding stallion for me. . . ."

Griff bit back a grin. "I prefer to think of it as using the right incentive to get what I want." He took her hand in his. "And I prefer to think that I got the best part of the bargain." He leaned closer.

She met him halfway. "I'll try to insure that you always feel that way, my lord."

"Will you indeed?" he breathed.

"Indeed," she promised, rising on tiptoe in order to give him full access to her lips. "I will." She smiled up at him.

"Your parents are in the next room," he warned.

"Probably listening at the door," she agreed.

"We *do* have permission," he whispered.

"Then, stop wasting time," she whispered back, "and kiss me."

"My pleasure," he breathed, seconds before he covered her lips with his.

Alyssa melted into his arms, returning his kiss with a passion that surprised both of them. She teased and tantalized and tasted him, engaging him an erotic duel, sweeping his mouth with her tongue, filling her taste buds with the essence of Griffin Abernathy.

"We have to stop." He forced himself to end the kiss.

"You're the second person today to tell me to stop doing what I want to do," she complained, brushing his lips with hers.

Griff buried his nose in her hair. "You smell of roses," he replied. "Fields of roses. And lavender."

"Much better than the sulfur and peacock feathers, don't you think?"

"Much," he murmured. "What were you doing? Bathing in the essence of roses and lavender?"

She shook her head. "Distilling it."

Griff blinked.

"You spent the afternoon closeted with my father while I spent the afternoon making rosewater."

Griff stepped back. "I didn't spend the entire afternoon closeted with your father. Believe it or not, I somehow managed to work in a bit of shopping at Dalrymple's Jewelers."

"Prove it," she challenged.

Griff reached into his jacket pocket and pulled out a ring. "Will you do me the honor of becoming my wife?"

Alyssa gasped at the beauty of the ring as he withdrew it from its velvet drawstring bag and offered it to her.

The delicate gold ring contained a large purple center stone surrounded by a ring of smaller green stones, and accented by several diamonds. It looked like a purple flower blooming in the midst of bright green leaves sparkling with droplets of rain or dew. Alyssa instantly adored it.

"It isn't the traditional Abernathy betrothal ring,"

Griff told her, "but this one is unique. I thought you might like a betrothal ring no one else has ever worn. And with your love of gardening, I thought this one was particularly apropos." He slipped the ring onto the ring finger of her left hand. "Besides," Griff grinned, "I like amethysts, peridots, and small, tasteful diamonds. But if you prefer otherwise . . ."

"It's beautiful!" Alyssa exclaimed. "And it fits perfectly." She held out her hand to admire the ring. "However did you manage it?"

"I'm afraid you're missing a pair of gloves, my lady."

"Am I?"

"Yes, indeed."

She pursed her lips. "I don't remember dropping them."

"That's because I asked your butler to appropriate your gloves for me to take to the jeweler's."

"Then I'm happy to sacrifice them," Alyssa said, wiggling her fingers, admiring the way the light reflected off the stones in her betrothal ring.

"Prove it," he challenged.

And Alyssa did, wrapping her arms around his neck, kissing him to show her pleasure in his gift.

"Ahem."

Lord Tressingham cleared his throat in polite warning as he and Lady Tressingham reentered the library.

Alyssa dropped her arms from around Griff's neck and would have moved completely out of his reach, but Griffin stopped her by catching hold of her wrist and interlacing his fingers with hers.

"That's not the Abernathy betrothal ring," Lady Tressingham complained the moment she caught sight of the ring on Alyssa's finger.

"It is now, Mama," Alyssa said, "for I'm about to become the new Viscountess Abernathy."

"The *original* Abernathy betrothal ring contains a priceless yellow diamond," her mother retorted, "and that isn't it."

"No, it isn't," Alyssa said. "But I'd rather have this one."

Lady Tressingham shook her head. "I don't understand you, Alyssa. I'll never understand you—"

"No matter, Puss," Lord Tressingham interrupted. "The original Abernathy betrothal ring is still at the jeweler's. If the gel is happy with the new ring, so much the better, for she'll receive the other one after the wedding. It's like getting two rings for the price of one. Besides, the contract is signed and the gel is no longer your concern."

"She is until she's married," Lady Tressingham reminded him.

Lord Tressingham rubbed his palms together in anticipation. "Then all I have to say is: When shall we have the wedding?"

"A proper wedding will take months of planning," Lady Tressingham said.

"It will take seven days," Alyssa answered. "For that's all the time we have before Lord Abernathy leaves to join his regiment."

Lady Tressingham gasped. "Seven days? That's impossible!"

"Not for me," Alyssa announced. "We will be married at Saint Paul's and host a wedding breakfast for two hundred guests here following the ceremony. And we'll do it in seven days' time." She glanced up at Griffin. "You lived up to your end of the bargain, my lord. Now, I'll live up to mine."

Griffin met her gaze with a smile, suddenly completely at peace with his choice. He knew in his heart that Lady Alyssa Carrollton *would* live up to her end of the bargain. She wouldn't fail him.

Chapter 12

"My bride-to-be is planning our wedding with all the precision of a general planning a military campaign. My role is minimal. I've been asked to show up at all appointed times in order to escort her to the rounds of parties, and fetes, and to stay out of the way otherwise. I'm following those orders."

—Griffin, Lord Abernathy, journal entry, 26 April 1810

An hour later, Griff straightened the folds of his neckcloth, splashed on bay lime, and ran a brush through his hair. He turned from the mirror as his valet appeared with a black evening coat.

"Lord and Lady Weymouth are waiting for you downstairs, my lord," Eastman announced.

Griff shrugged into his evening coat. "Am I late?"

Eastman shook his head. "Not at all, sir. You've made splendid time."

Griffin had burst through the front door of his parents' town house an hour earlier and hit the stairs running. Eastman had a tub of hot water and his evening clothes prepared. Griffin had rushed through his bath, dressed as quickly as possible, and now, garbed in evening wear, stood ready to join his parents for light refreshments before escorting Alyssa and her mother to Lady Harralson's party.

"Lords Grantham and Shepherdston sent word that they will be expecting you to join them for brandy and cigars at the club once your duty as escort to Lady Alyssa and her mother is concluded."

Griff pocketed the handkerchief Eastman handed him, then walked over to his writing table and scribbled a note to Colin and Jarrod informing them that he would meet them when Lady Harralson's ball concluded. He folded the note and gave it to Eastman. "Send this around to the club."

"Won't Lords Grantham and Shepherdston be making an appearance at Lady Harralson's?"

"God, I hope not," Griff admitted. "I shall get plenty of grief from Lady Tressingham. I shan't need additional grief from my boon companions."

Eastman bit the inside of his cheek to keep from smiling. "Anticipating mother-in-law difficulties, sir?"

"With every breath she takes," Griffin answered. "Until she finishes venting her spleen over her disappointment in getting me for a son-in-law instead of His Grace."

"Perhaps her displeasure will be short-lived," Eastman offered.

"Perhaps." Griffin didn't sound convinced. "But since you and I will be joining my regiment in ten days, I'll only have to endure Lady Tressingham's temper for a little while longer. I'm afraid my bride won't be as fortunate."

"Your bride will be safely ensconced at Abernathy Manor," Eastman reminded him. "Far away from her mother."

"Mothers have been known to visit," Griff said, "with or without an invitation, and countesses outrank viscountesses." He frowned. "Another point in Sussex's favor. If Lady Alyssa were marrying His Grace, she wouldn't have to worry about her mother pulling rank."

"She isn't marrying the duke; she's marrying you," Eastman replied. "Perhaps a word in Lady Weymouth's ear will do the trick, sir."

"Mother doesn't outrank Lady Tressingham," Griff reminded his valet. "They're both countesses."

"Lady Weymouth is higher in order of precedence and is beloved of the queen. Her disapproval carries a great deal of weight with the ladies of the ton, and she's sure to disapprove of anyone who gives her son's bride a difficult time."

"Including the mother of the bride?"

"Most definitely, sir," Eastman replied. "Because Lady Alyssa is *your* bride, and your mother won't allow anyone to question your choice or cause difficulties or distress for her. Especially while you're away at war."

"Assuming my mother approves of Lady Alyssa."

"If you chose her, how could she not?"

Griff grinned. "I hope you're right."

"Count on it, sir."

He would have to, Griff decided. For he had no other choice.

Moments later, Griff entered the main salon and found his mother and father waiting.

He crossed the room and embraced his mother, placing a kiss on her cheek. "Sorry to keep you waiting."

"That's all right, my dear," Lady Weymouth replied as soon as Griff released her. "Your father and I have only been downstairs a few moments ourselves.

Griff shook hands with his father and then turned back to his mother. "You look beautiful, Mother."

"Of course I do," she teased, a twinkle in her blue eyes. "I'm wearing almost all of my sparkly Countess of Weymouth finery."

"You don't need your sparkly Countess of Weymouth finery in order to look beautiful, Mother," Griff told her fondly. "It only enhances what you've already got."

She laughed. "Spoken like a doting only son."

"I am that," Griff assured her. But even had he not been Cicely Abernathy's only child, he would have spoken the truth. She was a beautiful woman with delicately formed features, shimmering silver blond hair, and the same bright blue eyes as her son. She wasn't an especially tall woman, but she was reed slim with the graceful, willowy body of a ballerina and the vivacious personality and the energy of a six-year-old boy.

Griffin adored her.

She looked up at him with the same blue eyes he faced in his shaving mirror every morning. "Your father says you've something you want to tell us."

Lord Weymouth poured his wife a glass of sherry and handed it to her, then poured one for himself and one for his son, giving Griffin a moment to compose his thoughts before making his announcement.

Lady Weymouth lifted a perfectly arched eyebrow. "That bad, eh?"

"Not at all." Griff accepted the glass of sherry from his father, then took a deep breath before blurting out the news. "You see, I'm getting married."

Lady Weymouth sat up straighter. "To whom?"

"Lady Alyssa Carrollton," he replied. "The announcement will appear in the morning papers. I wanted to tell you in person before you read it in the papers."

"This is a bit sudden, isn't it?" She stared at Griffin, pinning him with her direct gaze. "And a bit rash, considering that you are about to leave for the Peninsula." She took a deep breath, and her voice trembled. "You could make the girl a widow."

Griff didn't flinch. "I know. The fact that I may not return from the Peninsula is all the more reason I should get married before I go. Ensuring the future of our family is the right thing to do."

"That sounds exactly as if it came from your father's mouth instead of yours," Lady Weymouth commented, glancing at her husband, who remained conspicuously silent.

"It's still the right thing to do," Griff answered.

"For us," his mother replied. "But what about your bride?"

Griffin sighed. "I'd like to think that it's best for her as well, but the truth is that I don't know."

"Does she?" Lady Weymouth asked.

"She understands the situation, and she agreed to it." Griff lifted his glass and swallowed a mouthful of sherry. "She chose me over the Duke of Sussex."

His mother smiled. "I don't blame her. She sounds like a sensible girl."

Griff nodded.

"She's Penina Tressingham's youngest daughter, isn't she?"

"Yes."

"I've heard she's quite lovely."

"She's one of the season's Incomparables," Griff offered.

His mother frowned at him. "I don't doubt that she's lovely on the outside. My hope is that she's just as lovely on the inside."

"You won't be disappointed," Griff replied.

Lady Weymouth glanced from her husband to her son. "Trevor forced you into this, didn't he?"

"Yes, he did," Griff admitted. "But he didn't choose Lady Alyssa: That choice was mine."

His mother reached over and patted him on the hand. "I don't imagine Penina is too happy about losing the Duke of Sussex for her youngest daughter. She already has two earls and a viscount."

Griff shrugged. "It's done. She'll get used to it. Besides, I'm not marrying Lady Tressingham. I'm marrying Lady Alyssa."

"I'm sure I'll like Alyssa very much. When do we meet her?"

"Tonight."

"Tonight?" she repeated.

"At Lady Harralson's. Didn't Father tell you?"

Lady Weymouth turned to her husband. "No, he did not. But that explains our unexpected foray into the ton tonight and your father's suggestion that I wear my Countess of Weymouth finery."

Weymouth cleared his throat, then drained his glass of sherry. He looked at the clock. "Griffin, you'll want to be on your way—"

"On *his* way?" Lady Weymouth asked. "I understood that Griffin was riding with us."

"No, my dear," Lord Weymouth explained. "Griffin is escorting his intended and her mother to Lady Harralson's. We're meeting them there." He looked at his son. "I've ordered your carriage brought around. It's waiting out front."

"Thanks, Father."

Lord Weymouth smiled. "You don't want to be late."

Griff placed his sherry glass on a marble-topped table, shook hands with his father, and then leaned down and kissed his mother on the cheek. "Good-bye, Mother. I'll see you at Lady Harralson's."

"I'm looking forward to it."

Chapter 13

"My first test of endurance comes tonight. I must learn to endure my future mother-in-law's enmity."

—GRIFFIN, LORD ABERNATHY, JOURNAL ENTRY, 26 APRIL 1810

Griff wished he could say the same. Not that he wasn't looking forward to seeing Alyssa. He was. Very much. But he wasn't looking forward to spending an evening in the company of her mother.

Despite what he'd said to his mother, Griff was well aware that marrying Alyssa meant marrying her family as well. Griff knew that better than anyone. Hadn't he lured her father into accepting his proposal by dangling the prospect of joining their families and their possessions?

Marrying Alyssa meant joining her family, however briefly.

Unfortunately, it also meant suffering the chaperonage of an angry Lady Tressingham. At least until the wedding.

Griffin exited his carriage before it rolled to a complete stop in front of the blue door of Number Three Grosvenor Square. He bounded through the wrought-iron gate and up the steps to the front door.

The door opened to his knock, and Needham allowed him entrance. "Lord Tressingham is at his club, sir. But Lady Tressingham is awaiting you in the lesser salon."

"I'm not here to see Lord Tressingham," Griff answered. "I'm here to escort Lady Alyssa to Lady Harralson's soiree. Where is she?"

"She'll be down directly," Needham answered.

Griff glanced at the long case clock standing in the curve of the entryway beneath the stairs. "I expected her downstairs before I arrived."

"Quite, sir," Needham replied. "Lady Alyssa is ready. But she has been instructed to remain upstairs until Lady Tressingham sends for her."

"I'll wait here for Lady Alyssa," he said. "Please inform her of my arrival."

"But Lady Tressingham—" Needham began.

"May join us here any time she wishes," Griff interrupted. He'd had enough private interviews with parents for one day. "Otherwise, my parents, Lord and Lady Weymouth, will be happy to serve as chaperones on the way to Lady Harralson's."

"Lady Tressingham won't be pleased," Needham warned.

Griff smiled. "Something tells me that nothing I do will please Lady Tressingham at the moment. That being the case, I've decided to suit myself. And Lady Alyssa."

"Very good, sir." Needham bowed.

Griff paced the entrance hall while he waited for Alyssa to come downstairs. He didn't venture anywhere near the lesser salon, but it didn't take long for his future mother-in-law to find him.

"I asked Needham to tell you that I was waiting in the lesser salon."

Griff turned from his perusal of a collection of blue and white Chinese porcelain to find Lady Tressingham standing in the entryway. "He relayed the message," Griff said calmly. "I chose to ignore it."

"How dare you!"

Griff looked her in the eye. "I dare, Lady Tressingham, because I've endured enough of your tirades and temper tantrums for one day. I'm here to escort your daughter to Lady Harralson's. As far as I am concerned, you're accompanying us for the sake of appearances."

"I am accompanying you because I've no wish to see my daughter compromised and her reputation ruined," Lady Tressingham informed him icily.

"Then you've no need to worry," Griff retorted, "because neither do I."

"That's what you say now," she argued. "I wonder if you would say the same thing if I allowed you and Alyssa to share a darkened, closed coach without me." She glared up at him. "This sudden wedding will set tongues to wagging, and you can bet that certain ladies in the ton will be shaking their heads and counting the months when your first child is born."

Griff snorted in contempt. "Most of the ladies in the ton to whom you refer are rather weak in mathematics. I doubt they can count that high, for it's likely they never had to do so before their own children were born. And you, Lady Tressingham, may rest assured that when my eldest child comes into the world, it will be a full nine months after his parents' wedding."

"I don't trust you," she said flatly. "Not where Alyssa is concerned."

"That's your prerogative," Griff replied. "But what I'm saying is true, nonetheless. I may only be a viscount, but I'm entirely capable of keeping my word and controlling my desire—even where your daughter is concerned."

"Why did you offer for her?" Lady Tressingham demanded. "Why ruin her life when she could have been a duchess? You're not in love with her."

"Neither is His Grace," Griff reminded her.

"Perhaps you're right," she admitted, "but *he* won't break her heart."

"And you think *I* will?" Griff pinned Lady Tressingham with his sharp gaze.

"I know you will," she replied. "The minute you leave her and ride away to join your regiment."

"Lady Alyssa knows I'm leaving."

"Her knowing won't make any difference. You're going to leave her—with or without a child—and when you do, Alyssa will never be the same."

"I think you underestimate your daughter, Lady Tressingham." Griff took a deep breath. "Lady Alyssa is made of sterner stuff. You needn't worry that she will

pine away with love for me. Your daughter and I understand one another."

"You understand. Alyssa is an innocent."

"She may be an innocent, but she is a woman fully
grown, and she knows exactly what she wants out of
life."

"And that is?"

"A home of her own." *Far away from you,* Griff
added, silently. "I can give her that."

Lady Tressingham looked Griff in the eye. "You offered for her, and my husband accepted that offer against
my better judgment. I can't change that. But, you should
understand, Lord Abernathy, that I don't—"

"Want me for your daughter?" Griff snorted once
again. "Believe me, madam, I would have to be deaf,
dumb, and blind not to understand that. And I am none
of those things. You don't like me? Fine. You aren't
required to. But you will have to endure my presence
for the next week, so I suggest you make the best of it
for Lady Alyssa's sake. If you'll agree to be civil to me
when Alyssa is present, I'll do my best to keep my opin-
ions and comments to myself, and I'll do everything in
my power not only to please Alyssa but to stay out of
your way. Agreed?"

Lady Tressingham hesitated.

"You won't get a better offer from me," he warned.

"Agreed," she reluctantly replied.

Griff and Lady Tressingham had reached an understanding by the time Alyssa joined them downstairs.
They were polite and civil to one another when they
were forced to engage in conversation, but they kept the
conversation to a minimum.

Unfortunately, their new agreement did not include
Alyssa, and Lady Tressingham decided her daughter was
fair game.

"This is madness, Alyssa," her mother told her as
soon as they were seated comfortably in the carriage.
"You cannot accomplish so large a task in so short an
amount of time."

"Watch me."

"If you attempt to pull off a society wedding and fail, you'll make us the laughingstock of the ton."

"I have no intention of making you, me, or Lord Abernathy and his family the laughingstocks of the ton," Alyssa said calmly. "Because I don't intend to fail. I will use every resource at my disposal in order to accomplish my task. Invitations go out tomorrow afternoon by special post. Two hundred select members of the ton will be invited to attend the wedding of the season." She leveled her gaze at her mother. "You can help, or you can stand aside and watch."

Lady Tressingham heaved a theatrical sigh. "You're my daughter, and I'll not let it be said that your father and I failed to give you a proper society wedding. . . ."

"I'm impressed," Griff said softly, stealing up behind Alyssa in the receiving line at Lady Harralson's and leaning close.

It had been nearly an hour since they arrived, and Griff had had the devil's own time keeping track of her in the crowd.

Lady Tressingham had stepped down from the carriage, grabbed her daughter by the hand, and whisked Alyssa out of the carriage and into the crush of arrivals. Griff, waylaid by several acquaintances, barely managed to catch up.

"With what?" Alyssa turned slightly and looked up at the underside of his jaw. She leaned back against his shirtfront, enjoying the novelty of being surrounded by his strength and his warmth.

"With you," he whispered. "And the way you handled your mother."

She shivered as his warm breath tickled her ear.

"Cold?" he asked, placing his hands on the flesh of her upper arms left exposed by her evening gloves and her sleeveless gown.

She shook her head. It was impossible to be cold, surrounded as she was by so much heat, but to her delight, Griff kept his hands where they were, increasing the soothing friction. "The trick to handling my mother is to take charge of the situation before she does," she told him. "And you were doing an excellent job of it when I joined the two of you downstairs."

"You heard that?" He felt the color rise in his neck, felt the heat of it in the tips of his ears.

"Not all of it," Alyssa said. "But enough to know that the two of you have reached an understanding." She nodded toward a group of chattering women.

Griff glanced over to where Lady Tressingham stood holding court among a group of her society friends. "Our understanding is that your mother hates me."

Alyssa giggled. "She doesn't hate you, Griffin. She just dislikes you—a lot."

"I like the sound of that," he murmured.

"What? The fact that my mother doesn't hate you?"

"No." He shook his head. "I like the sound of my Christian name on your lips. And I like the sound of your laughter, Alyssa."

"So do I." She smiled. "I like the sound of my Christian name on your lips."

"That's good," he teased, "because I've called you by your Christian name since we were introduced, my lady."

"I like it better when you don't put the title of lady in front of it, my lord."

Griff gently tightened his grip on Alyssa's upper arms. "Did I remember to tell you that you look beautiful tonight?"

"No, but I thank you all the same."

"You're welcome," he said. "And I apologize for failing to tell you sooner."

"There is no need for you to apologize, Griffin. Compliments are never late."

Griffin didn't have to see her face to know Alyssa was smiling. He reached down and lifted the dance card hanging from a silver cord looped around her wrist. Opening the card, he squinted at the names penciled in beside the list of scheduled dances. "I don't see a partner for the next dance."

"No," she replied, "I'm free."

"That's not entirely true," he reminded her. "I believe we established that fact this afternoon."

"I'm free for the next dance." Her voice became low and husky. "If you need a partner . . ."

Griff stepped up beside her and offered Alyssa his arm. "I would very much like to dance with you, my lady, but there is someone I would like you to meet first."

Alyssa tucked her hand into the crook of his arm. "I've already met our hostess."

"Have you met Lord and Lady Weymouth yet?"

"No, I . . ." She shook her head. "Lord and Lady Weymouth . . . You mean . . ."

He nodded. "My mother and father. They braved the crush here tonight in order to meet you."

Alyssa inhaled sharply, then smoothed the front of her ball gown and touched her hair. She glanced around for a mirror and, failing to find one, turned to Griffin instead. "Do I look all right?"

Griffin laughed. "Fishing for more compliments, my lady?"

"Just reassurance," she answered honestly.

"Then rest assured that you look as beautiful now as you did a few moments ago." He looked down at her. "You've nothing to worry about."

"It isn't every day that one meets one's future in-laws."

"Thank God!" Griffin breathed. "Once is enough." He made a face at her.

Alyssa laughed.

"Just be yourself," he advised, "and my parents will adore you."

"What about you?" Alyssa couldn't believe she'd spoken her thoughts aloud.

"I already adore you," he answered smoothly, flashing her his most winning smile.

A smile that looked more convincing than it felt. Alyssa lifted her chin a notch higher and pasted a smile on her face. What did she expect? She'd put him on the spot and asked him to declare his feelings. He'd traded a prized breeding stallion and the rights to his father's stables and kennels to her father in order to gain consent to marry her. She'd been sold for a horse and a litter of puppies. What could she expect? That he really did adore her?

If only that were true.

Alyssa did her best to follow Griff's advice, but she couldn't quite conceal her nervousness as Griffin escorted her through the crowd and across the room to where the Earl and Countess of Weymouth sat talking to each other.

"Father, Mother, may I introduce you to Lady Alyssa Carrollton?" Griff made the introductions. "Alyssa, may I present my parents, the Earl and Countess of Weymouth?"

Alyssa sank down into a perfect curtsy. "A pleasure to meet you, ma'am, sir."

"The pleasure is ours, my dear." Lord Weymouth stood up and helped his wife to her feet, then assisted Alyssa as she rose from her curtsy.

Lady Weymouth leaned forward and kissed Alyssa on both cheeks in the Continental fashion. "We're delighted to meet you, my dear."

"Thank you, ma'am."

Lady Weymouth glanced at her husband and son. "Would you two mind fetching us some champagne?"

Recognizing a dismissal when he heard it, Griffin looked to Alyssa for confirmation that she was comfortable spending a few moments alone with his mother.

Alyssa nodded. "That would be nice. Thank you, Lady Weymouth, for suggesting it."

Lady Weymouth glanced pointedly at her husband and son once again. "Run along, my dears. Lady Alyssa and I are going to have a little chat." Lady Weymouth waited until the men left, then turned and patted the arm of the chair Lord Weymouth had vacated, gesturing for Alyssa to sit. "First things first," Lady Weymouth said. "I hope you don't mind, but I'm simply dying to see it." She sat down beside Alyssa and leaned close. "When you get to know me better, you'll learn that I have a sense of curiosity equal to that of a schoolroom full of excitable little boys." She sighed. "It can be a nuisance, but . . ." She shrugged her shoulders in a gesture Alyssa was beginning to associate with her son. "I know your engagement isn't public yet and that you shouldn't be showing it about, but may I see your ring?"

Alyssa beamed. "Yes, of course." Extending her left arm, she unbuttoned her opera-length glove. Alyssa tugged the glove down her arm and off her hand. She held up her hand and wiggled her fingers, admiring the unique design of her betrothal ring and the way the light sparkled off the amethysts, peridots, and diamonds. "Isn't it beautiful?"

Lady Weymouth was as enchanted with the ring as its owner. "It's perfectly lovely." She lifted Alyssa's hand and studied the ring. "It looks to be one of Mr. Dalrymple's designs. You're fortunate. This ring is ever so much prettier than the bird egg."

"The bird egg?"

Lady Weymouth laughed. "The Abernathy betrothal ring. I call it the bird egg because it's a big canary yellow diamond set in a chunk of heavy gold. It's all anyone talks about when they talk about betrothal rings. It's worth a fortune, but good heavens! It's so big and gaudy. . . ." She looked at Alyssa. "You wouldn't think anyone could make a priceless diamond so unattractive, but there you have it. . . ." She shuddered in distaste. "It's part of a set you'll receive as a portion of your wedding settlement. And when you get it, thank your lucky stars that, unlike his Great-grandfather Abernathy, my son has exquisite taste in jewelry and in his choice of a bride."

"Thank you, ma'am," Alyssa murmured.

"You're welcome, my dear." Lady Tressingham smiled at her future daughter-in-law. "I know you haven't much time to prepare for a wedding, so tell me, what can I do to help?"

"Well," Alyssa began, "I only had two hours in which to work after I learned I was to marry your son. He says we should invite two hundred for the wedding so, I've begun making lists and organizing . . ."

Chapter 14

"My second test of endurance is about to begin——the meeting with my fellow Free Fellows at White's."

—GRIFFIN, LORD ABERNATHY, JOURNAL ENTRY, 26 APRIL 1810

"*How did it go?*" Jarrod, fifth Marquess of Shepherdston, asked when Griffin joined him and Colin, Viscount Grantham, at their usual corner at White's an hour or so after the conclusion of Lady Harralson's soiree.

Griffin grunted in reply.

"We expected you earlier," Colin informed him.

"I've been vetted by Lord Tressingham," Griff answered. "And blooded by his wife. That takes a while." He sank down onto his favorite chair, propped his elbows on the arms and his feet on the leather ottoman before the fire, and let out a sigh.

"As does escorting one's intended and her mother to Lady Harralson's soiree." Jarrod smirked.

"How would you know?" Griff shot back. "Have you got an intended or a future mother-in-law?"

Jarrod laughed. "No, but you do."

"And the rumor about town is that Lady Tressingham is none too happy. The wags all say she was hoping to snag Sussex for her daughter," Colin offered, reaching over and pouring Griff a snifter of brandy from the carafe on the table beside him.

"That was no rumor," Griff told him, shoving the ottoman out of the way with his foot before pulling his chair closer to the table Jarrod and Colin were sharing.

"That was fact. The wags are right. And Lady T makes no bones about it. She would most definitely prefer His Grace to me."

"Odd that you haven't been able to win her over," Jarrod replied. "You're usually most adept at charming the ladies."

"Not this lady," Griff said ruefully. "Not unless I suddenly inherit and I've no wish for my father to turn toes up just to please Lady Tressingham."

Colin nodded his head in understanding. "Aye, as a mother, she wanted a loftier title for her daughter."

"Much loftier," Griff agreed.

"So her preference for His Grace has nothing to do with you," Jarrod said. "It isn't personal."

Griff took a swallow of brandy. "It's very personal. She hates me."

"She can't hate you," Jarrod said. "She doesn't know you well enough." He smiled at Griffin. "You've only had one day in which to become acquainted. Perhaps she simply hates the fact that you're a viscount instead of a duke."

"Or a *marquess*." Griff lifted his snifter of brandy in salute to Jarrod.

Jarrod raised an eyebrow.

"Don't look so surprised," Griff said, "or so smug. Surely, you realize you were next on Lady Tressingham's list—behind His Grace."

Jarrod held up both hands. "She was barking up the wrong tree with me. You know I'm not the least bit interested in Lady Alyssa or any other debutante at Almack's. I'm not looking for a bride, and no one is coercing me into accepting one. I'm a Free Fellow."

"We're all Free Fellows," Colin reminded him.

"We *were* all Free Fellows," Griff retorted. "My status as one seems to be coming to an end."

"Once a Free Fellow, always a Free Fellow." Jarrod lifted his glass. "We're brothers, remember? Blood brothers. Nothing can change that. Not even wives." He winked at Griff. "Here's to your future, Brother."

Griff lifted his glass, clinked it against Colin's and

Jarrod's, then swirled the warm liquor around in the bottom before draining the contents. "Here's to Lady Tressingham learning to live with her disappointment."

"She's not the only one." Jarrod met Griff's gaze over the rim of his glass. "His Grace is none too happy about the situation."

"He knows? So soon?"

Colin nodded. "Apparently, your father-in-law felt honor bound to send His Grace a note informing him that Lady Alyssa was no longer available."

"How did you find out about this?" Griffin asked.

"We're spies," Colin whispered. "We haven't spent nearly a year slipping in and out of France without learning something about gathering information."

Griff stared at Colin. He and Jarrod *were* spies. While Griff had been attached to the Quarter Master General's office at the War Department, Colin and Jarrod had trained under Lieutenant Colonel Colquhoun Grant, known in British military circles as the Spy Maker. While Griff had been memorizing military strategies and learning the business of supplying and moving vast armies of troops across continents and oceans, Colin and Jarrod had been learning the art of subterfuge and code breaking, consorting with smugglers, and slipping in and out of France at will. "Have you been gathering information on Sussex or on me?"

"Neither." Jarrod snorted. "He's foxing you. We know everything there is to know about you. And although he's a duke, Sussex is a rather nice and boring sort of fellow. Not worth expending the time or the energy to follow—at least until a few hours ago."

"What do you mean?" Griff demanded.

"His Grace came into White's a few hours ago, drank a bit more than is his custom, and let it be known that he'd been eliminated from the list of suitors of a certain young lady whose father cared more about his horses and hounds than he did her welfare. He let slip that he'd lost out to a certain viscount who had used a prized Thoroughbred stallion to bribe the father." Colin shook his head. "Did you *really* trade Apollo for Lady Alyssa?"

"Is that what Sussex is telling everybody?" Griff shoved his fingers through his hair, then slid his glass forward, motioning for Colin to refill it.

Jarrod took a deep breath. "Fortunately, His Grace, although deep in his cups, didn't take complete leave of his senses—"

"Just his sense of self-preservation," Griff retorted.

"He made his remarks to *us,*" Colin said. "Here at the club. His Grace said he knew he'd find us here because everyone else was at Lady Harralson's or Madam Theodora's. And he was right. The club was practically empty. His Grace called us your 'fellow cohorts' and said he was certain we would see that you got the message. Apparently, he has some feelings for your bride-to-be, because His Grace took exception to the fact that a gentleman would actually bribe another gentleman with *livestock*—his words, not ours—in order to secure a bride."

"He ought to take exception to the fact that Tressingham could be so easily manipulated and bribed by the promise of *livestock.*" Griff fought to control his rising temper. "I did."

"That didn't stop you from bribing him," Jarrod pointed out.

"Of course it didn't." Griff pinned Jarrod with a sharp look. "It wouldn't have stopped you, or Colin, or His Grace, either. I wanted Lady Alyssa, and I used whatever weapons I had at hand to win her. Fair and square. His Grace is upset not only because he lost to a mere viscount but because he didn't put forth any real effort into winning her."

"Who did you win?" Jarrod asked. "Lord Tressingham or his daughter?"

"Both. Blister it!" Griff slammed his glass down on the table. "I had to win Tressingham to get his daughter. But he was only a means to an end. Sussex gave up too easily. The truth is that I would have ended my pursuit of her if I had thought she cared anything about the duke."

"Would you?" Jarrod questioned.

"Yes," Griff answered. "I wouldn't have enjoyed it, but I would have stepped aside if she had wanted to be a duchess—or a Marchioness." He looked at his two blood brothers. "I didn't deprive her of the life she wanted. Quite the contrary. She prefers a lesser title. She wants to be a viscountess. She chose me and Abernathy Manor over His Grace and his too-perfect gardens."

"I'll be damned." Jarrod whistled. "I've known lots of women who settled for less, but I've never heard of any woman who actually wanted less than she could have had."

"Why not?" Griff demanded. "You know men who want less complicated lives. You are one."

Jarrod smiled. "Why, yes, I guess I am."

"Why should women be any different? You've always said you'd rather be a marquess than a duke any day. It's the same for Lady Alyssa and many other women. Why take on the responsibilities of a higher rank when you know you could be perfectly happy with a lesser one?"

"I never thought about it like that," Colin admitted.

Jarrod nodded. "I suppose you're right."

"And you should thank your lucky stars Lady Alyssa had lower aspirations, else you might find yourself with Lady Tressingham as *your* mother-in-law."

Jarrod grinned. "You seem to think the bride is worth the aggravation."

"She is," Griff confirmed.

"Good, because His Grace may not give up as easily as you think."

"He'll have to. Lady Alyssa and I have an understanding. She has dreams of her own that make her the perfect sort of wife for a Free Fellow." Griff finished his brandy, then held up his index finger, indicating that he would like one more glass of brandy.

"So . . ." Colin drawled, pouring the final round of drinks. "When's the wedding?"

"The announcement will appear in tomorrow's edition of the *Morning Chronicle* and the *Times*. And I believe Mother and Alyssa decided the wedding will be Friday morning," Griff replied, matter-of-factly. "At Saint Paul's. And we're leaving for Abernathy Manor right after the wedding breakfast." Griff glanced from Colin to Jarrod and back again. "I'd like to ask you to stand up for me, but . . ."

"Free Fellows don't attend weddings," Colin said. "Except our own. When we've no other choice."

"We won't be there," Jarrod said. "But our thoughts will be with you." He whistled through his teeth. "I must confess I'm impressed. I didn't think it was possible to put a society wedding together that quickly."

"Alyssa is determined to make it possible." Griff smiled. "Earlier this evening, she and my mother were planning to mobilize an army of household staff to make it possible."

"You know you're welcome to mine," Jarrod offered. "My London staff and the staff of Shepherdston Hall. Will you be stopping off at the hall on your way to Abernathy Manor?" Griff had made a habit of breaking up the daylong journey from London to Abernathy Manor with a stopover and change of horses at Shepherdston Hall. It had become such a habit that Jarrod had given Griff a permanent suite of rooms at the hall and kept a team of Griff's horses in his stables so Griff was able to exchange one team of his horses for another team of his own horses.

"For a brief respite and a change of horses," Griff said. "If you don't mind."

"Why should I mind?" Jarrod said. "I'd be pleased to have you and your lovely bride as guests. I'll send word to the staff to expect you. I won't be acting as your host though." Jarrod paused to take a drink of his brandy. "I'll be in London."

"As will I," Colin added.

Perpetually short of blunt, Colin kept suites of rooms at Griffin's rented town house in London and at Jarrod's country house. "Oh, and I'll be relinquishing my suite of rooms in your town house," Colin said.

"You don't have to do that," Griff told him.

"I'm afraid he does," Jarrod said. "You're getting married in a few days. Your bride may want to come to London for the remainder of the season and take up residence in your town house."

"She can't do that with me in residence," Colin said. "It wouldn't look right."

"She won't come to London while I'm gone," Griff told them. "She doesn't want a London season. She wants a home of her own far away from London. She wants Abernathy Manor."

Colin held up his hand. "Doesn't matter. I've already arranged to move my belongings into Jarrod's town house."

Griff took a deep breath, then cleared his throat. "She'll have her parents," he said. "And my mother and father, but she'll be alone at the manor." His voice cracked, and Griff took a moment to compose himself. He cleared his throat and tried again. "I was hoping you two would check on her from time to time while I'm away."

"Of course," Jarrod said.

"That goes without saying," Colin agreed. "We're brothers. We take care of our own."

"Thank you." Griff stood up.

"Good luck, Griff. Don't worry about Lady Alyssa or the manor. We'll take care of the home front," Jarrod promised.

"Take care of yourself," Colin reminded him. "And keep your head down."

Griff smiled. "It's been a hell of a day."

Jarrod stood up and clapped him on the shoulder. "And the coming week is going to be equally challenging."

Colin laughed. "Go on home, man. Get some rest. With a wedding, a honeymoon, and the joining of your regiment, you're going to need it."

Chapter 15

"For better or for worse, I am married."

—ALYSSA, LADY ABERNATHY, DIARY ENTRY,

04 MAY 1810

Planning a society wedding for two hundred guests in less than a week's time required the skill of a military genius, the negotiating arts of a practiced diplomatist, and the stamina of a dozen men. Execution of the plan required the talents of a huge, loyal, and dedicated household staff—several huge, loyal, dedicated, and talented staffs. And lots of ready cash.

By dawn on the morning of the wedding, Alyssa had pressed the Tressingham household staffs in London and at Tressingham Court, as well as Lord and Lady Weymouth's London staff, Griff's rented staff, the staffs of her sisters—Amelia, Lady Brookestone; Anne, Lady Garrison; and Adelaide, Lady Hastings—and the Marquess of Shepherdston's London staff into service.

It seemed that nearly every merchant and tradesman in London had something to do with the wedding of Lady Alyssa Carrollton to Lord Griffin Abernathy. Vast sums of money changed hands on a daily basis. The services that couldn't be bought—even at unusually exorbitant prices—were purchased with favors owed and the promise of future favors. Every string that could be pulled had been pulled, and every account ever owed had been settled and then some.

Even the Prince of Wales contributed by commanding his personal pastry chef and several of the chef's assis-

tants to fashion the wedding cake as Alyssa, Lady Tressingham, and Lady Weymouth mobilized an army of
domestic and trades help in order to create a miracle.

The wedding party itself was rather small and intimate. Alyssa had four attendants: her three sisters and
the only real friend she had made during her two London
seasons, Lady Miranda Saint Germaine. Lady Tressingham had objected to having her three married daughters serve as Alyssa's bridesmaids, insisting that the
bridesmaids be *maids* instead of *matrons*—one of whom
had to be hastily churched and the other two of whom
were increasing, although it was not yet noticeable or
common knowledge. Lady Tressingham had pushed for
eight bridesmaids, all unmarried debutante daughters of
the ton, but Alyssa had stood firm. She wanted only four
attendants, her sisters and Lady Miranda.

Lady Tressingham didn't like the fact that Lady Miranda had a reputation for being the ton's perpetual
bridesmaid, but Alyssa didn't care. She asked Miranda
to be her maid of honor, and Miranda agreed.

Griffin's only choice as a groomsman was his father.
Lord Weymouth agreed to stand up for his son by serving as best man. Alyssa wondered why Griffin hadn't
asked his close friends to be groomsmen, but she didn't
question him about it. She simply pressed her brothers-
in-law into service as groomsmen, charging them with
the duty of seating guests before the ceremony and accompanying their wives down the aisle immediately after it.

Like her choice of wedding decorations, the bridesmaids' gowns were elegant and understated, expensive
but not ostentatious, sheaths of iridescent pale green silk
trimmed in exquisite Honiton lace.

Griffin and the groomsmen wore single-breasted
morning coats of navy blue superfine and light gray trousers.

Alyssa's gown of shimmering white satin was one of
two gowns that had been created for her presentation at
court. The hem of the ball gown and the four-foot train
were decorated with hundreds of tiny seed pearls sewn

in an elegant trailing vine pattern accented with tiny diamonds.

In place of the regulation three white egret feathers and diamond clips she would have worn for her presentation, Alyssa wore a small wreath of orange blossoms and a veil made from the same Honiton lace as that used to decorate her attendants' dresses.

Sixteen seamstresses had worked nearly around the clock to make her attendants' gowns, and another sixteen, their assistants, glovers, milliners, and cobblers had worked just as hard to fashion the gifts for the lady's maids, each of whom were given complete ensembles of the latest style as a gift from the bride and groom.

Alyssa's gown had been the easiest to prepare. It had required little more than a pressing and the addition of the lace veil and wreath of orange blossoms. As she glanced at her reflection in the full-length mirror, Alyssa thought that a darker color might have been more flattering for her light brown hair and blue eyes, but debutantes were forbidden from wearing more dramatic colors until after their presentation at court.

Alyssa had already made her curtsy to Queen Charlotte and to the Prince of Wales, who was acting in his father's stead, but in choosing to wear her second court gown, she had limited herself to white. This one, made from a heavier satin fabric for warmth, had been hanging in her armoire unworn, and Alyssa saw no reason to waste it. It was, in her opinion, a perfectly practical choice for a wedding gown.

She had dispensed with the necessity for a bridal trousseau since she had yet to wear over half of this season's wardrobe. Her only concession had been to allow the seamstresses to fashion three sets of bridal lingerie—a set for each of the three nights she would spend in Griffin's bed.

Alyssa was nothing, if not practical.

On Monday morning, her husband would leave to join his regiment. There would be no need for an expensive trousseau or the dozens of articles of intimate apparel one usually contained.

She would be alone at Abernathy Manor once Griffin left for the Peninsula, and since her goal was to restore the house and the grounds to their previous splendor, her current wardrobe would suffice.

Once she had decided on her wedding attire and saw to the completion of her attendants' gowns, Alyssa concentrated her attention on the details of the wedding breakfast—providing the food, drinks, flowers, and gifts for two hundred guests.

Alyssa had given everything one final check before she'd begun dressing for the wedding. Elegantly decorated buffet tables lined the perimeter of the ballroom in the Tressinghams' town house, and smaller tables, set with crystal and silver, were placed about the room, and all of the rooms adjoining the ballroom had been opened up. The adjoining rooms had been decorated to match the ballroom; the furniture in each had been removed, and the carpets had been rolled up and stored, and additional tables, set with more silver and crystal, placed there to accommodate the crush.

All in all, she was pleased with her efforts.

The Prince of Wales's pastry chef and confectioner had crafted a four-foot-high wedding cake frosted in white and decorated with sugared roses and topped with orange blossoms. It was joined by another cake frosted in chocolate and decorated with candied fruit, fresh mint sprigs, and chocolate shavings. Separating the two cakes was a massive ice sculpture of a bride and groom framed beneath an arch bearing a viscount's coronet, its single row of pearls clearly visible.

The ice sculpture of the bride and groom had been Alyssa's idea. Having them stand beneath an arch bearing a viscount's coronet had, of course, been her mother's. Alyssa suspected it was her mother's way of reminding the ton—and perhaps, Griffin—that the most spectacular wedding of the season, thus far, had been that of a *mere* viscount.

Gunter's, the confectioner in Berkeley Square, was providing the wedding breakfast. It consisted of cold meats, chicken, fish, ham, roast beef and lamb, prawns and lobster salad, as well as oysters and tongue, a hot and cold soup, truffles, candied fruits, jellies, raisins, dates, and pastries and biscuits of every form and filling laid out on tables covered with snowy white tablecloths and trimmed with pale green satin ribbons. On the end of each of the tables were silver urns of tea and coffee, and at the other end were flavored ices.

Sugared pomegranates, whole oranges dusted with sugar and cinnamon, and bouquets of orange blossoms decorated each table. Alyssa had arranged each one and chosen the green satin ribbon. The yards of ribbon were an extravagance, but Alyssa used them anyway. She tied the bouquets of cascading roses and lilies her bridesmaids carried with the colored ribbons and draped more ribbon around the buffet tables, fashioning lavish bows at the corners of each table.

And Alyssa, her bridesmaids, mother, and future mother-in-law had tied satin ribbons around each of two hundred tiny engraved silver saltcellars to be presented to each guest as a memento of the wedding.

She would have preferred more personal gifts, but engraved silver saltcellars were the current rage among the ton, and Lady Tressingham had her heart set on presenting them as gifts. Alyssa had agreed, partly because her mother had worked so hard in helping her with the wedding preparations and partly because her mother enjoyed the novelty of being the mother of the first bride to present such fashionable wedding mementos.

On the eve of the wedding, as was the custom, Lord and Lady Weymouth had hosted a dinner for the wedding party.

Griffin used the occasion to present each of Alyssa's bridesmaids and his groomsmen with gifts. He gave the ladies heart-shaped diamond pendants on delicate gold chains to wear with their bridesmaids' gowns, and he gifted his groomsmen with silver flasks engraved with their coats of arms and provided his father with the coin to present to the clergymen, the clerk, the pew opener, and the choir.

The gifts for the household staff and the wedding

guests would be presented at the conclusion of the wedding breakfast. Alyssa had chosen to give each of the female staff members lace shawls, kid gloves, or handkerchiefs, depending upon their service. The housekeepers of each household were to receive silver chatelaines, and the cooks of each household, silver lockets. The exception being Alyssa's lady's maid and the lady's maids of the other women, who all received a complete ensemble in the latest style. Each of the butlers of the eight households would be given gold watches, and the footmen and grooms would receive kid gloves and cash.

Alyssa smothered a yawn, then pulled on her gloves. She hadn't had more than two or three hours of sleep a night in over a week. Her days had been filled with rounds of at homes and bridal fetes and the myriad details of planning the wedding, and her nights had been spent attending the balls, musicales, soirees, and midnight suppers to which she and Griffin had been invited. Lady Weymouth had insisted on an early evening for last night's supper for the wedding party. She had called an end to it at eleven, for which Alyssa was grateful because she had been up since five.

Her wedding day was no different. Alyssa had, once again, rolled out of bed at five to put the finishing touches on the decorations and to oversee the setting of the tables. She was weary. Tired to the bone. And elated. All at the same time.

She'd done it. She had managed to put together a wedding in which her family and Griffin's could take pride in less than seven days. And she hadn't forgotten about the members of the household staffs who had worked so hard to make it possible.

Once the wedding breakfast ended, every member of all the household staffs would have the afternoon and evening and the next two days off with full pay.

The Earls of Tressingham, Weymouth, Brookestone, Garrison, and Hastings, and the Marquess of Shepherdston and their families and houseguests, were going to have to fend for themselves until Monday morning.

And no one seemed to mind, because everyone Alyssa

had talked to planned to use their days off to catch up on their sleep.

Only the staff of Abernathy Manor was excluded, and that was because Lord and Lady Abernathy would be honeymooning there.

"It's time, Alyssa."

Alyssa turned from the mirror to find Lady Miranda Saint Germaine holding a huge bouquet of roses and daisies tied with white satin ribbons and her own bouquet of cascading roses and lilies.

"Your sisters have already lined up to start the walk down the aisle," Miranda told her. "It's time for us to follow."

"I'm almost ready," Alyssa told her.

"Griffin asked me to give you these." Lady Miranda set her bouquet aside before untying a soft white leather pouch from around Alyssa's bouquet. Smiling, she handed the pouch to Alyssa. "A present from the groom. Could it be the famous Abernathy family jewels?"

Alyssa frowned. "I hope not," she admitted, "because everyone will expect me to wear them, and Lady Weymouth says they are hideously large and gaudy."

"Then, don't keep us in suspense," Miranda urged. "Open it."

Alyssa untied the strings and opened the pouch. "Oh! Miranda, look!" She pulled out a strand of perfectly matched pearls crowned with a brilliant pendant of amethysts and peridots. Along with the necklace was a matching bracelet and a matching pair of earrings.

Alyssa held the jewelry so Miranda could see it.

"They're beautiful," Miranda breathed.

"The gems match the stones in my betrothal ring." She smiled. "And the pearls match those sewn onto my wedding dress."

"Then you'll want to wear these."

"Of course." Reaching up, Alyssa began fumbling with the clasp of the cameo locket she'd worn to complement her dress.

"Let me help you," Miranda said. "Turn around."

Alyssa did as she asked, and Miranda quickly un-

hooked the cameo locket and replaced it with the strand
of pearls.

When she finished fastening the pearl necklace around
Alyssa's neck, Miranda clasped the bracelet over
Alyssa's gloved right wrist and replaced Alyssa's tiny
cameo earrings with Griffin's gift.

"You look beautiful," Miranda murmured, handing
Alyssa her bouquet of flowers. "Just the way a bride
should look."

"Thank you," Alyssa replied. "So do you."

Lady Miranda glanced at her reflection in the mirror.
The mint green color of her dress was most becoming.
It complemented her light auburn hair, the green of her
eyes, and her flawless ivory complexion. In it, Miranda
felt almost beautiful. Or as close to beautiful as one
could feel when one stood a hair under six feet tall in
one's stocking feet and would never possess the small
rounded bosom, the slim hips, or twenty-inch waist currently in vogue.

Miranda shook her head. "I'll never be anyone's idea
of the beautiful bride. I'm too big and tomboyish for
that." She shrugged her shoulders. "I'm destined to be
everyone's favorite bridesmaid and nobody's chosen
bride."

Alyssa's mouth dropped open. Was it possible that
Miranda didn't know how truly lovely she was? "I think
that one day soon, you'll make someone a beautiful
bride."

Miranda gave Alyssa an affectionate hug. "Let's make
you a beautiful bride first," she teased. "We'll work on
making me one after you're married."

"Agreed," Alyssa said.

"Good," Miranda answered, reaching for her own
bouquet. "Now, let's go. Your groom is waiting."

Miranda led the way out of the antechamber and into
the church sanctuary.

Alyssa followed, grasping her father's elbow and taking her place at the back of the line as the choir began
to sing Alyssa's favorite wedding chorale by Handel.

Griffin turned and looked down the aisle as the final

note of the chorus faded away. His first glimpse of Alyssa took his breath away. She radiated beauty and serenity. Griffin waited until her father stepped aside, then moved into place at Alyssa's side and took her hand in his. Smiling down at Alyssa, unable to take his gaze away from her face, Griff nodded to the bishop.

The bishop cleared his throat and began the service. As he listened to the bishop, Griff's thoughts turned to his bride. Although he'd despaired at relinquishing his Free Fellows status and being forced to marry when his father forced the issue, Griff decided that he had chosen well. In addition to being lovely, Alyssa had proven herself to be an extraordinary woman. She'd managed to create a miracle wedding, and he had yet to hear her utter a single word of complaint. Griff glanced heavenward and said a silent prayer of thanks for the spark of attraction that had flared the first time he'd seen her and for his good judgment in recognizing it.

"Griffin Abernathy, seventeenth Viscount Abernathy and twenty-second Baron Maitland, wilt thou have this woman to thy wedded wife, to live together after God's ordinance in the holy estate of Matrimony? Wilt thou love her, comfort her, honor, and keep her in sickness and in health; and, forsaking all other, keep thee only unto her, so long as ye both shall live?"

"I will." Griff's answer was strong and firm.

He smiled at her, and Alyssa recognized the steady light of confidence that seemed to glow in the depths of his blue eyes. Griffin had just promised to love her. The fact that he did so in such a strong and firm tone of voice took her by surprise. *She* knew he didn't love her. She knew he didn't want to marry her or anyone else. She had heard him say so. She had heard him affirm his loyalty to the Free Fellows League. Whatever that was. But his manner and his certain answer said something else entirely.

He had been the perfect companion for the past few days, escorting her to myriad parties and socials and enduring the company of countless grand dames of the ton. He had listened to hours of endless conversation

about the wedding and had tolerated a thousand interruptions to his daily routine in order to accommodate
her requests and offer assistance. He had trusted her
judgment and allowed her to make the decisions, patiently staying out of the way until he was called upon
to help smooth the way with his name and his reputation,
enlisting his staff and his friend's staff to help without
uttering a single word of complaint in her hearing.

Alyssa smiled at him. He didn't love her, nor had he
wanted to marry, but he was making certain that everyone within earshot thought that he did. He might never
grow to love her or feel affection for her, but he had
given himself to her before God and witnesses. He was
hers for the keeping, and Alyssa intended to make him
proud.

"Lady Alyssa Carrollton, wilt thou have this man to
thy wedded husband, to live together after God's ordinance in the holy estate of Matrimony? Wilt thou obey
him, and serve him, love, honor, and keep him in sickness and in health; and, forsaking all other, keep thee
only unto him, so long as ye both shall live?"

She wasn't completely certain she would always obey
him, but Alyssa promised to try. She looked up at Griffin
and answered just as strongly and firmly as he had done:
"I will."

Alyssa listened as Griffin repeated his vows and she
repeated hers in kind until the bishop paused.

"It's time for the ring," he prompted.

Lord Weymouth handed his son a gold wedding band.

Griffin waited as Alyssa removed her gloves and
handed them to her maid of honor.

Griff took Alyssa's left hand. "With this ring I thee
wed, with my body I thee worship, and with all my
worldly goods I thee endow: In the Name of the Father,
and of the Son, and of the Holy Ghost. Amen," he repeated, sliding the slim gold band onto her ring finger.
When the wedding band was in place, Griff gently
pulled her betrothal ring from her middle finger, where
she'd moved it before the ceremony, and slid it alongside.

The slim band and the amethyst and peridot betrothal ring matched perfectly, and Alyssa stood admiring them before she closed her eyes and bowed her head in prayer.

"Alyssa?"

She hadn't realized the prayer was over until Griffin said her name.

"You can open your eyes, now." She heard the teasing note in his voice. "The worst of it's over. We're done, except for the signing of the register."

She looked up.

Griffin blew out a little sigh of relief. "Are you ready?"

She nodded.

"All right, let's go." He tucked her hand in the crook of his arm and led her down the aisle to the vestibule to sign the parish registry.

He signed his name with a flourish and handed her the pen: Alyssa *Abernathy*. She halted the pen in mid-motion, and Griff leaned over her shoulder and whispered, "Viscountess Abernathy and Baroness Maitland."

She gave him a grateful smile.

"We've done it," Griffin said.

Yes, they had done it. For better or for worse, they were husband and wife.

Chapter 16

"The wedding went off without a hitch. I'm amazed that Alyssa managed to accomplish so much in so little time. I hope I shall be as fortunate when I begin my journey to join my regiment."

—GRIFFIN, VISCOUNT ABERNATHY, JOURNAL ENTRY, 04 MAY 1810

"*That's the last of them,*" *Griffin said, lifting* Alyssa's hand to his lips in salute as the final few guests passed through the receiving line and on to the buffet tables.

"Are you certain?" Alyssa glanced around as Griff let go of her hand and breathed a heartfelt sigh of relief when she saw that the line had disappeared. "I know I sent out two hundred invitations, but I feel as if I've greeted two thousand people."

She shifted her weight from one foot to the other, and Griff automatically placed his hand at the small of her back to steady her. "I believe I recognized everyone on the guest list," he said. "With a few exceptions."

Alyssa leaned against him, allowing Griffin to support her weight as she rested her aching feet.

The trust in that intimate gesture took him by surprise. His chest expanded with pride, and he smiled at her. "I suppose that means we welcomed a handful of gate crashers along with the guests, but who can blame them for crashing when you managed to provide such a dazzling feast? Everyone who is anyone in the ton seems to have snatched an invite."

"Everyone except your friends." Alyssa frowned. "I don't remember being introduced to them."

"How could you not?" Griff teased. "Over half the people here were put on the guest list at the suggestion of my mother and father."

"That doesn't explain why Lord Grantham and Lord Shepherdston didn't come. I distinctly remember sending their invitations."

"Grantham and Shepherdston couldn't come," Griff told her. "They're Fre—" He bit his tongue.

"They're what?" she asked.

"They're friends," Griff improvised, "from my bachelor days." He'd almost proclaimed them Free Fellows. "As such, I'm sure they sent their regrets. It's generally understood that it's bad form for bachelors to attend a friend's wedding, even when invited to do so."

"But they're your friends," Alyssa protested. "And I didn't want them to feel excluded."

Griffin pulled her closer, so that she fit neatly into the curve of his side, and then gave her waist a reassuring squeeze. "They weren't excluded," he said. "You invited them. Shepherdston and Grantham sent regrets because they're gentlemen and they understand how and why things are done the way they are." He frowned. "Unfortunately, His Grace doesn't subscribe to the same sensibilities, or he wouldn't be here, either."

"I didn't invite . . ." Alyssa turned to find the Duke of Sussex striding through the door. "His Grace."

"Well, someone did," Griff said.

He and Alyssa looked at one another and then spoke in unison.

"Your mother."

"My mother."

Alyssa sighed. "It had to be my mother—or my father. . . ."

Griff shook his head. "Your father is a gentlemen. Gentlemen do not refuse another gentleman's offer for his daughter's hand in marriage and then invite him to the wedding. It's poor form."

"Then it must have been Mama. She wants so much to be considered one of the premier hostesses that it would never occur to her not to invite a duke. *Any* duke."

"Nevertheless . . ." Griff scowled. "His Grace should have had the decency not to attend. He knows the ways of society. He understands that we were rivals for your hand." Griff gritted his teeth until his jaw muscles ached. "He may have received an invitation," he continued, "but he knows he didn't come at *my* invitation."

Alyssa widened her eyes. "You don't suppose he thinks he came at *mine?*"

"Not unless you gave him reason to hope—" Griff began.

"I haven't spoken to him since we were children," Alyssa said. "And *I* wouldn't have provided him with reason to hope, even if such a thing had been possible, because *I* didn't want to marry him. *I* didn't want to become a duchess."

"Well, buck up," Griff said, tightening his grasp on her waist ever so slightly in what could only be called a masculine show of possession. "Because he's coming over to offer his felicitations."

"As if either of us wanted them," Alyssa muttered. She understood exactly what was taking place, and none of it had anything to do with His Grace offering his felicitations on their wedding. Alyssa had seen this behavior before. If Griffin or His Grace had been one of her father's hounds, they would have been busily engaged in the business of marking their territories.

"May I offer you congratulations on the occasion of your wedding, Lady Abernathy, and offer you many happy returns of the day?" His Grace, the Duke of Sussex, bowed before Alyssa.

"Thank you, Your Grace," she answered.

"And congratulations to you as well, Abernathy." Sussex offered his hand to Griffin. "I cannot profess to believe that as a husband, you are the best choice for Lady Alyssa, but—"

Griff looked Sussex in the eye but made no move to shake his hand. "I don't care what you profess, Your

Grace," Griff said. "As a husband, I was *Lady Alyssa's* choice."

Sussex lifted one elegantly arched eyebrow as he dropped his hand back down to his side. "Indeed? I was given to understand that Lord Tressingham's acquisition of a prized stallion induced him to make the choice."

"Be careful, Your Grace," Alyssa warned in a fierce whisper. "For I have been told once too often today that my father bartered me in exchange for a horse." She stared up at the handsome duke. "And I promised myself that I would shoot the next person who suggested it." She smiled sweetly. "I've never shot anyone before, and I never dreamed I would have to begin with so august a personage, but I am willing to start at the top—if you are. . . ."

Griffin smiled at his wife before turning to the duke. "As you can see, Your Grace, you have been misinformed. Your understanding of the situation is incorrect. And I would not go around repeating so inaccurate a statement, were I you."

Sussex stiffened. "But you are not me."

"On that we are agreed." Griff smiled at the young duke. "For I am Lady Alyssa's husband. You are not." He offered Alyssa his arm. "Now, if you will be so kind as to excuse us, Your Grace, there are other wedding guests who wish an opportunity to offer us their felicitations."

Sussex inhaled sharply. One did not *dismiss* a duke. One waited until the duke dismissed *him*. But, His Grace admitted, one didn't normally challenge the bridegroom on his wedding day, either. "It's been understood for some time now, that I would take one of Tressingham's daughters to wife."

"I'm afraid you missed out, Your Grace," Griffin responded, taking a step toward the duke. "Four times. Lady Abernathy's sisters preceded her in marriage. And Lord Tressingham hasn't any other daughters."

"Only horses and hounds," Sussex said, refusing to give ground.

"Stop this at once!" Alyssa stepped between the two

men. "I am not chattel to be bartered for in exchange for a horse, nor am I a bone to be fought over by *gentlemen* who persist in behaving like hounds marking the lamppost boundaries of their territory." She eyed her husband and his onetime rival. "I know where my father keeps his firearms. And I am quite an accomplished target shot. This is my wedding day, and since you two gentlemen seem determined to spoil what remains of the wedding breakfast, I must tell you that at the moment, I am not averse to depriving Bonaparte of another English cavalryman target or of depriving His Majesty of one of his 'right trusty and right entirely beloved cousins.' If I am to be made a widow, I prefer to do the making. As of this moment, your bit of territorial marking is over." Alyssa glared at the duke. "Do you understand, Your Grace? Or must I gain your attention in a more violent manner?"

Griffin bit the inside of his cheek to keep from laughing at the look on the young duke's face. "I believe, my lady, that this episode, as you call it, stems from the fact that you have already gained His Grace's attention."

"I recognize the honor His Grace has paid me with his attention, but in truth, I did not seek it prior to my marriage, and I do not seek it following my marriage." Alyssa looked up at the duke. "I do, however, appreciate His Grace's unexpected felicitations on this, my wedding day."

The Duke of Sussex's second dismissal wasn't quite the surprise the first one had been. He bowed once again over Lady Abernathy's hand. "By your leave, milady." He gifted Alyssa with an indulgent smile before turning to Griffin. "Unlike you, my lord, I'm in no rush to join a regiment and become cannon fodder. I can wait."

"Yes, you can, Your Grace," Griff shot back. "You appear to be quite adept at waiting." He tucked Alyssa's hand in the crook of his arm and led her to the bride and groom's table to begin the toasts and the distribution of presents to their guests and to the members of the household staffs.

After all the toasts to the health of the bride and

groom and to the health of the bishop had been exchanged and Alyssa and Griffin had presented the gifts, Alyssa went upstairs to change from her wedding dress into a traveling dress.

She emerged from her bedchamber half an hour later, said her good-byes to her family and the many loyal retainers who had served the Tressinghams since before Alyssa was born, and joined with Griffin on the east portico to say his.

Tossing her wedding bouquet toward the cluster of unmarried girls and debutantes, Alyssa laughed when Miranda caught it, then gasped as the gathered crowd began throwing old shoes and fistfuls of rice. Griffin took her by the hand and nodded toward the coach. Gathering her skirts in hand, Alyssa ran with Griffin to the coach, dodging handfuls of rice and old shoes as they made their way through a gauntlet of well-wishers.

Alyssa climbed into the coach, sank down onto the velvet-covered cushions, and heaved a sigh of relief as the coachman slammed the door of the coach shut behind them. She started to put her feet up on the opposite seat, then thought better of it.

"Go ahead," Griffin invited. "It's as much your coach as it is mine. And I know your legs and feet must be killing you."

Alyssa nodded.

"How long have you been on your feet today?" he asked.

Alyssa thought for a moment. "Since five."

Griffin moved to the opposite seat, then reached down and gently encircled her ankle, carefully lifting it onto his lap. He untied the ribbons that held her slippers on her feet and slid her shoe off. Positioning her foot in the cradle of his thighs, Griffin began to massage the ball of her foot.

"You can't." His hands and fingers were magical; still Alyssa made a halfhearted protest.

"Why not?" Griff asked. "We're married."

"We're taking up too much room," she explained, biting back a moan of sheer pleasure as he kneaded a particularly tender spot in the arch of her right foot with the pads of his thumbs. "Where are Durham and Eastman going to sit?"

"It's our coach," Griffin reminded her. "We're allowed to take up as much room as we like. And your lady's maid and my valet are riding with the luggage in a separate coach. We've a long journey ahead of us, and I thought you might like to rest before we get there."

"That would be heavenly," Alyssa admitted.

"Then close your eyes and go to sleep," Griff advised.

"You don't mind?" She smothered a yawn.

Griff shook his head. "Not at all. Go on, close your eyes. I'll wake you at the first stop."

She didn't have to be prompted twice. She closed her eyes, leaned her head back against the velvet cushion, and allowed the tension in her body to melt away as Griff massaged first one foot and then the other.

Chapter 17

"Needlepoint cushions in varying sizes and lap robes of cashmere or woven cotton make useful additions to any lady or gentleman's traveling coach."

—ALYSSA, LADY ABERNATHY, DIARY ENTRY, 04 MAY 1810

Alyssa jolted awake. She opened her eyes and discovered that she was lying on her side on the coach seat with her face comfortably pillowed against a firmly muscled thigh covered in buff-colored breeches. The thigh she was using as a pillow and the buff breeches covering it puzzled her. When she'd left her parents' London town house, she'd been sitting across from Griffin, and he'd been wearing his wedding suit. The trousers were pale gray.

Alyssa stared down the length of the gentleman's leg and noted the glossy black leather Hessian boot gloving his well-molded calf and his foot. Her heart thudded in her chest, and her blood roared in her ears. She struggled to sit up, but the rocking motion of the coach over rough terrain made it all but impossible.

"Sssh, Alyssa. If you need to sit up, I'll help you, but you're perfectly fine where you are." His voice calmed her. It was warm and familiar and as soothing as the touch of his hand on her hair.

She relaxed, shifted her weight onto her back, and smiled. Looking up at him seemed the most natural thing in the world. "Where are we?"

Griff leaned forward and returned her smile. Feeling an almost overwhelming urge to kiss her, he bent close enough to feel the whisper of her breath against his mouth. He paused, waiting for some sign that she wanted him to continue. But she didn't seem to notice his desire, so Griff sat back and answered her question with words instead of kisses. "About a mile past Shepherdston Hall. If you need to make a privacy stop, I'll order Myrick to turn the coach around."

Alyssa remembered Griffin mentioning that Shepherdston Hall was a little over halfway between London and Abernathy Manor and that he often stopped there to rest, refresh, and change horses. "Why didn't we stop there?"

"We *did* stop." He brushed her hair from her forehead and smiled indulgently as if she were a little girl. She'd managed several hours of sleep, but her eyes were still ringed by dark bluish circles that spoke of extreme exhaustion. "We changed horses, and I changed into more comfortable traveling clothes."

She smothered a yawn and blinked up at him. That explained the change from trousers and black shoes to breeches and Hessian boots. It didn't explain why he hadn't awakened her. "You promised to wake me."

"I did wake you," he told her. "And you told me to go away and let you sleep."

"You left me sleeping alone in a coach while you changed clothes?"

Griffin shrugged his shoulders. "It seemed the thing to do, short of bundling you in a lap robe and carrying you inside."

"I could have walked inside," Alyssa replied.

"Not unless you were awake and not in your current state of undress," he said, eyes twinkling.

Alyssa glanced down, surprised to find that she was not only using Griffin's thigh as a pillow, but that until she'd been jolted awake by the movement of the coach, she'd apparently been sprawled all over him wearing nothing more than her chemise, stockings, gloves, the very brief and thin pair of lacy drawers the dressmaker insisted she wear beneath her traveling dress, and a soft wool lap robe with his jacket draped over it. Alyssa shivered, enveloped in the musk and citrus scent of the cologne emanating from the collar of his jacket. "You removed my dress?"

"I did," he admitted, tucking his jacket and the lap robe more firmly around her shoulders to ward off the cool air. "Before it became hopelessly crumpled, I might add." He made a wry face. "I didn't think you would want to arrive at Abernathy Manor looking so travel worn."

"Where is it?"

"Abernathy Manor?" he asked. "It's in Northamptonshire."

"No," she said. "Where is my dress?"

"There." He nodded toward the opposite seat, where her dress and jacket were neatly folded. Her bonnet lay atop her dress and beside it lay his hat, gloves, and neckcloth. Her shoes were beneath the bench seat.

Alyssa realized that she was nearly naked, while he remained fully dressed except for his hat, gloves, and cravat. "Oh."

"It started raining two hours out of London—"

"Rain on our wedding day," Alyssa interrupted. "I don't think that's a good sign. I believe it means we'll have bad luck."

"I believe it means we live in England where it rains quite a bit." He tilted her chin toward him with the tip of his index finger. "If everyone in England who had rain on their wedding day was destined for bad luck, we'd have been overrun by plague and pestilence centuries ago." He smiled at her. "I believe we make our own luck."

"I suppose you're right."

"We only stayed at Shepherdston Hall long enough for me to change clothes and for the coachmen to change horses. I didn't want to tarry because of the rain. Because I want to get home as soon as possible. And you were sleeping so soundly when we arrived, I saw no reason you shouldn't continue." He paused for a moment. "I left you sleeping while I changed clothes and the coachmen and grooms exchanged the spent horses for the fresh ones. But you were never alone. Durham and Eastman took turns watching over the coach while I was inside the hall. And I've been with you ever since."

"How long?" Her throat was dry and scratchy, and her voice sounded foreign to her ears.

Griffin shifted his weight to his left side in order to reach his watch pocket. He pulled out the watch, flipped open the cover, and stared at the hands. "A little over four hours."

"Four hours!" Alyssa covered her eyes with her forearm and groaned. "I can't imagine what came over me."

Griffin tinkered with a tiny knob on his timepiece, then returned it to his watch pocket. He stretched his arms overhead, scraping the ceiling of the coach with his knuckles. "It must have been my scintillating company," he said dryly.

Alyssa giggled.

"Or exhaustion." He yawned. "You've been working practically around the clock for the past six days. Flitting about town seeing to an overwhelming number of details like a hummingbird going from blossom to blossom in the garden. But even hummingbirds rest." He frowned. "I'm not sure when or how they rest, but I'm convinced that they do—sometimes. After all your hard work and sleepless nights spent planning the wedding, it's perfectly natural to for you to need a nap." He stretched his arms over his head once again. "In fact, I was tempted to stretch out beneath you and take one myself."

"Why didn't you?" She surprised herself with the question, and he surprised her even more with his answer.

Griff answered honestly, "I was afraid you might find me entirely too comfortable. Afraid I might enjoy it too much. Afraid I might succumb to temptation."

"Temptation?"

"I'm a man, my sweet, not a eunuch. You may find me entirely comfortable and cozy as your pillow, but the picture of you lying sprawled atop me is more than I could stand." The fact that a lap robe and his jacket

covered her was proof. He'd spent most of the journey
with her sleeping on him, and the image he carried in
his brain of her lying with her head in his lap and her
firm, rosy-tipped breasts nearly spilling out of her transparent chemise had been enough to nearly do him in.

He'd been hard and aching and almost afraid to move
for fear of exploding since he'd been foolish enough to
try to preserve her clothing from the ravages of travel.
Griffin looked at her. "And, my sweet, no bride should
wake up to find she's lost her virginity in the coach on
the way to her honeymoon."

He didn't seem to notice the endearment, but Alyssa's
heart caught at the sound. "I believe you're stronger than
you think. I slept upon your lap for nearly four hours,
and I felt entirely safe in your company. I knew no harm
would come to me."

Griffin chuckled. "Which shows how little you know
of randy young bridegrooms. Harming you wasn't what
I had in mind, my lady." His voice was low and husky,
filled with meaning.

The timbre of his voice and the expression on his face
intrigued her. "I know nothing of bridegrooms, randy or
otherwise. For you are my first," she replied in a voice
equally low and husky and filled with meaning. "What
did you have in mind, my lord?"

"I told you, my sweet. I was tempted to do something
no gentleman would ever do."

"And what was that?" Suddenly warm, Alyssa pushed
his jacket and the lap robe off her shoulders and sat up.

Griffin bit back a groan as she bared her near naked
chest for him to view and brushed the vee of his thighs
with her fingers. His body tightened even more. "Relieve
you of your innocence while you slept, so that I might
ease the aching in my groin."

"Was it *possible* for you to relieve me of my innocence while I slept?" she asked.

Griffin closed his eyes and nodded.

Recalling the conversation she'd overheard between
the members of the Free Fellows League, Alyssa smiled.
"I've heard that losing one's innocence is a messy, un-

comfortable, and shockingly distasteful business. Especially on one's wedding night. And that young ladies seldom find *pleasure* in the marriage bed."

Griffin opened his eyes and narrowed his gaze at her. "Who told you that? Your mother?"

"Oh no," she explained. "I just heard it somewhere." She had also heard Griffin proclaim that the husbands of those young ladies were ignorant fools—and that he was neither. Alyssa waited for him to repeat that proclamation.

"You shouldn't believe everything you hear," he warned.

Alyssa was disappointed until Griffin continued speaking. "Especially the kinds of conversations you often hear when women gather at parties to talk. You see, my lady, a great many women are married to ignorant, overbearing fools. You are not."

Alyssa beamed at him. "Then the marriage bed needn't be a terrible place?"

"Not at all," he assured her. "I'm told it can be a bit uncomfortable for the woman the first time." Griffin cleared his throat. "But the marriage bed should be a heavenly place. A place of supreme satisfaction and enjoyment." And he was eager to experience it, for Alyssa's transparent chemise offered him an enticing view of the joys to be had as soon as he reached the marriage bed. He clamped his teeth together as the twin points of her breasts formed tight, dark pink buds against the delicate lawn fabric.

"Is there any way to ease the discomfort?"

Which discomfort? Hers? Or mine? Griffin groaned. "There is."

"How?"

"A little wine. A little whisky. And a game of seduction."

"I'm intrigued." Alyssa leaned closer. "Tell me about this game, my lord."

Griffin cleared his throat once again. "Why bother telling you, my lady, when we can go right to the instruction?"

"I like to be well-informed," Alyssa teased, watching as her husband's blue eyes darkened. "How do you play it? I want to know the rules."

"Well," he drawled, "seduction is a teasing game, and there is only one rule, my sweet. And that's to ease the ache by giving only pleasure."

Alyssa frowned at him. "Will I lose my innocence in the coach?"

Griffin laughed. "You'll lose a great deal of it," he promised, "but we shall add a caveat." He looked at her. "Because you are a bride, and because no bride should lose her complete innocence in a coach on her way to her honeymoon, we're allowed everything that gives pleasure—except consummation. That shall have to wait until we're properly settled in the great, big comfortable bed in the master's chamber at Abernathy Manor. In about three hours. Agreed?"

Alyssa held out her hand. "Agreed."

Griffin stared at the elbow-length glove encasing it. He took her hand, turned it palm upward, and unbuttoned the tiny buttons of her glove before pulling it off. "I think we can dispense with the gloves," he said, suddenly wondering at the wisdom of agreeing to three hours of extreme arousal. "This is a momentous occasion, but no longer an especially formal one." He winked at her as he unbuttoned her remaining glove and pulled it off, too. "Nothing to warrant opera-length gloves."

"Where shall you begin?" Alyssa asked.

"I don't begin," Griffin answered, a twinkle in his eye. "You do."

"*I* do?"

Griff heard the astonishment in her voice. "But, of course." He grinned at her. "Ladies first."

Alyssa reached out and put her hand on his thigh. "Where does it ache, my lord?"

"Here." Griffin covered Alyssa's hand with his and moved it over a few inches, resting it atop the hard ridge pressing against the front of his breeches.

Chapter 18

"It is important to make travel by coach as enjoyable as possible. And there are a great many pleasurable ways in which to pass the time. Especially during long journeys."

—ALYSSA, LADY ABERNATHY, DIARY ENTRY, 04 MAY 1810

"Shall I kiss you and make it better?" Alyssa whispered, keeping her hand right where it was despite the hot blush she knew colored her cheeks. He was hard beneath her hand and hot, and the intimacy of such a hitherto forbidden touch excited her.

Griff caught his breath. Was it possible? Had he died and gone to heaven? Or had his innocent wife just asked him if she could kiss him in the place he craved it most? "Please," he managed.

Alyssa leaned forward and kissed him, pressing her soft lips against his mouth. Her kiss was hot and sweet enough to tempt an angel. And he enjoyed it immensely, but it wasn't the sort of kiss he'd been expecting.

Alyssa pulled him to her until she could press herself against him. She flattened herself against his chest, feeling the heat of his flesh as she deepened the kiss.

The twin points of her breasts pressed into him. Griffin groaned.

Encouraged by his response, Alyssa wrapped her free arm around his neck, forcing him to bend closer. She pressed her other hand harder against the front of his breeches, massaging him in a slow, circular motion that increased the heat and the pressure beneath her palm.

Griffin groaned again. His tongue mated with hers as he showed her what he wanted.

Alyssa continued her exploration. She trailed her hand from his neck, over his shoulders, and down his back as far as she could reach, then trailed it back up again, only this time, she moved over his shoulders, up the nape of his neck, where she buried her fingers in his hair. And when she'd explored every lock of hair on his head, she repeated the procedure, working her way back down his body.

Griff turned on the seat and slipped his free arm around Alyssa's waist. He kept one arm around her waist, supporting her. He pulled her close, then lifted his other hand from hers. He caught hold of her wrist when she would have pulled her hand away and pressed it back against him, urging her to continue the motion by breaking their kiss long enough to murmur, "Don't stop."

His muscles bunched and rippled under her hands as Griffin held her tightly, half-lifting her off the coach seat as he ground his hips against her, rubbing his throbbing erection against her hand. He pulled his mouth away from hers and began to trail hot, wet kisses on her face, her neck, her throat, and over to her earlobes.

"Sweet Alyssa," Griffin whispered close to her ear, "I want to feel your hands on my flesh. I want to taste you. And have you taste me."

The muscles in his arms began to quiver. Alyssa felt them through the thin fabric of her chemise. "How?" She breathed the question against his forehead as he worked his way from her earlobe, down her neck, and over her chest to the edge of her chemise.

"Buttons," he answered, moving her hand from his throbbing groin to the waistband of his breeches. "Undo the buttons on the right side of my breeches."

She did as he asked, reaching around to unfasten the line of buttons at his waist.

Griffin braced his feet against the floor of the coach, lifted his hips from the seat cushion, and slid out of his breeches. It wasn't the first time he'd shucked his breeches in a vehicle. He'd changed clothes in his coach numerous times when traveling, and on several occasions, he and a willing female companion had played the seduction game to break up the monotony of a long journey, but he hadn't done it in quite a while, and his movements weren't as smooth and practiced as they'd once been.

Alyssa watched as Griffin pushed his skintight breeches over his lean hips and down his thighs. He couldn't wriggle all the way out of his trousers because his boots stopped their progress, but his movements were smooth and practiced, and Alyssa thought he must have had other opportunities to polish the maneuver.

He didn't wear undergarments. The thought popped into her head as the paler flesh of his muscled buttocks came into view. Of course, it was probably impossible to get undergarments beneath those breeches. She was so fascinated by the play of muscles along his flanks and buttocks that she didn't notice the arrow of dark hair pointing toward the thick nest of curls at the juncture of his thighs until his prominent male member sprang forward.

Alyssa's eyes widened, and she inhaled sharply at the sight.

Griff chuckled. "So much for subtlety."

Leaning closer, Alyssa studied that portion of his anatomy that made him indisputably male, unable to believe that the long hard ridge she'd massaged and traced with her fingertips could be so easily concealed and contained beneath his tight breeches. "Is it always like this?"

"Only during the past week or so." He met her gaze, waiting until he saw understanding dawn in her eyes. "That's right," he nodded in approval. "It's been like this—more or less—nearly every day since I first met you."

She reached out to touch him, then stopped short. "It looks painful."

"It can be very painful," he told her. "But only if you don't touch me."

As she continued to watch, Griffin stripped off his

waistcoat and lawn shirt. He tossed his clothes into the corner of the opposite seat beside Alyssa's traveling dress.

Wanting to see him completely naked, Alyssa impulsively moved to the opposite seat and began tugging at his boots.

Griffin helped, toeing off his Hessians and stripping off his stockings and breeches before leaning back against the velvet squabs so his inquisitive bride could get a look at him in all his male glory.

Alyssa stared. She had known he was handsome. But she hadn't realized he was beautiful until he sat sprawled before her like a gypsy slave on display. A blue-eyed gypsy slave . . .

Alyssa's breathing increased. The sight of him fascinated her. She loved the way he challenged her and answered her curiosity, spreading his legs and planting his long, elegantly arched feet on the floor of the coach to give her an unencumbered view of the mysteries of the male body.

His wide shoulders tapered into a narrow waist, into slim hips and strong thighs. His chest was covered with a patch of dark curly hair that also tapered down into a long slim line that encircled his navel and pointed to the hard erection jutting from another nest of dark curls. He was big. He was all male. And he was hers for the taking. Her blue-eyed gypsy lord. All he needed was a wide gold arm cuff to complete the picture and perhaps an earring . . .

"Well?" he drawled.

She said the first thing that came to mind. "I've never seen a naked man before."

Griffin gifted her with a broad smile. "I can't tell you how delighted I am to hear that, my lady."

"You just did," she said. "But then, you obviously cannot say the same."

"That's because I see a naked man in my mirror each time I step out of my bed." His broad smile became an amused chuckle.

Alyssa bit her lower lip to keep from laughing with

him. "I meant that you obviously couldn't say that you have never seen a naked woman before."

Griff arched one eyebrow in an elegantly lazy gesture that spoke of generations of noble ancestors. "I don't see one now."

Alyssa looked down at her chemise, realizing for the first time how very transparent it was. "Close enough."

Griff shook his head slowly from side to side. "Not close enough."

"But you've seen a naked woman before," she protested, suddenly inexplicably modest.

"I've never seen my wife naked." He met her gaze, then softened his voice to what could best be described as a soft, rumbling purr. "I've never seen *you* naked. And I want to, Alyssa. Very much."

"All right." Her assent was nearly lost amid the patter of rain on the roof of the coach and the noise of the team.

He'd hired post riders as protection, and it was a relatively safe drive with the moon nearly full, but accidents could happen, and heaven help them if they lost a wheel, became bogged in the quagmire that passed as the post road, or encountered highwaymen, Griff thought as Alyssa reached up to untie the drawstring ribbon resting along the curve of her breasts. No doubt, his driver, Myrick, and the coachmen and groom, and the driver of the other coach—not to mention Alyssa's lady's maid and his valet—would be scandalized by their game of seduction. No doubt it was worth it. Griff smiled like the cat that ate the cream and crooked his index finger at Alyssa. "Closer."

She scooted to the edge of the opposite seat.

Griff patted the seat beside him. "Closer."

Alyssa moved to sit beside him.

"Allow me." He faced her, then reached over and untied the white satin drawstring ribbon holding her chemise in place. When he'd successfully unknotted the bow, Griffin looped a finger in the gathered neck of the garment and tugged. The chemise slipped off her shoulders, sliding down her chest until it hung suspended on the slope of her upturned breasts.

Seeking a solution to the problem, Griffin leaned forward and kissed the hard, rosy tips of her breasts through the fabric of her chemise.

Alyssa closed her eyes and arched her back as Griffin teased her with his tongue, pulling her nipples into his mouth, dampening the fabric before breathing upon it, forcing his hot breath through the wet material. The sensation sent delightful shivers up and down her spine.

"Like it?" he asked, leaning back just far enough to breathe the words against her breasts.

She nodded.

"Good." He placed his hands on either side of her ribs and palmed her undergarment off her breasts, trailing it over her stomach, motioning for Alyssa to lift her hips so that he could push the chemise down her thighs and allow it to fall in a puddle of delicate lawn fabric at her ankles.

Pressing his back against the wall of the coach, Griffin shifted Alyssa's weight until she was able to lie comfortably on her back against the velvet seat cushions. He knelt over her and cupped her bottom with his hands. Leaning forward, he placed his mouth against the dark triangle of hair beneath her lacy drawers and blew warm, moist air through the fabric, then he slid her drawers and her stockings off her hips, down her legs, and over her feet.

Alyssa kicked free of the remainder of her clothing, sighing with relief, welcoming her nakedness as clothing—any clothing—had suddenly become a hindrance. She wanted to feel him against her skin.

Griffin surprised her by sitting back on his heels and declaring, "Your turn."

Achy and trembling with a need she couldn't name, Alyssa pushed herself into a sitting position and reached for him. She placed her palms against his chest and then traced that intriguing arrow of rough hair down to its base.

His skin rippled beneath her delicate touch, and he gasped aloud as she gripped him.

The feel of him caught Alyssa by surprise. She expected the hardness, but she never expected the exquisitely soft feel of the flesh that encased it. He was hard yet velvety soft, and the contrast intrigued her. She discovered that she enjoyed caressing him, enjoyed experimenting with the weight and feel and the motion of him. And, she discovered, she loved the sense of accomplishment she felt when she gave Griffin such obvious satisfaction.

Griffin quivered with pleasure and came very close to spilling himself in her hand as Alyssa fondled him without shyness and with what could only be termed a natural talent.

"No more," he muttered, leaning his head against her breast.

"More?" she asked, pumping him slowly and gently.

"No!" Griffin reached down and placed his hand on her wrist, forcing her to cease the exquisite torture.

"Don't you like it?"

"I love it," he groaned, panting for breath. "But there is a limit to how much I can endure."

His rationalization captured her imagination. How much could he endure? And what happened when he could no longer endure? What would be the outcome of her teasing? Alyssa decided to ask him. "What happens when you exceed your limit of endurance?"

Griff struggled to catch his breath and process her question. "I reach satisfaction by spilling my seed." He opened his eyes and focused his gaze on her. "Right into your clever hand, my lady." Or her mouth. Or the intimate part of her his body was begging to explore.

Alyssa wasn't ignorant. She had no practical experience, but she was very well read. She knew enough to know that, in the Bible, men spilled their seed all the time—often with undesirable results. She knew it could be done; she had simply never seen the process. . . .

Except when she'd sneaked peeks while Abrams and the stable hands were breeding the studs and mares.

She'd seen the stallions about to cover the mares. And she knew that about a year after the mares were successfully covered, the foals arrived.

Alyssa glanced down at the hard member in her hand. The equine and the human male anatomy was remarkably similar. She supposed the results would also be similar should Griffin cover her and deposit his seed in the right place at the right time. Somehow, she didn't think her hand was the right place.

Alyssa gently released her grip on him, then smiled ever so sweetly and whispered, "Your turn."

"You're very good at this game, my lady," Griffin praised her.

"I'm very good at everything I do, my lord," Alyssa informed him.

"And modest, too," he teased.

"Yes," Alyssa retorted. "And I'm certain you were able to discern that little trait just by looking at me."

"But of course," he agreed, staring down at her. By Jove, but she was beautiful. And witty and intelligent and as uninhibited as a wood nymph. He ought to be on his knees thanking the gods for his good fortune in having her choose him.

"Lord Abernathy?" She caught his attention by trailing her fingers along the top of his thigh, dangerously close to the conflagration she'd aroused.

"Yes, Lady Abernathy?" Griffin decided he liked the sound of his name and his title on her lips.

"Aren't you forgetting something?" she asked.

He also discovered that he liked teasing her. "And what might that be?"

"It's your turn."

"How could I forget?" Turning his attention back to her breasts, Griffin dipped his head and trailed his tongue along the valley between them, licking at the tiny beads of perspiration he found there. Moving closer, Griff cupped one smooth, satiny globe in his hand and touched his lips to the rosy center.

Alyssa sucked in a breath at the wonderful sensation his tiny kiss evoked. Desire gripped her. She tangled her fingers in Griffin's thick, dark hair and held his head to her breasts. "More," she ordered.

Griffin obliged. The scent of her perfume filled his nostrils. It was warm and inviting—a mixture of old roses and fresh lavender—and it was all Alyssa.

Griff took the time to savor her, despite her urgent command for more. He touched and tasted and gently nipped at the hard bud with his teeth. And then he suckled her, careful to give equal time to each perfect globe, and Alyssa thought she might die of the pleasure as her nerve endings became gloriously alive and sent tiny electrical currents throughout her body, igniting her responses. He continued at a leisurely pace, working his way from the rosy aureole of her breasts, down into the valley between them, the soft rasp and moisture of tongue igniting little brushfires wherever he touched her.

He tasted the skin above her rib cage, trailed his tongue over her abdomen, circling her navel before dipping his tongue into the indention. And while Griffin tasted her with his tongue, he teased her with his fingers.

Skimming his hands over the sensitive flesh covering her hipbones and outer thighs, Griff felt his way down her body, finally locating and tracing the deep grooves at the juncture of her thighs with the pads of his thumbs.

Easing his way ever closer, Griffin massaged the womanly flesh surrounding her mound and then tangled his fingers in the lush brown hair covering it.

Alyssa reacted immediately, opening her legs ever so slightly to allow him greater access. She couldn't seem to get close enough to him. Her anticipation rose to a fever pitch. She began to quiver and make little moaning sounds of pleasure as he traced the outer edge of her folds with his finger before gently plunging his finger inside until Alyssa squirmed. She arched her back to bring herself into closer contact with Griffin.

Griffin gritted his teeth. The slick warm feel, the smell of her perfume, and the scent of her arousal nearly drove him mad. The swelling in his groin grew until he was rock hard and close to bursting. He was naked. She was naked. He couldn't wait any longer. He had to have her.

He had to feel himself inside her, feel her surrounding him, feel them joined together the way men and women were meant to be joined. He sat up and positioned himself between her thighs. He ached with the need for release. He throbbed with the need for satisfaction. It was there within his grasp. All he had to do was . . .

Stop, Griffin realized. He had to stop before he reached the point where he couldn't. Squeezing his eyes shut, he prayed for the strength to stop.

And the gods heard his prayers, for the coach bounced through a rut in the road, jostling the occupants and banging Griff's head against the paneling.

He saw stars. And in that brief moment, he forgot about his need for release. All he felt was pain. And gratitude.

The knock on the head brought him to his senses, reminding him that he was the fool who had set the rules of the game. And he would not break them.

He would not tumble his bride in a coach on the post road to Abernathy Manor.

And that meant that it was time he delivered on his promise to give only pleasure. Time to give Alyssa her first real understanding of the delights of lovemaking. So that she might spend the remainder of the journey anticipating their arrival at the manor and the culmination of the hours spent learning the game of seduction.

He slid his fingers inside her.

Alyssa sighed her pleasure, thrusting against him as he touched her in ways she could not have imagined.

"Griffin?" Her voice was higher than normal, her breathing ragged.

"I'm with you, my lady." Griffin skimmed the pad of his thumb through her slick womanly folds and pressed against the hard little bud hidden there.

Alyssa's eyelids fluttered open, then closed again. Somewhere inside the coach a tiny bell began to chime. Alyssa gasped.

Griffin ignored the sound of the chime and focused all of his attention on his bride. He leaned forward and covered her mouth with his own before increasing the exquisite pressure—with his lips and tongue and with his fingers. He kissed her tenderly, fiercely, possessively, hungrily, then tenderly once more, over and over again, skillfully plying his talented fingers until he felt her scream her pleasure as she shuddered against him.

Chapter 19

"I have discovered that honeymoons are worth all the fuss and bother of planning the wedding that precedes them."

—ALYSSA, LADY ABERNATHY, DIARY ENTRY, 05 MAY 1810

"*Is it my turn already?*" *Alyssa opened her* eyes and found her husband cradling her in his arms. She stretched like a cat, arching her back, luxuriating in the aftermath of an exquisite release of the tension Griffin had managed to build within her. The tips of her breasts brushed against the hair of his chest, and his insistent male member rubbed against the soft flesh of her hip.

"No, it's mine." Griffin smiled tenderly. "I think you just had your turn."

His double entendre was lost in her sense of fair play. "Oh, no," she protested. "That thing you did—the way you touched me with your fingers—was your turn. I believe it's my turn to seduce you."

Griff shook his head.

Alyssa frowned.

"Don't look so disappointed," he said. "You'll get your turn. I promise you'll have ample opportunity to seduce me once we reach the manor."

"But that's hours away. . . ."

Griffin chuckled. "Not anymore." He turned his head, glancing toward the opposite seat. "Hear that chiming?"

She nodded. "What is it?"

"My pocket watch," Griff answered, helping Alyssa sit up before he reached over and grabbed his breeches.

"I set it to chime before the last half hour of our journey so we would have time to—" He cleared his throat. "Prepare for our arrival." He retrieved his timepiece and pressed a tiny lever that ended the chime.

Alyssa couldn't believe it. It seemed as if the last two and a half hours of the journey had passed in the blink of an eye. *Or in the space of a kiss.* "We're there?"

"Almost. We've probably already crossed onto Abernathy land, but the road is a winding one, and it will take a bit longer to reach the manor. We should arrive shortly." He shrugged his shoulders. "So, you see, my lady, your seduction of me will have to wait a little longer."

Alyssa heaved a theatrical sigh worthy of one of her mother's. "I'll do my best to endure the wait."

Griffin grinned at her. "Buck up, my lady; at least you achieved a measure of satisfaction. Many women live their entire lives without reaching that sort of bliss." He glanced down at his rigid member and managed a mocking smile. "And at least you'll be presentable when we get to the manor. I doubt that I shall be so fortunate. My breeches are made tight to prevent chafing when riding and to endure the rigors of travel. They are not made to accommodate my present condition."

"I wondered how you managed to confine all that." She reached out and caressed the velvety-soft tip of his member with her finger. "Inside your breeches all the time without anyone noticing."

Griff closed his eyes, bit his bottom lip, and fought to control himself. "It isn't like this all the time," he reminded her. "And until I met you, I was able to *confine* it on a regular basis. Even after I met you—so long as I didn't allow myself to think about . . ."

"Seduction," Alyssa offered, trying to be helpful.

"Quite." Griff bit out the word, then sighed as the image had the predictable effect and his anatomy grew more insistent and rigid. "Well," he exhaled. "There's certainly no confining it now."

"What do we do?"

He leaned back against the wall of the coach. "We still have several options."

"What are they?" she asked.

Griff knew the answer to his present condition. There were only three ways to solve it satisfactorily, and one of them was prohibited by the rules of the game, since he'd promised himself he wouldn't take his bride's virginity in the coach. He could take matters into hand, so to speak, but that was not something a gentleman normally allowed an innocent to witness, or he could persuade his bride to take matters into her talented little hand. *Or into her mouth. Or between her thighs. Or between her breasts.* But he didn't think that was quite the thing a gentleman would suggest to his bride on their wedding night. So . . .

He pretended to ponder the solution. "We can wait," he said. "We can get you dressed, then sit quietly and see if that helps solve my present condition. If that doesn't work, we can get you dressed, then have Myrick drive past the manor for a mile or so before doubling back."

Alyssa frowned. "Wouldn't your driver and the staff wonder why we passed the manor?"

"Probably," Griff said. "But Myrick is too polite to inquire. And there would be a great many more questions if we drove up to the manor and stayed in the coach until I can safely make an appearance."

"There has to be a way." Alyssa bit her bottom lip and then looked up at him and gave him a brilliant smile as she came up with the solution. "What happens if you spill your seed?" she asked, nodding toward his erection. "Will it go down?"

Griffin's tongue was firmly in cheek when he spoke. "It will indeed."

"To a size that can be confined inside your breeches?"

He nodded.

"Then that's the answer," she announced. "Can you take care of it yourself, or will you need me to help?"

Griff closed his eyes and breathed another prayer to the gods, thanking them for sending Alyssa Carrollton into his path. Still, Griff felt compelled to warn her that what she was about to do might be considered advanced lovemaking and not something one would ask of a bride. "I would prefer your assistance, Alyssa," Griff answered honestly. "But, as this act is something I'm not quite sure a gentleman would ask of his bride right away, I'm quite capable of taking the problem in hand myself."

"Is that why you stopped me before?" She asked. "Because you're not certain it's proper for us to do it on our wedding night?"

"*In the coach* on our wedding night," he clarified wryly.

"Oh, well." Alyssa became very logical and practical. "I'm not certain any of this"—She lifted her hand and gestured toward their pile of discarded clothing, indicating her nudity and his—"is proper in a coach where we might be discovered at any time. But I think, perhaps, that's part of the allure of the game."

"I think you may be right, my lady."

"Is the act perverse? Or sinful?" She asked.

"Some will say so," he admitted. "I prefer to think of it as natural. And pleasurable. Either way, I'm entering new territory. I've never asked such a thing of a lady before or performed it myself in front of one. It's something I've only done in private or in the comp—"

Griff could have bitten out his tongue. He seemed to be violating quite a few tenets of gentlemanly behavior this evening. And now he'd gone and done it again. For a gentleman never spoke of Cyprians in the presence of his wife, much less the presence of his bride of less than a day. Unfortunately, Alyssa was very easy to talk to. She invited conversation and confidences with her wit and her intelligence and her questing nature.

"Only in the what?" she wondered.

"Only in the company of Cyprians," he told her.

"Of course," Alyssa replied thoughtfully. "Of course, a Cyprian can participate in intimate acts ladies consider improper. They aren't bound by the same constraints that bind us. They have more freedom."

"Not necessarily," Griff said.

"Cyprians have less freedom than debutantes?"

"No, of course not. Only that the life of a Cyprian isn't always pleasurable."

"It is when she's with you," Alyssa told him.

Griffin's mouth went dry. His heart began to pound, and his male member began an insistent throb. It took him a moment to find his voice, and when he did, all he could manage was, "Alyssa?"

"We are still playing a game of seduction, aren't we?" she asked.

He nodded.

"Then pretend I'm a Cyprian, instead of a lady," Alyssa invited. "Because I intend to watch as you take matters into your hand."

"You *intend* to watch, my lady?" Griff asked, shifting into a more comfortable position on the coach seat. "Or you *want* to watch?"

She looked him in the eye. "I *want* very much to watch. And when we reach the manor, I *want,* very much, for you to teach me all the things a proper Cyprian should know about pleasuring you and about pleasuring herself."

Griff leaned over, pulled her close, and kissed her, hard.

Alyssa closed her eyes and kissed him back. She used her tongue to tempt and tease him as they played the age-old game of seduction—of advance and retreat, of give and take, of mutual surrender. She followed his lead until he relinquished control and followed hers. They played the game over and over again, leading each other on a merry chase, deepening their kisses with every stroke of their tongues as they teased and tormented each other with kisses that were so hungry and hot and wet and deep that Griffin was finally forced to end them.

"Are you certain?" he asked.

"Quite," she answered. "Why should Cyprians have all the fun?"

"Why indeed?" He met her steady gaze, then reached down, took hold of his burgeoning erection, and began the familiar motion. "Watch and learn, my lady Cyprian, for you shall surely be tested later."

Chapter 20

"For weeks, I've been counting the hours until I could join my regiment and fulfill my destiny. Now, I count the hours for an entirely different reason. Now, I am willing to admit, that while I will go to take my commission in His Majesty's Army, my destiny may lie much closer to home...."

—GRIFFIN, VISCOUNT ABERNATHY, JOURNAL ENTRY, 06 MAY 1810

Griff and Alyssa barely managed to don their clothing before the coach pulled up to the front door of Abernathy Manor. But they were entirely presentable, if a little flushed and wrinkled, by the time the coachman opened the door and pulled down the steps of the coach.

It was half past ten in the evening, and it continued to rain. The rain had subsided from a steady downpour to a persistent drizzle, but even so, the staff of Abernathy Manor, each with umbrellas, had lined up to greet the master and his bride.

"Welcome home, my lord." The butler, Keswick, was the first to greet them as they descended from the coach. "May I be the first to offer felicitations on your wedding?"

"But, of course. Thank you, Keswick." Griffin moved back half a step to allow Alyssa to step forward. "Allow me to present my bride, Alyssa, Lady Abernathy. Alyssa, this is Keswick, the butler here at Abernathy Manor."

Keswick bowed.

"A privilege, Keswick." She looked up at the staff, dressed in their best livery and uniforms, lining the way to the entrance. "Thank you all for coming out on such a dreary night. I am deeply honored." Alyssa knew that tradition dictated that the butler, housekeeper, head footman, and groom turn out at each arrival or departure of the lord of the manor and that the entire manor staff turn out in full livery to welcome a new member of the family.

Griffin had explained the tradition while she was buttoning his waistcoat and he was tying the ribbons of her bonnet.

She knew that they were expected to greet each member of the staff and bestow wedding tokens. At Abernathy Manor, the lord of the manor generally bestowed coin, having learned that the staff preferred it to more personal gifts.

It was a miracle they hadn't been set upon by highwaymen, for Griff had traveled from London to Abernathy Manor with a purse full of gentleman's coin. And as he led Alyssa down the long line, introducing her to each member of the staff and allowing each of the servants to bow or curtsy, Griff distributed the coin, pressing a gold sovereign into each one's hand. The coin was given as reward for the service Griff had received while he was a bachelor and for the service he and his new bride would receive in the future.

Now that he had brought home a bride, the staff no longer answered solely to him. Abernathy Manor had a mistress to serve and to obey.

Griff and Alyssa understood there were traditions that must be observed before they could resume the game of seduction they'd begun in the coach. But enduring them was agony.

Every smoldering glance, every tantalizing brush of the fingers, every moment spent standing politely side by side instead of in each other's arms was pure torture.

Alyssa's body ached with anticipation of what was to come next. And it had been aching ever since she'd watched Griffin pleasure himself.

She was amazed at the trust and the confidence he'd exhibited in allowing her to share his intimate act. She couldn't get the memory of it out of her mind. She couldn't forget the expression on his face as he sought satisfaction, couldn't forget the way his strong male body strained for release, the way that same powerful body had trembled uncontrollably as he found it, and the slight flush of embarrassment when he'd opened his eyes and discovered that she hadn't just witnessed his private moment, but relished it.

She had handed him a handkerchief on which to catch the stream of liquid pulsing from the tip of his member. Griffin had made use of the square of linen and then carefully folded it and laid it aside. Alyssa had it now, tucked in the top of her bodice in the valley between her breasts, where the musky scent of him mingled with the scent of her rosewater and lavender fragrance.

Alyssa literally trembled with need. Her breasts were swollen to the point of aching, the peaks hard and puckered, the place between her thighs pooled with moisture, her knees were weak, and she shivered involuntarily as Griffin placed his hand at the small of her back and ushered her forward.

Theirs was a game of seduction run amok, where the current need for clothing inflamed their passions rather than cooled them. Alyssa craved to touch him and to feel him touch her. Her brain burned with hitherto forbidden images, and she desperately wanted to practice what she'd observed. And what's more, Griffin knew it.

"Steady, my lady," he whispered, as they neared the end of the long line of servants. "Almost done."

Alyssa breathed a sigh of relief and shivered once more.

Griff thanked the last footman and maid, pressed the gold sovereigns in their hands, then turned, bent at the knees, and swung Alyssa up into his arms.

"I can walk," she murmured.

"I've no doubt that you can do anything you are in mind to do, my lady." Griffin smiled down at her. "But

I believe it's customary for the groom to carry the bride over the threshold, is it not?"

"I'd forgotten," she admitted.

"I didn't," he replied.

"Then, please, get on with it," she whispered. "I'm on fire for you and the lessons you've yet to teach me."

"I understand completely," he whispered back. "As I have a condition that requires your attention."

"Is Lady Abernathy all right, sir?" Keswick asked.

"Tired," Griffin answered the butler. "Lady Abernathy is tired. It's been a long journey, Keswick, and it's time we retired."

The butler nodded. "The master suite is ready, sir. The beds have been turned down, and there are fires in the grates of both Your Lordship's and Your Ladyship's chambers. Your man and Lady Abernathy's maid are already upstairs."

"Thank you."

The staff cheered as Griff ascended the front steps and entered the house. "Huzzah! Huzzah!"

"Will you be wanting a supper tray, sir?" Griff halted on the master staircase, turning to face Mrs. Jernigan, the cook.

Griff looked down at Alyssa. They hadn't eaten since the wedding breakfast, and the light fare they'd nibbled there had long since disappeared.

She nodded.

Griff agreed. He needed sustenance for the hours ahead of him.

"I made a nice beef and potato stew, and we've fresh bread and cheese and butter and jam. Oh, and I also made your favorite spice cake—as a wedding cake of sorts—to welcome you and your bride home. We've waited to cut it until you arrived."

Griffin's stomach rumbled.

"That sounds wonderful," Alyssa said. "And I would be honored if you would cut the cake on my behalf and share it with the staff."

"Break out the wine and the ale," Griff added. "For the staff. And send a bottle of whisky and a nice sherry for my wife and me up with the supper tray as soon as possible." Griffin turned and continued his climb up the stairs. "We'll ring if we require anything else."

"Yes, sir." Mrs. Jernigan bobbed a curtsy and hurried back to the kitchen.

Griffin continued up the stairs. He didn't set Alyssa on her feet until they reached the privacy of the master's chambers. Griffin paused at the massive double doors, then leaned down. Alyssa opened the door, and he carried her over the final threshold, across the sitting room that connected the master bedchamber with the mistress's bedchamber, to the rug in front of the fireplace where he set her on her feet.

"Alone, at last," Griffin teased, untying the ribbons of her bonnet, the same ribbons he'd hastily tied three-quarters of an hour earlier. Tugging the bonnet off, he tossed it to the floor.

Someone gasped.

"Not quite," Alyssa replied, peeling off her gloves.

Griffin followed her gaze and discovered Alyssa's lady's maid sitting quietly in a wing chair before the fire. Blister it! Would they never have any privacy? How many more gauntlets would they have to run before they could consummate their first game of seduction?

Alyssa took charge. "My lord, you remember Winifred Durham, my maid?"

"Yes indeed, Miss Durham," Griffin acknowledged.

"Winifred, my husband, Lord Abernathy."

"M'lord." Durham bobbed a curtsy to Griffin, hurried to retrieve Alyssa's discarded bonnet, then turned to face her mistress.

"I had them bring hot water for your bath." She set the bonnet on a table and nodded toward the metal buckets lined up in front of the hearth. "And I unpacked your things and left your night rail on the foot of your bed while you were meeting the rest of the staff, miss"— Durham glanced up at Griffin—"I mean, my lady."

"Thank you, Durham, you may retire to your own bed now," Alyssa told her.

Durham looked confused. "But, miss . . . I mean, my

lady, I always assist you in your preparations for bed."

"And I thank you for that," Alyssa answered more firmly. "But I don't require any assistance tonight."

Durham's eyes grew as round as saucers. "But who's going to help you out of your dress and into your night rail? Who's going to unpin and brush your hair for you? Who's—"

"*I* am." Griffin placed his hands on Alyssa's shoulders.

"Go to bed, Durham," Alyssa said.

"But, Lady Alyssa—"

"What my wife is politely trying to tell you, Miss Durham, is that I will provide whatever assistance she requires tonight and every other night and morning I am in residence. I will see to her dressing and undressing and tend to her most personal needs."

Durham opened her mouth, but Griffin forestalled further comments by holding up his hand. "Didn't my valet explain this to you on the journey?"

"Yes, sir," Durham said.

Griffin was momentarily at a loss for words. He had given Eastman his instructions before the wedding and had asked that his valet apprise Lady Abernathy's maid as to the situation. It had never occurred to Griffin that the lady's maid might choose not to listen or do as instructed. "And what did Eastman tell you?"

"He said that as you and Lady Alyssa—I mean—"

"We know what you mean," Griff interrupted.

Durham continued. "Well, your man said that as you and my lady were on your honeymoon, our assistance wouldn't be necessary—except for the packing and unpacking. He said you had instructed him that there were to be no interruptions. He was to bring hot water for shaving and bathing and coffee and a pot of hot chocolate to the door of the master's bedchamber every morning and leave it. He said you would see to the choosing of your own clothes and that I should follow his example and wait until I was called and to never enter the master's suite or my lady's chamber without knocking."

Griffin nodded in confirmation. "Those were my instructions." He leaned down to whisper in Alyssa's ear. "Tell me, my lady, is she slow or simply disobedient?" He wasn't being unkind; he simply wanted to learn the correct way to approach Alyssa's lady's maid in order to get results.

Alyssa frowned. Durham had always been an efficient lady's maid. She had never appeared to be slow or given to disobedience, but she was young and away from home for the first time and, like Lady Tressingham, she had had her heart set on having Alyssa marry the Duke of Sussex. There was more cachet to being a duchess's lady's maid than a viscountess's. "Why didn't you follow his advice?"

Durham's expression was mutinous. "Because I'm a lady's maid," she answered. "I was trained to be lady's maid to a duchess. I don't take my orders from a viscount's valet. I take my orders from Lady Tressingham or you, and no one else."

Griffin and Alyssa exchanged glances.

"I take it—" he began.

Alyssa nodded. "My mother hired and trained her."

"That explains it." Griffin bit the inside of his cheek to keep from smiling as Alyssa continued to look at him, silently asking for advice. He shrugged his shoulders. "She doesn't take orders from me, sweet. She only takes orders from you or your mother."

Alyssa took a deep breath. "Listen, Winifred, and listen closely . . ."

Durham leaned closer.

"My mother isn't here. Your instructions come from me now and from Lord Abernathy. This is *our* home. And if you want to be a part of the staff here, you'll obey the instructions Lord Abernathy and I give.

"So, go to bed. Get out of here. Leave us alone. I appreciate all you've done, and I promise to call you if I need you, but in the meantime, Lord Abernathy and I are going to begin our honeymoon." When Winifred didn't budge, Alyssa looked her in the eye and elaborated. "That means that Lord Abernathy is going to take

off all my clothes and I am going to remove all of his
and then we are going to fall into bed together, make
mad, passionate love to one another, and do every
naughty and pleasurable thing you've ever heard whispered about."

"And a great many things you haven't heard about,"
Griff added. "So, unless Lady Abernathy decides to in-
vite you in to watch or to join us in our fun and games,
I suggest you find some other way to occupy your time."

He hadn't thought it possible for his erection to grow
harder or for the little lady's maid's eyes to grow wider,
but it was.

Durham turned and scurried for the door, slamming it
behind her in her haste to escape with her virtue intact.

"That should keep her away for the next two days,"
Griff said.

"Or keep her away forever." Alyssa grinned mischie-
vously. "I may be needing a new lady's maid."

"Yes, well . . ." His blue eyes smoldered with passion
when he looked at his wife. "I may be needing more
than that. You certainly have a way with words, my
Lady Cyprian." He unfastened the buttons on her short
jacket.

Alyssa quickly shrugged out of it in order to give
Griffin access to the row of tiny buttons at the back of
her dress.

"I *am* well read, my lord." She shoved his coat off
his shoulders at the same moment he unfastened the last
button on her dress.

Griff cocked an eyebrow. "Is that so?" He teased.

She shimmied out of her dress.

"There's much to admire in the written word." Griff's
mouth went dry at the silhouette she made standing in
front of the fire in her transparent chemise, her dress
lying at her feet. "And more to admire here." He bowed
to her. "You also have a way with disrobing, my lady."

"I excel at everything I do." She dropped to her knees
beside the wing chair Durham had vacated, then crooked
her finger and beckoned him forward.

"Do you now?" Griffin stepped closer.

Alyssa patted the seat of the chair.

Griffin sat.

She slipped between his thighs. "It's simple really." Alyssa looked up at him from beneath a veil of thick, dark eyelashes, and Griffin knew he had never seen anyone as beautiful.

"A little scientific observation." She reached up and unbuttoned his breeches.

His erection sprang forward, nearly hitting her in the nose.

"A little practice." She grinned like the cat that ate the cream, then slid her tongue up the length of him.

Griffin nearly jumped out of his boots.

She cupped him, weighing the twin sack at the base of his male member before wrapping her hand around his shaft and beginning the motion in the rhythm she had watched him use. "A little experimentation."

He closed his eyes, relaxed his facial muscles, and licked his lower lip.

Alyssa mimicked his gestures, closing her eyes, leaning forward, and tasting him again with the tip of her tongue as she continued to pump him with her hand.

Griffin moaned.

Alyssa lifted her head. "And suddenly I'm a master at whatever I try."

There was, Griff decided, no doubt about that. She was definitely a master at whatever she attempted. And he thanked his lucky stars that she was doing her damnedest to seduce him.

Moving to the edge of his seat in order to accommodate her, Griff exploded in a rush of hot passion. He bucked and writhed beneath her talented hand and her clever little mouth and tongue until he could stand no more.

"Ride me." He groaned the order, pulling Alyssa from the floor and onto his lap with a speed that surprised them both. In a near frenzy of passion and need, Griffin positioned her on his lap, lifted the hem of her chemise, and penetrated her through the convenience slit of her lacy drawers.

There was a moment of searing pain.

Tears sprang to her eyes. Alyssa blinked them away, but not before Griffin saw them. Not before he felt the membrane tear. Not before he realized what he had done.

Alyssa recognized the look of profound remorse and opened her mouth to speak, to tell him that the pain had already subsided when he covered her mouth with his own.

He kissed her gently, tenderly, and softly, telling her with his tongue and mouth what he could not say with words. Griffin held her close, surrounding himself with her as he waited until she began to move against him. Wanting, needing more.

He resumed the rhythm, slowly at first, then faster. Deeper and harder until he felt the first tremors, then a wave of tremors, grip her. She broke the kiss, crying out her pleasure, holding onto his neck, kissing his hair, pressing his face to her breasts, shedding tears of wonder, of gratitude, and of joyous release as she achieved perfection. For nothing could be more perfect than finding her destiny, discovering where and to whom she belonged.

Seconds after Alyssa achieved her bliss, Griffin joined her. He called out her name and held her tightly as he filled her with the seeds of their future.

When they recovered, Griffin sat holding Alyssa on his lap.

She clung to him, looping her arms around his neck and resting her head on his shoulder. She burrowed into his warmth, pressing against his chest, unable to get close enough, unable to express the emotions she felt until she began showing him by placing soft kisses against his neck and the underside of his jaw.

Griff held her as if she were the most precious thing on earth, rocking her softly, murmuring soothing nonsense phrases and words of apology.

"Alyssa, my sweet, I'm so sorry," he whispered. "I

never meant to lose control. I never meant to take you that way." He squeezed his eyes shut. "Good God, I never meant to cause you pain. Alyssa, I'm sorry . . ."

"Sssh!" Alyssa lifted her head and placed two fingers against his lips. "No remorse," she told him. "No regrets. You did what you had to do. I did the same."

"But I lost control. I took your virginity with no regard for—"

She placed a kiss beneath his earlobe. "It only hurt an instant, and then it was more wonderful that I could ever have imagined."

"But you cried. . . ." he protested, determined to do penance.

"So did you," she said, reaching up to trace the damp tear track on his cheek.

Griffin shook his head. "Christ! What you must think of me . . ."

"I think you are wonderful," Alyssa answered honestly. "I think I'm very fortunate that you chose me." She nipped at his earlobe with her teeth. "I think you've more lessons to teach. I think I'd like us to do this again—only in a bed instead of a chair."

Griffin laughed. "I think I've created a monster. An insatiable Lady Cyprian."

Alyssa took his face between her palms and met his gaze. "I may only have two days. When they are over, I may never see you again. I want you to leave me with beautiful memories of our wedding night. I want you to carry beautiful memories of our wedding night away with you. I don't want you to look back and regret what we did or what we didn't do. For these two days, I am not just your bride but your wife and your Cyprian . . . I am whatever you want me to be. And you shall be my lo—" She almost said her love, but at the last moment she amended her words. "Lover and my hero."

His stomach rumbled, and a knock sounded at the door almost simultaneously.

"One moment."

Griff carefully disengaged himself, rose from the chair, and placed Alyssa on it. "Stay here," he whispered, kissing her tenderly. "I'll be right back."

Ignoring the droplets of blood on him, Griff buttoned his trousers. He scooped up Alyssa's clothing as he made his way across the sitting room to the mistress's bedchamber. He deposited her traveling suit, bonnet, and gloves on the foot of the bed, then rummaged through Alyssa's garments until he found a dressing gown he liked.

Griffin carried it back to her and waited until she'd pulled it on before he opened the door and allowed the footman to hand over the supper tray.

They ate their fill of the supper Mrs. Jernigan had prepared, and then Griffin filled the washbasin with warm water and tenderly bathed his bride and carried her to bed. His bed. Where she slept the sleep of the exhausted.

He lay beside her. Watching over her as she slept, he wondered, suddenly, how the devil he was ever going to manage to leave her? How was he ever going to force himself to ride away?

Sometime later, Griffin awoke to find Alyssa exploring certain parts of his anatomy.

She pulled her hand away as soon as she realized he'd opened his eyes and was watching her. Griffin reached over and put it back, right where he wanted it.

"I woke up," she said. "You were still asleep, but the covers were—well . . ." She paused, searching for the right word. "*Tented*. And I wondered if you were . . ." She blushed. "If you had a condition I might take in hand. . . ."

"Be my guest," he invited. "But beware, my lady, turnabout is fair play."

It was. Griffin proved it twice by waking her in a similar manner after Alyssa fell asleep following their bouts of energetic lovemaking.

They didn't leave the master chamber for three nights and two days, and in that time, nothing was prohibited. They slept. They ate. They bathed each other. They made love. And in between, Alyssa and Griffin talked.

There was no request he wouldn't fulfill. No question he wouldn't answer. But still, Alyssa failed to put him to the test. Failed to ask about the Free Fellows League or the dangerous mission he was about to undertake.

And for the three nights and two days of their honeymoon, Alyssa pretended he loved her.

She pretended he had changed his mind about leaving to join his regiment and decided to stay, pretended he had discovered he loved her. Because anything else was unthinkable.

She had married Griffin Abernathy because she'd wanted her independence and a home of her own. He had willingly granted those things in exchange for the opportunity to make an heir.

Theirs was a business arrangement based on mutual like and respect.

Love had nothing to do with either bargain.

Unfortunately, sometime between his outrageous proposal and her second morning as Lady Abernathy, Alyssa had fallen madly in love with the lord of the manor.

Since she could not bring herself to burden him with the knowledge of her love by saying the words, Alyssa did the only thing she could do. She showed him how much she loved him with her all her heart and soul. And each time she awoke to find him still sleeping, Alyssa prayed that Griffin would understand her silent message and somehow find a way to return to her from war whole and unhurt.

And she promised herself that when he returned, he would have the most wonderful house in England to come home to.

Chapter 21

"There is no turning back from the course of action I have set for myself. I have done my duty to my family and fulfilled my obligation. Now, my regiment awaits....But leaving my bride is the hardest thing I have ever done."

—GRIFFIN, LORD ABERNATHY, JOURNAL ENTRY, 07 MAY 1810

He awoke her well before dawn on Monday morning.

Intent on making love to her one last time before he left, Griff kissed her awake. He fought the battle with his conscience and lost. For he knew she was mentally, physically, and emotionally exhausted. He recognized the purple bruising beneath her eyes and knew Alyssa needed uninterrupted sleep, but Griff was selfish.

He needed her.

Holding her in his arms, cradling her against his heart throughout the night wasn't enough. He needed to be with her. Inside her. He needed to surround himself with the taste and touch and scent of her. Once more before he left.

Alyssa smothered a yawn and opened her eyes.

A fire flickered in the fireplace. Griffin lay propped on his pillow, leaning on one elbow, staring down at her as if he was trying to memorize her face. She could see him clearly, could read his expression. "Is it time?"

Griff shook his head. "We've a couple of hours yet."

"Oh." Alyssa burrowed closer to his warmth. She'd slept alone all of her life, and yet she was amazed to discover that in the span of three nights, she had learned

to crave his hard-muscled warmth and the steady beat
of his heart beneath her ear. Sleeping with him seemed
the most natural thing in the world, and she was loath
to return to sleeping in a solitary bed.

"You'll write me as soon as you know if you're increasing?" he asked.

Alyssa nodded. "Of course." She added, "I'm going
to write you regardless."

"Send your letters by messenger to my father at the
War Office," Griff instructed. "He promised to include
them in the military dispatches. And don't hesitate to
send word to him if you need anything. And he and
Mother wanted me to tell you that if you tire of being
alone here at the manor, you are more than welcome to
stay with them in London. Promise me, you'll take them
up on the offer or that you'll invite your mother or your
sisters or a friend—like Lady Miranda—to keep you
company. Invite someone. Anyone. Just don't keep too
much to yourself. Or work too hard." He smiled at her.
"And, remember, the Marquess of Shepherdston's
county seat is only three and a half hours by coach,
faster by horseback if you need to get word or have
problems. . . ." He was speaking quickly as if he were
in a terrible rush to get everything out and to make certain she understood all of his instructions. "And Shepherdston and Grantham promised to drop by whenever
they're in the vicinity. . . ." Griffin had actually made
them swear that one of them would drop by at least
every month, but Alyssa didn't need to know that. "I've
arranged for a monthly sum to be placed in an account
from which you can draw funds. And I always keep a
ready reserve in the safe." Somehow he didn't worry
about Alyssa overspending the monthly allotment. He
had known from the moment she confessed her reasons
for not wanting to marry the Duke of Sussex that she
would be the perfect steward for Abernathy Manor.
"Should you need anything and not be able to reach my
father. Shepherdston and Grantham will take care of it
. . . You can reach them through the War Office or
through Shepherdston's majordomo at Shepherdston

Hall. Pomfrey always knows how to reach Lord Shepherdston. Don't hesitate to let them know. They're my oldest and dearest friends. The three of us are like brothers. You can count on them to do whatever you need. . . ." He paused for a moment. "About the manor . . ."

"Sssh, Griffin, I know." She moved closer and kissed him.

But he couldn't be distracted until he was certain all the details had been settled. "About the manor . . . There's a copy of my will in the safe behind the Vermeer in the sitting room." Griffin gestured toward the door that connected the bedchamber to the sitting room. "I wrote the combination down for you. It's behind the miniature in your diamond locket."

"I don't have a diamond locket," she said.

Griffin pulled a heart-shaped diamond locket from beneath his pillow, handed it to her, and grinned. "You do now."

"Oh, Griffin . . ." she breathed. It looked just like the gifts he had given her attendants, only larger.

"I had it made when I ordered the bridesmaids' pendants. But yours is a locket." He shrugged his shoulders in the boyish gesture that had become so familiar and beloved. "I intended to present it to you before now, but we've been rather busy. . . ."

She opened the locket to find a miniature of him. A perfect, true-to-life image of Griffin dressed in the uniform of His Majesty's Eleventh Blues. Alyssa touched the portrait with her finger, then carefully closed the locket and fastened it around her neck. "Thank you, Griffin. I love it. It's—"

"So you won't forget what I look like," he said. "In the event that—"

"Sssh." Alyssa stopped his words and the thought with a brush of her lips on his. "As if I could . . ." She whispered when she could speak once again. "I know every inch of you, Griffin Abernathy. Every freckle. Every scar. Every strand of hair. You are emblazoned in my memory."

Griffin swallowed hard, then cleared his throat. "At any rate, you'll have a more recent portrait to show our child than the one hanging in the petite salon."

"I've yet to see the petite salon," Alyssa reminded him. "Or your portrait."

"I was eight. I sat for it shortly before I went off to school at Knightsguild." He snapped his fingers. "That reminds me; if I should happen not—"

"Griffin, please," her voice quavered. She wanted to beg him not to leave her. But Alyssa stopped herself. She loved him enough not to add to his mental burden.

He took a deep breath. "If you've conceived our son, you need to know that I don't want him sent to Knightsguild so long as Norworthy is headmaster there. Send him to Eton or anywhere else you choose, but not Knightsguild. If it hadn't been for Jarrod and Colin, I'd have been miserable there."

"All right."

"Promise me," he insisted.

"I promise," she said. "I don't believe little boys should be sent away at all. I believe they should stay home until they're old enough for university."

"Fair enough," he said. "Now, remember, the combination is written on a slip of paper behind my miniature. My father knows the combination as well, but you'll need it should you require a large amount of ready cash or access to the Abernathy jewels. Or the wedding set I gave you. Eastman left everything in my bedchamber the night we arrived, and I put it all in the safe."

"I didn't realize . . ." Alyssa remembered now that she had taken her pearl necklace and bracelet off when she changed into her traveling dress after the wedding. She had given the box containing the jewelry to Griffin, who had turned it over to his valet for safekeeping.

Griff kissed her on the nose. "There's no reason you should. You were sound asleep."

"Nevertheless," Alyssa teased. "My mother taught me better than to be careless about the whereabouts of my jewelry."

Griffin frowned. "I expect she did. By the way, the

bird's egg is in the safe, should you need to show it off to your mother."

"And have her hound me about wearing it everywhere I go for the rest of my life so she can boast about it to the ton? Not bloody likely!"

He laughed. "I'm going to miss you, Alyssa."

"I'm going to miss you, too."

Griffin blinked. "I never thought I would say that," he admitted. "I never believed it possible."

"Me, either."

"Aren't we a fine pair?" He smiled crookedly.

"Yes," she answered softly, rolling over to push him to his back so that she could straddle him. "I believe we are."

Griffin buried his fingers in her hair and pulled her face down to his. "And to think your father gave you to me for the loan of a horse. . . ."

Alyssa wiggled her bottom against his erection. "Not just any horse," she reminded him, "but a prized breeding stallion."

"Your father did seem to be quite happy with the arrangement. . . ." He looked up at her. "Seemed pretty happy to be rid of his youngest *gel.*" Griffin managed a perfect imitation of Lord Tressingham's voice.

"No more happy than I," she said. "Of course, I'm a bit surprised he knew who I was. As my sisters and I are neither horses nor hounds, he tends to get us confused."

"Not at all," Griff corrected, "Your father knew exactly who you were." He waggled his eyebrows at her and imitated her father once again. *"Alyssa, don't you know? Filly. Light brown mane, streaked with blond. Nice big eyes. Blue, if I'm not mistaken. Good ground manners. Hasn't been broken to ride. But that's only natural as she lacks an adequate handler."*

"Imagine that," she pretended to marvel, taking him in hand to guide him where they both wanted him to be. "Papa found an adequate handler who could break me to ride in only three nights."

Griffin groaned. "And he still imagines he got the best part of the deal."

"Well," Alyssa drawled as she moved up and down on him. "You did throw in a breeding for Carrollton's Fancy Mistress to your father's famous King George's Prince of a Fellow. For Papa, that is a better deal. All you got was a breeding to me."

He rolled out of bed and began to dress at dawn.

Alyssa wanted to dress and go downstairs to see him off, but Griff would have none of it.

"No," he whispered, staring at her, committing everything to memory. "Stay there. Just as you are. I want to remember you like that. Lying in bed with your hair spread out across the pillows, with your skin still flushed with lovemaking, your lips swollen from my kisses, your eyes dark with passion as if you're waiting for me. . . ."

"I *will* be waiting for you," she promised, watching as he pulled on his boots. *Always.*

Griff turned away, unable to bear the look in her eyes. "There is something I need to tell you. . . ."

Alyssa strained to hear his words, strained to keep from sitting up, and from running to him. *Tell me you love me. Please.*

He cleared his throat. "Abernathy Manor is yours," he said.

"*What?*" His words came as a shock. They weren't at all what she expected. Abernathy Manor was his ancestral home. He couldn't give it away, even to his wife.

"Short of selling it to anyone but my father, it's yours to do with as you please." He turned around to face her. "You deserve a home of your own."

"But Griffin, what about your parents . . ."

"I discussed it with my father before I left London, and he agreed." Griff met her worried gaze. "And I intend to stop in and say good-bye to them before I sail for the Peninsula. But don't worry. I'm an only child and heir, Alyssa. My father is a very wealthy man, and

I am wealthy in my own right. One day, everything my father has will come to me. Or to my heir. If the manor was our family's only holding, I couldn't deed it to you. But Abernathy Manor is just one of several family homes, and I'm giving it to you."

"But it's your *ancestral* home."

"Now, it's *your* ancestral home," he said softly. "It's done, my lady. My solicitor in London has a copy of the documents giving you full authority over the manor and everything on it."

"I'm overwhelmed," she whispered.

"Don't be." Griffin smiled tenderly. "My solicitor is the same one I used for our marriage contract. He and my man of affairs will assist you with any business decisions you need to make."

"I don't know your man of affairs," she said. "I've never heard you speak of him."

Griffin blushed. "Actually, it's Colin."

"Colin?" She drew a blank.

"Lord Grantham. He doesn't have any real money yet, as his father managed to gamble everything but the title away, but he's accumulating a tidy sum investing for me and for Shepherdston. He takes a commission from everything he makes for us. And he's proving to be a genius at making money." Griffin looked up at her. "He doesn't advertise, and we haven't any formal agreement. It's just something we do for one another. And I'd be grateful if you didn't let on to anyone else that he acts as my man of affairs. Having everyone in society know that he's short of blunt is hard enough. He doesn't need to have to defend his venturing into trade."

"I won't say anything."

"Thank you." He reached for his coat. "I knew I could rely on you."

Alyssa stopped him. "Griffin, I have something for you, too." She squeezed her eyes shut to keep from crying. "A gift. But you asked me to stay here, and now I can't get up to get it."

"Where is it?" he said, gently. "I'll get it."

"In my traveling case. In my bedchamber. It's the small black box."

Griffin left the room. He returned moments later with the box. Crossing over to the bed, he handed it to her.

"Close your eyes," she ordered. "And bend so that I can reach your neck."

He followed her instructions to the letter, bending far enough so that she could loop her arms over his neck.

"Now, raise up and open your eyes."

Griffin did and discovered that he was wearing a small gold medallion depicting Saint George slaying the dragon.

Alyssa's eyes sparkled with pleasure at the sight of her gift shining beside the buttons of his uniform. "I bought it for you the morning after we met at Almack's because I wanted you to have something to protect you in your noble quest. Even if Papa refused your suit." She drew her brows together, concentrating on his earlier words. "I intended to present it to you before now, but we've been a little busy."

"I'll wear it with pride and honor," he told her. *And love.* The words popped into Griffin's mind, but he pushed them aside. Love hadn't been part of the bargain. She had married him not because she wanted a husband but because she wanted to escape her parents' dominion. Because she wanted a home of her own.

Love had never been part of the deal. Besides, he reminded himself, he was a lifelong Free Fellow and sworn never to love his wife. He could like her, admire her, and respect her. But he could never love her.

There was a discreet tap at the door.

"It's time, sir." Eastman called softly.

"I'll be right there," Griff answered.

"Please Griffin, let me see you off."

"You *are* seeing me off," he answered. "And I am seeing you the way I want always to remember you." He leaned down and placed a kiss on her forehead, on her eyes, on her nose, and finally on the corner of her mouth. A kiss that was the merest brush of his lips against hers. A kiss so poignant she thought her heart might break. "Good-bye, my lady." *My love.* "God keep you."

"And you," she whispered.

Chapter 22

"Hard work is nature's antidote to grief. There is no remedy for a broken heart. Hard work alone makes the condition bearable. There would be no reason to get out of bed otherwise."

—ALYSSA, LADY ABERNATHY, DIARY ENTRY, 10 JUNE 1810.

She was inconsolable for two days after Griffin left to join his regiment, but she finally emerged from their room on the third day with firm resolve, a clear vision, and a handful of letters addressed to Griffin, Major Lord Abernathy, His Majesty's Eleventh Blues, that she gave to Keswick to post.

Keswick rewarded her with three letters from Griffin that had arrived by special messenger that morning. The butler directed Alyssa to the conservatory, where the morning sun provided perfect reading light and where he knew she would be undisturbed while she read Lord Abernathy's letters.

After reading and rereading each of Griff's letters, Alyssa sought the library, where she immediately began drawing up and implementing her plans for the changes and improvements she hoped to make.

She adapted surprisingly well, absorbing the routine of the manor as she renewed her acquaintances with the staff by touring the house and taking notes.

Alyssa recorded the household routine: the number of staff members, the work schedule, cleaning schedules, the inventories, and special projects. Then she began interviewing Keswick and Mrs. Lightsey, the housekeeper, and Cook.

With Keswick's and Mrs. Lightsey's approval, Alyssa spoke with the household staff, seeking suggestions and gathering ideas for improvements, and then she turned her attention to the out-of-doors staff.

Griffin had spoken the truth that night at Almack's when he'd told her he had an estate with a badly neglected garden. Once a masterpiece of Tudor design, the garden wasn't the only part of the estate that had been neglected.

The manor appeared to be a substantial and financially sound holding—and Alyssa supposed it was—but the strong foundation on which it was based—that of a self-sustaining agrarian society—was crumbling. Unemployment in the village was high, due in part to the manor's reduced circumstances, and the villagers were flocking to London and Liverpool and Birmingham in substantial numbers.

Alyssa learned that while there was a dairy on the property, there weren't enough freshened cows to keep it running at full capacity. And although the manor showed great potential for the production of flax and hops and wool, no one had thought to utilize it. As a result, Cook often purchased milk and dairy products from the dairyman in the nearby village of Haversham. Men and women, who might once have found employment farming or managing the livestock at the manor or who might once have worked the empty looms, spinning wool into fabric, were now seeking employment elsewhere.

There were skilled craftsmen in the village and at the manor with few opportunities to practice their crafts. Because the master was so seldom at Abernathy Manor, the staff was kept to a minimum, and the cultivation of crops and livestock had steadily decreased.

No one criticized Griffin for the lack. His employees and tenants were, in fact, quick to defend him. The manor hadn't suffered from poor management. It ran as efficiently as possible under the circumstances, but there had been no real attention paid to it since the previous master had inherited the title of Earl of Weymouth.

The earldom of Weymouth came with its own county seat, and the earl had been forced to divide his attention between the management of Weymouth Park and the running of Abernathy Manor.

Lord Griffin had been at Knightsguild. At the time, he'd been too young to assume control of the manor, and from Knightsguild, Lord Griffin had gone to university and from university, he had gone to London and his work in the War Office.

Like the enchanted castles in the fairy tales of old, Abernathy Manor had been waiting for someone to come along and notice its decline. It had been waiting for someone to restore it to its former glory. It had, it seemed, been waiting for someone like Alyssa.

And Alyssa was more than equal to the task. Accustomed as she was to resistance to change and tradition at Tressingham Court, Alyssa had been prepared to find the same resistance at Abernathy Manor. But what she found was unwavering loyalty and unquestioning support.

She discussed her plans with Keswick and Mrs. Lightsey, and Cook, with the head gardener, groom, and yeoman as she formulated them. She listened to their suggestions, learned from their experiences, and sought their approval before barging ahead with her new ideas for improvement and expansion. And there was no question that she got it.

And Alyssa was glad for it. For she needed the challenge of restoring Abernathy Manor. The planning of the improvements and her determination to push herself to oversee the beginnings of them had served a vital purpose. It kept Alyssa occupied. She planned, she implemented, and she recorded all of her plans in her diary and in the long, descriptive letters she wrote to Griff, telling him all the goings-on at the manor. She pushed herself hard, filling her days from dawn to darkness with tasks to be accomplished. Until she was tired. Too tired to miss Griffin—except late at night when she lay in the big bed in the master bedchamber, to tired too wonder and worry.

She had been so busy attending to the needs of the manor and its staff in the month since Griffin had left to join his regiment that she neglected to pay attention to herself—until the morning her body reminded her.

Alyssa recognized the signs and knew in her heart what they meant, but she waited two full days before putting pen to paper. Waited to be certain. But now, there was no doubt. She couldn't wait any longer. She had to tell him. He had the right to know.

10 June 1810
Abernathy Manor
Northamptonshire, England

Dear Griffin,
*   As there is no easy way to tell you this, I write with the news that my monthly courses arrived two days past. I waited two days to write to you because I had hoped that the signs were false and that I might have better news.*
*   But there is no doubt.*
*   I, who boasted of becoming a master at everything I attempt, have been unsuccessful in that most basic of wifely responsibilities. I can only say that I am sorry to disappoint you and to have failed in keeping my end of the bargain.*
*   I send my best to you and to Eastman and pray that God and Saint George will keep you safe.*

*   As ever,*
*   Alyssa*

Alyssa blotted and sanded the letter before folding it. She dropped a puddle of crimson-colored wax onto the fold and pressed the Abernathy family seal—the seal, Keswick had assured her, that belonged to all the lords and ladies Abernathy—into the wax, sealing her very private missive.

She finished sealing her letter and then rang for the butler, who carried it from her sitting room to the messenger waiting to hand-deliver it to Lord Weymouth at the War

Office in London. She watched at the window as the messenger rode through the huge wrought-iron gates of Abernathy Manor, keeping him in her sights until he disappeared from view.

When she could no longer see the messenger in the distance, Alyssa turned from the window and fled to the master bedchamber. Quietly closing the door behind her, Alyssa flung herself, fully clothed, onto the huge bed, drew the covers up around her, buried her face in Griffin's pillow, and cried.

She had failed. There was nothing of him left inside her. Nothing except the memories she carried. All she had was his name and the manor, and all she wanted was Griffin and a family. Restoring the manor would be all for naught if Griffin didn't return to share it with her.

Alyssa didn't come downstairs to supper or answer the knocks on her door for nearly a week. Sleep, along with pots of hot tea and brandy, eased the physical discomfort, and spoonfuls of broth from the supper tray Cook sent up each night and the pot of morning hot chocolate she sent up each morning kept Alyssa nourished, but nothing could ease the ache in her heart.

She needed time, Alyssa decided. Time alone to come to terms with her disappointment. Time to rest. Time to reflect and grieve for her loss. And when she was done with sorrow, she would write to Miranda and ask her to visit.

The rest of the staff quizzed Durham with questions about her ladyship's health and her state of mind, but Durham was of little help. Alyssa's lady's maid couldn't tell if her mistress had nibbled on any of the food on the tray Cook sent up or if she was truly ill.

The only thing Durham knew for sure was that Lady Abernathy hadn't left her room except to make use of the earth closet down the hall in days and that the reason for her sudden change of behavior was that her ladyship's monthly courses had begun.

Realizing Lady Abernathy's maid hadn't yet grasped the significance of her ladyship's withdrawal and her apparent sorrow, and that the maid would not be able to offer helpful suggestions for handling the problem, Keswick sent a messenger to Shepherdston Hall, seeking advice.

"The staff is concerned about her," Jarrod announced to Colin after reading the note Keswick sent from Abernathy Manor.

The two lords were still in London, but Pomfrey relayed the note by messenger to Jarrod's town house with the news. Since Jarrod and Colin weren't in residence when the messenger arrived, having gone to their club for dinner, Jarrod's butler had sent the note around to White's.

"You know Keswick, and you know he isn't given to alarm, but Alyssa withdrew to her room and hasn't emerged from it for any length of time in several days," Jarrod explained.

"She's probably just upset," Colin said. "After all, she's a new bride without her groom."

Jarrod ran his fingers through his hair. "That's possible, but somehow, I don't think so. Everything I've heard about our new Lady Abernathy suggests that she isn't given to fits of crying or bouts of withdrawal. She knew Griff meant to join his regiment, so there must be another reason for her behavior. Something that's happened since he left. But what?" He paused for a moment, then began stating his case. "Let's look at this logically. Griff married her. She's Viscountess Abernathy, no matter what. And Griff deeded the manor to her and gave her a generous allowance with which to manage it." Jarrod shook his head. "And she should know by now that Griff isn't the sort of fellow to renege on a deal regardless of . . ." He snapped his fingers. "That's it. Keswick wouldn't write of anything so personal, but that must be the answer."

"What answer?" Colin demanded.

Jarrod shot Colin a disgusted look. "She's failed to conceive."

"Impossible," Colin proclaimed. "Griff . . ."

"Griff is an only child," Jarrod reminded him. "And it's no secret that the Abernathys have never been prolific. The reason Lord Weymouth forced this marriage is because the Abernathys have been so unprolific. According to Griff, his father told him that he and Lady Weymouth have been trying to provide Griff with a sibling from the time he was born until now."

Colin shuddered. He had nothing against Lord Weymouth attempting to give his only son a sibling or to give himself the heir and a spare, but Colin didn't especially care to know that the quest continued. Weymouth was fifty if he was a day, and although still an extremely attractive woman, Griff's mother had to be pushing forty-five.

"I mean, all you can do is work at it. . . ." Jarrod shrugged. "And from what I've gleaned from Keswick, Griff did his damnedest working at it . . ." He tapped his fingers on the table. "So she must have failed to conceive the heir. Why else would she be so upset?"

"Unless she's changed her mind about refusing *him*," Colin speculated, nodding toward the Duke of Sussex, who had just entered the club.

"She didn't refuse him," Jarrod corrected. "His Grace offered too late. After Tressingham had accepted Griff's offer. Alyssa had little say in the matter."

"That's not what I heard," Colin murmured.

"Oh?"

"We should have attended the wedding breakfast," Colin said ruefully. "Because the talk among the ton who were in attendance was that she turned His Grace down flat there. She didn't give him the cut direct," Colin continued, warming to his subject. "Not Griff's bride. No, she *told* His Grace she chose Griff over him. And threatened to shoot the duke if he didn't stop trying to ruin her wedding day." Colin gave a low whistle of admiration. "Just when you think they're all cold-hearted mercenaries, they go and surprise you by telling a duke that they'd rather be a viscountess than a duchess."

"I can't believe *His Grace* had the ill manners to attend," Jarrod said.

Colin chuckled. "Why's that so hard to believe?"

"He's had the benefit of the best schooling. He was taught better manners," Jarrod answered, secure in the knowledge that one could always count on a gentleman to behave honorably.

"He's a duke," Colin retorted. "Have you ever know a duke who didn't bend the rules of etiquette whenever it suited his purpose? Especially a bloody arrogant *English* duke?"

Jarrod shook his head before resuming their discussion. "Suppose for the sake of argument that she's changed her mind. Suppose that after failing to conceive his heir, Griff's viscountess is mourning the fact that she chose to become a viscountess instead of a duchess." Jarrod frowned. "I admit that it doesn't seem likely, nor do I necessarily believe it, but it's possible and could also explain her behavior. Because she had everything else she could want and nothing to lose . . ."

"Except Griff and the child she might have borne him." Colin looked at Jarrod. "What if all she really wants is Griff?"

"She *has* Griff." Jarrod helped himself to the whisky decanter, pouring a glass for himself and for Colin.

"What she has is a title and a house," Colin told him. "That's all."

"So?" Jarrod demanded. "It's what she claimed to want."

"So she changed her mind," Colin suggested. "Not about the duke, but about Griff. What if what she wants is Griff? Or some part of him. Jarrod, think about it. Griff is in Spain, and we all know, whether we want to admit it or not, that he'll be damned lucky to make it back in one piece." He met Jarrod's gaze. "Lord knows, I know very little about *ladies*, but I do know women and I think Griff's bride may have fallen in love with him."

"Fat lot of good it's going to do her with him a sworn Free Fellow," Jarrod muttered.

"She doesn't know he's a Free Fellow," Colin reminded him. "She doesn't know the Free Fellows exist, why we exist, the work we've undertaken for the good of our country, or the charter we've sworn to uphold."

"Blasted female! What a tangle! Damn, but I hope she doesn't make herself ill!" Jarrod threw back the glass of whisky and stared at Colin. "We gave our solemn oath that we would take care of her in Griff's absence. He'll have our hides if word of this reaches his ears."

"It isn't going to reach Griffin's ears," Colin said.

"And how do you plan to keep it from him?" Jarrod asked. "Keswick's note said that immediately before she retired to her chambers, Alyssa sent a letter addressed to Griffin by messenger to Lord Weymouth's office."

Colin pursed his lips in thought. "If we're right about her failure to conceive, we can't keep her from telling Griff about it. He has a right to know and she is the person who should tell him. But he doesn't have to know she's taking the news so badly. He isn't going to have to worry about her not eating or sleeping or taking care of herself." Colin nodded, pleased with the course of his thoughts. "He's at war. He has to worry about keeping himself alive. He can't worry about his viscountess, too. Besides, what can he do? He's in Spain."

"The question isn't what Griff can do," Jarrod answered thoughtfully. "The question is what are we going to do in his place?" He faced Colin. "Well?"

"We're going to come up with a way to snap Lady Abernathy out of her fit of depression."

"Fine. How?" Jarrod prodded.

"Damned if I know," Colin admitted.

Jarrod laughed. "A fine pair of guardian angels we turn out to be."

"At least we have a plan," Colin said.

"Are you certain?" Jarrod asked. "Because I disagree. I believe that all we have is an inkling of what we should do and no idea how to go about it."

"We don't have the details." Colin dismissed Jarrod's argument. "But we have a plan." He thought for a moment. "Part of the problem is that she's alone at Abernathy Manor."

"All alone with a full-time staff of sixty," Jarrod snorted.

"You're a fine one to talk," Colin reproved. "Until you started working for Grant, you'd never been alone a day in your life."

"That's true," Jarrod admitted. "I had, however, been alone in a room—*once*."

Colin laughed at Jarrod's joke.

It was no secret that the Marquess of Shepherdston had been born with a longer silver spoon in his mouth than most of his peers.

What was remarkable was that he had finally learned to joke about it.

Jarrod had grown up surrounded by wealth and luxury and a half a dozen households full of doting servants. And as the heir to a vast fortune, he had never wanted for anything—except parental affection.

Colin and Griff had learned to overlook Jarrod's arrogance and many of his increasingly cynical views of marriage over the years, because Jarrod had been brought into the world by parents who cared no more for him that they did yesterday's scraps.

Theirs had been a marriage of state, an alliance of two important families and Lord and Lady Shepherdston had despised the sight of one another—from the day they met until the day Lord Shepherdston died—and beyond.

Unfortunately for Jarrod, his loss of parental regard had been more than compensated by false regard, provided by a succession of sycophants and playmates his parents hired to keep him entertained and out of mischief. Colin and Griff had been Jarrod's first real friends. The first acquaintances he'd ever met who didn't give a rip about his name, his title, or his fortune.

Jarrod's lofty birthright hadn't mattered a whit to Griff because Griff was secure in his own birthright. He was secure in his parents' love and in the position to which he was heir.

And Colin had simply disregarded Jarrod's status and regarded the boy, first as an unworthy adversary and then as a friend because, although Colin had no real money, he had charm and intelligence and prospects. Colin was Scottish. His ancestors had spent centuries learning to survive and thrive in the *Sassenach* world, and he was the beneficiary of that training.

Colin had no qualms about trading a title that had existed before the time of Macbeth for a fabulously wealthy heiress, preferably one that would be suitably impressed by his title, if not his person. He considered it a fair trade. He was, after all, a Scot and superior to the English in every way that mattered.

"And what did you learn from that one time experience?" Colin asked, setting himself as Jarrod's gull.

"That people need other people around them—for entertainment, if for no other reason." Spoken like a true cynic, but Colin and Jarrod both understood that Jarrod didn't quite believe it. "I suspect company would be good for Lady Abernathy right about now. She needs cheering up."

"Who do you suggest we send?" Colin asked.

Jarrod snorted. "I was going to suggest you go," he answered honestly.

Colin shook his head. "Can't. I'm going fishing in Scotland. I leave tonight. You'll have to go."

"Can't." Jarrod answered as succinctly as Colin. "I have to remain in London and see to some unfinished business at the 'change."

Anyone who happened to overhear their conversation would think they were old friends discussing upcoming schedules. Lord Grantham was leaving for a fishing holiday in Scotland, and business kept Lord Shepherdston near the financial district and the stock exchange. But their conversation had a different meaning for Jarrod and Colin. They knew that the day's code word was *fishing*.

Translated, their conversation meant that Colin was leaving for France on the evening tide, and that Jarrod would remain in London to process information they'd already received from their broad network of spies and smugglers.

"Well?" Colin asked. "Who do you suggest? Her mother?"

It was Jarrod's turn to shudder. "I suspect that if Lady Abernathy wanted her mother, she'd have sent for her."

"How do you know she hasn't?"

"Apparently, someone is reading her mail." Jarrod grinned. "Alyssa hasn't contacted her mother since the wedding. And besides, Lady Tressingham is attending Lady Buckingham's masque tonight. She's going as Juliet."

Jarrod's ability to ferret out information never ceased to

amaze Colin. But, then, Jarrod was invited everywhere and knew everyone. "How?"

Jarrod gave Colin a look that said, *Don't ask*.

"Never mind."

Jarrod gave Colin an innocent look. The snippets of information one could pick up at Gentleman Jackson's Boxing Saloon constantly amazed him—and his superior at the War Office. "There were seven at last count," he added just to tantalize Colin.

"Seven what?"

"Juliets."

"Good lord!"

"The Duchess of Devonshire is one of them."

"Are you going?" Colin asked.

Jarrod shrugged. "Depends on how much work I have to do."

"I'm glad I'm going to Scotland," Colin said. "Less excitement." He was silent for a moment. "What about one of her sisters?"

Jarrod shook his head. "One has an infant and the other two are increasing."

"Too much like rubbing her nose in it," Colin agreed.

"We need someone who will rouse her from her megrims. Someone whose presence would demand she get out of bed and attend them."

"What we need is Griff," Colin remarked dryly.

Jarrod's eyes lit up. "Or the next best thing . . . at least according to Lord Tressingham." He glanced across the room.

"Oh, Christ!"

"He fits the bill," Jarrod said.

Colin nodded. "Agreed. But this could blow up in our faces. Especially if she is reconsidering her decision to become a viscountess instead of a duchess. She might learn to like his company too well."

"She chose Griff once," Jarrod said, his voice full of conviction. "I am willing to bet that she will again."

Colin nodded. "Now, how do we manage to make our little proposition attractive to *himself*?" he asked in the well-modulated Scottish burr that sent shivers of anticipation up the spines of his favorites at Madam Theodora's.

"That's easy." Jarrod poured another dram of whisky for himself and for Colin. "We negotiate. He's been nosing around us for weeks. He's not working for Grant or for anyone else we know, so my guess is that he wants something we have. We discover what it is and offer it to him in return for this favor."

"How do we accomplish that?"

Jarrod smiled. "We ask him."

"Bloody hell!" Colin took a deep breath, then exhaled it. "All right," he said finally. "Invite His Grace over."

A similar conversation was taking place at the Weymouth town house on Park Lane as Lord Weymouth broke the unhappy news to his wife.

"Have you seen her, Trevor? Have you spoken to her?" Lady Weymouth asked.

"No, my dear, I'm afraid I have not," Lord Weymouth answered.

"Then how did you discover that she isn't—"

"Breeding?" Lord Weymouth said the word they had both been avoiding.

"Yes."

"I read the letter she posted to Griffin," he replied matter-of-factly.

"You what?" Lady Weymouth was shocked. "You read her private correspondence?"

"Of course I did, my darling Cicely," he cajoled. "I read everything that goes into the military dispatches. It's one of the responsibilities of my position. We are at *war*, my dear."

"Don't patronize me," Cicely snapped. "I realize we're at war. My son is on the Peninsula fighting it. But you know as well as I that Alyssa's letters hardly fall into the realm of military secrets."

"That doesn't mean they can't bring harm to our son," he told her.

"I don't understand."

"I may have forced him into marriage, but Griffin chose the young lady." Weymouth faced his wife. "You saw the way he looked at her, Cicely. Whether the boy knows it or not, he's beginning to care for her. Perhaps, even love her . . ." He paused for a moment, searching for the right words. "What if she doesn't return his feelings? What if she decides, now that she's had a taste of it, that she doesn't like being married or having the responsibility of the manor? Or worse yet, what if she decides, now that she's no longer a virgin, that she doesn't like sleeping alone?"

"Trevor!"

"Well?" he demanded.

Lady Weymouth stared at her husband as if he'd just announced he was preparing for his coronation as king. "Trevor Abernathy, did you not pay any attention to what was going on around you?"

"Of course I did," he replied. "I saw the way Griffin treated the girl, the way he looked at her, touched her."

"Well, you should have paid more attention to the way *Alyssa* was looking at Griffin." She sighed. "She refused a duke, for heaven's sake! For our son."

"That fool father of hers refused the duke."

"And Alyssa refused him as well—at the wedding breakfast." She reached across the arm of her chair and took hold of her husband's big hand. "Trust me, that girl loves our son."

"I should hope so," he grumbled.

"Have you heard anything different? Anything that might lead you to believe she doesn't?"

Weymouth shook his head. "I did get the news that she's locked herself in her room and is refusing to eat. Keswick sent a message to Shepherdston, and Shepherdston sent a message to me. Said she'd locked herself in her room after writing that letter to Griffin and that she hadn't come out yet."

"Good gracious! Have they checked on her? Is she all right?"

He nodded. "She appears to be fine, except that she weeps quite a bit. The staff were quite alarmed by it, especially since she's been so happy rearranging the manor."

Lady Weymouth wanted to smack her husband for being so obtuse at times. "She's grieving."

"What?"

"She's grieving. For Griffin and for the loss of a child."

"She wasn't with child."

"She might have been! And that's what matters. Goodness, Trevor, have you forgotten how heartbreaking it was for me each time we lost a child? Each time my monthly courses came to dash our hopes? After we'd believed it was possible? Don't you realize that after all these years, I *still* cry each time I'm proven barren and old?"

"No, my dear." Weymouth dropped to his knees and took his wife in his strong embrace. "I haven't forgotten. I apologize for upsetting you so." He kissed her cheek and then her lips.

"You should apologize to Alyssa," she scolded him. "That girl is grieving for the loss of her hopes and dreams. She is grieving because she knows that she may have lost the only chance she had to give our son a child. She loves him, Trevor. Didn't you see how she wore her heart upon her sleeve?"

"I thought so," Lord Weymouth said. "But I had to be certain. She is, after all, the daughter of a man who traded her to Griff for the loan of a stallion and the possibility of a litter of puppies. I forced the boy into marrying. I had to make certain his bride was all she seemed to be." He met his wife's unerring gaze. "How was I to know she wouldn't be as shallow?"

"How indeed?" Cicely's blue eyes blazed fire. "Because Griffin chose her, and there isn't a shallow bone in his body. Besides," she added, "by forcing the situation, you, in effect, traded our son to the Tressinghams for the possibility of a grandchild."

"Yes, well, the Tressinghams didn't want Griffin. *He* wanted a litter of foxhound pups and his wife wanted the Duke of Sussex." He managed a smile. "You know, my dear, I was quite pleased with Griffin's choice—despite her father being a complete bore and her mother being a social climber. And I was vastly encouraged when I learned that her second sister has an infant son and that her eldest and the third are increasing." He squeezed his wife's hand. "Who would have thought that our little Alyssa wouldn't follow suit?"

Lady Weymouth smiled a mysterious sort of mother's smile. "Perhaps we should have. After all, she is unique among her family members."

"I am greatly disturbed by what I read in her letter," Lord Weymouth said. "She blames herself. She thinks she's at fault."

"She would." Lady Weymouth clucked her tongue in sympathy. "I did the same."

Cicely's words shocked her husband.

"*You?*"

She nodded.

"But why, my love? Everyone knows the Abernathys are notoriously unreliable breeders."

Cicely shook her head. "What everyone else thinks doesn't matter. I believed *I* was at fault. Alyssa believes *she* is at fault."

"Why?" he asked.

"Because in our eyes, the men we love *have* no faults."

That simple statement brought Lord Weymouth to his knees once more. "How shall we go about helping the girl?" he asked.

"She'll be all right," Lady Weymouth said. "In time. But she mustn't dwell on it. She must find some sort of diversion."

"The manor was her diversion, and the staff says she's shown no interest in it at all."

"Then we must arrange something else." Lady Weymouth tapped her fingers on the arm of her chair as she pondered a solution.

"We could invite her here," Lord Weymouth suggested.

Lady Weymouth shook her head. "Not yet. We're Griffin's parents. She doesn't need to feel she's disappointed us as well. She needs someone young. Someone vivacious. Someone as independent and free-spirited as she is. She needs . . ." She looked at her husband as they spoke in unison. "*Miranda.*"

Chapter 23

"Lord Wellington reviewed us on the 19th. We looked well. Today the entire regiment moved up about two leagues to the front. We marched at daylight, passing the Coā at the bridge of Almeida in order to join Crawford. The banks are rugged and inaccessible. Everything is parched and brown. I long for the news of home and for Alyssa. Her letters have been a godsend. They are my lifeline."

—Griffin, Lord Abernathy, journal entry, 04 July 1810

"What is it you want?" Jarrod asked as soon as the Duke of Sussex joined them at the table.

Sussex cocked an eyebrow. "I want?" He leaned forward. "You invited me to join you, Shepherdston, not the other way around."

"You've been nosing around us for weeks," Colin said. "What are you up to?"

"The question is, what are you up to?" The duke replied.

"We're trying to discover why you are still interested in courting Abernathy's bride." Jarrod got to the point.

"Heard about that, did you?" Sussex smiled.

"Of course we heard about it." Colin shouted. "You haven't exactly kept it a secret."

"That's because I wanted to get your attention," Sussex told them. "And I knew that continuing my pursuit of Lady Alyssa would do it."

"Our attention?" Jarrod frowned. "Why?"

Sussex leaned closer and lowered his voice to just above a whisper. "You are the leader of a group known as the Free Fellows, aren't you?"

"Where did you hear that?" Jarrod asked warily.

"I've heard it for *years,*" Sussex said. "Almost since you formed it."

"Impossible," Jarrod said. "There's no such organization."

"Is that so?" Sussex queried. "Because I heard you and Abernathy and Grantham formed a secret society while you were at Knightsguild. I've known about it since Knightsguild."

"Might I remind Your Grace that you did not attend Knightsguild?" Colin offered.

"No, I did not," Sussex replied. "But Manners did. He told me about it." The duke watched as Shepherdston and Grantham exchanged looks. "I see," he mused, "that your secret society wasn't as secret as you supposed."

Jarrod shrugged. "Manners had the cot next to mine. Naturally, he wanted to be a part of our group of friends and was always whining and threatening to follow us or report us to Norworthy."

"Didna' have the guts to actually do it." Colin's Scottish burr was thick with disgust. "But I see he lived up to his reputation as tattle."

The duke inclined his head. "He's a distant cousin who, before he inherited, often prevailed upon me to augment his allowance."

"You bribed him," Jarrod corrected flatly. "For information about us? When we were boys?"

Sussex nodded. "I, too, wanted to be a part of your group of friends. And now that I know that your secret group is working to defeat the French, I want more than ever to become a part of it."

"So, you've been pursuing Abernathy's bride?" Colin asked.

"She wasn't Abernathy's bride when I began pursuing her. She was the girl my mother selected for me. But she caught Abernathy's attention."

"If there *was* a secret organization," Jarrod began, glancing at Colin to make certain he followed, "any new member would naturally have to meet each old member's approval."

Colin picked up Jarrod's thread of conversation. "And would naturally have to meet and pass a series of, shall we say, challenges in order to prove himself trustworthy?"

"Naturally," Sussex agreed. "What would you have me do?"

Jarrod clenched his jaw to keep from grinning. "Before we have you do anything, Your Grace, we have to know two things. Why? And what are your feelings for Alyssa Abernathy?"

"Why?" Sussex repeated. "Because I grew up in similar circumstances to yours, Shepherdston. A lonely boy surrounded by sycophants and hired companions. I begged to be allowed to attend Knightsguild because you and Abernathy and Grantham were there, and I wanted to be like you. I still do." He looked away, unable to face Jarrod and Colin after baring his soul, afraid of having them turn him down. And while Daniel, Duke of Sussex, knew that Shepherdston and Grantham might not believe him, every word of what he had told them was true. He had bribed Manners into relating all of the Free Fellows of Knightsguild's adventures, every escapade, every punishment, every triumph Manners knew, so that he could feel as if he were one of them instead of one of the many miserable buggers at Eton. Manners pretended to be one of the fellows, too. But, he was whiny and irritatingly timid—too timid to actually be a Free Fellow, so he had claimed the role of historian and secretary. Sussex grimaced. Manners was the closest thing to a friend he had ever had, and the only thing they had had in common was Shepherdston, Abernathy, and Grantham—the Free Fellows League.

"What about Lady Abernathy?" Colin demanded.

"I like her," Sussex answered honestly. "Or rather, I like everything I know about her. Her mother and my mother inhabit the same circles of friends. They thought it a good match. Now that I am five and twenty, my mother has been hounding me incessantly to marry. Lady Alyssa seemed the perfect choice. I thought she would make a fine duchess." He gave a short, self-deprecating laugh. "She apparently disagreed."

"Are you in love with her?" Jarrod asked.

"Of course not," Sussex retorted. "I don't even know her. The first words I've exchanged with her since we were children were spoken at her wedding breakfast. I think it's apparent that she prefers Abernathy."

"Yet you promised to continue your pursuit. . . ."

Sussex blushed. "Yes, well, I don't like to lose, and if you check the betting books over there"—he nodded toward White's betting books—"you'll find there are several significant wagers betting that I would win Lady Alyssa's hand. Several of them placed by business rivals and, well—" He cleared his throat. "I can afford to lose the sums wagered, but I would much prefer that they did."

Jarrod laughed. The young duke sounded very much like he should be one of them. "You weren't serious?"

"I would have courted and married her," Sussex admitted, "if her father had accepted my suit, and I would have made her a good husband, but . . ." He glanced down at the toes of his highly polished boots. "In truth, I'm in no hurry to marry or procure an heir. I simply wanted an end to my mother's haranguing."

Colin poured the duke a dram of whisky and slid it across the table to him. "What do you know about gardening?"

"Nothing."

Jarrod snorted. "You possess the finest gardens in England, man, yet you know nothing about gardening?"

"The gardens have been in place for nearly two hundred years," Sussex said. "And professional gardeners have always come with the garden. I simply enjoy the results. Why?"

"Your first challenge is to become a master gardener and pay a call on Lady Abernathy." Jarrod's smile was wicked. "She's missing her husband and needs a bit of cheering up."

Sussex groaned. "You do realize she threatened to shoot me at her wedding breakfast?"

"Aye," Colin answered. "We heard."

"So, why me?"

"Two reasons," Jarrod said. "The first is to prove how trustworthy you are. You pay court to Lady Abernathy, but you don't touch." He shot the handsome duke a scathing look. "Not so much as a stolen kiss as long as she is Lord Abernathy's wife."

"Contrary to my hotheaded words at the wedding breakfast, I do not make a habit of seducing other men's wives—especially when they appear to be in love with their husbands."

"That's good, Your Grace," Colin said. "But we have to make certain. And this is the best way to kill two birds with one stone."

Sussex stared at Colin as if he'd lost his mind. "Surely, you can't believe that I'm the person best suited to lift Lady Alyssa's spirits?"

"Why not?" Jarrod demanded. "Who better to lift a lady's spirits than an old suitor?"

Sussex frowned. "Do you mean to challenge her fidelity as well as my own?"

Jarrod took a deep breath. "Let's just say we're giving Lady Abernathy a reason to get up in the morning."

"If only for the pleasure of turning you away from her front door. Just be careful that you don't give her cause to shoot you, Your Grace," Colin added. "Or us, either."

⌒

Griff broke the seal on Alyssa's latest letter. They had been on the move for almost three weeks, and it had taken the post longer than usual to catch up with them. His regiment was joining General Crawford in the push across Portugal, into Spain toward the siege of Ciudad Rodrigo.

Griff unfolded the parchment and read the brief note, then carefully refolded it and held it beneath his nose. The faint scent of roses and lavender filled his nostrils, bringing with it memories of the three nights he had held her in his arms. Griff gritted his teeth and squeezed his eyes shut, blocking out the noise of the camp, the jangle of bits and bridles, the rattle of swords and sabers, and the incessant droning of a black fly trapped inside the tent. He gently tucked the letter inside the ribbon tied around the packet of all the other letters she'd sent him.

Griff hadn't realized he'd made a noise until Eastman, who sat on a camp stool polishing the brass buttons of one of his coats, spoke. "News from home, my lord? From Lady Abernathy?"

Griff swallowed the lump in his throat and nodded.

"Good news? More descriptions of Lady Abernathy's plans for the improvement of the manor? Does she still intend to grow hops and flax? Have the new dairy cows arrived? Did she send any more skin lotion?"

Griffin didn't answer, and Eastman turned to look at him. "Sir? Is everything all right back home?"

Alyssa's letters full of sketches and ideas and bits of household gossip had brightened his and Eastman's days. She told him of ripping out sections of the overgrown hedges and replacing them with smaller varieties of boxwood and holly. She detailed the events of her day, wrote of Mrs. Lightsey's and Cook's surprise when Alyssa commandeered a portion of the kitchen storerooms in order to produce her herbal concoctions. And she always sent samples of new scents, sprinkling her pages with rose and lavender water or imbuing the sealing wax with rosemary or peppermint or spearmint or bayberry or lemon balm. She often included small packages of soap for Griff and Eastman and for the men in his command who needed them. The bright blue ribbon Griff used to tie her letters had come from around a parchment-wrapped bar of vanilla and chamomile soap. Griff had given it to a young second lieutenant whose face had been badly chafed from the sun and wind and the strong lye soap he'd been using to shave.

Her letters were unfailingly bright and cheerful, and Griff spent his time alone at night reading them over and over again.

When he complained in one letter of sunburn and the biting flies, Alyssa sent a flask of lotion to soothe the skin and repel the insects.

It had arrived in her last packet, and now he and Eastman were the envy of the regiment.

Griff imagined Alyssa creating the lotion in Cook's
kitchen, smiling as he recalled the memory of the way
she had smelled the day he and Lord Tressingham had
concluded the wedding settlement.

"No descriptions of the plans for the manor this time.
Or samples." He took a deep breath and slowly exhaled
it. "She writes with the news that there will be no heir."

Eastman sighed. "I am deeply sorry, my lord."

Griffin bit the inside of his cheek. "So am I, my
friend." He glanced at the valet who had willingly become his aide and comrade-in-arms. "I didn't realize
how much I had come to depend upon good news and
the confirmation that I had done my duty to my family
as well as my country."

"How is my lady taking the news?" Eastman asked
as if the event was current instead of almost a month
past.

"She blames herself." Griff cleared his throat.

"She mustn't."

"I agree," Griff told him, somehow managing a slight
smile. "But there are tear stains on the paper, which is
why I intend to take advantage in this lull in the march-
ing and skirmishing and disabuse her of the idea."

"I'll leave you to it," Eastman said, laying the coat
aside as Griffin took a sheet of paper from his traveling
desk, took out a pen and nib, and uncapped a bottle of
ink.

04 July 1810

My dear Alyssa,

*It took three weeks for your letter to reach me. We
have been on the move since mid-May. I cannot tell
you where were are for fear that these letters fall
into the wrong hands. The enemy, numbering ap-
proximately eight thousand, is nearby, and we are on
the alert. We never unsaddle excepting in the eve-*

nings, and then it is merely to clean the horses. We sleep in full appointments with our bridle reins in hand, ready to turn out on the instant and at two of the clock in the morning, the whole regiment remains on high alert until the pickets are relieved and return unharmed and all is quiet. The firing is very brisk. It begins at first daylight, ceases during the heat of the day, and resumes at night. Eastman and I remain unhurt, but my horse, Samson, sustained a slight wound when a minié ball grazed his hip. I used your drawing ointment and the lotion to repel the flies, and I am relieved to say that he is recovering very nicely.

As for your sad news, I am very sorry that I could not be there to hold you close and assure you that although I am disappointed, I am not disappointed in YOU.

There is no shame or fault in failing to conceive. These things happen in their own time and cannot be forced.

The ability to conceive is beyond your control. It is in the hands of a Higher Power. Please do not blame yourself. And please don't cry anymore. Everything will be all right. My last words to you were prophetic. I miss you. You are on my mind a thousand times a day. I think of you in the kitchen preparing herbal decoctions and supervising the replanting of the gardens—using massive amounts of the "tea" you prepare from the stable muck, and of course, I think of you as you looked the way I last saw you . . . and I remember what we shared. So I thank you, my sweet bride, for helping to relieve my burdens while I fulfill my duty.

Your husband, Griffin.

PS: I shared your chamomile soap with a young lieutenant of whom I have become very fond. He has a very fair countenance, and his skin has suffered mightily from the elements. Not the least of which *was the soap he used for shaving. His face is much improved, and Lieutenant Hughes begs me to send his deepest appreciation and admiration.*

G.

Chapter 24

"Letters from home are a lifeline for soldiers. There is, I believe, an art to the writing of them. They should be filled with the news of home, more heavily weighted with good news than ill, for soldiers should always have something for which to look forward."

—ALYSSA, LADY ABERNATHY, DIARY ENTRY, 16 JULY 1810

"*What are you doing here?*" Alyssa asked when she entered the morning salon and found the Duke of Sussex in it.

"I was in the neighborhood and wanted to pay my respects," he told her.

Alyssa narrowed her gaze at him. "According to my last calculations, Park Lane is an eight-hour drive by coach. I hardly think you were just in the neighborhood."

"Touché, Lady Abernathy." Sussex applauded. "At another time your calculations would be correct, but as it happens I am your nearest neighbor."

Alyssa groaned. "Don't tell me that Haversham House is *your* county seat."

"All right," the duke replied agreeably, "I won't. I will tell you, however, that Haversham House traditionally belongs to the Dukes of Sussex, the sovereign's right trusty and most beloved cousin."

"Mama was right," Alyssa muttered, beneath her breath. "I *should* have memorized Debrett's before I married."

"Pardon?" he inquired politely.

"Touché, Your Grace." Alyssa curtsied.

"Pax, Lady Abernathy." Sussex held up his hands. "I come in peace."

"As you appear to be our nearest neighbor, I appreciate the peaceful overture, Your Grace," she said. "But I am puzzled by why you would deign to come at all. Especially without invitation."

"I have an invitation," he informed her. "Your charming mother bade me call upon you when she learned I was traveling this way. She's been concerned about you."

"She could not have been too concerned," Alyssa remarked, "or she would have come in person." The smile she gave the duke told him, in no uncertain terms, that she knew how false his statement was. In fact, the last thing Lady Tressingham said to her youngest daughter before Alyssa boarded the coach that would bring her to Abernathy Manor for her honeymoon had been: "I did my best by you. You could have been a duchess, but you made your bed, Viscountess Abernathy—now lie in it."

"She did ask me to call upon you," he answered, truthfully this time.

"No doubt hoping that I've become a widow already." Alyssa looked up at the duke and met his unrelenting gaze.

He cocked an eyebrow. "There is always that possibility."

"Yes." Alyssa closed her eyes and counted slowly to ten. There was no question that the Duke of Sussex was one of the most gorgeous examples of the human male she had ever seen. But he also appeared to be one of the most arrogant, most ill bred, most obstinate and obtuse peers of the realm she had ever met. The man simply could not take a hint. "There *is* always that possibility, Your Grace. It's called war. And it makes a great many widows. But I am married. You are not. That means that it's quite improper for you to call upon me in spite of your lofty rank."

"Not at all, my lady," he replied. "For a duke is welcomed in any household. And it's quite proper for me to call so long as we are properly chaperoned and so long as I bring a wedding gift."

"We are not chaperoned." She glanced pointedly at his empty hands, and then turned her attention to the morning salon. There wasn't a sign of a wedding gift anywhere in sight. "And I don't see a wedding gift."

"Outside," he told her. "My wedding gift is outside."

Alyssa narrowed her gaze at the duke. "It had better not be a horse," she warned. "Or a foxhound."

Sussex laughed. He reached out to take her by the elbow. "Come, Lady Abernathy, let me set your mind at rest."

Intrigued in spite of herself, Alyssa allowed the duke to lead her out of the morning salon and through the front door.

A beautiful bay stallion stood tied to a wagon.

"He's not yours," Sussex informed her. "He's mine. What's in the wagon is yours."

He led her closer. Inside the bed of the wagon were two canvas-covered squares, one larger and one smaller. A carefully packed crate sat beside the covered squares.

His Grace lifted the canvas aside to reveal the two wooden cages beneath it. Inside the larger of the cages was a pair of mute swans.

The duke grinned. "I heard, my lady, that your intent is to transform Abernathy Manor and its gardens and grounds into an estate to rival Sussex House's gardens and grounds. Since every magnificent garden comes complete with swans, I found these very apropos."

"Thank you, Your Grace, they're lovely," Alyssa answered honestly.

"They are that," His Grace agreed. "But swans can be very ill-tempered creatures. Especially when they're mating . . ." He gave Alyssa a meaningful look. "They mate for life, you know."

"Yes," she said quietly. "I know."

The duke glanced down at the toes of his boots. "Well, in any case, I thought you and Lord Abernathy would appreciate that quality."

"I do."

"I, on other the other hand, appreciate the fact that these particularly nasty tempered creatures are mute," Sussex elaborated. "Unlike their new owner."

It was Alyssa's turn to laugh.

Sussex exhaled the breath he had been holding. "Oh, and I brought you these." He nodded toward a pair of peafowl—a male peacock and his hen. "A bit of competition just to make certain the swans don't become too full of themselves."

Reaching into the wagon, the duke removed a delicate looking potted plant from the padded crate, then untied his horse from the back of the wagon before nodding toward the driver of the wagon and the laborer who had accompanied him. "Take the peafowl around to the . . ." He turned to Alyssa.

"West lawn," she answered.

"West lawn," he repeated. "And take the swans to the pond. Don't worry," he said to Alyssa. "Their wings have been clipped."

"I wasn't worried." Alyssa waited until the wagon rumbled down the drive toward the west lawn and the pond at the far end of it. "And thank you once again, Your Grace," she murmured. "What is a garden without swans and peacocks?"

"Or exotic plants." Sussex handed Alyssa the plant. "This is for your conservatory. It's an orchis plant."

Alyssa smiled. "Yes, Your Grace, I recognized it as such."

"Of course." He smiled. "The head gardener at Sussex House developed this one. It's a new variety. The only one of its kind."

"You should keep it for your conservatory, Your Grace. It's much too valuable to give away," Alyssa protested.

Sussex held up his hand to forestall her. "This one no longer belongs in my conservatory," he informed her. "You see, my mother had it registered with the Royal Botanical Society as an *Orchis alyssium*." He winced. "A bit prematurely it seems, but she intended the flowers to be used in your bridal bouquet. At our wedding." He shoved the pot toward her. "Please, take it. As you can no doubt imagine, it's best, under the circumstances, that there be no reminders of my failure to bring that plan to fruition."

Alyssa accepted the plant. She motioned for one of the gardeners' assistants, then asked him to carry it to the conservatory.

"Give it the care it needs," Sussex instructed, "because it's as unique as its namesake."

"Your Grace . . ." she began, suddenly uncomfortable with the turn of conversation.

"I have to ask." He met her gaze. "Out of curiosity. Nothing more."

"Ask what, Your Grace?"

"Why Abernathy and not me?"

"You know the answer to that, Your Grace. Everyone who knows my father knows the answer. You don't keep a kennel."

"I'm not asking why your father refused me; I'm asking why you did."

Alyssa sighed. "I have nothing against you, Your Grace. But I didn't want to be a duchess. I wanted to be my own person, and duchesses are rarely allowed that freedom."

"I don't follow."

"Don't you?" she asked. "Because I would think that you of all people would understand." Alyssa paused. "You're perfect on paper, Your Grace. No one in her right mind would refuse a young, wealthy, handsome duke, but I didn't want a perfect world that's existed in much the same way for generations. I wanted a world I could perfect. For me. I didn't want to fit a mold," she explained. "I want to make one." She shrugged her shoulders in a gesture her mother would frown upon, but one she'd come to associate with Griffin. "Lord Abernathy was willing to give me that opportunity and I—" she broke off as a carriage came up the drive.

Shielding her eyes with her hand, Alyssa strained to see who it might be.

Sussex ignored the approaching carriage. "You were saying . . ." he prompted.

But Alyssa wasn't listening. "I'm not expecting anyone, unless it's—"

"It's Lady St. Germaine," he told her.

Alyssa blinked up at him.

"It's Lady *Miranda* St. Germaine, come to cheer you up and to act as chaperone."

"How do you know?" she sputtered.

The duke took a deep breath and then exhaled. "I passed her carriage on the road yesterday. We stayed at the same coaching inn."

"Together?" Alyssa was surprised.

"Of course not," the duke replied. "The marchioness and I dislike one another. We simply happened to choose the same inn. I recognized her coach and driver when I left at first light this morning for Haversham House. She apparently got a late start, or she would have arrived sooner." He stared as the coach rolled to a stop, and Miranda alighted from it.

Miranda walked toward Alyssa, but came up short when she saw the Duke of Sussex.

"Your Grace." She bobbed a quick curtsy. "Are you following me?"

"I arrived first, Lady Miranda," he pointed out. "I cannot be following you."

"What are you doing here?"

"A pleasure to see you, too." Sussex chuckled.

"Then the pleasure is all yours," she retorted.

The duke fought to keep from smiling at her turn of phrase. Miranda St. Germaine was known for her intelligence and wit as much as for her inability to snag a husband. "I'm surprised you gave up on the season so soon." He smiled at her. "What are you now? Four and twenty?"

She returned his smile with a too-sweet one of her own. "I'm the same age as you, Your Grace. As well you know."

"You left London prematurely," he said. "There were a few likely prospects left. If you'd stayed for the duration, you might have finally managed to walk down the aisle as a bride instead of an attendant."

"And if you'd invested in a few hounds, you might have managed to please your mother and become a bridegroom."

Alyssa stepped forward, embracing Miranda, defusing the scene between her two guests before it became more heated. "Miranda, how good of you to come!"

"It was good of you to invite me," Miranda replied. "Unfortunately, I didn't realize you already had a visitor." She glared at the duke.

"His Grace stopped by to present us with wedding gifts," Alyssa explained. "He brought us a pair of swans, a peacock and peahen for the gardens, and a plant for the conservatory."

"That was nice of him." Miranda spoke as if the duke had already left. She sighed. "And I only came bearing letters."

"Letters?"

Miranda grinned as Alyssa's eyes lit up. "Lord Weymouth received a packet of letters in yesterday's military dispatch pouch. They were all addressed to you, Lady Abernathy, from your husband."

Alyssa couldn't contain her squeal of delight as Miranda reached into her reticule and brought out a bundle of letters and handed them over.

"Oh, thank you." Alyssa flung her arms around Miranda's neck and hugged her.

"You're welcome, Alyssa." Miranda smiled down at her friend. "Why don't you go read them?"

Alyssa hesitated, torn between indulging her greatest need and entertaining her guests. She glanced from the Duke of Sussex to Lady St. Germaine and back again. As Miranda was the Marchioness of St. Germaine and a peeress in her own right and Sussex was a duke, protocol forbade Alyssa from withdrawing from their presence without their permission.

"Go on," Miranda urged. "I can entertain myself while you read your letters."

The duke nodded. "If you'll excuse me, Lady Abernathy, I'll take my leave of you and your guest as well."

"Thank you, Your Grace," Alyssa breathed, clutching the packet of letters to her chest. She curtsied and withdrew, practically running up the front steps and into the house in her haste to read the letters.

Sussex tipped his hat. "Lady Abernathy." He waited until Alyssa had disappeared inside the house before turning to Miranda and adding, "That certainly cheered her up. It seemed your letters trumped my gifts, Miranda."

"Letters from a husband have a way of doing that, Your Grace," Miranda replied.

"So you're an authority on husbands, are you?"

"Only on what I see from my vantage point at weddings," she answered in a low, pained voice.

The duke felt a flush of red creep up his neck. "It was nice of you to bring the letters and to allow her privacy in which to read them, Lady Miranda."

"Once upon a time, most of my friends and acquaintances thought I was a nice person, Your Grace. But that was before I learned to hide my bitterness and disappointment with a sharp wit and an acid tongue."

"I apologize for my cruel words, Lady Miranda," he said quietly.

"No need, Your Grace. You only said to my face what others say behind my back. Now, if I may have your leave?" Miranda replied in a dismissive tone.

But the duke wasn't to be dismissed so easily. "How long will you be staying?"

"Three or four weeks at least."

"Then, I'll be certain to stop by again."

"Don't bother on my account," Miranda jibed.

"Don't worry, my dear marchioness," Sussex drawled. "It's no bother. Now that you're here and we're all suitably chaperoned, paying a call on Lady Abernathy is no bother at all."

Miranda let him have the last word, but she stuck her tongue out at him as he turned his back to leave in a gesture that was completely immature and immensely satisfying.

Chapter 25

"After giving much thought to the matter, I have decided that letters from loved ones fighting abroad are as much a lifeline for those of us who wait for their safe return as our letters from home are for them. Those of us who wait hope for news with every breath and dread the same for we know not what it may bring. We dwell in the realm of make-believe. Where we make believe that our loved ones are fine, that they suffer no hardships, and that they long for home and the comfort of our arms. We pray it will be so. But we know that for many of us, that will not be the case. . . ."

—Alyssa, Lady Abernathy, diary entry, 16 July 1810

Alyssa didn't see Miranda again until sup- per that night. She had spent the afternoon reading and rereading Griffin's letters. And when she finished reading them, she began making lists of the items she would need for a new batch of herbal remedies for him and for his men, especially Eastman and Lieutenant Hughes. She lost track of time and forgot about Lady Miranda's presence until Durham reminded her that she had a houseguest.

Alyssa hurried into the petite salon where a table had been laid for two. She had decided to use the small salon for dining, as it was an easier trek from the kitchens for the staff than the much larger dining hall. And she liked dining beneath the watchful eyes of the portraits of Lord and Lady Weymouth and that of the eight-year-old Griffin.

Alyssa curtsied as she entered the room. "I apologize for leaving you alone all afternoon, Lady St. Germaine, and for not being here"—she glanced around the salon—"when you appeared for supper."

"Not at all, Alyssa." Miranda waved Alyssa to her feet. "And please, no formalities. I know I'm a marchioness and you're a viscountess, but this is your home now. You shouldn't have to curtsy to anyone in it. Besides, we've become friends. You're to call me Miranda, and I will call you Alyssa."

"Thank you," Alyssa said. "And for bringing my husband's letters and allowing me a few private hours in which to read them. I'm afraid I've been a very poor hostess."

"Not to worry," Miranda said. "I made myself at home in the library." She frowned. "It took me a few moments to discover the shelving system. I remembered it as being alphabetical."

"I rearranged it," Alyssa told her. "And I decided that since one can't always remember the author or the name of the book one is seeking, shelving them according to subject matter made the most sense." She glanced over at Miranda. "Of course, the subjects are grouped alphabetically. I created a sketch of the shelf arrangements in the library, labeling each subject, and posted copies on the tables beside each chair. I do hope you located the book you wanted."

Miranda nodded an affirmative. "I used the sketch to locate Shakespeare's works. I chose a volume of the bard's comedies." She smiled at Alyssa as they sat down for the first course. "Tell me, how is Griffin?"

Alyssa took a deep breath, then slowly expelled it. "He remains unharmed."

"I'm delighted to hear it."

Alyssa nodded. "I have been so very worried about him." She turned to Miranda and related the impersonal bits of Griffin's letters that could be shared. She had been disappointed to note that with the exception of his letter releasing her from all responsibility in her failure to live up to her end of their bargain by conceiving his heir, there was very little that Griffin wrote that couldn't be shared with others.

Alyssa hoped he would share his feelings with her, but his letters gave only the merest hint of them. It was almost as if their nights together had never happened. He spoke of missing her, but not of loving her. And he rarely mentioned his physical need for her.

She understood.

Logically, she understood that Griffin had distanced himself from her. She had done the same.

He wrote of his life as a soldier.

She wrote of her life as mistress of Abernathy Manor.

Neither spoke of their deepest feelings or fears. And although she knew he had married her to fulfill an obligation, Alyssa never gave up hoping that one day, Griffin would speak of his feelings or at the very least, sign his letters with love.

"What about the Duke of Sussex?" Miranda asked.

"What about him?" Alyssa was puzzled.

"He's going to continue to call on you."

Alyssa sighed. "I wish he would not. I haven't done anything to encourage him and everything I know to discourage him."

Miranda gave a short laugh. "I must admit I'm a bit surprised that he's being so persistent. His mother must be determined to have you for the next duchess; otherwise, Sussex would have given up. He certainly didn't devote nearly as much effort into courting the last young woman he thought would make a suitable duchess."

"Who was she?" Alyssa asked, more out of a sense of curiosity than anything else.

"Me," Miranda answered.

Alyssa gasped. "Oh, Miranda, I'm so sorry. I didn't know."

"There's no reason you should," she answered. "He only called upon me four times, and that was years ago during my first season."

"What happened?"

"Her Grace, the dowager duchess, did not approve of me. As you've no doubt noticed, I don't look the part of a dainty debutante or of a darling daughter-in-law."

Alyssa widened her eyes, and understanding dawned. "You love him." It wasn't a question but a statement.

"Not that he bloody deserves it," Miranda answered belligerently. "But yes, I love him. I think I've loved him from the first moment I met him and will probably continue to do so unto the day I die."

"Does he know?" Alyssa asked.

Miranda shook her head. "He thinks I despise him," she said. "And I like it that way."

"But Miranda—"

"No, buts." Miranda was firm. "I'd rather have his dislike and his contempt than his pity. I'm a wealthy marchioness in my own right. I don't need to marry, and I certainly don't need any man's pity."

"Did you accept my invitation to visit because you knew he would continue to pay me court?"

Miranda paused before answering honestly. "I didn't know for certain if he would continue to court you, but . . . Well, anyone with half an eye—anyone except Sussex, that is—can see that you're crazy about Griffin. Let's just say I hoped if I were here, he'd remember I was alive and available."

Alyssa smiled. "Then I'll see what I can do about encouraging him to visit."

⌒

The days and weeks and months passed, one rolling into the other.

The gillyflower, sweet pea, feverfew, chamomile, hollyhock, larkspur, mallow, nasturtium, and roses bloomed in the garden. Alyssa marked the days on the calendar, noting the blooms in the garden as a way of passing the time.

She took great satisfaction in the renovations, noting the newly designed and carefully tended herb garden with its well-defined borders of low-growing perennials. She kept detailed sketches of the wild, overgrown, and unruly beds that had yet to be redesigned, marking each plant with colored threads as to whether she intended to keep, relocate, or discard it. And Alyssa spent her time identifying plants and drawing the extensive sketches needed to keep track of their locations throughout the garden. Noting the blooming dates helped, for the greenery was often the same and only the colors of the blooms distinguished one species or variation of a plant from another.

Miranda and the Duke of Sussex often accompanied Alyssa on her garden expeditions. Miranda often pitched in with the chores of weeding the beds and gathering herbs for Alyssa's concoctions. Sussex carried baskets of cuttings and carted easels and paints about the garden, moved chairs and benches and the occasional statue, as the ladies painted and sketched and planned the renovations of the established flower beds.

It was a glorious way to spend the late summer.

They often dined al fresco in the garden, and Miranda twice extended her visit. Miranda's company kept Alyssa from working from sunrise to sundown, for the marchioness enlisted Alyssa's aid with the numerous county charities.

One afternoon they moved the pianoforte into the redesigned section of the west lawn and hosted a garden party for the children confined to the Haversham poorhouse, and the next afternoon they hosted another garden party for the women confined there.

They rode each good day, exploring the countryside as Alyssa learned the boundaries of the estate and met the tenants and the villagers who worked there.

Miranda's visit lasted longer than either of them expected—from Saint Swithin's Day until the end of the season.

Surprisingly, the Duke of Sussex's visit to his country home lasted almost as long. Both Alyssa and Miranda were surprised that the popular duke had forsaken the remainder of the season in order to keep them company in the country.

During the weeks Miranda was in residence and the duke was at home in the country, Alyssa became the mistress of Abernathy Manor. And as mistress and hostess of Abernathy Manor, she kept her word, inviting Sussex to the manor on an almost daily basis, using every excuse she could think of to persuade him to accept, then using just as many creative excuses to find ways of leaving him and Miranda alone and unchaperoned.

Alyssa thought her plan of throwing Miranda and the duke together was working until Sussex announced he was going north to his grouse moor two days before Miranda was to leave Abernathy Manor. He offered to delay his departure in order to escort Miranda to her country home in Cheshire on his way north, but Miranda coyly refused. Sussex left in a huff, and Miranda departed the manor two days later.

Alyssa missed Miranda's companionship almost as much as she missed Griffin.

But she wasn't left alone for long, for Miranda and the duke of Sussex were only the first in a line of visitors who came to call once the season ended.

Parliament had adjourned, and the great migration north for the autumn hunting season began.

Now that there was a lady in residence at Abernathy Manor, family, friends, and acquaintances paid visits, stopping over for days on end in order to break up their journeys to Scotland and the North Country.

Lord and Lady Weymouth were the first to pay a visit. They stayed a fortnight, taking the opportunity to get to know their daughter-in-law and admire the changes she had made to the manor before retiring to their country home for the autumn and winter months.

Parliament might be adjourned, but the war continued, and with it continued the work the war generated. Lord Weymouth made it a point to stay over at the manor during his frequent journeys to and from London for so long as the war continued, Weymouth intended to play a vital role in the fight against the French.

Alyssa's mother and father paid a brief visit in late August while on their way to Tressingham Court for the September cub hunting. Lord Tressingham invited Alyssa to join them. Although she loved to ride, Alyssa had never been one to relish the hunt, especially cub hunting. The September cub hunts served as training for the young fox hounds and Alyssa found them to be much too cruel and bloody. She declined the visit by pleading the need to stay at Abernathy Manor.

Alyssa knew Lord Weymouth's messengers would deliver Griffin's letters to Tressingham Court or anyplace else she cared to visit, but Alyssa couldn't bear the thought of another few hours or days of not knowing, of not hearing from him. She kept busy organizing the manor, renovating the gardens, supervising the preparation of the land for the spring planting of hops and flax, and increasing the herds of dairy cows and the flock of sheep. She played hostess to her guests, and she continued to work on her book of recipes for herbal remedies.

Griffin's letters kept her going, as did the visits from Griffin's two closest friends, the Marquess of Shepherdston and Viscount Grantham.

She lived for the days the mail arrived from London or when Keswick or Durham relayed the news that Shepherdston or Grantham or both had come to call.

Neither gentleman ever stayed the night. Alyssa didn't extend offers for them to stay unless she had other houseguests, but even then, Shepherdston and Grantham refused. And Shepherdston had made it quite clear on his first visit that spending a night beneath the same roof as the wife of one of one's closest friends when one's friend was unable to do the same was not at all the sort of thing a true gentleman would do. He appreciated the offer of hospitality but told her that, as a bachelor, he would seek his lodging elsewhere.

Alyssa never asked where. She assumed he and Grantham lodged at the nearest coaching inn or in the village or returned to Shepherdston Hall, a mere three hours by coach and a bit over two hours on horseback.

She never knew when they might appear, as their visits never occurred on a regular schedule and, unlike most of her other guests, the mysterious Free Fellows did not confine their travel to moonlit nights. Neither Shepherdston nor Grantham appeared to have any trouble navigating the darkest country roads, no matter how late they stayed.

But Alyssa liked them both despite their secretive ways. She also liked knowing that neither Grantham nor Shepherdston had any idea that she knew they and Griffin made up the roster of a secret organization. No one knew she knew. Not even Griffin. Alyssa had never breathed a word about the conversation she'd overheard. And although Miranda had expressed a certain curiosity about her sudden wedding, Alyssa had never confided the circumstances leading up to Griffin's proposal.

Everyone in the ton seemed to know that Griffin had been ordered to marry before he left for the Peninsula. Why he chose to marry her didn't seem to be all that important to anyone except her and friends like Miranda, who had grown to care about her. And the truth of the matter was that most of the gossips were more interested in learning if she regretted the loss of the duke enough to become his mistress. For it was no secret that the Duke of Sussex had continued to visit her at Abernathy Manor.

Alyssa sighed. No one seemed to notice or care that Lady Miranda St. Germaine had been in residence at Abernathy Manor each time the duke came to call or that, like the two other bachelors who visited, Sussex had never spent a night beneath Lady Abernathy's roof.

The nastier gossips proclaimed that the length of the duke's stay was of no consequence. One didn't necessarily need darkness or a roof over one's head to make a lady one's latest mistress. Other society gossips simply dismissed the marchioness's presence as chaperone and forgot all about Lady Abernathy's repeated refusals of the duke's suit.

Some said she was playing hard to get. Others said she wasn't playing at all.

Alyssa only prayed that Miranda and Sussex would manage to come to some sort of agreement so that her reasons for allowing the duke to continue to call at Abernathy Manor would come to light.

The truth was that Lady Abernathy wasn't playing hard to get or already gotten. She was playing matchmaker for the Marchioness of St. Germaine and the duke. Unfortunately, her matchmaking efforts seemed destined to go unnoticed and unrewarded.

Chapter 26

"I must endure. That is the essential duty of the wives of soldiers. To endure the wait, the worry, the loneliness—no matter what."

—ALYSSA, LADY ABERNATHY, DIARY ENTRY, 04 MAY 1811

"*I hear His Grace, the Duke of Sussex, paid* you a lengthy visit."

Alyssa sat in the main salon on a sofa across from the Marquess of Shepherdston and Viscount Grantham, watching as Shepherdston gracefully balanced a cup and saucer on his knee and Grantham attempted to do the same—but not nearly as gracefully.

"You and everyone else in the ton," she muttered.

"How's that?" the marquess asked.

"I said His Grace paid calls during his recent stay at Haversham House." Alyssa sighed. Shepherdston was a bit more slender, and his eyes were a light, almost golden brown instead of blue, but he reminded her very much of Griffin. Griffin would never be quite as elegant or refined because he was bigger—taller and broader of shoulder and hip. But his voice . . . She struggled to keep from trembling with longing at the sound of it because Jarrod's voice was nearly identical to Griffin's—or her memory of Griffin's voice—and Shepherdston and Griffin appeared to share a great many mannerisms: the lift of the eyebrow, the tilt of the head, the way they both frowned when deep in thought.

"Then the rumors are true," Colin said.

"That depends upon the rumors, Lord Grantham." Turning her attention back to the marquess, Alyssa added, "His Grace paid the first call in order to present me with a gift to celebrate Lord Abernathy's and my wedding."

"What sort of gift did His Grace bestow?" Grantham demanded in a thick Scottish burr that did nothing to conceal his disregard for the duke.

Alyssa concentrated on the viscount, studying him at length. He was very handsome and charming in a rougher sort of way than Griffin or Shepherdston. A fraction shorter than both his friends, Grantham had a stockier build with wide shoulders and heavily muscled thighs. His hair was sandy blond, and he wore it longer than was fashionable, but it was his grayish green eyes and the cleft in his stubborn chin that seemed to define his looks. Looks that were the antithesis of the Marquess of Shepherdston's. "A pair of mute swans, a peacock and his hen, and an orchis plant his mother named in my honor."

"The Dowager Duchess of Sussex named a plant in your honor?" Shepherdston shook his head. "As a wedding gift?"

"An *early* wedding gift." Alyssa emphasized the word. "In honor of her son's bride." She watched as the expression on the marquess's elegantly handsome face went from confusion to complete understanding.

"Since I married Griffin, the duke could rightfully assume that Mir—the woman he marries—the future Duchess of Sussex—might object to having a rare flower named for some other lady on the premises. So he made me a gift of it." She couldn't be certain, but she thought that Griff's friends were deliberately baiting her—testing her to see how she'd react.

"That was nice of him." Colin's reply was laced with sarcasm. "Seeing as how you are married to Abernathy."

But Alyssa refused to be baited. "I thought so," she said. "After all, the plant is very rare and very valuable to collectors."

"People collect plants?" Shepherdston was intrigued despite himself.

Alyssa leveled a look at him. "Does it surprise you,

my lord? Surely, you understand that people collect many things, especially rare and valuable things."

"Including mistresses," Colin added.

Alyssa glared at him. "I've done nothing to encourage His Grace to continue to pay me court."

Jarrod cocked an eyebrow. "And yet he paid a call here nearly every day he was in residence at Haversham House. And you invited him." Jarrod didn't like baiting her, but he wanted to make certain Griff's wife hadn't changed her mind about Sussex. After all, he and Colin had sent the duke.

"Only because Miran—" She broke off, then looked up to meet their curious gazes. She took a deep breath. "I invited His Grace to visit because Lady Miranda was here."

"To act as chaperone for the two of you?" Colin asked.

"No, you . . . you . . ." Alyssa did something she almost never did. She lost her temper. "You lackwit!"

Colin blinked. "I beg your pardon?"

"You should beg my pardon!" Alyssa snapped. "I not only married your fellow Free Fellows League member, but I was foolish enough to fall in love with him."

Colin froze, brought up short by her anger and her slip of the tongue. "I can't believe Griffin confided in you."

"Griffin didn't confide in me!" she exclaimed. "Griffin doesn't know that I know anything about your secret League."

"Then who?" Colin demanded.

"You," she answered, meeting Colin's stare. "And you." She glanced at Jarrod.

"That's impossible." Jarrod shot Colin a warning glance before he narrowed his gaze at Alyssa. "No such organization exists."

"Yes, it does," she contradicted him.

"All right," Jarrod answered in a soothing tone of voice designed to humor her. "Tell us about it. Tell us what you think you know of a league of Free Fellows."

Alyssa repeated the conversation she'd overheard at Almack's.

"How?" Jarrod demanded.

"I was standing behind the potted palms," she answered. "I couldn't make my presence known without revealing that I'd overheard. And, quite frankly, I was fascinated by your conversation."

Colin frowned. "You agreed to marry Griff after hearing all of that? Knowing he didn't want you?"

She smiled at Colin. "He wanted me," she answered. "He didn't want a wife. There's a difference, Lord Grantham."

"Very good, Lady Abernathy," Jarrod applauded.

"I may have been innocent when I married him, but I recognized that look in his eyes the first time I saw him. I didn't know what it meant at the time, but I knew it sent tingles up and down my spine, and that was more than any other man had ever managed to do."

"Including Sussex?" Colin drawled.

"Especially Sussex!" Alyssa snapped. "I wish everyone would stop pushing him at my head. He was never my choice, only my mother's. I didn't want him before I married Griffin, and I'm not interested in becoming his mistress now."

"What about his duchess?" Jarrod asked.

"I could have been his duchess if that's what I wanted. Ask Griffin. He knows." She threw her hands up in a gesture of pure frustration. "I only allowed His Grace to call at Abernathy Manor because Lady Miranda St. Germaine wants him."

Jarrod shook his head. "Not likely. Those two despise one another. Have for ages."

"Think again," Alyssa said. "Miranda didn't act as chaperone for me. I served as a chaperone for her." She looked at each of the Free Fellows. "At least, it was supposed to appear that way." She shrugged her shoulders. "Unfortunately, I'm not much of a chaperone."

Jarrod took her measure. "You're in love with Griff?"

She nodded.

"Does he know?"

"No," she answered.

"What if he doesn't love you in return?" he asked.

"He isn't required to love me in return." Alyssa met their gazes steadily. "I married him knowing that he did not. That doesn't alter the fact that I love him."

"What are you going to do?" Colin wanted to know.

"I'm going to love him," she replied. "That's all."

"You aren't going to try to change him? You aren't going to try to make him settle down here at Abernathy Manor with you once he returns from the Peninsula?" Jarrod asked.

"I pray every day that Griffin will return from the Peninsula safe and sound," she said. "And in exchange for his safety, I promised God I wouldn't try to make Griffin do or be anything he doesn't want to do or become. I'm in love with a Free Fellow, and I won't make any claims upon him beyond those in the marriage settlement. He has fulfilled his obligation to me. He's free to be whatever he wants to be. And wherever he wants to be."

"Even if it's not with you?" Colin asked.

"Even so." She bit her bottom lip to stop its quivering as she nodded.

"About the Free Fellows—" Jarrod began.

"No need to worry," Alyssa assured him. "Your secret is safe with me."

"Is it?" Colin challenged.

"As safe as it is with you," she retorted.

"Fair enough," Colin answered.

They reached an understanding that night—Alyssa, Jarrod, and Colin. And what they all understood was that each of them, in his or her own way, had Griffin's best interests at heart.

Alyssa respected and admired his friends for that. And they learned to respect and admire her. She loved their friend, but she promised to make no demands upon him.

Griff was as free as he'd ever been. Unless he chose otherwise. And Jarrod and Colin knew that he would never break his word. And neither would they. The Marquess of Shepherdston and Viscount Grantham continued to call upon Griff's bride as often as they could and at least once a month as they had promised, secure in the knowledge that the secret of the Free Fellows League was safe.

She knew only what she'd overheard at Almack's, and Alyssa, Lady Abernathy, would never reveal her husband's secret association, endanger the current work of the League, or keep her husband from seeking his destiny.

She would never bind Griff with the bonds of love. Not because she didn't want to but because she had given her word. And she intended to honor it.

Griff was a Free Fellow for life, unless he chose otherwise, and Jarrod and Colin knew that Griffin would never choose otherwise. He had given his word and made a blood oath, and he intended to honor it.

e ɔ

The time passed. Alyssa continued to mark off the days on her calendar.

The war on the Peninsula raged on. The fighting lulled, but the troop movement did not. And through it all, there were minor skirmishes, raids and reconnoitering, baggage to guard, and pickets to man.

She learned the language of war from Griffin's letters and the news he relayed.

She learned the nature of war by surviving as he survived each day.

The siege of Cuidad Rodrigo began in mid-June and ended in victory with surrender at six P.M. on the evening of July tenth. A few days later, Griffin's regiment was on the march once more to begin the siege of Almeida in Portugal. When Almeida fell on the twenty-eighth of August, the Eleventh Blues began the march toward Bussaco.

Alyssa nearly worried herself sick at the news of a major engagement at Bussaco, but Griffin's name didn't appear on the casualty lists, and a letter from him soon confirmed that once again, his regiment was on the move.

They moved from Bussaco toward Badajoz.

Alyssa sent letters and small gifts of her soaps and lotions, stationery and ink, sewing kits, packets of buttons and playing cards for him to share with Eastman and the young Lieutenant Hughes—anything she thought might ease the hardships and the boredom of his life as a soldier. And she never made him wait for word of home. Alyssa responded without fail to Griffin's missives with letters of her own, often two and three letters a day.

Autumn gave way to winter.

Alyssa spent half of the Christmas season with her family and half with Griffin's. She knitted scarves and socks and mittens for him and Eastman and Lieutenant Hughes and sent new uniforms as Christmas gifts for Griffin and Eastman.

She returned to the manor after the new year and waited until winter eventually gave way to spring.

The early crocuses, tulips, and daffodils emerged from their winter beds at about the same time the members of the ton began leaving their winter homes, heading south toward London and the opening of parliament and the season.

Life at Abernathy Manor went on, the cycle seemingly unchanged. The gardens bloomed. The trees and shrubs grew taller. The swans and the peafowl bore young, trailing through the garden paths and across the surface of the pond with their hatchlings following close behind.

The dairy cows birthed calves, and the sheep bore lambs. The fields left fallow were planted in flax and hops, and Alyssa, Lady Abernathy, celebrated her first wedding anniversary alone.

Chapter 27

"We've returned to the border village of Fuentes de Oñoro eight miles from the French garrison at Almeida and are preparing for battle. Our goal is to prevent the Prince of Essling from resupplying his forces there. Today is the first anniversary of my wedding to Alyssa. I hope I am alive to celebrate it when this is over."

—GRIFFIN, LORD ABERNATHY, JOURNAL ENTRY, 02 MAY 1811

"Happy anniversary, my lord." Eastman opened the pockmarked low wooden front door of the house to which he and Griffin had been billeted and ducked outside. He crossed the minuscule patch of ground separating the yard from the dirt street and walked to the line of cavalry officers' cots surrounding the village well.

Dusk had fallen, and Griffin sat hunched over his writing desk on the cot. Like all his fellow cavalry officers who would lead charges at dawn, Griffin had moved his bed outside to the village square in order to sleep with his bridle in hand. A small lamp hung suspended from a pole above his cot, the pool of light barely bright enough to illuminate the surface of Griffin's writing desk.

His favorite mount, Samson, fully recovered from his hip wound, stood quietly in full battle gear, his rein looped over Griffin's arm.

"The mail pouch Lord Weymouth sent made it up from the back of the line," Eastman announced. "A subaltern just delivered it." Griffin closed his journal and put it away, then straightened and stretched before he recapped the inkwell and set his writing desk aside.

The army had been on the march for two full days, and Griffin hadn't slept in three nights except in snatches when he and Samson both managed to doze.

The cavalry had been kept at the ready, and this morning they would lead the charge into the enemy lines.

"There's a bundle of letters and a package for you from Lady Abernathy." Eastman reached for Samson's reins at the same time he handed over the leather dispatch pouch containing the letters and the package.

Griffin accepted the pouch.

"Anything from Lady Abernathy?"

Griffin looked up to see Lieutenant Hughes bounding toward him, doing his best to balance three tin mugs of steaming hot coffee.

Lieutenant Hughes or Hughey, as the men had dubbed him, had quickly come to anticipate the arrival of the mail pouches as much as Eastman and Griffin and on the days the mail pouches arrived, he and Eastman joined Griffin for coffee and the reading of Alyssa's letters.

Hughey enjoyed hearing the news from Abernathy Manor almost as much as Griffin, and Eastman and took a childish delight in collecting whatever surprises Alyssa sent to them.

Griffin smiled. Hughey's exuberance and easy going nature had made him a favorite among his fellow officers and the men, and Griffin had gladly taken the younger man under his wing. Hughey reminded Griff of a half-grown mastiff trying desperately to find his place and to please.

Like Eastman, Hughey rarely received mail of his own, his mother being deceased and his father being a poor and unreliable correspondent. And also like Eastman, Hughey had become the beneficiary of Alyssa's largesse. She showered him with gifts of soaps and lotions to try, and with Christmas and Boxing Day gifts.

Hughey treasured the scarf and stockings and mittens

Alyssa knitted and the woolen blanket she sent for his horse, Bay.

Griffin had written of the lieutenant's loneliness, his lack of mail, and his lack of funds to purchase the little luxuries Griffin and Eastman took for granted, and Alyssa had responded by sending the young man the kinds of gifts a mother or female relative would send.

Hughey had proclaimed himself madly in love with Lady Abernathy and swore that if anything happened to Griffin, he would journey to Abernathy Manor and sweep the widow off her feet.

The lieutenant sat down on the cot beside Griffin. "What's happening at the manor? Have the tulips she planted bloomed yet? Did she send us anything?"

Eastman laughed. "It's their anniversary," he informed the younger man. "Anything Lady A sends this time is sure to be for my lord."

Hughey blushed. "Good lord, sir. Today's your anniversary? Why hasn't anyone mentioned it before now? Did we send her anything? You know how ladies are about anniversaries. Lady A will be heartbroken if we forgot."

Griffin gave the lieutenant an indulgent smile. Anyone listening to the conversation would think that Alyssa was their wife as well as his. "Our wedding anniversary is the fourth," Griffin explained. "And *we* didn't send anything." He looked at Eastman and Hughey. "I sent the pair of blue topaz earrings and the matching pendant I purchased before we sailed. My father will see that she gets it on the fourth."

"That's not enough," Hughey pronounced, glancing at Eastman for confirmation. "Lady A has been so kind to us. We must send something else. Something unique. Something from here in Spain."

Griffin cleared his throat. "Hughey . . ."

"With your permission, of course, sir," Hughey added hastily.

"He's right, sir," Eastman concurred. "Lieutenant Hughes and I would like to send Lady Abernathy something to mark the occasion." He frowned. "A *belated* anniversary gift if you will."

Griffin grinned. "We've shared everything else since we've been here. We might as well share this."

"Capital, sir!" Hughey was fairly bubbling with excitement.

"Though what you'll find to send her from here is beyond me." Griffin fixed his eyes on Hughey. "She would be most upset to think you'd sent her a gift plundered from some poor unfortunate Spanish or Portuguese woman."

"Not to worry, sir." Hughey grinned a big, broad-toothed, guileless grin. "I know just the thing. The old lady who billeted us has several, and she'll be glad to part with one for English coin."

"Part with what?" Griffin asked.

"A lemon tree," Hughey said.

"What?" Griffin and Eastman replied simultaneously.

"A small lemon tree in a pot," Hughey said. "It will be perfect for the conservatory at the manor." Hughey's big blue eyes twinkled merrily. "And you know she'll love it."

Eastman, ever the fashionable valet, frowned. "I was thinking more in terms of one of those lace mantillas the women here wear to church." He turned to Griffin. "If you don't think that too personal a gift, sir."

"Who am I to object if you wish to send her lace?" Griffin chuckled. "I'm just the lady's husband."

"Good. It's settled," Hughey said. "Eastman will send the lace thing, and I'll send a potted lemon tree. Together with your jewelry that should be enough to brighten Lady A's anniversary day." He lifted his tin coffee cup in a toast. "And when the battle is over, we'll celebrate our victory and our anniversary with a skin of that Spanish wine—*la tinta de la Mancha*. Agreed?"

Griffin nodded. "Agreed."

"Agreed," Eastman replied.

"Good," Hughey pronounced. "Now let us see what Lady A has sent Major Lord Abernathy and hear the news. I'm eager to know if the tulip beds turned out the way she wanted. . . ."

Griffin obliged.

She sent him a gold watch. Griffin opened the cover and smiled. The inside of the front cover unfolded to reveal a double frame containing a miniature copy of her father's Lawrence portrait of his foxhound bitch, Fancy, and a miniature of Apollo. A reminder of what he'd traded and what he'd gotten, her letter had said. Griffin had laughed aloud as he passed the watch around for Eastman and Hughey to admire. The front cover miniatures weren't the only ones. Inside the back cover was a miniature of Alyssa wearing the jewelry he had given her as a wedding gift. Her letter informed him that she had ordered the miniature when she sat for her formal portrait as Viscountess Abernathy. The larger version now hung in the portrait gallery of Weymouth Park, his parents' country seat.

"Good God! But she's as beautiful outside as she is inside!" Hughey exclaimed, staring down at Alyssa's likeness. "I didn't think it possible." He looked up at Griffin. "I'll be sure to watch your back tomorrow, sir. You must return to her in one piece, or she'll never forgive me."

"What happened to your vow to marry her should I fail to clear the French lines?" Griffin teased.

Hughey stared at the miniature for a moment longer before carefully closing the watch and returning it to Griff. When he looked up, he wore the most pensive expression Griffin had ever seen. "Lady A is much too fine for the likes of me, sir. I'm an odd-looking fellow with my pale skin and hair." He gave a self-deprecating laugh. "Why, most folks don't realize I have eyebrows and eyelashes! A fellow like me could never do Lady A justice. She should walk on the arm of the finest and most handsome gentleman in England." Hughey met Griffin's gaze. "I should not have joked about such a thing. For it's quite plain that Lady A is your match in every way. I'm honored to have your friendship, sir. It was wrong of me to joke about coveting your wife." Hughey stood up and saluted Griffin. "I won't let you down tomorrow, sir."

"Hughey . . ." Griffin got to his feet and returned the salute. "Lieutenant Hughes . . ."

"Sir?"

"My wife is as honored by your admiration for her as you are by her gift of friendship to you. She would be a lucky woman indeed if so fine and loyal a fellow as you relieved her of a burdensome widowhood."

"Thank you for saying so, sir."

"I only spoke the truth, Lieutenant. Remember that, if tomorrow's battle proves unfavorable and I fall."

"You won't fall, sir," Hughey promised. "You're protected by Saint George, by Lady Alyssa's prayers, and by Lieutenant Nolan Hughes." He winked. "Good night, Eastman. Good night, sir. Bay is waiting for me to turn in."

"Good night, Hughey."

Griffin watched until Hughey disappeared around the corner. He and Hughey and Eastman had spent a companionable evening meal.

As Hughey and Eastman said their good nights, Griffin took out Alyssa's letters and read them once again, saving the most recent for last.

15 April 1811
Abernathy Manor
Northamptonshire, England

Dearest Griffin,
   Congratulations! You are now the proud godfather of a litter of very fine foxhounds whose parents, Fancy and Prince, are quite enjoying the spoiling that goes along with the accomplishment. You aren't, I'm afraid, the recipient of the pick of the litter. That honor went to Lord Weymouth, who is quite overcome by the gift. You were offered second pick of the litter. Papa pressed me to choose, but I declined by

saying that a man should pick his own hounds. A sentiment I am certain you will appreciate.

However, I did not decline the offer of first pick of the foals Apollo has bred upon the mares he covered. Nor did I allow my father to retain ownership of all the others. You will be happy to know that on this point, I stood quite firm. Papa was most unhappy with the bargain, saying the mares belong to him and therefore the foals, but I pointed out there would be no foals without the loan of Apollo, and although you did not attach strings to the loan, you did not expect Apollo to be used to cover all of Papa's broodmares. Since that was the case, I felt you should derive some profit from Apollo's exertions.

If all goes well with the foaling, we shall increase our stables by twelve over the course of the spring. Papa will have to absorb the loss should any of the foals not be born whole and hardy. I was quite put out with him for taking advantage of your generosity in such a way, although he assured me that Apollo was none the worse for wear and that he quite enjoyed the duties placed upon him. But for Papa to enhance his stock in such a manner . . . Suffice it to say that Papa is, at present, not on speaking terms with me. In his estimation, I am nowhere near the worth of twelve foals and Fancy's second pick of the litter. But your father was very pleased with my bargaining ability and says I am worth much more despite our unfortunate setback in producing an heir. I hope you feel the same.

At any rate, please accept my best wishes and my offering on the first anniversary of our nuptials. I know the date on my letter does not correspond to the date of our actual wedding, but I am putting this in the dispatch pouch early in hopes that it will reach you on the appointed day. I never thought to ask if you wanted to celebrate the day of our nuptials. I'm afraid I simply took it for granted that you would choose to do so. I am enclosing this letter along with my anniversary gift to you. A not too very subtle re-

minder of me, I'm afraid, but I beg your indulgence, for I am married a year and yet barely a bride, and as such, I believe brides are entitled to a bit of sentimentality.

Shepherdston and Grantham continue to pay brief visits on your behalf. They never stay the night and have been the most circumspect of gentlemen and loyal friends. Thank you for asking them to look out for me in your absence.

I pray God and Saint George will keep you safe.

Your devoted wife,
Alyssa

PS: Please give my best regards to Eastman and Lieutenant Hughes and assure them that the gardens are beginning to bloom and I will soon have a batch of fresh rosemary and sheep's milk soap to send. It sounds repulsive, I know, but it does wonders for the complexion. Oh, and I remembered to enclose the gold braid Lieutenant Hughes asked me to send.

Griffin had opened the folds of the letter the first time he'd read it, but there was no sign of the gold braid that should have been enclosed.

This time Griffin reached into the bottom of the dispatch bag and discovered it lying there. He hadn't discovered the braid earlier because he'd been too busy reading the other four letters to stop and look for it. And afterward, he and Hughey and Eastman had been so engrossed in studying his new watch they'd forgotten to look for the braid Hughey needed to refurbish his uniform coat.

Griffin fished the length of gold braid out of the leather pouch and placed it in his coat pocket. He would give it to Hughey tomorrow after the battle when Eastman would certainly elect to make repairs to all of their coats.

Griffin carefully refolded the letter, then opened the drawer of his portable writing desk and removed the packet of letters he kept there. He untied the blue ribbon holding them together and added the five new letters to the packet, briefly stopping to inhale the faint scent of roses each one carried. He painstakingly retied the blue ribbon and gently deposited the packet back inside his escritoire.

This time, she signed the letters: "Your devoted wife, Alyssa." Griffin's eyes felt gritty and moist. Squeezing them shut, he rubbed the sockets with his fingers, massaging away the ache.

He had hoped that she might sign them with love . . . but perhaps that was an unreasonable hope from a lonely soldier who dared not burden her with his feelings by doing the same.

He opened his eyes, unfastened the back cover of his new watch, and stared down at the miniature of his wife.

A year ago he hadn't wanted a wife. Now that he had a devoted one, Griff realized he wanted a loving one. A year ago he couldn't wait to join his regiment. Now, all he wanted was to go home to his wife and see if he might help her go from devoted to loving with a few hundred kisses and a lifetime of passion.

Griffin awoke with a start to find Samson nicker-ering in his ear. Griff reached out to caress the gelding's soft muzzle.

The camp was beginning to stir, and Samson wanted his morning treat. Griff tugged off his leather cavalry gloves, then reached into his pocket and brought out a small square tin. He opened the square and removed a lump of sugar candy for Samson.

"She didn't forget you, boy," Griff glanced over at the miniature of Alyssa in the watch lying atop the writing desk where he'd placed it earlier in the evening.

Samson nickered a bit louder, and Griffin fed him the candy.

Alyssa had been making and sending the sweets since he'd arrived in Spain. She had read somewhere that soldiers in battle required frequent doses of sugar, and she'd made certain that Griffin kept an ample supply.

Since Griffin preferred his sugar in the distilled liquid form, he had taken to sharing the candy with Samson.

After feeding Samson his sugar lump and a handful of

grain from the supply in his kit, Griffin loosened Samson's girth and began to clean beneath the saddle and the blanket.

Eastman appeared with a bucket of fresh water from the well and a washbasin. Griffin removed Samson's bridle to feed and water him, then cleaned the bit and checked the leather for cracks and wear before he replaced the bridle and tightened Samson's girth.

Once his horse's needs had been met, Griff washed his own face, cleaned his teeth, and shaved. He buttoned his collar, straightened his uniform jacket, then took Samson by the reins and led him down the street to the house where Colonel Jeffcoat was billeted. Other officers of the Eleventh Blues milled about, having turned out for the regimental briefing and morning assignments.

Hughey was there waiting.

"You're up early," Griffin teased.

"I had an important errand to run." Hughey smiled. "I delivered a potted lemon tree and a lace mantilla to the dispatch rider before daylight. I hope she likes it."

"She'll love it," Griff said. "You know she married me for my garden."

Hughey laughed, and Griffin clapped him on the back.

"It's true," Griff assured him as he led the way into the colonel's quarters.

Ten minutes later, General Crawford's Light Division, including the Eleventh Blues under command of Colonel Raleigh Jeffcoat, set out for the ridge above the village to join Picton's Third Division, Spencer's First Division, and Houstun's Seventh Division.

The French, under command of General Junot, sent ten battalions against Colonel Williams and the twenty-two hundred men garrisoned in the village.

The fighting was desperate and nasty, with skirmishes lasting throughout the day.

The French took the town in the second assault on Colonel Williams' troops and Lord Wellington began amassing three regiments to retake it.

The Eleventh Blues never made it to the ridge. They were called back to join Wellington in the afternoon hours.

Griffin led the Eleventh Blues' second cavalry charge,

following Colonel Jeffcoat's first assault. Lieutenant Hughes, who normally rode at Griffin's side, was assigned to lead the third charge.

"Don't worry, sir," Hughey called as Griffin readied himself to lead his charge. "I'll watch your back."

Griffin saluted. "Thank you, Lieutenant. I'll see you in the village."

Hughey snapped a salute. "I'm right behind you."

Griffin watched as Colonel Jeffcoat led his men into the battle, then urged Samson forward.

"Remember what I told you, Lieutenant," Griffin called over his shoulder.

"I'll remember, sir," Hughey answered. "You remember what I told you. You've Saint George, Lady A's prayers, and Nolan Hughes watching over you."

"I couldn't ask for anything better." Griffin turned to his bugler. "Sound the charge."

The bugler followed his order. He sounded the charge, and Griffin led his men into the thick of the French line, cutting and slashing his way through the French defense, rallying his men into the breach of the village wall, urging them forward.

Spotting a gap in the French line defending the wall, Griffin led his men through it. Musket balls whizzed past his head as Samson jumped the wall, but Griffin and Samson made it through alive and unharmed.

Dismounting quickly, Griff sent Samson toward the safety of the rear of the line where Colonel Jeffcoat and his men were dispatching the French with deadly efficiency.

Griffin and his men began clearing the French from the wall, making room for Hughey and the men following his lead.

Hughey. Griff felt the hairs on the back of his neck stand on end. He kicked the corpse of a French grenadier off the point of his sword and looked up over the wall in time to see Hughey unhorsed.

"No!" Griff shouted.

He watched as Hughey rolled to his feet and began running to retrieve the regimental colors from the fallen color-bearer.

Griffin reacted without thinking. Grabbing the reins of the closest horse, Griff mounted and rode back through the breach onto the battlefield.

The field began exploding beneath his horse's hooves as a group of French gunners regrouped and began lobbing shells at the mounted cavalry. The rear cavalry scattered as the shells ripped through the ranks, but Griffin rode on through it all.

A cheer went up through the ranks as Griffin slashed his way through the French infantrymen who were struggling to close the ranks around the cavalry. He barely felt the saber slash across his thigh or the balls that struck him—one through the flesh beneath his right arm and the other that fractured his collarbone.

Another cheer went through the English ranks as Griffin surged through the French surrounding Hughey as Hughey rescued the fallen regimental colors.

Hughey grabbed for the reins of a loose horse but missed. The horse galloped past into the lines of the fourth advancing charge of English cavalry.

"Hughey!" Griffin leaned down and held out his hand. "Grab hold!"

"You saved me, sir!" Hughey grinned as he grabbed hold of Griffin's hand.

It was the last thing he ever did.

Chapter 28

"I have become a national hero for rallying the men on the field at Fuentes de Oñoro in time to turn the tide of battle. The irony is that I'm not a hero at all. I was only trying to save my friend, and in the end, he saved me."

—GRIFFIN, LORD ABERNATHY, JOURNAL ENTRY, 02 JULY 1811

"I haven't had any mail in over three weeks." Alyssa greeted the lone rider as soon as Keswick opened the front door. "I've been worried sick."

"Lady Alyssa . . ."

Alyssa's knees buckled when she recognized Lord Grantham standing on the stoop. He wore a formal tailcoat and trousers instead of his usual riding clothes and there was a black mourning band pinned to his right arm.

"Catch her!" Colin ordered, stepping forward as Keswick hurried to keep Alyssa from hitting the hard marble floor of the vestibule.

She opened her eyes a few moments later to find herself sitting on a low chaise in the conservatory and clutching fistfuls of Viscount Grantham's shirtfront. "I was expecting the dispatch rider from Lord Weymouth's office." Her voice quavered as she sat up and automatically smoothed her hair and straightened her clothing.

"He sent me instead."

Alyssa paled once again and began to shake. "Please, tell me he isn't."

"Oh no," Grantham rushed to reassure her. "He's coming home."

"He's coming home," she parroted, staring at Colin's

armband, barely able to comprehend Grantham's words.

Grantham nodded. "Tomorrow's *Morning Post* is printing the casualty lists from Spain. Lord Weymouth asked me to come break the news to you before you had the misfortune to read it in the papers." Colin followed her gaze and quickly snatched off the armband and stuffed it in his pocket. Of all the fool things to have done! He'd frightened Alyssa into a faint and all because he'd forgotten to take off the armband he'd worn to Lord Corwin's funeral. Colin hastened to apologize. "Cripes, Alyssa, but I'm sorry. The band isn't for Griff. It was for Lord Corwin—the undersecretary of the army. His funeral was this morning and everyone in the War Office turned out to pay respects. That's where I saw Lord Weymouth. He knew I was coming this way, so he asked me to bring you the news."

"Then, Griffin—"

"His name appears on the casualty lists. But he's fine." Colin rushed to reassure her. "He was wounded but—"

"Wounded?" Alyssa's voice rose in alarm.

Colin held up his hand. "He was wounded in the battle of Fuentes de Oñoro, but he survived and is making a satisfactory recovery. Shepherdston has gone to Spain to help Eastman bring Griff home."

"Has he been invalided?" Alyssa was almost afraid to ask. To be invalided out of the army meant that his wounds were serious enough that he could not return to active duty. And while she prayed Griffin wouldn't have to return to the front, Alyssa also prayed that he could.

"No, not invalided, Lady Alyssa." Colin grinned at her. "After your husband reached the safety of the village wall, he turned and charged back onto the battlefield. His heroic charge back rallied the troops and turned the tide of battle. When it was over, Lord Wellington retook the village and won the day. My dear Lady Abernathy, your husband has become England's greatest hero since Lord Nelson."

Alyssa didn't care that Griffin had become England's greatest hero since Admiral Lord Nelson. All she cared about was Griffin. "How badly is he hurt?" She demanded, already preparing to make a mental list of the herbal potions she would need.

"He suffered a series of wounds, but none of them are disfiguring." *So far*, he added silently. There was no need to alarm her by mentioning that first reports had stated that the saber cut to the thigh might cost Griff his leg.

"What kind of wounds? How many?" Alyssa stared at Colin, daring him to prevaricate. "I need to know what remedies to prepare."

"That won't be necessary, Lady Alyssa. He's receiving the best of care."

Alyssa didn't honor that platitude with a reply. The streets of London were full of maimed beggars who had fought against the French and suffered not only their wounds, but also the care of the best military surgeons. "What sort of wounds?" she repeated. "And where?"

Colin heaved a sigh. "I'm not certain where all of his wounds are located. When I left London Lord Weymouth hadn't received all of the injury reports. I do know that Griff was shot several times during his charge across the field. He suffered a saber wound to the thigh and was bayoneted after the battle," Colin said.

"Bayoneted? After the battle?"

Colin could have bitten out his tongue for letting that bit of information slip. He looked at Alyssa and started to lie, then thought better of it and decided to tell her the truth. "The French aren't taking any prisoners at present. Wounded enemy soldiers are bayoneted after a battle to put them out of their misery."

"Oh, dear God!" Alyssa gasped at the horror, then covered her mouth with her hand as her stomach threatened to revolt.

"Griff survived the bayonet wounds. He's being attended by Lord Wellington's personal surgeon and is recovering."

"I want to see him," Alyssa said.

"That's why I'm here," Colin told her. "Lord Weymouth also asked that I escort you to London."

"London?" She didn't want Griffin recuperating in the dirt and noise that was London. She wanted him home at Abernathy Manor where she could take care of him. "Isn't he coming here? To Abernathy Manor?"

"That was the plan, but His Royal Highness has requested Griffin's presence in London. Griff is to receive The Order of the Garter. Jarrod is going to bring him home to London first," Colin explained. "And if Griff wants to journey to the manor after the honors are awarded, we'll see that he gets here safe and sound." He reached for her hand and gave it a gentle squeeze. "My duty is to take you to London." He looked at Alyssa. "I've already taken the liberty of ordering your coach brought around. How long will it take you to pack?"

"I can be ready within the hour." Alyssa turned to Keswick. "Please find Durham and ask her to pack only the essentials. I can purchase whatever else I need once I get to town."

She took a deep breath to calm herself and breathed in the strong clean scent of the lemon blossoms permeating the air of the conservatory. Alyssa glanced at the potted lemon tree that had arrived from Spain a fortnight earlier, accompanied by an exquisite white lace mantilla and notes from Eastman and Lieutenant Hughes wishing her a very happy first wedding anniversary. The two gifts and the notes from Eastman and Hughes had been the last thing the dispatch rider had delivered to the manor. There had been no word from Griffin in all that time and now she knew why.

Alyssa looked at Colin and noticed, for the first time since his arrival, that he was dusty and travel-stained. "Keswick." She stopped the butler with a word.

"Yes, my lady?"

"Please see to Lord Grantham's comfort while I assemble my remedies."

"Right away, ma'am." The butler bowed to Alyssa before turning to Colin.

"If you will follow me to Lord Abernathy's study, my lord, I am certain we can provide you with gentlemanly refreshments."

Grateful for the offer of refreshments more potent than tea or coffee, Colin rose from the sofa and started to follow Keswick out of the room.

Alyssa's softly spoken inquiry caught Colin off guard. "How is Eastman? And Lieutenant Hughes?"

Colin cleared his throat. He turned toward her, but his gaze didn't quite meet hers. "Eastman is well."

Alyssa cried the whole time she was in the kitchen gathering her herbal remedies. She packed a bar of vanilla and chamomile soap into her canvas bag, then slowly removed it and replaced it on the shelf.

It was Lieutenant Hughes's favorite.

Alyssa knew she would never smell those mingled scents or the scent of lemons and not think of the young lieutenant who had thought enough of her to send her a present on the first anniversary of her marriage to his commanding officer.

She closed her eyes against the flood of tears and recalled his note.

03 May 1811
A village on the Spanish and Portuguese border

My dear Lady Abernathy,

Please accept this lemon tree as a reminder of tomorrow—the first anniversary of your marriage. I pray that it may serve as a token of the high esteem in which I hold you and the friendship you have bestowed upon me.

As I look about my quarters, I am constantly reminded of you, Lady Abernathy, though we have never met. Your presence is in the scent of the shaving soap you made for me, the scarf and the stockings and the mittens you knitted me for Christmas, in the lotions and ointments you sent to ease my suffering. And in the wonderful thick new blanket you sent for my gallant steed, Bay.

I have been deeply fortunate to serve with your

noble husband and to be allowed to share in his very great fortune in having you as his lady.

Please consider this gift from Spain and Portugal a small memento of my good wishes and good fortune. Major Lord Abernathy has been kind enough to share the letters you have sent him, and I feel as if I know every inch of Abernathy Manor, for I have seen it through your eyes, shared it through your dreams and plans . . . If I close my eyes I can picture the conservatory and the empty corner you despaired of filling. I knew when I saw this tree that it was exactly right. I close my eyes and see it in my imagination, filling the corner of the conservatory of Abernathy Manor with the scent of lemons for years to come, providing fruit for your remedies and ease for those who benefit from them.

And in some tiny measure, I hope that as it grows, you will be reminded of the soldier who celebrated your special day in the company of your spouse and was deeply moved by your deep devotion to one another.

I look forward to the day I will visit Abernathy Manor and have the pleasure of meeting you in person and seeing for myself how all of your grand plans for the manor have come to fruition.

Until then, I remain,

Your devoted friend and admirer,
Lieutenant Nolan Hughes

PS: I enclose a note and a gift from Eastman. He is as deeply appreciative of your kindnesses as I and wished you to have an anniversary gift from him as well. Major Lord Abernathy agreed and graciously allowed us to presume upon the annual celebration of his nuptials. And don't worry, ma'am, I promise to see that the major returns home to you.

Alyssa wiped her tears and murmured a prayer for Lieutenant Hughes and a profound prayer thanking God for al-

lowing the lieutenant to keep his promise, for allowing him
to see that the major returned home.

Griffin was alive. His wounds—whatever they were—
would heal, and Griffin would come home to Abernathy
Manor and to her. And she would be there to greet him.

She was waiting for him at the dock in London
two days later when his ship came into port with the tide.

Alyssa's teeth chattered as she stood in the cold, early
morning breeze, flanked on one side by Lord and Lady
Weymouth and the Prince of Wales and on the other side
by Viscount Grantham and the prime minister. Directly behind Alyssa stood her mother and father, her sisters and
their husbands. Behind them were the relatives and friends
of the other men aboard HMS *Semaphore*.

Griffin's ship was supposed to have been met only by
the family and friends of the men aboard it, but the Prince
of Wales's and the prime minister's appearance at the wharf
had dashed that possibility.

It seemed that much of London had turned out to witness
the arrival of England's new hero. She glanced over her
shoulder as the sailors aboard HMS *Semaphore* prepared to
lower the gangway.

A crowd of well-wishers and onlookers stood behind the
wooden barricades. The barricades were in place because
the Prince Regent, like all royals since the revolution in
France, had a fear of crowds and mobs. He had made it a
practice wherever he went to have barricades erected and
to use the Horse Guards to keep the crowd at bay.

The crowd gathered at the docks this morning didn't appear to pose a danger to the regent, but the barricades kept
the people behind them from rushing forward to greet the
disembarking passengers.

The noise of the crowd alerted her. Alyssa looked up as
the soldiers and sailors began disembarking from the ship.
Viscount Grantham reached down and gave her gloved
hand a reassuring squeeze.

The ambulatory passengers were the first to leave, followed by those who required assistance, the bedridden, and finally, the gravely wounded.

Griffin was among the last of the ambulatory passengers to make his way down the gangway. Lord Shepherdston and Eastman closely followed him.

He was easy to recognize. His height set him apart from most of the other passengers, and Griffin wore the distinctive dress uniform of His Majesty's own Eleventh Blues.

He hadn't yet spotted them, and Alyssa took the opportunity to feast upon the sight of him and take careful note of the changes.

The sun had burnished his face and neck, but Alyssa could see that he was pale and thin. His coat hung on his muscular frame, clearly marking the loss of a stone or more of weight. His right arm was confined to a sling. He held a cane in his left hand, using it to support his weight as he inched his way down the ramp. His lush lower lip was compressed into a firm, determined line. He struggled valiantly to hide it, but anyone who knew Griffin could see that he was clearly suffering from the pain of his wounds and fighting the effects of overexertion.

"Jesus!" Colin breathed, squeezing Alyssa's hand once again, but this time more to comfort himself than to comfort her. "He looks as if he's aged five years."

Alyssa agreed. Griffin was still one of the most handsome men she had ever seen, but he bore little physical resemblance to the man who had left for the Peninsula fourteen months earlier.

This Griffin was leaner, harder, and the look in his eyes was that of an old man, one who had lost the sweet innocence of youth and desperately needed to recapture a glimpse of it. Alyssa shivered at the look of guilty anguish she saw on his face.

Lady Weymouth began to cry.

"Griffin!" Lord Weymouth called to his son as he patted his wife on the shoulder in a heartfelt gesture of comfort.

Refusing to greet him with tears in her eyes, Alyssa blinked them back and welcomed him with a smile.

Recognizing the sound of his father's voice above the noise of the crowd, Griffin turned his head sharply to his left and scanned the faces of the people below. "Where are they?" he demanded, squinting into the morning sun. "I can't see them."

"There!" Jarrod pointed. "A bit farther to the left at the end of the red carpet beside Prime Minister Sir Spencer Perceval and the Prince of Wales."

Griffin recognized the dandily dressed and increasingly corpulent form of the Prince Regent first and then fixed his gaze on his parents, who were standing beside him. "She's crying," he said softly. "I have become a hero, and my mother is crying—and in the presence of His Royal Highness."

"Of course she's crying," Jarrod replied in a tone of voice just above a whisper. "I'd cry, too, if I had to stand beside His Highness. Good Lord! Look at his breeches. That shade of green is enough to make anyone cry. Especially a woman of your mother's exceptional taste." Jarrod smiled at Griffin and was rewarded, for a split second, by a ghost of his friend's old smile.

Behind them, Eastman coughed to keep from snickering.

Jarrod turned to face his friend. "Those are tears of relief, you big oaf. Your mother missed you something fierce, and she's terribly grateful to have you home safe and sound."

"And only a little bit worse for wear." Griffin said the right thing, but his voice was tight with strain, and his smile was patentedly artificial. Looking back down at his parents, he caught sight of Alyssa shivering in the cold and sucked in a breath.

"I feel much better," Jarrod remarked dryly.

"You feel better?" Griffin challenged.

"Yes, indeed," Jarrod retorted. "Now, I know you're still alive."

Griffin shot his friend a nasty look.

Jarrod ignored it. "I was beginning to wonder. It's about time you took notice of your bride."

"I didn't expect her," Griffin said. "I thought she'd be waiting at the manor where I left her." *The way I left her.* He recalled the way Alyssa had looked lying in bed with her hair fanned out across the pillows, the rosy tip of one breast peeking out from beneath the sheets.

"Nearly all of London turns out for your arrival home, and you think your wife is going to wait in the country? Not likely," Jarrod said.

"I haven't written in weeks," Griffin admitted. "Not since . . ." He took a deep breath. "I didn't ask her to meet me. I didn't know when I was coming home or if she—"

"You didn't write to tell her you were coming home?"

Griffin shook his head.

"You would have left her at the manor?"

Griff nodded.

"Then it's a bloody good thing your father sent for her. You're a hero, Griff. I know you didn't want a wife before you left, but you got one, whether you wanted one or not. And since you've got one, do yourself a favor and remember that a woman will forgive you just about anything so long as you don't do anything to embarrass or humiliate her in public. If you had allowed her to miss all of this"— Jarrod waved his arm to encompass the celebratory crowd— "you would have publicly humiliated her."

"Who made you a bloody authority on wives?" Griffin retorted, suddenly ashamed of himself for being so caught up in his own feelings that he'd forgotten about Alyssa's.

"I'm not a bloody authority on wives," Jarrod replied. "I'm a bloody authority on women. And on that point, they're all alike from the lowest whore to the highest born lady. There's a great deal of truth to that woman-scorned proverb. Don't ever humiliate or embarrass them in front of their friends, family, or peers."

"I didn't think . . ." Griff broke off, drinking in the sight of her. Her deep-brimmed bonnet hid most of her face from view, but there was no hiding her form as the brisk wind plastered her cloak against her body, outlining its curves. "Damn, but she's beautiful!"

"She is that," Jarrod agreed.

Griffin shot him another nasty look.

"But she is out of reach. She's married you know," Jarrod continued as if Griffin hadn't just warned him about poaching. "To a friend of mine. And no matter how beautiful the gardener or how ripe the temptation, or how big the arse that owns it, I don't tend my friends' gardens." He returned Griffin's nasty look. "I can admire without wanting, Griff. And there's everything to admire about Lady Abernathy." He gave Griffin a little push as they reached the bottom of the gangway. "Go to her."

Griffin limped toward Alyssa as a cheer went up from the crowd.

"Do you think that's wise, sir?" Eastman leaned close to Jarrod.

Griffin's valet had been with him nearly every moment since he'd recovered him from the battlefield at Fuentes de Oñoro. He knew the damage Griffin had suffered and knew the extent of his physical wounds and knew that while the physical wounds were well on the way to mending, the emotional wounds he'd suffered were far from healed.

Jarrod hadn't been privy to all of Griffin's suffering, but he'd seen enough to recognize that at the moment, Griffin was hanging on to his composure by sheer force of will. There had been times during the crossing from Spain that Jarrod had thought Griffin's reason had left him. "I honestly don't know," Jarrod said. "But if *she* can't help heal him, no one can."

Alyssa watched, unable to take her gaze off him, as Griffin limped toward her. She wanted to run into his arms, but her feet stayed firmly rooted in place.

"Go on," Colin urged quietly, placing his hand at the small of her back. "Go to him. He needs you."

She gave Grantham a grateful smile, then moved toward Griffin.

But the Prince of Wales stepped forward at the same time. "Welcome home, Lord Abernathy, our brave and true hero, our most beloved right trusty *cousin.*" The Prince Regent embraced Griffin, kissing him on both cheeks after the Continental fashion.

The crowd roared its approval as the regent embraced the hero of Fuentes de Oñoro.

Griffin looked over the prince's shoulder to where Alyssa stood behind him. He'd been within a few feet of having his wife in his arms once again and ended up being embraced by the Prince of Wales. "Highness." Griffin bowed.

The prince released Griffin, then clapped his hands together in delight. "We've arranged a small dinner party in your honor, Lord Abernathy. Tonight at Carlton House. You and Lady Abernathy, your parents and Lady Abernathy's parents are to be our guests at tonight's celebration."

"Sir, I'm deeply honored—" Griffin began.

"No more honored than we are to welcome England's newest hero to our home." The prince stepped back, then beckoned Alyssa forward.

She curtsied before the regent.

He took her hand and raised her to her feet, then kissed her cheeks. "We shall be most honored to welcome you and your dear husband to Carlton House tonight, Lady Abernathy."

"Thank you for your gracious invitation, sir," she answered.

"Your Highness," Griffin tried again. "I had hoped to convalesce in the country."

The Prince of Wales grinned. "Nonsense, sir! We are in the midst of the season, and everyone shall want to see you. You must stay in London until we arrange the ceremony of the awarding of the Order of the Garter."

Griffin bit his tongue to keep from groaning aloud. "As you wish, Your Royal Highness."

"We shall expect you at ten of the clock this evening," the prince said.

Alyssa curtsied once more, then stepped back, making way so that the prince might present Sir Spencer Perceval to Griffin, then speak to Lord and Lady Weymouth, and to her parents, to Eastman, Shepherdston, and Grantham.

When he was done, the Horse Guards cleared a path through the crowd for the Prince Regent and the prime minister to follow back to Pall Mall.

"Alyssa . . ." Griffin held out his hand as he breathed her name.

"Griffin . . ." She responded in kind.

His fingers brushed hers, and a spark of electricity shot through them.

Lord Weymouth walked over and cleared his throat. "Plenty of time for that once we get you home and completely recovered. No need to provide a spectacle for the crowd."

Lady Weymouth joined her husband, then reached up and embraced her son.

"Let's go home," Lord Weymouth said. "You need your rest, son." He frowned. "For you've received a royal summons to appear at Carlton House for dinner."

Heaving a heavy sigh, Lady Weymouth linked one of her arms through Griffin's and linked her other arm through Alyssa's, drawing them close to her. "I was hoping for a quiet evening spent with our immediate family," Lady Weymouth said, making eye contact with Jarrod and Colin, automatically including them as immediate family. "But it appears that we're going to be joined by two or three hundred of our closest friends *and* enemies. Come, children, we'll all need time to prepare for the evening ahead."

Chapter 29

"I worry that I shall never see a crowd of people without recalling the hours I lay helpless on a battlefield in a small village on the Spanish and Portuguese border."

—GRIFFIN, LORD ABERNATHY, JOURNAL ENTRY, 04 JULY 1811

*C*arlton House was ablaze with lights, the mansion and the grounds packed with people, by the time Alyssa and Griffin and the other members of their little party arrived.

They stepped from their carriage onto a red carpet and made their way into the house accompanied by a great fanfare of trumpets. Red-liveried servants led them to the long gilt dining room.

Griffin flinched. The sound of the trumpets reminded him too vividly of things he would rather forget. "I hate this," he murmured.

Alyssa reached over and took his hand. It was the first time she'd touched Griffin in over a year except for the merest brush of their fingers they had shared that morning.

Griffin had retired to his rooms as soon as they had returned to the Weymouth's town house.

Alyssa hadn't seen him again until they had met downstairs moments before they climbed into the carriage that brought them to Carlton House. "I know. I hate that you have to do this. I'm sorry."

"You're sorry?" Griffin was surprised. "Why? You didn't do anything."

"I'm sorry because you have to do something you'd rather not do."

Like leave you the morning after our honeymoon. He looked at Alyssa, and the heat between them was palpable. Griffin shrugged his shoulders. "I'm sorry, too. I know you don't care any more for these types of gatherings than I do."

Alyssa looked up at him and smiled a knowing smile. "Not like having dinner at Carlton House with the Prince Regent and England's newest hero? What woman wouldn't like that?"

"Lady and Lord Tressingham's youngest daughter." Griffin paused in the doorway of the Prince Regent's fancy dining hall. "You married me to keep from becoming the Duchess of Sussex because duchesses are always made to bear such close scrutiny from the public and from members of the ton. And now, I've gone and made you the center of attention." Griffin lifted Alyssa's hand to his lips. "And that is why I'm going to do the best thing for both of us."

Alyssa frowned. "Which is?"

"Let you go."

Alyssa opened her mouth in shocked protest, but the Prince Regent's majordomo interrupted by announcing their arrival. "Ladies and gentleman, His Royal Highness the Prince Regent invites all of you to join him in welcoming his guests, the *Duke and Duchess of Avon.*"

Griff and Alyssa glanced around for the duke and duchess, but all eyes were upon them.

The Prince Regent approached them, wineglass in hand. Signaling for a waiter, he stepped up on the dais and handed a glass of wine to Alyssa and then to Griffin.

"My lords and ladies," the Prince Regent announced. "Let us toast Our Right Trusty and Right Entirely Beloved Cousin Griffin Abernathy, first Duke of Avon and Marquess of Abbingdon, and Her Grace, Alyssa, Duchess of Avon and Marchioness of Abbingdon."

Griffin forced a smile as everyone present lifted a glass in his honor. Hell and damnation! He'd just become a duke. And Alyssa had just become the thing she had never wanted to be: a duchess.

The awarding of a ducal title was the sort of surprise the Prince Regent loved and at which he excelled. It was also a political coup. The Second Resolution of the Regency Bill of 1811 had restricted the Prince Regent's right to create peers except as a reward for some outstanding naval or military achievement. The prince used Griffin's heroic act that turned the tide of the Battle of Fuentes de Oñoro to create his first peer and to annoy the prime minister and his Tory supporters.

There was no doubt that Viscount Abernathy had acted heroically and in Lord Wellington's own words, "turned the tide of battle, enabling us to win the day and that most important village," but elevating him to the rank of duke was unprecedented in recent history. Wellington himself had only been awarded his viscountcy following his victory at Talavera.

The Prince Regent was, perhaps, the most delighted person at Carlton House. Delighted with himself for finding a way to thumb his nose at the Tory leaders of his government and delighted with Griffin for providing him with the means to do it. He clapped Griffin on the shoulder and offered Alyssa his arm as he led them into the gilt dining hall on the upper floor, where he seated Griffin on his right and Alyssa on his left.

The dinner dragged on interminably before the final course was brought in at half-past one in the morning.

Unaccustomed to the late city hours, Alyssa fought to keep from falling face first into whatever course was put before her and to carry on a reasonably coherent conversation with the Prince Regent and with the Marquess of Something-or-other who was seated on her left.

Griffin was struggling as well. He had removed the sling from his right arm, but that decision had been made prematurely. His collarbone still ached as did the bayonet wound in his shoulder and the hole where a ball had torn through the flesh of his upper arm. The heavy gold flatware caused him no end of grief as he did his best to eat without spilling soup or causing some other embarrassing mishap. His hand shook when he lifted his wineglass, and he shifted in his seat whenever he thought no one was looking in order to relieve the pain and stiffness caused by his wounds.

He was nearly soaked through with sweat, and the noise from the crush of dinner guests and the rattling of cutlery and dinnerware had his nerves stretched taut. He needed peace. He needed quiet. He needed to go home, far away from these shallow and petty people who cared more about gossip and politics and the manner in which their food was served than they did about the army of brave men who were dying on the battlefields every day.

The meal over, the Prince Regent pushed himself to his feet, tapped his crystal goblet with a gold knife, and announced that everyone should remove to the terrace for the special surprise of the evening.

A murmur of excitement rippled through the crowd as the throng of people moved through the great opened doors and onto the terrace.

The first explosion sent Griffin's heart racing, and the dazzling display of fiery sparks lighting up the night sky increased his sense of rising panic.

"Fireworks," the Prince Regent announced. "To honor our most gallant of heroes." He glanced over his shoulder and smiled at Griffin.

Griffin bared his teeth in what he hoped was a semblance of a return smile and reached blindly for Alyssa's hand. His whole body began to shake, and he reacted instinctively as the next barrage of explosions lit up the Mall.

Seizing Alyssa's hand, Griffin shoved her behind him, then pressed her against the shelter of the nearest stone column, shielding her with his body.

It was fortunate that nearly every pair of eyes in the place was looking upward. The unexpected sight of the nation's newest hero hiding behind a stone edifice would have been enough to make the Prince Regent rescind the honors he'd just bestowed on him. As it was, only five people witnessed his reaction and they all stepped forward in unison to cover Griffin's moment of panic.

Lifting his head, Griffin scanned the crowd and the distant horizon, searching for the cannons and the line of grenadiers, unable to comprehend the fact that Jarrod and Colin and Weymouth and Lord Tressingham and the Duke of Sussex had formed a ring about him. Didn't they realize the danger they were in? Didn't they understand the horrible things that could happen when cannon balls rolled through the lines? Or the damage done by shells and shell fragments that rained from the sky? His father and Lord Tressingham were too old to be sent into battle, and his friends were too young. Too young to die. Too young to have their bodies ripped apart and their limbs scattered all over the battlefield. He had to warn them of the danger. Had to save them . . .

"Get down!" he screamed. "Take cover! For God's sake, get down!"

"Sssh! Sssh, Griffin. It's all right," Alyssa spoke softly, hoping to soothe the violent shudders that racked his body with each explosion.

He didn't move. He sat frozen in place, shielding her body, protecting her from unseen horrors as his friends and their fathers protected him from prying eyes and vicious tongues.

Alyssa wrapped her arms around him and held on as he struggled against his paralyzing horror. "Sssh, my darling, you're safe. Nothing bad is going to happen." She pressed her lips to his, quieting his anguished cries, swallowing the high-pitched keening that sounded like the whimpers of a wounded animal, as the extravagant fireworks display continued. Her heart broke at the sight of her strong, proud husband brought to his knees by the horror of what he'd suffered. But she refused to let him to see it.

As the last skyrocket ripped through the sky, Alyssa coaxed Griffin's lips apart and began to kiss him in earnest.

Awareness returned with a vengeance as Griffin realized he was soaked with perspiration and that he was holding his wife's upper arms in a white-knuckled grip and kissing her as if his life depended on it.

The Prince Regent turned back to the new Duke of Avon to gauge the young man's reaction to the honors he'd received and the magnificent fireworks display and discovered the Earls of Weymouth and Tressingham, the Marquess of Shepherdston, Viscount Grantham, and the Duke of Sussex standing where the new Duke of Avon and his wife had been.

"Lord Weymouth, where is your son the young duke?" the Prince Regent asked.

Lord Weymouth moved one step to his left.

The Prince Regent chuckled at the sight of the new duke and duchess kissing in the shadow of the stone columns. "Ah, young love . . ."

"Indeed, sir," Jarrod remarked. "It appears your most extraordinary fireworks display has sparked an additional display of fireworks."

Lord Weymouth spoke for the first time. "My son has been serving on the Peninsula for over a year, sir. And as you no doubt recall, he married Her Grace only three days before. They barely managed a honeymoon." Lord Weymouth gave the regent a smile. "We are hoping they might produce a family heir. We appreciate the honors you've bestowed on our family, sir, and the efforts to which you've gone to entertain us this evening." He shrugged his shoulders. "If you would kindly grant permission for my son and his bride to withdraw from this evening's celebrations . . ."

"Grant a *by our leave* so that they might celebrate in private?" The regent smiled broadly.

"Exactly, sir," Lord Weymouth said.

The regent turned back to Griffin and Alyssa. "Your Grace, we're hereby granting you and your bride permission to withdraw from our festivities in order to attend to your own celebration."

Alyssa broke the kiss in order to answer. "Thank you, Your Highness."

"Go." The regent waved his beringed fingers at Alyssa. "So we can pursue our own pleasures."

"Please," Griffin murmured against her lips. "Get me out of here."

Alyssa let go of Griffin long enough to drop a graceful curtsy, then took hold of her husband's hand and backed out of the regent's presence.

"Go on," Lord Weymouth urged. "Lady Weymouth and I will beg a ride from your parents."

Alyssa nodded.

Although his demeanor gave no indication of it, Griffin leaned heavily against her as Alyssa led him to his father's carriage.

Griffin sank down into the cushions of his coach and heaved a sigh of exhaustion.

Alyssa spoke to the driver. "Take us home."

Myrick lifted an eyebrow in question.

Alyssa nodded. "Home."

Alyssa stared out the window as the coach rumbled through the countryside. Griffin dozed on the opposite seat. Her last journey to London marked Alyssa's first trip to town as Lady Abernathy. This journey marked her first trip home as the Duchess of Avon.

It was only the fifth journey she'd made since her marriage. The first had been her wedding trip to the manor and the second and third trip had been her travel to Weymouth Park and Tressingham Place over the Christmas holidays. Her fourth trip, made two days ago, had been from the manor to London in the company of Lord Grantham.

Alyssa smiled at the flood of memories. She was traveling the same post road she and Griffin had traveled on the day of their wedding, but this trip was markedly different. She had slept in the coach on her wedding day and awakened in Griffin's arms. She and Griffin had done things in this coach that made her blush and at the same time, ache with longing for her husband.

Now Griffin slept fitfully, sprawled in the corner of the coach. They had barely exchanged two words since he climbed inside it. Griffin had simply closed his eyes and fallen asleep.

Yes, Alyssa thought, this trip was very different. The

last time they'd traveled to the manor, they had played a game of seduction. Griffin hadn't wanted a wife, but he'd wanted her. This time, he wanted neither.

He intended to let her go. His Free Fellows League past had come back to haunt her. He had told her he was going to do what was best for both of them and let her go. But letting her go wasn't best for Alyssa and from what she'd seen tonight, letting her go wasn't what was best for him either. He might think so. He might hope so. But she knew better.

She loved him.

And whether he knew it or not, Griffin needed her. And as long as he needed her, Alyssa intended to be by his side. *Be the thorn in his side if necessary.* Whatever it took to convince him that letting her go would be a terrible mistake for them both.

If only she could persuade him to play a nice little game of seduction . . .

Chapter 30

"My husband has been elevated to the rank of duke. I am now the Duchess of Avon. The thing I did not want to be has become the thing I am. Unfortunately, Griffin intends to set me free. Fortunately, I recognize a challenge when I see one. My husband needs to know if I think he's worth fighting for. Worth saving..."

—ALYSSA, DUCHESS OF AVON, DIARY ENTRY, 05 JULY 1811

*G*riffin awoke shortly after they changed horses at Shepherdston Hall. He yawned, then stretched his arms overhead, scraping the ceiling of the coach with his knuckles. Opening his eyes, he looked at Alyssa. "I must have dozed off."

"You might say that," Alyssa answered.

"How long before we get home?" He asked, automatically reaching in his coat pocket for his timepiece, only to remember that he no longer had a timepiece. He patted his pocket. "I seem to have lost my watch."

"About three hours."

Suddenly alert, Griff sat up in the coach. "Three hours? It doesn't take three hours to go from Carlton House to Park Lane."

"We aren't going back to Park Lane," Alyssa told him. "We're going home to Abernathy Manor." She leveled her gaze at him. "You might say I'm kidnapping you."

Griff raked his hands through his hair before he narrowed his gaze at Alyssa. "You're kidnapping me? For what? Ransom? Do my parents know about this?"

"No one knows," she answered.

"They'll be worried sick," he predicted.

"I sent a message to them while we were at Shepherdston Hall."

"Why didn't you tell them before you left Carlton House?"

"I couldn't," Alyssa said. "Because the idea came to me on the spur of the moment."

"Why?" he demanded.

"Because I'm not ready for you to let me go."

"You should be," he answered in a warning tone.

"Why?" It was Alyssa's turn to ask for answers.

"After what happened tonight, I should think it would be quite obvious." He snorted. "I'm not the man you married. I've changed. I don't know who I am anymore."

"I know who you are," Alyssa answered. "You're my husband, Griffin Abernathy."

"I *was* Griffin Abernathy. I'm not sure who I am now. Or who I'll be tomorrow. England's greatest war hero or the man hiding behind a stone column because he's frightened of fireworks." He shook his head. "All I know is that I'm not the sort of husband you need. You deserve better than what you got tonight."

"Let me be the judge of that," Alyssa answered firmly. "Because you're in no position to judge what's best for me or for yourself. You've just come home from war, Griffin. I can't begin to imagine what that is like, but I do know that no man comes home from war unchanged. You may not be the same man I married, but that doesn't mean you aren't exactly what I want in a husband."

"My, but your standards have fallen, Lady Abernathy." He smiled with his mouth, but the smile didn't reach his eyes. "Last year you married me for my neglected manor and gardens and because I wasn't a duke. Now, even that has changed."

"Everything changes, Griffin," she said softly. "Nothing stays the same."

"You have." Unable to resist the need, Griff reached over and loosened her hair from its topknot. "You stayed the same. You're exactly the way I remembered you."

Alyssa smiled a slow, sweet smile. "Then your memory is faulty, my lord. We had just made love the last time you saw me. I was lying in bed. And I was naked."

Griffin's mouth went dry, and his body reacted immediately. The only part of him that hadn't been aching until now began to throb. "Don't, Alyssa," he said when she reached up to unbutton her evening gown.

"Don't what, my lord?"

"Don't try to tempt me with a game of seduction." He stared at her. "You may win the battle, but the victory will be a hollow one for both of us."

"I wouldn't dream of tempting you with a game of seduction," Alyssa retorted. "We've gone far beyond seduction. The only game I'm playing with you is the marriage game."

"Then you shall lose, madam," he said. "For there's no longer a reason for us to continue the marriage game."

The pain of his words ripped through her. "There's every reason for us to continue the game of marriage," she told him.

"Indeed?" He cocked an eyebrow.

"We spoke vows," she said simply. "For better, for worse. For richer, for poorer. In sickness and in health. Till death us do part. Those vows bound us to one another for life. And I intend that we shall keep them."

"Then prepare yourself, my lady," he warned once again. "For I'm afraid that you've enjoyed the better and are about to experience the worst."

Alyssa looked him in the eye. "I've just become a duchess," she reminded him. "I'm prepared for anything."

They arrived at Abernathy Manor at half past three in the afternoon, after traveling through the night. Alyssa was bone weary, emotionally and physically exhausted. Although he tried hard not to show it, she suspected Griffin was even more so. She had only made the journey from the manor to London and back. He had traveled from Spain.

The staff was lined up to greet them, and Myrick drove the carriage up the circular drive to the front door. A footman opened the door and unfolded the steps, and Alyssa quickly alighted from the vehicle.

Griffin moved more slowly, gingerly flexing the muscles of his right leg before he grabbed his cane with his left hand and eased off his seat and out of the coach.

The staff cheered when they saw him, and Griffin did his best to smile through the pain as he greeted each member of the staff on his way into the house.

"Welcome home, my lord," Keswick said.

"Good to see you again, sir," Mrs. Lightsey echoed.

"Thank you," Griff answered. "Thank you all."

Griffin was nearly faint from fatigue and leaning very heavily on his cane when Alyssa turned to one of the footmen. "Please help His Grace up to the master suite. I'll be up to tend his wounds as soon as I retrieve my supplies."

Keswick dismissed the staff and turned to Alyssa. "Did I hear correctly, Lady Abernathy? Did you refer to Lord Abernathy as His Grace?"

She waited until the footman and Griffin were out of earshot and the rest of the staff had returned to their duties before she plopped down to sit on one of the lower steps of the grand staircase and confirmed her earlier statement. "Yes," she answered. "His Grace Griffin Abernathy, first Duke of Avon. First Marquess of Abbingdon. Seventeenth Viscount Abernathy. Twenty-second Baron Maitland. We arrived in London as a viscount and viscountess, and we left a duke and duchess."

"My word!" Keswick breathed.

"We'll have to work hard to live up to that standard," Alyssa teased. "For Haversham House is no longer the only ducal household in the county, and Sussex is no longer the only duke."

Keswick sniffed. "We surpassed Haversham House's standards the day you became Lady Abernathy."

There were tears in her eyes as Alyssa looked up at the butler. "We've still got our work cut out for us," she admitted. "For Lord Abernathy—I mean, His Grace—has suffered greatly in the earning of his new title." She searched Keswick's face. "Restoring his health won't be a simple matter. I shall require your assistance and depend upon your discretion to keep the details from becoming common knowledge."

"You can count on me, my lady—uh—" He turned red. "I beg your pardon. Your Grace."

"It does take some getting used to," she mused. "Ironic isn't it?"

"What, Your Grace?"

"I chose to marry Viscount Abernathy in part because I didn't want to be a duchess, because I didn't want to be bothered by the silliness or the watchful eyes of the ton. And now, Griffin has become a national hero and a duke."

"There will be no escaping the eyes of the ton, now," Keswick said. "But as a duchess, you have a certain power and freedom a viscountess cannot command."

Alyssa massaged her temples with the tips of her fingers. "Let us hope so," she said. "Because I fear I'm going to need all the power I can command in order to keep my husband."

"Keep him?" Keswick was understandably puzzled.

Alyssa sighed. "You might as well know the truth, Keswick. His Grace is here against his will."

"His Grace didn't want to come home to Abernathy Manor?"

Alyssa shook her head. "His Grace didn't want to come home to Abernathy Manor with *me.*"

Keswick released a heavy sigh. "It's that Free Fellows League business, of course."

Alyssa was surprised. "You know of the Free Fellows?"

"Yes, indeed," Keswick replied. "From the time they formed it when Lord Abernathy was a little chap. He always wanted to be a cavalry officer and a national hero."

"He succeeded." Alyssa couldn't keep the note of pride out of her voice. "Unfortunately for me."

"The Free Fellows are completely loyal to one another and entirely honorable," Keswick confided. "But that may work to your advantage—if you choose to fight to keep him."

"How?" She wondered.

"He'll be completely honorable and noble and act accordingly." He faced the new duchess, gauging her mettle. "What are you prepared to do?"

"Whatever it takes."

"Then I'm prepared to assist you."

Alyssa gave a rather unladylike snort. "Any advice?"

"Don't be so bloody noble." Keswick grinned. "Use every measure at your disposal. Fight dirty."

❧

"Lie down," *Alyssa ordered as she entered the* master suite and found Griffin sitting on a chair near the window, gazing out over the refurbished grounds and gardens. "You're dead on your feet. You need your rest."

He ignored her. "It's magnificent, Alyssa. You've created a slice of paradise."

"I thought so," she told him. "But now I realize it's missing something it desperately needs."

Griffin stared out at the carefully manicured lawns and the beautiful arrangements of flower beds and statuary, at the gravel path that wound its way through the gardens and the stone benches and resting areas.

A pair of swans and their cygnets glided across the water's surface and a peacock spread his tail feathers in an impressive display near the fountain of Diana. A flock of sheep grazed in the distance, and in the field beyond that, he could hear the lowing of dairy cattle.

Abernathy Manor had become the perfect vision of a country home. Any man would be proud to own it. Proud to call it his home. But Griff suddenly felt about the manor the way Alyssa had once felt about the Duke of Sussex's gardens. It was so perfect, there was nothing

left to do. Certainly nothing left for him to do. Alyssa
had proven herself to be far better at taking care of the
manor than he had ever been.

His whole life had been spent preparing to serve in
the cavalry. He'd given little thought to what lay beyond
that goal. Perhaps because he'd never thought that there
would be anything beyond that goal. He had only known
that he would become a cavalry officer, and that he
would fight and probably die a glorious death on the
battlefield.

But Griffin had learned that there was no such thing
as a glorious death on the battlefield. Death was ugly
and dirty and final. There was no glory in killing. There
was only pain and suffering, remorse and guilt. Guilt
because he had survived the odds, and so many of his
friends and fellow soldiers had not. Guilt because he had
been handsomely rewarded for failing so miserably.

He had wanted to change the world. But nothing had
changed.

Alyssa was wrong. Nothing really changed.

He had spent months fighting over the same bits of
Spanish and Portuguese land, and nothing had changed.
He had thought himself a soldier and a good leader and
discovered that deep down, he was really a frightened
little boy, horrified by the things he had done and seen.

He had fancied himself a savior, a chivalrous knight
of old. But Griffin knew in his heart of hearts that he
had destroyed much more than he had managed to save.
His men hadn't really been prepared for war. Griff had
done the best he could, but he hadn't had time to train
them, hadn't realized how little practical training the
men in his command had until he'd seen them in action
during their first skirmish. The seasoned French troops
had decimated the inexperienced lines and Griff had
railed in frustration and grief at the multitude of unnec-
essary losses. He had led men into battles they could not
win. He had watched many of them die. And their faces
haunted him. He saw them in his dreams.

He saw them all—the men he'd tried to lead and protect and the men he'd had to kill. The men he'd fought

with and the men he'd fought against. He remembered them all, for they visited nightly in his dreams. The French grenadier. The Prussian cavalry officer. The Spaniard who had fought so bravely at Ciudad Rodrigo. Hughey.

Griffin was haunted by the dead scattered across the battlefield. He saw their faces and heard the pitiful moans of the wounded who begged for water, for warmth, for comfort, for prayers, for God's mercy, for their mothers, and for death.

And now he had come home again to find there was no place for him here. This was Alyssa's slice of paradise, and he had committed far too many sins—had too much blood upon his hands—to find refuge with her.

He had spoiled his slice of paradise. Griffin had sought salvation, but his sins had followed him home. And he'd been rewarded for them. He hadn't been back in England a whole day before he had become the thing Alyssa had railed against marrying. He had become the one thing she had never wanted.

He turned away from the window and looked up at her. "You've done a tremendous job, Alyssa. Abernathy Manor is every man's dream of a home: safe, secure, comfortable, beautiful. What could it possibly lack?"

"Children."

An honorable man would let her go.

Griff prayed for the strength to find the honor he needed to do it.

Chapter 31

"A man must have honor. He cannot live without it."

—GRIFFIN, DUKE OF AVON, JOURNAL ENTRY, 10 JULY 1811

*Griffin's sleep brought no refuge from the ter-*ror. The dark early morning hours ushered in his nightmares.

The sound of his anguished cries penetrated the walls of the master chamber. Alyssa bolted from the bed as soon as she heard them and raced to Griffin's room.

He was dreaming. Bad dreams. Horrible dreams. Dreams that made him cry in his sleep. Alyssa climbed up on his bed and struggled to hold him down and to calm him.

But Griffin fought back, and Alyssa found herself fighting to protect her face from his flailing arms.

She lay almost atop him, holding the covers close about his body, forcing him to stop thrashing. "Griffin." She spoke softly but firmly. "You're having a bad dream. That's all it is." She noticed the beads of perspiration forming on his upper lip and placed her palm against his forehead.

He was feverish.

And it was his own fault, Alyssa thought uncharitably. The stubborn man hadn't listened to her when she had warned him his wounds needed attention. And his stubborn refusal to allow her to tend his wounds had caused him more pain.

Griffin wouldn't allow her to tend his wounds while he was awake, but he'd have no say in the matter from now on. She'd simply tend them while he was asleep. But first, she had to soothe him.

"Go away. Please, go away. Leave me alone. Let me die. Please." Griffin twisted his head from side to side on the pillow in an effort to evade the soft hand stroking his damp hair as hot tears slid down his cheeks and onto the pillow slip.

"Sssh," Alyssa soothed, easing her weight off him.

His thrashing about had caused him to slip off the mound of pillows she and Keswick had propped beneath his injured shoulder and at his back after Keswick, acting a valet, helped Griffin shave and retire to the bed. "I'm not going to hurt you. I'm only going to prop your pillows around you so you'll be more comfortable."

"Hot," Griffin whispered. "Water, please. I beg you." He opened his eyes, but he was still lost in the throes of his nightmare, and his brilliant blue eyes showed no spark of recognition.

Alyssa sat up and reached for the water carafe on the bedside table. She poured a small amount in a glass, then propped him up and pressed the glass to his lips.

"Hot," he said again, after she'd managed to dribble a bit of water through his parched lips without drowning him.

Alyssa set the glass on the bedside table and then flipped back the covers.

She gasped at the sight. His magnificent body was a mass of cuts and bruises. A big purple and yellow bruise marred the area below his collarbone, and another bigger bruise surrounded the bandage on his right shoulder. Alyssa untied the bandage and removed it, immensely relieved to find the bandage clean and fresh.

A stab wound about four inches long marked the point of a bayonet. The cut had been neatly stitched, and the stitches had held. Although the wound was an angry pink color, there was no sign of infection.

Glad that she'd had the presence of mind to leave her remedies in Griffin's room, Alyssa slid off the bed and grabbed her canvas bag from its resting place upon the dressing table. Rummaging around inside, she pulled out a jar of soothing and drawing salve and returned to the bed.

The salve would soothe the skin and prevent the wound from scarring as badly as it would if left unattended. Pushing the bedclothes aside so she could view his naked body, Alyssa found more wounds: another bayonet wound, this one in the calf of his left leg; he had been shot in the fleshy part of his right arm, and he had sustained a deep and nasty saber cut to his right thigh.

Staring at the stitches securing the flesh and muscle of the saber cut, Alyssa murmured a prayer of thanks that he hadn't lost his leg or the use of it. It would take time, but the saber cut would heal. At the moment, though, it was hot and red and irritated from the fabric of his uniform breeches, no doubt, and from the fact that he had been on his feet much longer than he should have.

There were other wounds, lesser ones. A small puncture wound and a thin line at his throat. She stared at the wound more closely. Dear God! It looked as if someone had tried to . . . as if someone had tried to cut his throat. At the top of his right thigh above the saber cut was the bruised imprint of a horse's hoof, and there across his abdomen was the clear mark of a wagon or cart wheel. Alyssa blinked back a flood of tears as she set about slathering his body with a liniment meant to ease the discomfort caused by deep bruises. It was a miracle his hip bones hadn't been crushed. It was a miracle he'd survived. Because someone had driven a horse and cart over him.

Alyssa's mouth tightened into a thin line. Tension strained every muscle in her face. "Don't worry, my love," she whispered. "I'll take care of you. You're hurt and you're tired of fighting, so rest. I'll keep the nightmares at bay."

Alyssa smoothed the liniment over his chest and arms, following the line of his chest hair down over his abdomen, upper thighs, calves, and legs, and back again where his male member lay cradled in the nest of hair between his thighs.

He was so beautiful. And he'd been so terribly hurt. So dreadfully battered and bruised. Reaching out, Alyssa gently traced the length of him with the slightest touch of her fingertips and then tenderly cupped her hand around him.

"Touch that portion of my anatomy again, madam, and I'll kill you!"

Alyssa cried out as Griffin caught her wrist in a painful grip. "Griffin, please, you're hurting me." She met his gaze and saw a look of hatred so intense it frightened her. She opened her hand. "I didn't mean to . . . to . . . trespass. I'm sorry."

Moments passed. Griffin stared at her without recognition, then slowly closed his eyes, took a deep breath, and fell into a deep, exhausted sleep.

Alyssa pulled her wrist from beneath his sweaty palm. There would be bruises there in the morning, but nothing like the bruises Griffin had suffered. Nothing like the pain he'd endured.

Alyssa lifted his hand, turned it over so that the palm faced upward, then leaned over and pressed her lips against it. "I love you, Griffin," she whispered. "And I'm never going to let anyone hurt you again. I promise."

Smiling, Alyssa closed her eyes and slept.

The morning sunlight bathed the room in a wash of pale yellow when Griffin awoke.

He stretched his sore muscles and automatically swiped at the irritant tickling his face.

The clean scent of roses and lavender assailed his sensitive nostrils. Griffin opened his eyes, suddenly wide awake.

He lay half on his left side and half on his stomach, with the majority of his body curved around his wife's slender form. His shoulder hurt like the very devil, but his long legs were intimately entwined with Alyssa's sleek, satin ones, and his injured arm rested lazily across her narrow waist. To Griffin's way of thinking, the pleasure of having her close was well worth the pain.

He sighed contentedly, and Alyssa stirred in her sleep, moving closer to the comforting warmth radiating from his body until her baby-soft bottom rested familiarly against him.

Griffin groaned aloud as the root of him instantly sprang to life, standing proudly erect, prodding her softness, seeking entrance. His brain flashed a sudden warning that told him he should leave while he still had the chance, but Griffin ignored the warning.

A year had passed since he'd held his bride in his arms, and Griffin fully intended to enjoy these few precious moments, these marvelous moments between waking and sleep, when instincts urged him to pull her closer. Moments when he could indulge in the pleasure of having her share his bed without discovery.

Griffin breathed in the fragrance of her silky light brown hair, allowing his warm breath to caress the tender flesh at the nape of her neck while he traced the outline of her ribs through her thin silk nightgown as his brain envisioned her passionate response to his lovemaking.

God, but it would be heaven to kiss that soft mouth again and bury himself deep within her. It would be sheer paradise to wake up to her like this every morning for the rest of his life.

And for the next four mornings of his life, he did wake up to her just that way. Griffin studied the bluish crescents beneath Alyssa's eyes and knew that he was the cause of her lack of sleep. Every night he retired to the master chamber and she retired to the mistress's chamber, and yet every morning for the past five days, he had awakened with her in his bed.

He didn't remember them in the morning, but he knew his nightmares had returned. All the familiar signs were there. His jaw ached from clenching it. His muscles ached from the strain of reliving each sword thrust and saber slash, and his eyes were swollen and gritty from the tears he'd shed in his sleep.

His nighttime terrors were interrupting Alyssa's sleep. And sleep was something she needed. She worked hard from shortly after sunup to well beyond sundown every day. And the wear was beginning to show in the dark circles beneath her eyes.

And the strain of pretending to sleep as she stole out of bed, of ignoring his body's insistent early morning response to her closeness, was beginning to tell on him. He couldn't pretend he didn't want her. His reaction to her nearness was a constant reminder. He wanted her, all right. But he didn't intend to satisfy his desires.

After five days of bed rest, Griffin felt it was time to get up. He needed to regain his strength and make arrangements for his return to London.

Taking great care not to wake her, Griffin slipped out of bed and donned a floor-length dressing gown and slippers before making his way out of the bedchamber and inching his way out of the master suite. Leaning heavily on his cane, Griffin limped down the staircase toward the breakfast room.

He arrived to find it empty. Stopping a passing footman, Griff asked, "Where might I find a bit of breakfast?"

"There, sir," the footman pointed. "There was more light for her to read her letters by, so Lady—I mean, Her Grace—decided to move breakfast in there."

Griff followed the young man's directions and was in the conservatory before he realized it. Mingled with the scent of fried bacon and sausage, eggs, and toast spread out upon the sideboard was the unmistakable fragrance of lemons.

Tears stung his eyes as Griff turned toward the source and discovered Hughey's potted lemon tree occupying the place of honor in the corner of the conservatory Alyssa had despaired of filling.

Griffin stared at the little tree, then leaned his back against the nearest wall and slowly slid to the floor, unable to control the pain that doubled him over or the rush of hot tears coursing down his cheeks.

Alyssa found him that way an hour or so later when Keswick quietly alerted her to the fact that His Grace appeared to be in some distress in the conservatory.

She pulled a silk wrapper over her nightgown and quickly followed Keswick down the stairs to the conservatory. "Please close the doors to the conservatory. Send the staff elsewhere, and please make certain that we are not disturbed for any reason." She looked at the butler. "I don't want anyone to see this."

"Yes, ma'am," Keswick agreed. "I will personally see that you and His Grace are not disturbed." He waited until she walked through the doors of the conservatory, then carefully pulled the heavy green velvet draperies and the massive glass doors closed.

Alyssa knelt on the floor beside Griffin. He didn't hear her approach. His face was turned toward the wall, his back was to the door, and his broad shoulders shook from the force of his grief.

"Griffin." She placed her hand on his shoulder. He turned in her arms and Alyssa knew that she would never forget the look of naked anguish on his face, the grief in his eyes, as he wrapped his arms around her and held on for dear life.

Wiping the tears from his eyes with the back of his hand, Griffin held on to her as the words began tumbling out, one on top of the other.

"Hughey," he said, in a voice raw with grief and tears. "I saw the lemon tree, smelled the blossoms, and remembered . . . Dear God . . . Hughey . . ."

"Tell me." Alyssa pressed her lips against the soft brown hair at his temple. "Please tell me about Hughey."

Griffin told her what he remembered of the charge across the battlefield at Fuentes de Oñoro.

"Colonel Jeffcoat led the first charge. I led the second, and Hughey led the third." Griffin fought for control. "Samson and I made it through the lines without injury and I was grateful to have made it through alive."

Alyssa bit her bottom lip to keep from commenting.

"I dismounted as soon as Samson surged through the breach in the village wall and sent him to safety. The space was so narrow we were forced to fight hand-to-hand on foot." He paused. "I had just killed a French grenadier when I looked up and saw Hughey unhorsed.

I grabbed the nearest horse, mounted, and rode back onto the field." Griffin looked Alyssa in the eye. "Everything is a lie," he said, tears rolling down his face. "All of this . . ." He waved his arm to encompass the conservatory. "I didn't care about rallying the men. I didn't think of rallying the men or of becoming a hero. I never expected to be awarded the Order of the Garter or a ducal title. I only wanted to save my friend. And I failed."

Alyssa hugged him closer. "I'm so very sorry."

"I dream of Hughey. At night. Every night. I dream of reaching him in time. I dream of saving him."

"What happened?" Alyssa whispered, encouraging him to talk even though she knew it was terribly difficult for him to do.

"I crossed the field and made it to his side with only a few scrapes to show for it." The tears were rolling down his face at a faster pace, but Griffin remained unaware of them. "I leaned down and reached for him. Hughey looked up at me, clasped my arm, and declared that I had saved him." Griffin raked his fingers through his hair as he choked back a sob. "A second later, I was lying on the ground beneath the horse, holding Hughey's arm."

Alyssa gasped.

"That was all that was left of him." Griffin's voice shook. "He was hit by a twenty-four-pound shell and all that remained of my friend Hughey was his arm and part of his trunk. His head—" He broke off, pulled Alyssa closer. He buried his head against her shoulder and when he spoke, his words were muffled. "Dear God. I tried to put him together. I tried to reach him, but I was trapped beneath the horse and Hughey's head had rolled too far away." Griff squeezed his eyes shut in a vain attempt to blot out the image. "His eyes were open and he was smiling at me. I was holding his arm and half of his chest and Hughey's head lay several yards away smiling at me . . ." Griffin choked on his words as his sobs caught in his throat.

Alyssa pressed a kiss against the crown of his head.

Griffin looked up at her, his blue eyes swimming with tears, and she was lost. Alyssa kissed him again and although her kiss was meant to console, it became more. Much more.

She placed her hand over his heart and felt the steady beat of it before she slid her fingers through the thick mat of hair on his chest, tracing the pattern as it narrowed into a thin line over the hard contours of his abdomen.

Griffin caught hold of her hand to stop its progress before he kissed her back with a year's worth of pent-up passion.

Breaking the kiss, Alyssa took a deep breath, then untied the sash at her waist. She shrugged out of her wrapper, then reached up and loosed the ribbons at her neck of her gown and pushed her nightgown off her shoulders.

It slipped down her arms and settled at her waist, baring her breasts.

Griffin fought to maintain control. He narrowed his gaze until he was practically scowling. But Alyssa wasn't put off by his frown or the pulsing muscle in his jaw.

She scooted closer, lifted her arms overhead, and offered him her breasts.

Griffin gave up all thought of maintaining control. He ran his hands up her ribs before filling them with the weight of her breasts. He bent his head and then trailed a line of kisses across the tops of her breasts, dipping his tongue into the crevice between them before covering the rosy tip of the first one with his mouth.

Alyssa gasped as he suckled her, teasing the first breast before moving to taste the other.

She slid her fingers through his thick dark hair and pressed him closer.

He leaned into her, pressing the lower part of his body against the cradle of hers, and Alyssa parted her legs to grant him access.

"Turn around." He reached behind her and cupped her buttocks, urging her closer as he slipped his hand between her thighs and caressed the tiny kernel of pleasure hidden beneath the silky curls of her woman's triangle.

Alyssa turned.

Griffin held her close with his uninjured arm and carefully probed her entrance. He pressed his lips against the curve of her neck as he slipped deep inside her, sheathing himself to the hilt.

She was warm and wet and welcoming, and he was rock hard and consumed with wanting. Theirs was a perfect fit, and Griffin stroked her with a consuming urgency that bespoke his great need of her. She met him stroke for stroke, answering him in kind, taking as much as she gave.

They made sweet, passionate love throughout the morning, moving from the floor to the chaise longue.

They made love with a bittersweet sense of desperation, and when at last he collapsed on the pillow beside her and closed his eyes, Griffin knew that he was forever changed by her touch. She had left her mark on him, branded his heart and soul with her essence.

He knew with unshakable certainty that even should he live to be a thousand years old, he would never love anyone or anything as much as he loved Alyssa, but he was a Free Fellow and sworn never to love his wife.

So he kissed the top of her head, fanning her hair with his breath, and tried to convince himself that she deserved so much better. That the best thing he could do for Alyssa was to let her go. And he would, he swore. Just as soon as he found the strength.

❧

"I lay on the battlefield, buried beneath what was left of Hughey and the horse I borrowed, for seventeen hours," Griffin said softly when he and Alyssa lay on the chaise in the quiet aftermath of their love-making.

She knew he had been bayoneted twice, in the left leg and through the right shoulder, but she hadn't known how long the horror lasted or that he had been left for dead, left to rot unless a burial detail was dispatched to retrieve him. And as he lay in the darkness, unable to move, Griffin had suffered the fate of every casualty left to die on the battlefield.

"I was plundered by three different armies: the French, a group of German Hussars, and our Spanish and Portuguese allies. And when the armies had finished with me, the native villagers plundered the battlefield. My clothing and boots were stolen first and then my sword." He met her gaze. His admission surprised him. But it felt good to talk to her. "My Saint George medallion saved my life. There was a dent in it where a ball hit it. I saw it when the French soldier who bayoneted me ripped it from around my neck. My gold watch was taken with my waistcoat. I was stripped naked and about to have a precious part of my anatomy removed by a group of old women as a keepsake and my throat cut when Eastman found me."

He didn't tell her the worst of it, but Alyssa knew. She knew in her heart that what he didn't tell her was far worse than what he did. And she knew from the nature of his wounds and from his nightmares that Griffin had suffered far more than he could relate. She understood the horrors and the indignities he had endured. She also understood that she would have to help him come to terms with them.

Alyssa scored her hand through his body hair. Lower and lower until she was able to wrap her fingers around him.

Griffin froze.

He stopped kissing her. He stopped everything.

She caressed him, using the motion he had taught her in the coach on their wedding day, but Griffin shook his head. "No."

Alyssa widened her eyes in surprise at his answer.

"No." He placed his hand over hers and stopped her motion.

"But, Griffin . . ."

He removed his hand from over hers, then stared down at her fingers. "No," he told her. "Please . . ."

Suddenly, the words he had spoken the first night he'd

awakened her with his feverish nightmares made perfect sense. *"Touch that portion of my anatomy again, madam, and I'll kill you!"*

Alyssa gently released him, then looked up and into his blue eyes.

Griffin captured her face in his hands, plowed his fingers through her hair, and kissed her with a fierce passion, kissed her as if it had been much too long between kisses. And he kept on kissing her.

Alyssa kissed him back, and when she'd done kissing his mouth, she slid down his body and kissed him where she'd just held him.

He didn't pull away, and Alyssa, emboldened by his response, took him into her mouth and made love to him in an entirely new way.

She lavished love and attention on him until he exploded in blissful satisfaction.

He shuddered in her arms, and Alyssa held him as his deep breathing told her he had finally found refuge in sleep.

Closing her eyes, Alyssa slept cradled on the chaise longue beside him.

Chapter 32

He was gone when she awoke.
    She slipped out of the conservatory and tiptoed up to the master suite to dress. She met Keswick as she was coming down the stairs.

"Where is His Grace?" She asked.

"He left," Keswick answered.

"He left?"

The butler nodded. "He left instructions that you were not to be disturbed and ordered the coach brought around while I helped him dress. I am sorry, Your Grace, but His Grace has returned to London."

She looked stricken by the news, and Keswick pulled a letter from his coat pocket and handed it to her, then stepped aside to give her the privacy in which to read it.

My Dear Alyssa,

I shall always be grateful for the time we have shared and for the solace you offered me in my time of need, but I must set you free so that you might choose a man worthy of you.

I promised myself, in Spain, that I would not force my affections on you or interfere in your life in any way. Nor would I expect that you would return my affections or grant me further license to get my heir upon you.

But I have broken that promise this day. As it seems that I have no strength of will where you are concerned, I am removing myself from temptation.

If you should find a month from today that you are with child, you may reach me at my town house in London. If that is not the case, you may rest assured that I will refrain from settling my affections on you in the future—unless you desire them.

Alyssa finished reading the letter, and then crumpled it in her fist. "Unless I desire them," she murmured. "Of course I desire them. I thought I made that perfectly clear." Alyssa stamped her foot in frustration. "That fool! That pigheaded, noble, idiotic fool!"

"Your Grace?"

She looked up at Keswick. "He's setting me free again so that I might choose a man worthy of me." She rolled her eyes. "As if there was a man more worthy than Griffin." She sighed. "But I suppose I should give him back what he seems to crave: his Free Fellow status."

Keswick cocked an eyebrow. "Are you certain, Your Grace?"

"Most assuredly."

❧

She made herself wait a week before following Griffin to London and when she arrived, she went straight to his rented town house.

"I'm sorry, Madam," the butler apologized. "But His Grace is not at home."

"Then it is most fortuitous that His Grace's presence isn't required." She smiled at the butler. "I am the Duchess of Avon. Please see that my bags are brought inside and that Durham, my lady's maid, is settled in." She arched an eyebrow. "And I'll require tonight's invitations. Please see that they're brought to the master suite. Where is the master suite?"

"Up the stairs, down the corridor to the right."

Alyssa breezed past him and started up the stairs.

"But, Your Grace, His Grace said nothing to me of your impending arrival . . ."

"I decided to surprise him."

❧

And surprise him she did.

The Duke of Avon had become the toast of London. He was welcomed and feted everywhere, and everywhere he appeared Alyssa turned up, along with her flock of young admirers.

She curtsied to the Prince Regent and smiled proudly when Griffin received the Order of the Garter, but later that evening, she retired to her bedchamber without a word.

They were sharing a town house, but Alyssa didn't speak or acknowledge his existence unless guests were present and then only in the most coolly polite manner. She lavished attention on Colin and Jarrod and everyone who called at the house, but she gave nothing to her husband except a cold shoulder.

"What the devil does she think she's doing? Dressed like that?" Griffin glared over Jarrod's shoulder to where Alyssa stood, dressed in a daringly low cut gown of silver tissue, and surrounded by young bucks.

Jarrod bit back a smile. "Apparently, she knows exactly what she's doing."

"She didn't become an Incomparable for nothing." Colin gave a low admiring whistle. "Especially when only the best will do."

"What are you talking about?" Griffin demanded.

Colin squinted through the throng of people crowding Lord and Lady Tressingham's ballroom where Griffin's in-laws were hosting a huge ball in his honor. "Isn't that His Grace, the Duke of Sussex, asking your wife to dance?"

"Over my dead body!" Griffin exclaimed, grabbing his cane.

The other two Free Fellows watched in amused fascination as Griffin limped across the ballroom floor.

❧

"Good evening, Your Grace," Sussex *bowed to* Alyssa.

She smiled. "Good evening to you, Your Grace."

"I always believed you were meant to be a duchess," he teased. "Unfortunately, you weren't meant to be *my* duchess."

"You are not alone in your way of thinking, Your Grace," Alyssa admitted, glancing down at the toes of her dancing slippers. "Apparently, my husband shares your feeling."

Sussex frowned before he moved a step closer and lifted Alyssa's chin with the tip of his index finger so that he might look her in the eye. "You think so?"

"I know so," she informed him.

"Then, look again," Sussex said. "Because your husband is headed this way."

"Only because he dislikes you," she said. "I've flirted outrageously with every young bachelor here, and he has yet to notice."

"He noticed."

Alyssa snorted in disbelief. "Not likely."

"You're walking a dangerous path, Alyssa." Sussex took her by the hand. "And I wouldn't interfere if you appeared to be enjoying it, but you don't appear to be enjoying yourself. If you're going to play for high stakes, you need to learn to conceal your emotions a bit better."

"What do you suggest I do?" she asked.

"If you allow me escort you down that dangerous path you've uncovered, you'll find out." He gave her a challenging grin. "Are you game, Your Grace?"

Alyssa nodded.

"Shall we dance?"

"What of . . . your partner?" Alyssa glanced around.

"I came alone."

"Then, I'd be delighted."

❧

"Kindly unhand my wife." Griffin *barked the* order at the Duke of Sussex.

Sussex looked pointedly at Griffin's cane. "I thought

your wife might enjoy a turn on the dance floor," he replied.

"Not with you." Griffin smiled.

Sussex raised an eyebrow. "Is that your wish as well, Your Grace?" He turned to Alyssa.

"No," she answered, looking Griffin in the eye and daring him to contradict her.

Sussex offered Alyssa his elbow.

Griffin stopped them. "She can dance with me."

Alyssa stared at her husband. "I could, but I won't."

"Why not?" Griffin asked. "You've danced with nearly every man here tonight except me."

Everyone and everything in the ballroom seemed to recede into the background until Alyssa and Griffin were the only two people in the room.

"The other men here tonight don't find my presence a chore." Alyssa said.

"Alyssa . . ." Griffin began.

She glared at him. "You set me free, Griffin. Remember? You set me free to find a man worthy of me. You left me a letter telling me that's what you wanted, so you've no right to interfere if I choose to do so in your presence."

"Alyssa, you don't understand . . . I made promises . . ."

"So did I," she said.

"I promised myself I would fight the French and become England's greatest hero."

"You've succeeded," she reminded him.

"I know," he answered. "But I didn't expect to survive it."

"What?"

"I didn't expect to live through it. I'm a cavalry officer. I expected to die in battle."

"But you didn't."

"No," he answered. "Unfortunately, I never planned beyond it. I never planned for the future. I was never afraid of dying, I was afraid of not being where I was needed. And now that I'm home . . ." He looked at her. "I don't know what to do with the rest of my life."

"I heard you were returning to your regiment," she said. "I heard you'd been offered a command. Is it true?"

"You don't need me," he said. "You need someone

stronger. Someone who won't disappoint you. Someone who won't let you down."

She blinked back tears as she looked up at him. "I love you, Griffin. You've never let me down," she answered. "Until now." Alyssa turned back to the duke of Sussex. "Shall we?"

Griffin tried again. "Alyssa . . ."

"Go back to the cavalry," Alyssa told him. "Keep your promises to your Free Fellows League. Keep your promises to everyone except me. Leave. Go back and become England's greatest *dead* hero since Nelson, but please, stop setting me free. Stop breaking my heart." She reached for Sussex's arm, but her tears blinded her as Sussex stepped back and Griffin took his place. Neither of them noticed him slipping away.

"You love me?" Griffin asked, dumbfounded by her revelation.

Alyssa looked up at him. "Of course, I love you," she answered simply. "I've loved you since the moment you kissed me. Do you honestly believe I'd have turned down a duke to marry a viscount if I hadn't loved you?"

Griffin laughed. "Yes, I did. Because you said you didn't want to be a duchess."

"I was an idiot," she told him. "And you, an even bigger one."

"Why didn't you tell me?"

"How could I confide my feelings?" she asked, lifting her chin a notch. "Why should I? You didn't tell me anything except that you needed a wife before you left to join your regiment. You didn't tell me about your Free Fellows League, or the vows you took, or the full nature of the work in which you're engaged. You kept it a secret, but you made no secret of the fact that you didn't want me. I understood your loyalty to your league and your great love for the cavalry. I was under no illusion. I knew you intended to join your regiment and I understood that marrying me was simply a means to that end. But you aren't the only one cursed with a full measure of pride, Griffin. I share your affliction and I learned that it was better to keep my feelings to myself than to hear how little I mattered to you.

You only wanted me in order to get an heir and I failed to do that . . ." She hesitated, then took a deep breath and continued, "And now, you're trying to be rid of me. And although, I hate to admit it, I know it's only a matter of time before you succeed. You're a hero now. And a duke. Nothing is too good for you. There's no reason for you to remain tied to a barren bride. Once all the fuss dies down, you shouldn't have any difficulty petitioning the church for an annulment. That was, after all, the only reason you ever needed me. You had the Free Fellows and the cavalry and you didn't want anything else."

"You knew about the Free Fellows?"

Alyssa nodded. "I was standing behind the potted palms that night at Almack's. I heard you talking about the Free Fellows with Shepherdston and Grantham."

"And after hearing all that, you married me anyway?"

"Of course."

"Thank God," he breathed. "Because I don't want to let you go. And your ability or your inability to conceive an heir has nothing to do with it. I love you, Alyssa. I love you more than the cavalry. I love you more than the Free Fellows League. I love you more than life itself."

She frowned at him. "Well, you have a most peculiar way of showing it. You set me free."

Griff snorted. "I *tried* to set you free. I *tried* to be noble and do what's best for you . . ."

"You're what's best for me."

"Am I?"

"Of course, you are."

"I *want* to be the best for you," he admitted. "But I'm not at all certain that I *am* or that I ever *can* be." Griff stared at her, memorizing her features and the expression on her face. "When I was on the Peninsula, I believed I could be. I read your letters and I knew in my heart that you were my soul mate—my other half—and I believed that I was yours. I wanted to be. With all my heart. I thought I could be, but after everything that's happened—" Griff's words caught in his throat and he had to work to get them out. "I'm afraid," he whispered. "I barely sleep and when I do, I dream of war. I dream of all I've seen and done.

I see their faces and I wake up in a cold sweat. Christ, Alyssa! You've seen me. My hands shake. I ask you, what kind of hero has hands that shake uncontrollably? What kind of hero is afraid of crowds? Of fireworks?" He shook his head in disgust. "Bloody hell!"

"Bloody hell is right," Alyssa answered vehemently. "That's what you've been through. Of course, you're afraid. Who wouldn't be after all you're endured? You spent a year in hell. And you've only just returned home. You haven't given yourself time to heal. It will get better."

"Time heals all wounds?"

Alyssa nodded. "I believe it does."

"I hope so." Griff squeezed his eyes shut and gave voice to his greatest fear. "But what if it doesn't? What do we do if it doesn't? Can you stand to be awakened by my nightmares every night of your life for the next forty or fifty years?"

Alyssa blinked back tears. "I can if you can," she promised. "I can stand anything as long as I have you. As long as I can hold you in my arms. As long as you let me love you for the next forty or fifty years . . ."

"Oh, Lys," he murmured, "I don't want to hurt you. I don't want to break your heart. I don't want you to suffer with me when you might have a chance to be happy with someone else . . ."

"There is no one else for me," Alyssa promised him. "Only you."

"Then we're in complete accord." Griff pulled her close, then leaned down and took her in his arms and kissed her, his path in life suddenly, vividly clear. "I'm not leaving you, Alyssa. I'm not setting you free." He smiled down at her. "I refused the offer of a new command. My place is here with you. I spoke with the prime minister and with the regent and the senior members of the War Department about the conditions in the field—the food, the supply lines or lack thereof, the incompetence of officers and the lack of training of the common soldiers, as well as the burdens placed upon young officers, like Hughey, who are forced to supply their own equipment or forced to do without. We agreed that we must improve and reorganize the military.

From top to bottom. I believe there's a better, more efficient way, to run an army and I intend to find it. I'm buying Knightsguild and I'm going to use it to train military leaders—especially foolhardy and hot-headed cavalry officers. I want to make a difference. And I want you to help me."

"I'll help you in every way I can," Alyssa told him. "But I know nothing about the military except what I learned from you."

Griff laughed. "Alyssa, my darling duchess, you're the best field commander I've ever seen. You know all there is to know about organizing and mobilizing large groups of people and I want you to teach me everything you know."

Alyssa grinned. "That may take some time, Your Grace, for I have a vast store of knowledge on the subject."

"I'm counting on it taking some time, Your Grace," Griff answered. "Say, for the rest of our lives?" He leaned down and kissed her again. "I love you, Alyssa. More than anything and I intend to love you for the remainder of my life and beyond."

"Then we're in complete accord, my love," Alyssa whispered. "For that's exactly how long it will take."

Epilogue

"A man must have love. He cannot live without it."

—GRIFFIN, DUKE OF AVON, JOURNAL ENTRY, 19 JULY 1811

"*What are you going to do about Sussex?*" Griffin asked as he lay holding his wife in his arms.

"Nothing," Alyssa replied. "I'm a very happily married woman." She rolled to her side, within the circle of his arms, and faced him. "The question is: What are you going to do about Sussex?"

Griffin eyed her suspiciously. "Why do you ask?"

"Rumor has it he desperately wants to become a member of your Free Fellows League. Are you going to allow it?"

"Probably," Griff admitted. "So long as he proves his worth."

"I'll wager his future duchess isn't going to like that," Alyssa murmured. "Unless you do something about that horrid clause in the charter."

Griff arched an eyebrow and tried his best to appear annoyed. "What clause in what charter?"

"As if you didn't know," Alyssa retorted. "You talk in your sleep, Griffin. You *agonize* in your sleep. And a great deal of that agonizing could be remedied if you'd just get together with the other Free Fellows—whoever and however many there are—and amend the clause in the charter that forbids Free Fellows from loving their wives."

Griffin was astonished. He still suffered frequent

nightmares and he knew he talked in his sleep, but he had no idea that he'd been so forthcoming and coherent. Alyssa had never breathed a word of the secrets he spilled in his sleep—until now. "Do I mention specifics?"

"Incessantly."

"And what exactly are they?"

Alyssa shrugged. "The fact that you love me with all your heart and the fact that it goes against the charter and the blood oath you swore to uphold."

"Any idea what clause I'm agonizing over?"

Alyssa smiled. "The fifth one. You know the one that states that: you shall never be encumbered by sentiment known as love or succumb to female wiles or tears."

Griffin blushed. "And you think I'd sleep better if I call a meeting of the Free Fellows League and propose an amendment to that clause in the charter?"

"Most definitely."

"Any suggestions?"

"Why not simply amend it to read that: you shall never be encumbered by sentiment known as love or succumb to female wiles unless, of course, you want to be encumbered because the female is question is a wife who loves you to distraction and is dearly loved in return?"

"That's perfect," Griff said.

"I'm glad it meets your approval."

Griff laughed. "I'm easy to please. I have a vested interest in amending that particular clause to suit my purposes. I'm not so sure about the others."

Alyssa ran her fingers through the hair covering his chest. "I'd say you have an *unvested* interest in amending that horrid clause to suit your purposes." Her fingers inched lower. "And given time and the right incentive, the other Free Fellows will gladly approve the amendment you're going to propose."

"Have you any idea who'll be providing the other Free Fellows with the right incentives?" If his wife was playing matchmaker for Grantham or Shepherdston, Griff thought it prudent to have some warning of it.

"Only for Sussex," she answered.

Her answer piqued Griffin's curiosity. "Have you a future duchess in mind?"

"Lady Miranda," she said.

Griffin laughed. "That will never happen. They hate each other."

Alyssa smiled knowingly. "The same way we hate each other."

"Really? This I've got to see."

"Wait and you will." She traced the line of hair on his abdomen. "In the meantime . . ."

"Yes?"

"You tend to your garden and let Sussex tend to his."

Griff covered her hand with his and guided her to the place she'd been inching toward. "Now that you mention it," he teased. "I do have a few seeds that need planting . . ."

Alyssa giggled. "Then you've come to the right place for I happen to be an excellent gardener . . ."

Griff nibbled her earlobe. "Duchesses do seem to have the finest gardens," he allowed. "And my duchess has the finest garden of all."

Turn the page for a preview of

MERELY THE GROOM

The second novel in Rebecca Hagan Lee's

Free Fellows League trilogy

Chapter 1

He had sold his soul to the devil. An English devil. A *merchant* devil.

Colin McElreath, twenty-seventh Viscount Grantham, stared down at his signature on the smooth vellum paper as he pressed his signet ring into the puddle of melted red wax on the document. It was done. He was about to become a very wealthy man. And his new solvency had only cost him his good name, his title, his future, his freedom, and five hundred pounds sterling.

Colin was relinquishing his Free Fellows status, sealing his fate for cash, because duty required it. Because his father, the ninth Earl of McElreath, had squandered what had remained of the family fortune and because the man standing before him, the newly created baron, Lord Davies, was a rich silk merchant who urgently required a respectable son-in-law for his disgraced daughter.

"Welcome to the family," the baron said. "It's been a pleasure doing business with you, my lord."

Colin grunted in reply, wincing at the baron's choice of words. *Pleasure? What pleasure?* Colin's wince became a frown. A few bold strokes of his pen had forced him into the ultimate sacrifice. He'd sold himself for a few million pieces of silver, sentenced himself to a lifetime of *marriage* to a girl who had foolishly entrusted her heart and her virtue to a man who had eloped with, then abandoned her at a coaching inn in Gretna Green.

Colin didn't know whether to laugh or to cry at the irony. After a lifetime of avoiding society misses, he was about to marry one. His betrothed was damaged goods, but her good name and her place in society were safe.

Miss Gillian Davies was about to become a blushing bride.

He was merely the groom.